"Ignorant Am I? You Dare to Call Me That?"

While Tatyana swayed angrily in her softly fitted gown, her face in the candlelight glowed with indignation. Gregory towered over her.

"Women like you think you can get away with anything," he said in a furious undertone, "because you're so damn pretty." His eyes suddenly raked hers and in an instant Tatyana felt herself crushed in his arms. He kissed her hard.

Terrified by a kiss she had never before experienced, Tatyana struggled. But he held her fast, impervious to her resistance. Then, some deep animal instinct began to pulse within her, and a feeling of bliss came over her. Gregory's lips stayed on hers, plumbing the depths of her feelings. Her arms went slack, all that was real was their embrace, as the world seemed to vanish. Just as she put her arms about him, Gregory flung her away from him.

Dear Reader,

We, the editors of Tapestry Romances, are committed to bringing you two outstanding original romantic historical novels each and every month.

From Kentucky in the 1850s to the court of Louis XIII, from the deck of a pirate ship within sight of Gibraltar to a mining camp high in the Sierra Nevadas, our heroines experience life and love, romance and adventure.

Our aim is to give you the kind of historical romances that you want to read. We would enjoy hearing your thoughts about this book and all future Tapestry Romances. Please write to us at the address below.

The Editors
Tapestry Romances
POCKET BOOKS
1230 Avenue of the Americas
Box TAP
New York, N.Y. 10020

Snow Princess

Victoria Foote

A TAPESTRY BOOK

PUBLISHED BY POCKET BOOKS NEW YORK

An *Original* publication of TAPESTRY BOOKS

A Tapestry Book published by
POCKET BOOKS, a division of Simon & Schuster, Inc.
1230 Avenue of the Americas, New York, N.Y. 10020

ISBN: 0-671-49333-7

First Tapestry Books printing August, 1983

10 9 8 7 6 5 4 3 2 1

POCKET and colophon are registered trademarks
of Simon & Schuster, Inc.

TAPESTRY is a trademark of Simon & Schuster, Inc.

Printed in the U.S.A.

To my husband, Wayne Kendall Greenwell,
for his love, support, and patience,
and to Jill Gitlin Jones,
who helped make it all possible

AUTHOR'S NOTE

The Decembrist uprising, which took place in Russia in the early nineteenth century, is little known in the United States. I have used this historical event as the basis for *Snow Princess*.

In my research I drew both facts and inspiration from a number of historical and cultural works. Two of the most helpful sources were Mikhail Zetlin's *The Decembrists* and Suzanne Massie's *Land of the Firebird*.

Chapter One

December 1824, Russia

THE GLARING ICE STRETCHED AS FAR AS THE EYE COULD see. Under the winter sun there was only stillness and silence. But at last a black speck could be seen crossing the frozen brilliance. Bells began to tinkle in the air, accompanied by hoofbeats and music made by steel runners whisking over the snow. A red-painted troika that carried four people was dashing along the crests and valleys of white snowdrifts.

"Vpered, Sokoliki!" sang out the driver, who urged his three gray horses forward over the beaten snow, "Davay, davay!" The driver was big and round, and he did not seem to feel the cold through his green caftan cinched at the waist with a red sash that matched his hat. His long grizzled beard made a natural muffler as it poked out over the caftan and down his chest, and it bobbed up and down as he rippled the bell-studded reins of the horses. "Davay, davay!" he urged the horses faster.

His words were clearly meaningless to the small man who sat beside him gripping the rails of the driver's box in his gloved hands. Terrified by the speed at which they traveled, he winced every time the horses kicked up snow into his face. And each time he ducked down into his cloak to avoid the cold white spray, his large companion laughed out loud. The slight man ignored the driver but looked back occasionally into the scarlet sleigh, as if hoping some change in his comfortless state would issue from within. But none came.

In the sleigh sat two gentlemen talking. It was evident they were indeed gentlemen, for one wore a rich sable cloak and the other a greatcoat trimmed in silver fox. Over their knees were thrown wolfskin rugs to keep out the cold.

"You look pensive, my English friend," came the strongly accented voice of the young man in the sable cloak. Between his high collar and mink hat, little could be seen but a pair of laughing blue eyes. And when he occasionally lowered his collar in order to be better heard by his companion, one could glimpse a small, well-made nose and a short blond moustache.

"I am only wondering how many more hours before we reach your father's house," was the languid reply spoken in perfect English. But the dark brooding eyes that searched the frozen horizon belied the idle tone in his voice. He too would lower his collar to speak, though less frequently, and when he did so one glimpsed a long aquiline nose and the hint of side whiskers.

"Only a citizen of the British Isles would be presumptuous enough to wonder how many hours a trip should take," laughed the other. "Here, we measure distances differently. When in Russia, ask instead how many *days.*"

The eyebrows of the Englishman, if they could have been seen, would certainly have been lifted, and his Russian companion hastened to reassure him. "In this case, though, before I alarm you, let me say that by our standards my father's estate, Starlina, is almost within the gates of St. Petersburg. Starlina is only forty versts from the capital, or twenty-six of your English miles."

The young Russian waved his arm toward the great round figure in front of the sledge. "Platon, my father's coachman, is an excellent driver—the best in our district! Heaven to him is driving his beloved gray Orlovs at twelve miles an hour over any road—good, bad, or indifferent. But of course today, with all this snow, it will take us longer than usual, maybe six hours in all. So you see, we are nearly at Starlina."

The golden spires of the imperial city of St. Petersburg had been left far behind when this conversation between the two young men took place.

"Your voice is happy, Prince Dmitry," spoke the dark-eyed Englishman. "I believe you are glad to be going home, after all. And I believe, after all, that our good times in Paris are nothing to you compared to this dreary landscape of your fatherland."

Beneath his mink hat, the young Russian nobleman's blue eyes continued to smile, and he sat back contentedly in the sledge. "Yes, I admit it. It is very good to be coming home. I have not seen my family in so long. Two whole years is a long time for a Russian to be without his family."

At the Englishman's silence Prince Dmitry added, "You may patronize me for my homely affections, Gregory, because you have no thought or care for such tedious domestic preoccupations, but my family is a family worth coming home to. How much I have missed them!"

The young Englishman laughed sardonically. "If I remember correctly, you stomped about your flat in St. Germain and shouted at your father—as if he were sitting there—for summoning you back to Russia so peremptorily. And then you had to drown your irritation in a glass of vodka."

"Well, yes, that is true," admitted Prince Dmitry good-naturedly. "I admit I don't take easily to orders, and well, Paris is so bewitching, as bewitching as a beautiful woman! One doesn't notice the time fly by."

Gregory said nothing but drew his fox collar up higher around his face and continued to gaze on the empty white countryside.

The open troika continued to slide quickly over the snow. Nothing could be seen but an occasional clump of bare birch trees, the distant outline of pine forests, and the endlessly gleaming snow.

Prince Dmitry tapped his friend. "Many of your thoughts elude me, Gregory, but I know what you are thinking now. You are wondering why you accompanied me to my country. You are looking at this monotonous, cold landscape and thinking that you could be sitting in a warm café in Paris, holding sway over a crowd of Left Bank intellectuals, or dallying on the Italian Riviera. But I think I know the answer. I think you were bored and decided to see with your own eyes whether the rumors about my country are true, whether Russia is only a barbaric winter wasteland. But you will see, you will see. The Russian people long to follow in Europe's footsteps."

Gregory half smiled enigmatically and changed the subject. "Tell me, Prince, who is it we shall have to contend with at your father's house? Refresh my memory."

"My father, of course. I have told you about him. . . ."

"Of Prince Ivan Korbatsky I have heard at length," and he repeated as if by rote, "Prince Korbatsky the great Field Marshal and hero of 1812, wounded at the Battle of Borodino. Because of a war injury that shattered his leg, retired from military service. Now spends most of his time on his estate, where he lords over a small army of serfs. Have I got that right?"

Prince Dmitry blushed, then added energetically, "Yes, yes, but forgive me, Gregory, if I have bored you."

"No," interrupted Gregory, "you do not bore me, it is only I who bore myself. Besides, you see, I did forget one thing. That your father is also now preoccupied with threatening to disinherit you if you do not return home immediately."

"Yes, there is that, too," said Prince Dmitry, thoughtfully, and then he grinned. "So you see it is a very good thing for me to return home now."

Gregory glanced at the young prince with quizzical affection. "I may be jaded, Prince, but neither am I so foolish as to believe an idle threat of your father's would drag you across this everlasting ice-bitten tundra. No, besides your nostalgic family affections, there is another reason you are returning to your homeland. . . ."

Prince Dmitry glanced at Gregory with embarrassed shyness, and Gregory continued.

"It is not only the family and their affairs that draw you home, but the affairs of your whole nation. I have seen it happen to others. Europe and her ideals have gone to your head, and you have decided that to change the world—for nothing less would suffice—you have to start in the parental nest and spread your influence out in concentric circles. That is why you have come home. Correct me if I'm wrong."

Prince Dmitry smiled affectionately at his older friend. "You mock me, Gregory, but you are all too accurate, as always."

"I mock you not," said Gregory, still mocking, but his tone was affectionate. "Your motivations are highly laudable, and I envy you your dedication. I will be looking on, I assure you, with the greatest solicitude and interest."

Prince Dmitry turned and studied the inscrutable profile of his friend. "Can that be one of the reasons you decided to accompany me to Russia?"

"How clever you become in your old age," responded Gregory lazily, with the bare flicker of a smile.

Their conversation was interrupted when Platon the coachman gave a shout and the small figure beside him shrieked. They looked up to see the troika career off the narrow track and into a five-foot snowdrift.

The little figure shrieked again as he was pitched out of the sleigh and went sprawling into the snow. He jumped up and struggled out of the drift, muttering, *"Ça alors, ce voyage devient de plus en plus impossible, impossible! J'en ai assez!"*

"What is the matter, Anatole," laughed the young Englishman as he watched his French valet brush the snow off his coat with a fastidious sweep of his glove. "Had enough of this Russian winter—though by all accounts it has scarcely begun—or is it Biarritz you mourn for?"

"Monsieur Grandison," huffed the valet, trying to regain a measure of pride, "a gentleman's valet goes where his master bids him. It is not for me to say." But the look of injury he threw at his employer made it all too clear what he thought of their impulsive flight from civilization. He took his seat again up beside Platon but would not condescend to give him so much as a withering glance. Platon took this slight in good stride and applied himself to the fine Russian art of wheedling and coaxing his horses out of the snowdrift. *"Poshevelivaytes, Golubchiki! Milenkie! Davay! Davay!"* he repeated in a singsong, and soon the three gray Orlovs pulled the sledge back onto the beaten track.

"What exactly is your coachman mumbling?" asked Gregory Grandison. He had never heard of a coachman having an extended conversation with his horses.

"Roughly translated, he is saying, go on my darlings, my dear ones, hurry, hurry!"

"How fascinating," said Gregory, laughing, "and to what use does he put his whip?"

"It is a matter of great pride to a Russian coachman in private service never to resort to a whip. Obscenities, when he is angry, but never a whip."

When they were on their way again, the conversation returned to Dmitry's family. "Other than his stable of serfs, who else makes up your father's household?" asked Gregory.

"Tatyana."

"Tatyana? And who is Tatyana, pray?"

"My sister. I have spoken to you of her, haven't I?"

"Ah yes, the beautiful one," waxed Gregory, "who shuns the world and has given up her entire life to the service of your father."

Prince Dmitry was accustomed to Gregory Grandison's sardonic treatment of "family" and did not seem fazed by this irreverent remark. "She was a mere slip of a girl when I first received my commission in the Imperial Army," he said, "and I have seen her so few times in the past seven years, even before I went to Paris. And yet, I feel on the most intimate terms with her, for she has written me the most affectionate, declarative letters all along. What an angelic soul, and as I recall, the promise of so much beauty!"

Gregory stifled a yawn. "However much or little these flattering assertions bear on reality, it is certainly brotherly of you to say so. Then again, you have always been an admirer of the weaker sex." He paused and added, "For what reasons I cannot fathom. To me they are empty chatterboxes, not worth the ribbons they come wrapped in." He yawned again.

"Gregory, it is in the nature of most people to find much to say in the space of a five-minute conversation. But why do you always find that trait so appalling in a woman?"

"Because at least what comes out of the mouths of most men is not quite the drivel we are forced to listen to when in the company of ladies. With men at least one can argue or contest their imbecilities. But with the ladies one is forced to remain gallant, wincing inwardly as they find forty-nine absurdities to say about the weather. Or worse yet one is forced to lend an ear to the multitude of veiled insults they are glad to make of one another. Only the movement of their little fans keeps one from suffocating from such nauseating sweetness."

"You are harsh, Gregory," said Prince Dmitry. "Don't you find any charm in their surreptitious glances, their frivolous banter?" And Dmitry's eyes again began to smile as he recalled their evenings haunting the Paris salons of the *haut monde*. "By God, those little French dancers with their exquisite sense of dress, and the Italian contessas with their delectable accents. . . ."

"All a very pretty poison," remarked Gregory. "Like children, ladies should be seen and not heard, if they must be seen at all. For they do not mean what they say and they won't say what they mean, which is all for the better. Those tiny craniums have room for no more than an inventory of dresses and intrigues."

"Nevertheless, you are to be envied," said Dmitry in an affable tone, "for the contempt never seems mutual. How do you do it?"

Gregory laughed. "Don't follow my example. There are many ladies who would invoke the wrath of the gods upon my head."

"True, perhaps," said Dmitry, smiling. "They love or hate you, but they are never indifferent."

Gregory shrugged his shoulders, for the subject bored him.

This conversation had as a backdrop the encroaching dusk. Though it was only three in the afternoon, the sun was setting in the west and changing the golden fleece of snow to mauve. The sleigh raced along the silhouette of darkening pines, which increasingly surrounded them as they traveled north. The wind grew colder now. This drop in temperature as well as the thought that they neared their destination brought a halt to the young men's conversation.

For some stretch the only sound was the tinkling sleigh bells and occasional squeak of the sleigh runners skimming along the snow. Platon, too, had grown silent, only occasionally cooing to his horses. Then, in the cold but peaceful dusk, one of the gray Orlovs suddenly whinnied and Platon bellowed, *"Volki! Volki! Volki!"*

Prince Dmitry stood up in his seat and peered into the twilight, searching the edge of the woods. In Russian he addressed his father's coachman. "So early in the year, Platon?"

"That is no surprise to me, little father. These past few winters they have been hungry and mischievous."

Gregory scanned the unfamiliar gloom and understood what had prompted the coachman's shout. Against the outline of the trees he saw dark, low-slung animals with long sloping tails, loping along beside them. "Wolves," he muttered and counted eight of them. The wolves made no sound as they slinked along, keeping abreast of the sleigh but maintaining a certain distance.

"They aren't likely to attack us," announced Prince Dmitry. "There aren't enough of them, and it's too early in the year. Nevertheless, let's keep an eye on them." He pulled from his leather sabretache a pistol in which he began to fit a bullet.

Gregory leaned over and handed him a shiny six-chambered revolver. "Take this. These newfangled pistols were designed with a separate spring and give an excellent aim." Dmitry was surprised but accepted the handsome revolver, whose twin Gregory was already loading with his own bullets.

The three horses galloped swiftly along, whinnying with fear, and Anatole sat frozen to his seat beside the driver.

"Not too fast, Platon," prompted Prince Dmitry, "or we'll end up in another snow bank." Four pairs of eyes watched the wolves that kept pace with them.

Just as Prince Dmitry recognized the unmarked but familiar turnoff to Starlina, his father's huge estate, the wolves diverged from the woods and shot across the snow toward the tiny sleigh. Prince Dmitry panicked as the wolves bounded toward them, and his first few shots went wide. But even the sound of the blasts didn't deter the beasts.

A lean gray wolf came abreast of the troika and lunged at the outside horse. Gregory fired a shot and down the animal went, rolling over in the snow. A second wolf sprang up from the right and leapt at the horse on that side, but another blast of Gregory's revolver sent it spinning backward into its tracks. There was a moment when it seemed to Gregory that there were not a half-dozen wolves but a hundred of them. For like a hydra's head, when one wolf went down, another two immediately sprang up to take its place.

Platon tried to restrain the frightened horses, who now dashed headlong toward a snow bank, and only by a well-timed yank of the reins did he keep the sleigh from landing on its side. Onward wildly went the sleigh, turning and twisting in the icy darkness of the snow-covered forest. Anatole's shrieks punctuated the lunges of the wolves as they flung themselves at the frenzied horses.

Emboldened by the smell of blood and the horses' terror, one large wolf tried to jump into the sleigh itself. The animal clacked his teeth and lunged for Dmitry's boot just as Dmitry was cocking his pistol. *"Chort!"* exclaimed Dmitry, uttering an oath in Russian. "They're feeling frisky!" And then he fired his gun, which blasted the animal backward out of the sleigh.

A lurch of the troika made Prince Dmitry lose his balance. He was flung forward and his revolver went flying. "Damn it, I've lost my piece," he shouted at Gregory.

"And I've no bullets left," returned Gregory, who had just fired the last of his shot.

"Watch out," shouted Prince Dmitry once more, for a huge wolf, larger than the others, was bounding toward Gregory's side of the troika. The brute threw its whole body forward and landed in the sleigh. With its fangs bared, it lunged at Gregory. To Prince Dmitry's horror, Gregory shoved his left arm into the animal's gaping jaw. With its slathering teeth the animal crunched down and wrenched Gregory's hand with enough force to break the arm in two. An instant later Gregory raised his other arm and slammed the butt of his revolver on the animal's skull. There was a yelp, the animal's jaw went slack, and the dead wolf fell at Gregory's feet. Prince Dmitry shoved the carcass out of the sleigh.

"Your hand," said Dmitry fearing the worst.

Though his face was pale, Gregory smiled. "Safe," he said, and pushed his arm out of his coat, "I only fed the poor brute some fox fur." Dmitry saw that Gregory had pulled his arm all the way back into his sleeve so that the wolf bit only his cuff. "I'm damned impressed. What made you think of that?" asked Prince Dmitry.

Gregory smiled wryly. "However much I fight it I find that I too am susceptible to that primitive instinct called self-preservation."

Dmitry smiled at his friend's high-mindedness, but his relief was short-lived.

"There are two more upon us, little father," shouted Platon, as a brace of wolves, the last of the pack, eased in on the sleigh and its exhausted horses.

A feeling like despair suddenly overcame both friends as they saw the sinister shapes weave toward them out of the darkness. But the thudding of their hearts was superseded by a new sound, the sound of bullets singing through the frozen air. The wolves yelped and disappeared into the forest.

The trees began to crackle; the boughs of the firs trembled, and one human figure after another dropped from the snow-laden branches onto the ground. Within moments a dozen peasants encircled the sleigh. Gregory regarded their strange, exotic faces and primitive sheepskin coats with doubt until the men broke into a song that was happy and welcoming.

"My father's *mujiks*," said Dmitry, before he jumped down from the sleigh. Half the serfs fell on their knees in the snow and pressed the hem of Prince Dmitry's fur cloak to their lips. *"Ne nuzhno,"* commanded the young prince in their language and entreated them to rise. The *mujiks* good-naturedly ignored the entreaties of their master's son until he regained the troika. Then they trudged after him in the snow, chanting in the moonlight until the troika drove through the stone gate and the alley of pine trees that led to Dmitry's ancestral home.

As the troika came out from under the firs, Gregory saw in the moonlight a facade of large white columns and steps leading down from it to the drive. A dark mass swelled around these steps and behind the columns on what appeared to be a darkened terrace.

As the troika pranced forward the mass unexpectedly separated, and Gregory realized this moving shape, so like a swarm of bees, was a crowd of human beings. Here and there an arm held up a pine torch that illumined a small radius of faces. "More of my father's *mujiks*," said Prince Dmitry, glancing at the assembled serfs, among whom all the men wore beards, the badge of their station in life.

When Prince Dmitry leapt from the sledge, there was a murmur of voices. The crowd buckled before him, the torchlights dipped, and all the serfs sank down on their knees in the snow. As the master's son strode up the path they made for him, they reached out to kiss the hem of his cloak. On their faces Gregory saw only two expressions: love and abject servility.

But Prince Dmitry scarcely seemed aware just now of this teeming mass of obsequious humanity. His attention was focused elsewhere. Gregory allowed his eyes to follow the prince's. His upward gaze was intently riveted on something at the top of the stairs.

Chapter Two

ON THE TERRACE, FRAMED BY HUGE WHITE COLUMNS, stood a figure wreathed in light. And it was to this figure surrounded by a dozen serfs bearing flaming torches that Prince Dmitry made his way. Something in the stance of this apparition made Gregory realize it was a woman.

She was crowned with a headdress of glistening white pearls that encircled her shadowed face and draped around her neck and shoulders in long strands. Her body was covered with a fur-trimmed mantle of brocade on red velvet that fell in thick stiff folds about her. She was as immobile as a statue, and it seemed to Gregory that she must be some effigy or icon.

It was not a movement on her part that finally betrayed her human form, only the Russian winter. From her face, shadowed by her headdress and the darkness, Gregory saw her warm breath evanesce into the cold night air.

Prince Dmitry mounted the steps and crossed the terrace to her. She stared intently at him. A moment later, with slow ceremony, she dipped in a half-curtsy, half-

14

bow. Then, methodically, she took his gloved hands in hers and kissed them. Her movements were slow and formal, but Gregory sensed a great tension within her body. She stood up again, and gazed at Dmitry for several moments longer. Suddenly a sigh escaped her, and with an extraordinary strength and rapidity, she threw both her arms about his neck. Dmitry returned the passionate embrace.

"Mitya, Mitya, golubchik moy!" came her voice in a tone that was both sad and ecstatic.

Gregory had never witnessed such a strange and intense homecoming, betraying so many colors of emotions, and he had never in his life seen a woman embrace a man with the vitality of this unknown woman weighed down under the mass of pearls.

After some minutes, Prince Dmitry gently pulled away and indicated his companion. The woman turned distractedly toward Gregory. He now had a chance to glimpse a small straight nose and, in the light of the flames, the shadow of high, very wide cheekbones. Her lips were dark and round and partly opened as she turned to look at the other traveler. Her gaze was forthright and lacked any trace of self-consciousness or affectation. She glanced away a second later and again embraced the young prince as if she would never let him go.

Prince Dmitry laughed gently, said a few words of Russian to her, and then, in French, said, "Gregory, my sister, Tatyana Ivanovna." But she was still gazing into her brother's face.

Gregory felt disconcerted, for she scarcely seemed aware of his existence. "Her features are odd," he thought to himself. "Her cheekbones are too wide, and her lips are decidedly too full." It was a habit with Gregory when confronted by a woman, especially one that was young, to consider her looks with detachment and to make a mental note of any defects, just as he would with a racehorse or frock coat. "Yes, an unusual face, but not a beautiful one," he decided. "By no means beautiful at all. In fact, one might call her plain."

The young princess now briefly turned her attention to him again and said in polite French, "Gregory Grandison, you are Mitya's friend? Well then, you are very much welcome in my father's house." Her eyes instantly reverted to her brother's. "Let us go in, Mitya. Father will want to see you."

Gregory and Dmitry followed the young princess indoors, where she intermittently squeezed her brother's arm, repeatedly murmuring "Mitya," which was her pet name for him.

They passed through a wide entrance hall, where in typical Russian gesture of hospitality, Tatyana offered them black bread and salt from two silver trays. But now that she had abandoned all ceremony, she did this in an impulsive way, barely waiting till they had nibbled the offering before she prodded them into the drawing room.

They were greeted by the sweet and pungent smell of honey and incense as she opened the doors. Within, the room was furnished in the European style, with a lofty ceiling and mirrors and portraits hanging from the walls. At the end of the room, thick damask curtains hung from ceiling to floor, covering the huge double windows that were sealed with wax to keep out the cold. The room itself was dominated by a large stuffed leather ottoman. Elsewhere and around the walls was a profusion of mahogany tables and chests inlaid with gold and steel on which stood bronze candelabra, sculpted busts, and Grecian urns carved from malachite.

But on closer inspection, details were exotic and not to be found in an English or French drawing room. Against the inner wall reared a large firebrick stove covered in richly designed enamel tiles that reached to the ceiling. It was this stove that kept the room so warm, and one was to be found in every Russian household. And in one corner of the drawing room, a soft red lamp burned that illuminated a cluster of wooden crucifixes and icons set on a table, with one Madonna after the other set in ornate gold frames.

"You had best take off your coat, Gregory," said Dmitry. "You will find it very warm here otherwise." In the way that Dmitry waited for Gregory to remove his wraps, it was obvious how much he deferred to the Englishman and how deeply fond he was of him. Divested of their coats, the appearance of both young men contrasted like light and dark with each other.

Prince Dmitry was of medium height and strongly built. His blue eyes smiled out of a strong, square face and ruddy cheeks. He kept his dark gold hair cut short and straight but wore a moustache—the prerogative of a military man. His honest, energetic countenance and muscular build gave the impression of youthful vitality and optimism.

Gregory was in shade and substance Prince Dmitry's opposite. He was only a little taller than Dmitry but stood with the weight on his heels and his head thrown back, which created the illusion of more height. He was also impeccably dressed in a gentleman's bottle green frock coat, mustard breeches, and a pair of Hessian boots that came almost above the knee. He had the English fair complexion and a rather long, angular face. But his aquiline nose, too large on any other face, suited it well and suited the hollow of his cheekbones. There was even a slight indentation at his temples, framed by the short loose curls of his dark hair. He wore a moustache and his side whiskers had been exquisitely trimmed. When he moved, he did so with graceful ease and confidence. But the smoldering gaze of his dark eyes contradicted the lazy rhythms of his speech. His manner, combined with the affected tilt of his head, conveyed a sense of *hauteur*.

He unwrapped a saffron-colored scarf from around his neck and casually dropped it into Dmitry's outstretched hands. And it was only this movement that drew Tatyana's eyes reluctantly from her brother to their visitor. Something in the gesture bothered her, and she wondered if this person cared for her brother as much as Dmitry deserved.

Tatyana longed to embrace her brother again and to chatter with him at length in Russian. But remembering her father's injunctions about propriety, she addressed him in French, their second language and the language of the court. It was superficial and more lovely than Russian, and it did seem right in the company of a stranger. So in French she asked, "Did you have a safe journey?"

Prince Dmitry launched into an account of their trip and of the wolf attack. This raised a series of strong expressions in Tatyana's face, first of fear, then dread, then awe, then excitement, and then smiles of delight and laughter as she heard of their rescue by the *mujiks* sitting like owls in the trees.

"How good they are, father's *mujiks,*" she said with evident pride and pleasure. "The wolves have been so very bad these last few winters, more wily than ever. I keep urging father to post a bounty. In the next district they are offering five rubles for each dead wolf. Imagine, the serfs could grow rich in no time. Father hasn't had a chance to offer similar rewards. Perhaps, Dmitry, you can urge him to." And here she slipped her arm in his.

"Yes, yes," said the young prince eagerly. "There are many things I wish to speak to him about." Then seeing the questioning gaze on his sister's upturned face, he only said, "Let me have a good look at you. Into the light where I can see your face."

Obediently Tatyana turned her face up to the glow of the lantern and smiled at Dmitry. He touched her chin with his hands and scanned her face with its wide high cheekbones and green eyes.

"You have really grown up in two years, Tanya," he said with admiration. "You are radiant. Your soul smiles from your eyes."

Tatyana laughed, and indeed her face was radiant, with the love she felt for her brother evident in the look she gave him. The intimacy and shared past of the brother and sister heightened Gregory's aloof manner. Gregory had never found much to be jealous of in Dmitry and regarded him with an affection couched in his sense of his own superiority. But now for the first time he felt momentarily at a disadvantage. And the disadvantage ripened.

"She is a beauty, is she not?" Dmitry asked, in his enthusiasm wishing to draw in Gregory.

"As only your sister could be," Gregory murmured politely. But he barely glanced at Tatyana and turned his intent gaze elsewhere in the room. This maddening insouciance had enflamed many a feminine heart.

But the snub was lost on Tatyana. She had not noticed, and if she had she would not have cared. For to Tatyana, her beauty, if that was what they wished to call it, had no function except to please her father, and after him, her brother and perhaps her dearest friends. If these select few had found her ugly, her vanity would have been wounded. But if others thought her plain—which happened rarely—it meant not a particle to her.

Suddenly Tatyana tilted her head, and an expression of fear and exultation galloped across her features.

"Here he comes," she whispered, and she flew to the door of the drawing room. Neither Dmitry nor Gregory heard a sound, though they paused and listened. "Yes, here comes father," she exclaimed. She opened the door, and they heard a deep, gruff voice from down the hallway.

"Another hand, another hand, you fools, or you will drop me. I am not some tin samovar to be sloshed about. Have a care. Another hand!"

There was a rapid, excited conversation in Russian, the creak of wood, and the scurry of feet. As Tatyana stepped aside, a massive baroque chair carried by four young men in peasant costume came barreling into the room.

"Put me down now, put me down," roared the old man, who sat slumped in its cushions, half hidden under wolfskin rugs. The chair was immediately grounded. The old man clapped his hands in dismissal and the young peasants fled. Then he stared imperiously at the new arrivals.

Prince Ivan Korbatsky was dressed as a man of his generation. He wore a maroon caftan, a powdered wig, and a skullcap. The silver curls fell onto his shoulders, framing an ashen face with heavy jowls, partly hidden by a drooping white moustache. But the eyes that scrutinized the two young men were beady and very much alive.

"My son," he proclaimed loudly, and held out his hand to be kissed. Prince Dmitry went down on his knee and pressed the soft old fingers to his lips. "Papa, it is good to be home, and good to see you in such vigorous spirits," he said warmly.

"Did you expect to find me in my coffin?" demanded Prince Korbatsky, screwing up one eye.

"Papa, let me introduce my friend, Gregory Grandison, of whom I have written," said Dmitry, scarcely aware of this remark.

Prince Korbatsky raised his quizzing glass and studied the Englishman. He saw a well-built young man with handsome features who met his glance and matched it openly.

"You are welcome at Starlina," said Prince Korbatsky. As a former Field Marshal, Prince Korbatsky was used to examining those he came across without any self-consciousness. Another glance through the quizzing glass and he dismissed Gregory from his notice. Now the old prince turned to his son.

"You are not wearing a uniform, Dmitry Ivanovich," he said, laying particular stress on his son's patronym.

"No, father. As you know, I have been on leave from active duty for the past year."

Prince Korbatsky cleared his throat. "A year, is it? And what may I ask have you done with all that time?"

"Oh, father, I have written to you of my activities. I have learned a great many things—"

"I hope that you have learned your place is with the Imperial Guard," interrupted his father.

"In fact, father, I have learned the contrary," began Prince Dmitry, but he was again interrupted, this time by his sister.

"Oh, papa, they have had the most harrowing journey," said Tatyana. "They were pursued by wolves. Platon is out back right now taking care of the horses who were wounded."

Tatyana drew up a footstool beside her father's chair and began to tell her father all about the wolf attack. Prince Korbatsky did not seem to notice that his conversation with his son had been interrupted, and he listened closely to her account.

At last, when she was finished, he spoke. "Well, these two young men are in good health. If I cannot expect my own son—flesh of my flesh— to withstand a few underfed baggages of fur, what is the fatherland to come to after all?" But during the course of Tatyana's narrative, the prince had slowly pulled on the tips of his white moustache and even faintly smiled when Tatyana described Dmitry shooting one of the wolves who had leapt into the sleigh. And he did not again for the time being allude to Dmitry's lack of uniform. Instead he added, "Let us drink something to your return."

He clapped his hands for tea but then added, "Of course, the occasion might have been more pleasurable if your arrival had been made earlier." No one said anything, and he turned brusquely to the Englishman. "May I ask you, Mr. Grandison, were you a help or hindrance in getting my son back to me?"

Just then a house serf scrambled into the drawing room with a silver samovar shaped like a phoenix, and he set this down beside Prince Korbatsky.

"I have neither helped nor hindered him, Prince," answered Gregory. Prince Korbatsky raised his quizzing glass again to consider at his leisure the young person who had made this answer. "Tell me, Mr. Grandison," he said at length, "what is your opinion of our country?"

Gregory smiled. "Under so much snow it is rather hard to tell. Your wolves are ambitious. Your serfs—servants hardy. That is all that I have been able to observe so far." He paused. "Oh yes, and the Russian method of doing things seems very thorough, at least I think that is the word. Each one of my books was examined, and my passport checked at every posting station."

Prince Korbatsky fixed the young man with his beady eyes. He was no idiot and recognized the ironic criticism in the young Englishman's voice. And unlike many of his compatriots, he was no Anglophile. His memory was tapped by some written words of Dmitry's in a letter. "Ah, yes," he remembered to himself, "one of those insufferable young European idealists one hears so much of these days." But he kept this observation to himself and only said, "Yes, our Russian ways are very thorough, quite different from yours," and without waiting for an answer added, "and what, young man, will your family think of your leaving the civilized continent for the wilds of Russia?"

"It will afford no one either pleasure or pain."

"How is that, young man? It is usually a matter of some concern to parents when their sons leave home in order to traipse about the continent." Here he cast a baleful look at his own progeny.

"In my case, such human sentiments are spared. I have no family."

"No family?"

"Only a stepfather I have not seen in . . . many years. That is all."

"Many years?" repeated Prince Korbatsky, and he seemed so offended by this notion that he began to scowl.

"Are you all right, father?" asked Tatyana. "Is your leg hurting you?"

"No, Tatyana," said the prince in a fonder voice and stroked Tatyana's pearl headdress. He turned to his son. "Here is a dutiful child, a loving daughter who is always by my side and whose every thought is for my comfort in this life and my salvation in the next." He chucked Tatyana under the chin. "My loyal little snow princess."

This was Prince Korbatsky's pet name for his daughter. When Tatyana was six years old, she had built a snow sculpture in honor of her father's name day. It was mid-April, but there was still snow on the ground. She had worked until dusk, long after she began to shiver from the cold, in order to be completed for the following day. The next morning she was overcome with fever but proudly dragged her father out on his balcony to see the awkward statue she had built the night before.

Tears sprang into her eyes when there was no trace to be seen of the snow sculpture. "Papa, I built you a princess out of snow," she wept with the purity of grief only children feel, "and now she's run away!" Her father sniffed the warm air and laughed. "It is only the spring that took the snow away. My real snow princess is right here beside me." The title had stuck ever since, used in sentimental moments by her father.

"Yes," repeated old Prince Korbatsky, "my loyal little snow princess."

The not so subtle comparison between siblings might have irked the prodigal son, but Prince Ivan's intentions backfired as Dmitry turned bright eyes on his sister.

"Indeed, father, I am amazed at how much she has grown in my absence and how charming she looks in Russian dress." He lifted Tatyana up by her elbows. "You wore it in honor of my arrival?"

"Yes, yes, but don't you recognize this *sarafan?*" she asked, spreading the voluminous folds of the pyramid-shaped dress.

Dmitry looked puzzled.

"Nor my *kokoshnik?*"

And here Dmitry scrutinized Tatyana's pearl head-dress. "Was it mama's?"

"The *sarafan* and the *kokoshnik* were both your mother's," said Prince Korbatsky irritably.

"I am ashamed not to have remembered, father," said Dmitry. "But they do look wonderful on Tanya."

"Father presented this *kokoshnik* to mama at their wedding. Did you notice? Not just the ordinary river seed pearls, but real, oriental ones," said Tatyana proudly. "Is it true, father, there was one pearl for every soul she brought with her dowry?"

"True enough," said the old prince, and ordered Timofey, the house butler, to pour him another cup of tea from the samovar.

Prince Dmitry fingered a long strand of pearls from the *kokoshnik*. "Why, there must be five or six hundred pearls here father."

"Why do you look surprised?" countered Prince Korbatsky.

"Five hundred seems a lot for a dowry."

"Five hundred was a lot, but in my father's day, five hundred was less than it is now. Your grandfather owned sixty thousand serfs at the height of his career, most of them a gift from Catherine the Great."

"How many do you have now?" asked Dmitry innocently.

Prince Korbatsky began to stroke his droopy moustache. "The sum has naturally been eroded away in two generations. I'm not sure of the exact figure. It is only several thousand, I believe. My new steward would know."

"Father, stewards are a worthless lot, always out to better themselves at the expense of their employers and the serfs. Do you not keep track of the numbers yourself?" said Dmitry with surprise.

The old prince began to tug on his moustache as if he was annoyed. "The only reason he would know the exact figure is that he recently sold a number of villages for me."

"Oh, yes, we passed the Razlin forests on the way up. I stopped a *mujik* who I thought belonged to you and learned that he now belongs to Count Vasily Turburov, your neighbor."

"I didn't know you had sold some villages to the Turburovs," interjected Tatyana with surprise. "Father, you have always taken great pride in not selling the serfs and the land."

"Yes, yes, yes," snapped Prince Korbatsky, twisting sideways in his seat, and added as if feeling the need to justify himself, "The count has been gradually acquiring land, and since those forests abut some of his property, and since they are of no use to me, I told him I would sell them to him. And let me tell you, he offered me a very good price—a thousand rubles a serf." Then he added quickly, "What do I need with so many serfs?"

While his father spoke, Dmitry's face had become suffused with more color and animation than had yet been seen on it since his arrival. When he spoke, his voice was low but eager. "Father, what a great opportunity you have missed. You feel yourself overwhelmed with estate matters and your conscience troubled by our family's richness? Instead of selling the serfs, why didn't you give the land to the serfs themselves and grant them their freedom?"

Prince Korbatsky stared at his son as if he were one of those American Indians. "Grant my serfs their freedom?" he spluttered.

"Yes, father, emancipate them! A prince in Novgorod has done as much."

"Well, that prince is either a fool or so extraordinarily rich that he can no longer think straight. What absurd notions are these spoken by my own son? Is that what you've been up to in Paris, plotting ways to undermine your father's fortune?"

Dmitry shook his head. "No father, certainly not. And I did not wish to trouble you tonight, but to raise a crucial issue—the morality of owning men of flesh and blood like ourselves." But seeing his father's white eyebrows begin to knit in consternation, he changed his tack. "Father, giving the serfs their freedom could even be profitable for you. As it is the serfs are so discouraged you need two or three to do the work of one. They only cultivate enough for your subsistence and their own. If they were motivated—"

"I will not hear such rubbish in my house, by a son who has not once stepped over this threshold in twenty-four months, and for four years before that only twice a year. You speak out of ignorance, I assure you." He swept the air with his arm. "I am tired, Tanya, that wretched Timofey is never to be found when he is needed. Tanya, pour me some tea."

Tatyana instantly complied. But now Dmitry's face was flushed.

"Father, if the welfare of the serfs does not concern you, think at least of the peasant rebellions that have taken place. Such conditions cannot last. If we do not grant them their liberty, the peasants will some day take it themselves. Their vengeance will be great!"

"Mitya," exclaimed Tatyana nervously as she handed her father his cup of tea, "Father's souls would never rebel, would never hurt us. They are happy here. They don't want to be abandoned! Father takes care of them in the famine. Who but the czar himself would show such concern and felicity for those more unfortunate than he? Our serfs love father dearly."

"Tanya, you do not understand. If they were free, these men and women, these children of the earth would learn to take care of themselves, would learn how to set aside stores of grain for themselves in times of trouble. They would no longer be dependent on the fickle generosity of whoever happens to be their master."

"Father is no fickle master, Mitya," said Tatyana, a slight frown appearing on her smooth white forehead. "The souls love him and trust him."

"As a dog loves his master."

"Enough of this fantastic talk," interrupted the old prince, rapping the arm of his chair. "I have not lived to the age of sixty-nine to be told by my own son how to dispose of Starlina. But we will indeed resume this conversation at a later date. Now, Tatyana, be so good as to show your brother and our guest to their rooms." The prince clapped his hands and had himself carried from the drawing room after wishing them good night.

As Tatyana led the young men down the long corridor that led to their quarters, she turned to Dmitry with a worried look. "Mitya, what is freedom to the serfs? They do not cherish it."

"Not cherish their freedom?" said Dmitry excitedly. "When these poor folk must beg for permission to marry? When families are broken up by the outright sale of the land and the people that live on it? When they are beaten and whipped with the knout for minor trespasses? Not cherish their freedom?"

"But papa is not like that," said Tatyana, defending her father against the strange notions of her beloved brother, for that was all she heard in Dmitry's words. At the doors to their rooms, where they had now arrived, she added, "Only think, Mitya, what little good can come of such talk." She was surprised by her brother's outburst, for Dmitry had always been sensible and practical and realistic. He was not the kind to get dragged into issues that had no bearing on their lives. But as she spoke she happened to look up at Dmitry's friend and was struck by the ferocious look in his dark eyes fixed on her with obvious scorn. So this is where Mitya's notions have come from, she realized suddenly, scanning that high, wide forehead and dark brow. Who is this strange man who has come in our midst? she wondered as she kissed her brother's hands and wished them both good night. This homecoming was not the heartwarming scene she had for so long envisioned, and Tatyana went off to bed feeling curiously unsettled.

Chapter Three

"WAKE UP, WAKE UP, CHILD," URGED A WOMAN WHO STOOD in the morning sunlight shaking the feather comforter over her young mistress.

Tatyana lifted her head from her pillow. "Go away, Dunyasha, let me sleep."

"No, I won't," said Dunyasha, who had been Tatyana's *nyanya*, or nurse, almost from birth. She was a short, stolid peasantwoman with bright blue eyes and a red face. Despite her plumpness her step was light, and she reminded Tatyana of a bouncing red ball. This vigor was partly because she was still quite young, only forty-one, and because never having married gave her a girlishness. But the relationship between nurse and mistress was much like mother and daughter. It was to Dunyasha that Tatyana had always run as a small child for comfort, safety, and understanding.

"No, I won't go away, little mother," repeated Dunyasha. "You told me to wake you early, and it is past ten o'clock. Don't you wish to see the work on your gown?

Or don't you care what work your *nyanya* has gone to to see that you are the most beautiful young lady at the ball tonight? Tell me, do you want pearls on the sleeves as well?"

"Shush, Dunyasha," said Tatyana, pushing her *nyanya's* hand away. "Why should I wake to hear you squawking? I said to awaken me, not to frighten me to death. I thought the house was on fire."

The peasantwoman gasped and quickly made a sign of the cross. "Father in Heaven forbid such a thought! I wouldn't be speaking of pearls and such fineries if the house was visited by the Red Rooster."

"Oh, but Dunyasha, I did dream about a fire last night," said Tatyana, suddenly wide awake and sitting up in bed. "I really did. I dreamed that our English guest held a pine torch, flung it down, and set the house on fire!"

"Heaven forbid the thought," repeated Dunyasha, and again, since she was superstitious, crossed herself.

"How odd to dream of him," said Tatyana. "He has been here only five days. I hardly know him," and Tatyana absently curled a lock of her wheat-colored hair about her finger.

"It is no wonder that you dreamed of him," said Dunyasha, "for I heard your father say he thought the gentleman had enflamed your brother's thoughts."

"Yes," said Tatyana, "the house has been a little topsy-turvy! Why, at every meal it seems Mitya manages to find something wrong with Russia and to argue how much Russia should look to Europe. And that Mr. Grandison hardly says a word, but I can see the same ideas smoldering in those dark eyes of his that look like tunnels into the center of the earth." Tatyana shivered. "Maybe that is why I dreamed of him. He scares me a little."

"He does know how to make a body feel uncomfort-able," chatted Dunyasha, "but it's that valet of his who is driving us all out of our minds," she said, referring to the house serfs. "I'll tell you, that little midget wouldn't drink kvass with us last night; said he wanted wine, Bordeaux —like the master. Imagine a valet wanting wine! That Gregory Grandison has spoiled him awful."

Dunyasha began to lay out Tatyana's day dress.

"And such airs he has, that Anatole. You should see, little mother, those itty-bitty breeches he wears. They are made of calfskin. Imagine a servant wearing calfskin. And silver buckles on his shoes. I tell you," she said, winking and quoting a Russian proverb, "the devil is always dressed in the latest fashion."

Tatyana laughed while she lolled in bed, and Dunyasha rambled on. "And you should see the way he brushes his master's coats. No vigorous one-two, like one of our own hearty house serfs would do in half a minute. No, you'd think he was painting a holy icon, he is so very particu-lar." And here Dunyasha, with her voluptuous peasant figure, stuck her pinky in the air and in a burlesque manner proceeded to paint the air with tiny imaginary brush strokes.

Tatyana laughed, for she always found Dunyasha amusing. "You're just mad because the valet had the audacity to throw you out of his master's rooms while he was shaving Mr. Grandison."

"Not only that, he told me to knock on the door before entering next time," huffed Dunyasha, recollecting the insult. Like most house serfs, Dunyasha had always had complete access to any room in the house, day or night. So this injunction from a pipsqueak French valet was almost more than Dunyasha's peasant pride could bear. "And you know what else that Anatole did yesterday?"

"Spare me, Dunyasha. I have heard of nothing else the

past few days," interrupted Tatyana, "I want my breakfast first. You will have to handle Mr. Grandison's valet as
best you can, and if *you* can't do it, no other servant in
this household can."

Dunyasha grumbled but began gently to brush Tatyana's long shining hair while Tatyana gazed in the
mirror. "Have Mitya and Mr. Grandison breakfasted?"
asked Tatyana.

"Mr. Grandison is sleeping late, and your brother
breakfasted with your father. But it did not go well."

Tatyana's questioning glance was reflected in the mirror, and Dunyasha answered, "You know how your
father is—how punctual and ordered he is about everything, and how he becomes enraged if his breakfast is half
a minute late on the table? Well, Dmitry arrived after the
meal started. Your father then told Dmitry he had some
letters of recommendation for him, including one for the
Governor-General of St. Petersburg, General Milor—I
can't ever remember his name."

"General Miloradovich," tripped off Tatyana's tongue.
She was very fond of the handsome count, who was an
old friend of her father's and who, like her father, had
distinguished himself during the Napoleonic campaign.
"Yes, Dunyasha, what did Dmitry say?"

"Your brother said that he would meet with the
different gentlemen but refused to promise he would
accept a commission in the army." Here Tatyana sighed,
and Dunyasha continued. "Your father grew angry and
had himself carried away, saying he couldn't stomach
breakfast in the face of such foolhardiness."

Tatyana bit her lip. "I don't know what's come over
Mitya. He is just as charming and handsome and lively as
he always was, but he has a bee in his bonnet. And papa
is just tired of being stung. This is the first year papa said
he wouldn't go to the New Year's Ball at the Winter

Palace, but perhaps it's a good thing. After the ball Mitya will stay in the capital and see all the people papa's recommended. Then maybe he'll be sensible and go on to be a dashing young colonel in the Preobrazhensky Foot Guards, or maybe a captain in the Horse Guards. How handsome he would look in a white uniform and a scarlet cape!" Her smile crumbled. "I really do hope he obeys father. Tell me, Dunyasha, any word as to whether that Mr. Grandison will accompany us to the ball? I can't imagine he'd enjoy himself. He's so high-minded he would probably consider an invitation to the czar's ball a mere frivolity." As Tatyana said this she was gazing at herself in the mirror. "Dunyasha, am I pretty?" She scrutinized her features closely.

"How can you ask such a thing," answered her *nyanya*. "Who has greener eyes this side of the Neva, or hair the color of ripe wheat, and then on top of that, my *golubushka*, a complexion to put the snow to shame."

"But my cheekbones are too wide, my mouth is too big."

"You are fishing for compliments now, princess," said Dunyasha. "Your cheekbones are and should be your pride and joy. They are what hold your face up after all."

"They are rather interesting, aren't they?" agreed Tatyana with such artlessness that Dunyasha laughed.

"Don't worry, little mother, you will be the beauty of the ball."

"I hope so. I want to have fun no matter what, no matter how much Mr. Grandison looks down his long nose at us. And I want to look lovely for Mitya, so he can be proud of me tonight." She looked up at her nurse fiercely, and then smiled sweetly. "Now Dunyasha, if you please, please bring me a bowl of cherries. I have a ferocious appetite this morning."

A similar tête-à-tête was taking place at the other end

of the house, in the guest room set aside for Gregory Grandison.

Gregory Grandison had also slept late, and now he stood at the window, looking out on the snow and the sunlight, while he put his agate cufflinks through his shirt sleeves. He had one foot up on a stool, and Anatole, his valet, was polishing his boot.

"Hélas, monsieur, how long are we going to stay in this godforsaken country full of snow, serfs, and superstitious women?" heaved Anatole. "When are we to return to France and a proper existence, *monsieur?"*

"Always *la belle France!"* laughed Gregory. "What a xenophobe you are. I'm surprised at you."

"Ah, but *monsieur—"*

"You are a citizen of a country that rose up in arms to topple a monarchy and sent its pampered aristocrats to the guillotine. Look around you, you might learn something from this country."

"Yes," said the valet bleakly, "that they are two hundred and fifty years behind the times. Please, *monsieur,* let us return to the nineteenth century."

"Two hundred and fifty years," mused the young Englishman. "Curious and interesting that you should choose that number. There's more truth to your remark than you can guess. For that's almost precisely how long the Mongol horde occupied Russia, clapping its oriental bell jar down on progress of any kind. Russia was a thriving country and Kiev a brilliant metropolis until the advent of Genghis Khan." Gregory gave Anatole his other boot to polish. "So you see, Russia is hardly to be faulted if it is more primitive than Europe. And it wasn't until Peter the Great that any Russians were even allowed to travel to the West. No, there's nothing wrong with this country—except for the blasted cold. All Russia needs is to have its windows opened, its shutters rattled, and a little fresh air to kick up the dust—or, should I say, snow."

"So we are here to kick up the dust?" asked Anatole morosely.

"Not at all. We are foreigners you remember. But I think that if you will keep your eyes open, Anatole, you may just see some of Russia's own countrymen do precisely that."

"How do you know all these things, *monsieur,* Mongol hordes and the such like?" asked Anatole, waving his tin of polish. "I never understand it."

Gregory put on his silk embroidered waistcoat. "Reading, Anatole, and not just your giddy little French novels. Tell me, Anatole, does the name Voltaire mean anything to you?"

"Voltaire, Voltaire," muttered the little valet. "Is he the chemist off the Jardins des Tuilleries?"

Gregory laughed. "Of course, who keeps a parakeet named Jean-Jacques Rousseau. No, you nincompoop. Voltaire is the author of the satirical novel *Candide,* and perhaps the greatest of your countrymen to further the cause of the French Revolution. How ignorant you are, Anatole, of your native soil."

Anatole drew himself up to his full height, which was just up to Gregory's shoulder. "I am a gentleman's valet, *monsieur.* I have more important things to do than read." Then he knelt down and began vigorously to brush his master's boot. Gregory laughed again. "I am sorry, Anatole, if I have offended your sensibilities. I know that looking after me is a thankless job, and a full-time one." Gregory raised an eyebrow with amusement. "Especially since you have chased all the serfs away from me or my rooms."

"Believe me, *monsieur,* it was for your own good. These Russian servants are maniacs." The valet rolled his eyes. "It is I, not you, who am forced to take my dinner with them at night. They eat a wretched compote of cabbage and beets whose effect on my liver is too terrifying a notion to consider. And in the middle of this so-called meal they get drunk, break out into songs, and then into fist fights; weep, embrace like old friends returned from the grave, and then, on the table—beside the very food we have been eating—they begin to dance! It is just too *dégoûtant* for words!" Anatole mopped his brow at the memory of this terrible ordeal and, remembering something, added, "On top of all that, you return with some dignity to your meal and somebody cries, 'Shush, I think I hear a *domovoy.*' Well, I found out a *domovoy* is not a rat, or a bat, or a cat, but a ghost. And so then it's everybody down on their hands and knees to pray. And from the little I have seen, no wonder the *Bon Dieu* never responds to one's prayers. He is too beleaguered in this corner of the world with their endless petitions." Anatole ran his short fingers through his hair. "And on top of all else, they grease their hair with the stuff they drink, called kvass!"

Gregory laughed. "It will be impossible for me to sleep knowing how your sensibilities have been offended. Is there nothing redeemable about these Russian serfs?"

"Nothing, *monsieur,* nothing. And there is the young princess's nurse, who was put on earth, I believe, to drive me mad. She thinks herself so clever because she picked up a few words of French from her mistress. So it's always, 'Commant allay voo, mussya, see voo play?' all day long, and she curtsies and snickers when I go by."

Gregory smiled. "I wouldn't pay any attention to her mockery. After all, you are a free man, an independent spirit, and they are the possessions, like so many boots and bottles, of a free man like yourself. Remember, Anatole, *noblesse oblige.* If it is any consolation to you,

ignorance in Russia seems democratic. It is all Prince
Dmitry can do not to argue with his father every minute
of the day, for the notions in this family are positively
antediluvian. And it is not just a symptom of old age.
Both father and daughter are cut from the same cloth."

"Cut from the same cloth, *monsieur?*" asked Anatole
with a twinkle in his eye. "Father and daughter? I would
call the princess more of an eyeful than the old prince."

Gregory glanced at Anatole, who was now brushing
his coats. "You old Don Juan. So you like the princess's
odd looks?"

"*Oui, monsieur, tout à fait!* She is very unlike our
Western ladies, pretty in an exotic way. Besides, that
skin, those eyes—"

Gregory snorted in derision. "I can explain scientifical-
ly what you find so fetching. She has the Slavic coloring,
but the touch of Mongol in her aristocratic blood gives
her those bones and her almond eyes. That is what you
must find so fascinating."

"No, *monsieur,* it is not just her looks, *monsieur,* but
the way . . . she looks at you. You know, *sans artifice.*"

"Perhaps, but she is ignorant all the same," retorted
Gregory with a vehemence that startled Anatole. "Damn
it, I cannot get this stock right," he added, trying to adjust
his white silk neckcloth.

Anatole gazed at his master a moment and began to
speak. But then he stopped himself.

"What is it, Anatole?" asked Gregory irritably.

"Ah, nothing, *monsieur,*" said his valet, who went
back to brushing his master's greatcoat.

"She is a princess in the worst ways," said Gregory out
of the blue. "Good-hearted maybe, generous perhaps to
those she cares for, and yes, perhaps vivacious—and
clearly loyal. But!" and here he knotted his stock. "She is
also ignorant—absolutely ignorant—and lives her life

without the slightest inkling of what the world is really like, or of how others live. Her naiveté is simply unfathomable, in fact, almost criminal."

"*Monsieur,* you don't have to convince me," agreed Anatole, shivering. "These Russians could curdle vichyssoise!"

That evening Gregory, Dmitry, and Tatyana were driven by sleigh into St. Petersburg. They sat in a carriage attached to long steel runners. It gave them plenty of room and kept them warm throughout the many hours of travel.

"Perhaps balls are giddy events," acknowledged Tatyana affably, "but I do like them. I like them entirely. The dancing! When can one have so much fun as when dancing?" And her eyes sparkled as she peeked out through the curtained windows to see them draw up beside the Winter Palace.

The Winter Palace was the winter residence of the czar in St. Petersburg. It was here that the New Year's Ball was being held, to which Tatyana had looked forward breathlessly for so many weeks. It was almost as important to her as her brother's homecoming.

Outside, the night was crystal clear, and to Tatyana the palace seemed a vision in a fairy tale. The black sky swarmed with winking stars, and a full white moon cast its spell on the snowy square, turning everything it touched to silver. To Tatyana's excited imagination, the brightly lit palace with its fretted columns and statued minarets seemed like a filagreed crown of encrusted silver.

Every window was a blaze of light that spread its golden aura on the train of elegant sleighs that drew up and emptied its privileged contents under the palace portico.

When Tatyana, Dmitry and Gregory alighted from

their sleigh they were ushered into the Jordan entrance with its huge baroque staircase of white Carrara marble. Gilt bronze chandeliers boasting a hundred candles each illumined the gold and white interior. Along the walls guards stood at attention, dressed in scarlet uniforms decorated with the insignia of the Romanovs, a double-headed eagle.

Up the Great Stairs they were wafted while footmen in livery wandered sedately, waving censers that perfumed the gallery with the scent of jasmine, sandalwood, and patchouli. As they approached the Great Hall, Gregory saw blackamoors dressed in red pantaloons and white turbans who gracefully swung open mahogany doors forty feet high and all encrusted with gold. Here, before they entered the Great Hall, Tatyana slipped away to join the ladies.

Gregory and Dmitry entered the enormous ballroom, where they were greeted by the surprising smell of flowers against a background of music and French conversation. From the high ceilings a chandelier groaned under the weight of wax candles set in crystal whose flickerings danced in the reflection of the forty-foot high window panes. Against the paneled walls were shell-shaped silver basins choked with a profusion of gardenia and orchids, their petals multiplied over and over in the mirrors around the room.

But even more distracting than the opulence of the hall was the attire of the men and women. Every style of military dress was present, from sublieutenants in their simple court uniforms to field marshals so bedecked with gold braid, sashes, stars, and huge jewels that they looked to Gregory like upright treasure chests.

Even more resplendent than the gentlemen was the hazy gauze and glitter of tulle, taffeta, satin, and gem-encrusted velvet worn by their feminine counterparts.

Several ladies-in-waiting of the empress's entourage were so weighted down with diamonds and pearls that they could hardly move. Such extravagant richness, such ostentation, was something Gregory had never beheld even in the choice salons he had frequented, and he cast a long cold look of wonder at it.

His eye, cast upward at the ornately painted ceiling and the chandeliers, was momentarily distracted by a movement below. From across the room skimmed Tatyana, now divested of her red sable-lined pelisse, and she was looking for her brother.

The little fur bundle that had been laughing and jesting in the carriage with her brother and his friend had suddenly been transformed into a court lady. Their conversation dwindled. Both young men instinctively turned to look at her as she approached them in her little dancing slippers.

Tatyana wore a velvet ballgown the color of pine green forests. Its billowing skirt emphasized the smallness of her cinched waist, and the dark softness of the velvet made her bare bosom and shoulders seem even barer. The bodice was tightly fitted and worked with pearls and small emeralds that also sparkled along the length of the full gigot sleeves. Tonight her hair, normally parted in the middle, had been lifted up into curls on her head. These ringlets were intertwined with strands of pearls that cascaded down onto her breast. The style of her hair seemed to magnify those high, wide cheekbones of hers and framed her almond eyes made aquamarine by the color of her gown.

More extraordinary though than the unexpected sumptuousness of her beauty was the expression—or rather the expressions—in her eyes. At once bright and limpid, her eyes so easily conveyed delight and every hue and shade of feeling that a cynic would have accused her of insincerity and incapable of deep feeling. But Tatyana was not insincere, only young and ardent. And when made aware of some injustice to herself or others, her eyes could narrow and darken with such lively anger no impartial bystander could have doubted the integrity of her feelings.

To Gregory, the princess seemed an open encyclopedia whose delicate pages his penetrating eyes could rifle at will. But because he himself was secretive, he mistook her openness for superficiality of feeling. This openness in her nature made him feel superior to her, since she was so transparent. And yet, something in her open smile made him feel dissatisfied with himself and his own limitations.

For one instant, as she approached them, open admiration flitted across his face. But when she turned her laughing eyes toward those guests she passed, he observed cynically to her brother, "It is intriguing to see the many transformations young ladies undertake to make us think there is complexity in their characters."

But it was only in Gregory's eyes that deception had taken place. Tatyana still knew that she was Tatyana and would not have thought to be anybody else. Within the bone stays propping her up and the flow of green velvet, she was still the same person. It was Gregory who read the dress and misread the girl.

Tatyana beamed with pleasure at her brother and in an outburst of happiness impulsively dragged the young men across the floor in the dainty but sturdy crook of her arms. She had someone very special she wanted them to meet.

As she flew with the young men across the room, many eyes turned in her direction. There might have been other beauties there with more regular, classic features, but Tatyana's buoyant presence infected those about her, brought out the color in other ladies' cheeks, made the dull man witty; hers was not a charm of daintiness, or of serene elegance, but of raw vitality. Though she followed the Europeanized customs and dress of the court and spoke a flawless French, still she retained what she would have proudly claimed to be her Russianness. For without a mother, it was Dunyasha with her simple peasant values who had instilled her with her Russian exuberance and Russian values.

All through the evening Gregory's eyes kept turning back to her in spite of himself to see the play of decorum and spontaneity that struggled for supremacy within her. Always decorum was pushed to the brink by her strong feelings, and she gave in wholeheartedly to what she felt and wanted to say. She kept breaking from French and lapsing into Russian.

"Look who I found," she gushed, and Dmitry and Gregory came face to face with an elderly man, handsome and urbane, in full court dress. Across his chest he wore the sky blue ribbon and medal of St. Andrew, the highest order of the empire, awarded for exceptional valor. His coat was satin, embroidered with gold leaves.

"Count Miloradovich," said Prince Dmitry, bowing low to the Governor-General of St. Petersburg. "It is a great honor to see you again." Dmitry's words were not idle flattery, for the count was a very important personage in the realm, having been dubbed during the War of 1812 "the Bravest of the Brave."

The general was one of the few who stood completely at ease in the royal ballroom, and he shook Dmitry's hand with hearty affection. "It is good to see you home, my boy. Your father has hankered after you a good while. So what will it be? The Horse Guards maybe, or do you wish to be an aide-de-camp?"

"It is too soon to tell," said Dmitry quickly. "For the moment it is just good to be home, to see my father and sister."

The general turned his eye on Tatyana. "Yes, Tatyana has become a beauty in your absence, Dmitry Ivanovich. It is a good thing you have returned to look to your father, and to your sister's future as well." But she of whom he spoke suddenly whisked away, and reappeared a moment later with a lady she kissed affectionately and to whom she introduced Gregory. "This is Countess Sofia Stegorina."

The countess was dressed in a lilac gown of taffeta that complimented her delicate complexion and features. She had a quality about her of sureness and serenity that made her seem older than Tatyana, though there was only three years' difference in their ages. Her gray eyes were mild, and her voice low and even. When she took Gregory's outstretched hand, her grip was gentle but firm. But for all her calm and poise, her doelike eyes exuded the briefest hint of vulnerability. Gregory was more solicitous toward Countess Stegorina than to anybody else he met that evening. Tatyana noticed this with pleasure and was grateful to him.

"Where is my old friend Arkady?" asked Dmitry, who wore a ginger-colored frock coat, beige breeches, and a ruffled blouse.

"He will join us soon," said Sofia quietly. "You know, my husband is always talking with the men." She laughed softly, and without derision. "We come here to dance, my Arkady to debate and to listen."

The conversation was suddenly interrupted by three knocks on the marble floor of the Great Hall. Instantly everyone turned to see the master of ceremonies rap the floor with the bottom of his double-eagle cane. Immediately all trace of French repartee and the movement of silk fans came to a standstill, and it seemed a thick cord of electricity traveled through the room. There was no sound or movement, only the expectant hush of the courtiers, who knew that the double-eagle cane rapped three times on the marble floor heralded the arrival of the czar.

Chapter Four

"THEIR IMPERIAL HIGHNESSES," BOOMED THE MASTER OF ceremonies.

There was a clink of sabers as the gentlemen bowed and a rustle of gowns as the ladies dipped in curtsy.

Alexander I, wearing his white uniform and a sash of St. Andrew across his chest, appeared at the door. Beside him his wife, the Czarina Elizabeth, wore a dress made of cloth of gold with a train. They were followed in the procession by two of the czar's younger brothers, the Grand Duke Nicholas and the Grand Duke Michael. Behind them, walking in a stately manner, came the gentlemen of the bedchamber and the ladies-in-waiting.

As the czar entered the room, the national anthem played, and Tatyana listened with deep reverence. Gregory's dark eyes turned to Tatyana, feeling the intensity of her concentration. His study of her disturbed her from her reverie, and she glanced up at her brother's friend. Gregory looked particularly elegant tonight, in an evening shirt of finely pleated, embroidered linen, over which he wore a saffron-colored waistcoat with gold buttons and a black frockcoat fitted at the waist. The ruffle at his throat only added to his masculinity and emphasized the blackness of his eyes.

"Do you really feel devotion to the czar?" he asked loftily, tilting his head back as he surveyed the solemn pomp of ritual.

"Of course," whispered Tatyana, returning her eyes to her sovereign. "What an odd question." A smile broke on her lips, for she had forgotten what he said and had moved on to the next idea that pleased her. "Just wait, you will see that we open with a polonaise."

The czar and czarina took their places in the middle of the ballroom facing each other. Then, as the orchestra began to play a slow, melodious tune, other couples formed two lines with an aisle in between. To Gregory, the polonaise resembled less a dance than a parade as the czar and czarina toured the room, followed by the other members of the dance. They regained the center of the room, then started the same procession over again.

General Miloradovich had asked Tatyana to be his partner, and Dmitry was dancing with Countess Stegorina, so Gregory had more than enough time to watch this Russian court ritual. "How utterly boring," he commented to himself through closed teeth to no one in particular. "Having to do this once a month would make one addle-headed."

Shortly after the polonaise was over, Tatyana was approached by a lady-in-waiting to the empress. She wore a rose-colored gown made of tulle shot with steel and gold sequins. "Princess," she said with great formality, addressing Tatyana, "his imperial highness wishes to greet his goddaughter."

Tatyana curtsied. "The goddaughter of his imperial highness accepts this great honor." Gregory raised an eyebrow, for Tatyana had made no allusion to this special distinction. He looked at her, and she took his arm in hers.

"Dmitry is dancing with the Baroness Buxhoeveden. Would you escort me?"

At Gregory's nod, they were escorted by the lady-in-waiting to where the czar stood apart from the crowd. He was encircled by members of his inner sanctum, which consisted of several ministers and other notables. Tatyana and Gregory waited to the side until the czar should see fit to receive them. Tatyana touched Gregory's arm, keeping her eyes focused on the emperor. "If there is an opportunity, I will introduce you to Alexander."

They both stood silently and watched. The czar was tall and blond and at forty-eight still very handsome. Beside him stood a young man who resembled him and who like Alexander was dressed in full military regalia with the blue ribbon of St. Andrew also spanning his chest. This was one of the czar's younger brothers. He was handsomer than Alexander, but the expression in his eyes was harder, as if he expected iron discipline of himself and others. Gregory watched him thoughtfully.

The moment came, and Tatyana was ushered forward. She bent down in her velvet gown upon one knee and kissed Alexander's outstretched hand. "Beloved emperor," she whispered. "You do me a great honor." She raised her eyes, full of love and devotion, to the czar.

"Arise, little goddaughter," he said with placid charm. "You look lovely tonight." But the expression on his face conveyed no emotion.

"Thank you, your imperial highness."

"And how is your father? I am sorry he is not here."

"My father is well and deeply regrets absenting himself from your kindness and generosity." As she bowed her head, her curls and the strand of pearls swayed down her bodice. "It is a great honor for me to be here tonight."

The czar, by the slightest tilt of his head, turned his cool, blue eyes on Gregory. At this signal, Tatyana said, "May I present Mr. Gregory Grandison, here from England."

The czar smiled wanly at the Englishman. In a stilted but correct English he observed, "I hope you do not find our Russian winter too cold."

Gregory bowed. "The Russian cold is no match for the fiery determination of her people."

The czar gazed briefly at Gregory, as if he would again address him, but he seemed to reconsider. There were many others waiting eagerly for a chance to speak to him. He smiled faintly and by a nod of his head informed Tatyana and all present that the audience was finished. The interview over, Tatyana and Gregory were swept aside to let another honored guest be presented to the czar.

"What a good, dear man," said Tatyana, tears coming to her eyes. "I hope he will honor Mitya with an audience tonight."

"Thank you for managing an introduction for me," said Gregory abruptly and, seeing the diamondlike drops in her eyes, asked, "Would you like a handkerchief?"

Tatyana shook her head impatiently. "You were impressed by him, weren't you?"

"I had no impression of the czar whatsoever. No wonder the French always called him the sphinx of the North. His face was totally inscrutable. I could not see a hint of any feeling in him." Then half to himself he added, "There was so much promise in him at the beginning of his reign, and how little he fulfilled it."

"It is only because you are not Russian that you do not understand him or love him," sighed Tatyana.

"I admit he is an enigma to me, and I have no insight into him through his dress or behavior tonight. All I know

about him is what recent history tells me." Then Gregory
added, "Who was the tall young man with the blue
ribbon who stood beside him?"

"That was the Grand Duke Nicholas, Alexander's
younger brother."

"Will he be the next czar?"

"Not likely," responded Tatyana. "Alexander is still so
young and may yet have children. Besides, Nicholas has
his older brother Constantine before him in line for the
throne. No, he is not likely ever to be czar. Perhaps a
good thing," Tatyana added pragmatically, "since he is
not so popular."

"Well then, perhaps it is a good thing," echoed
Gregory, watching the young man across the room
whose bearing was so stiff and whose expression was so
rigid. "There was something disquieting in his eyes that
makes one think he would not be a good ruler to thirty
million people."

Tatyana scarcely heard him. "Come, you must dance
with Sofia Stegorina, and I have promised to dance the
mazurka with Dmitry."

Some half-hour later Gregory saw Tatyana again, this
time on the arm of a portly young man wearing a green,
short-waisted jacket that showed the bulge of his belly in
a pair of tight-fitting white breeches. Something in the
way he squeezed Tatyana around the waist attracted
Gregory's attention.

"Tell me, countess," he said addressing Sofia Stegorina, with whom he was dancing, "who is the officer
dancing with Prince Dmitry's sister?"

"That is Count Vasily Turburov. Surely you have heard
of Count Turburov?"

"The name is familiar, but why, I don't know," began
Gregory.

"His father was an active privy councillor of Alexander's and one of Count Arakcheyev's most trusted advisors. But he has been dead some years now, and his entire fortune passed into Vasily's hands."

"Arakcheyev," said Gregory repeating the name. "He is the minister who oversees the military colonies where the peasants are forced to do agricultural labour while fulfilling their twenty-five year military service?"

Sofia Stegorina nodded. "Count Arakcheyev is the most powerful man in Russia after the czar."

"Yes, I gather. He has a curious nickname—"

"The Vampire," said the countess in an undertone, and she almost blushed. "As you see, he is not very well liked."

"Is he here tonight?"

"He would have been, but he was called away to his estate. Apparently some of his serfs staged a rebellion, and he went to crush it."

Sofia's use of the word "crush" suggested some sympathy on her part for the rebellious serfs. Gregory did not allude to this but still made note of it. Gregory's eyes were again diverted to Tatyana and her partner. The way the young count squeezed Tatyana's waist close to him and bent near to her while he danced suggested lascivious designs on his part. By the words he whispered in her ear, he was evidently trying to flatter the young princess. She laughed up into his pasty-textured face and pointy nose. As he leered down over her, his double chin squeezed out over his tightly fitted gold braid collar.

"Count Turburov has a great many stars and seems much decorated," observed Gregory.

"Yes, he is a major-general with the Guards," said Sofia.

"He seems no older than I. How did he distinguish himself to have climbed so far?"

The countess did a ladylike version of clearing her throat. "Well, actually, nothing particular to my knowledge, but there is favoritism at court. His father, after all—and he too is now a favorite."

"A favorite of whose?" asked Gregory dryly.

"Of the Grand Duke Nicholas, Alexander's younger brother. They were in military training together. And of course, Count Turburov is very, very rich."

"No wonder the princess seems so happy to be dancing with him," remarked Gregory in a blasé voice, as he expertly maneuvered the countess through the crowd of dancers.

The countess looked up into Gregory's beautiful masculine face, flushed from the heat and incipient anger. "You misunderstand the princess, Mr. Grandison," she said gently, for she had caught something vulnerable in his battling brown eyes. "Tatyana would certainly not be after Count Turburov's money. He is a neighbor of the Korbatskys', and Tatyana is kind to everyone."

"How very open-minded of her," drawled Gregory. But noticing the gentle reproach in Sofia's gray eyes, he added, "You are right to reprimand me by your look, countess. She is the sister of my friend and daughter of my host, and my words are petty and ungrateful. Will you do me the honor of dancing with me once more?" And at Sofia's smiling nod, he became her partner in the following quadrille.

At the end of the quadrille, Tatyana and her hefty companion as well as another young lady who resembled Count Turburov approached Gregory and Sofia.

"Dmitry is off with his dancing partner, but here is Count Vasily Turburov and his sister Countess Irina," she announced gaily. "And this is Mr. Grandison, who is stopping with us this winter."

Count Vasily held out a plump white hand to shake Gregory's. He did so with the tips of his fingers, as if he were holding a skunk by its tail. And at the moment he shook hands he half pressed down on Gregory's and

pushed it away from him. It was a memorable handshake, and Gregory looked at the man who could convey
so much distaste and frigidity in that one gesture.

His face was mushroom white and flaccid, but his nose
was very pointed, and the eyes that looked out at
Gregory were small but shrewd. Gregory turned his gaze
to the sister, who was not fat like her brother. In fact, she
was neat and small. There were, however, other similari-
ties between brother and sister. The more one looked
into her face, the less one found in her that could be
described as pleasing.

Her face was pointed, with no forehead to speak of.
Her mouth was small and tight, and she looked out
suspiciously and narrow-mindedly on the world with
brown beady eyes. Even the choice of her dress was
unfortunate. The yellow hue of her ornate gown turned
her brown hair dull and made her Mongol coloring even
sallower. But when the countess saw Mr. Grandison's
dark eyes turned on her, a certain coyness appeared in
her gestures, and she simpered at him from behind her
fan. But even the simper was niggardly, for as was
betrayed in her ferretlike eyes, she entirely lacked
warmth or expansiveness. Even Prince Dmitry would
have been hard put to find her feminine charms.

Gregory seemed scarcely to notice Countess Irina's
demonstration of interest in him. It was something he had
had to endure many times before, and even more
attractive manifestations of the form had failed.

"Oh, Monsieur Grandison," said Countess Irina, pry-
ing herself near him and speaking in a highly accented
French. "We have heard so much about you in the past
five minutes. You have never been to Russia or St.
Petersburg before. Surely you must be disappointed by
our shabby imitation of the glories of Europe." Yet she
eyed the sumptuous decor of the ballroom smugly.

"As I am sure you know, countess, the Winter Palace is far more palatial and extravagant than any of its European counterparts—even the Chateau de Versailles. But of course, while the splendor always varies in degrees, the presumption that creates it is a universal trait among monarchs."

Count Vasily Turburov's sister didn't understand a word Gregory said, not because she wasn't shrewd but because the concept of his words was unfathomable to her. She twisted her face into the prettiest simper she could muster. "How true, how true," she cooed. "And what do you think of our capital? I have heard it called the Venice of the North. Of course, that may be too generous a description of our fair city. . . ."

Her cloying manner was beginning to bore Gregory, who would not feed her the compliment she was waiting for, and she finished lamely. "Certainly Mr. Grandison, you must admit St. Petersburg is a tribute to the czar who built it."

While the little countess was speaking, Gregory's eyes strayed to Count Turburov, whose eyes glazed over as he peered at the dazzling whiteness of Tatyana's bosom. He seemed scarcely aware of his sister or the conversation going on beside him.

Gregory spoke. "Yes, indeed, Countess Irina, it was clever of Peter the Great to think of building his imperial city on the Gulf of Finland, almost directly within earshot of Europe. But I did not know he was the one who actually built it and deserves your tribute."

Gregory continued casually, taking a pinch of snuff from his snuff box. "I had read somewhere that St. Petersburg was built by thousands of unpaid peasants, many of whom froze to death dredging the wretched swamps around it. I may not have my figures straight, but if I recall, only in Egypt during the building of the pyramids did so many slaves drop like flies. Perhaps that was one of the wonders of the world."

The pointy-faced Irina did not register Gregory's casual double-entendre, but Tatyana did, and she looked at Gregory in surprise. Count Vasily had also heard, and he resentfully reverted his gaze from Tatyana to the Englishman.

"It seems curious to me," he commented acidly, "for someone who is a guest to criticize our country and her foundations."

"I beg your pardon if my words were misconstrued," responded Gregory, raising an eyebrow in cynical amusement. "My intention was to honor those unremembered Russians who sacrificed their lives to pave the way for our present entertainment."

Tatyana spoke up, unable to contain her thoughts any longer. "Mr. Grandison, I can see by your look that you think tonight's activities and its setting somehow vainglorious. But surely there must be some reward for those who have the oppressive responsibility of guiding nations. The Winter Palace, for all its beauty, does not begin to compensate our beloved czar for all the worries and care he takes in governing our people."

"Virtue should be its own reward, don't you think, Princess?" returned Gregory softly. "Otherwise it is not the virtuous who reign, but those who wish power for its own sake. The czar is only a man, no better or worse than others, and not above the baser motivations of common men."

The question of the czar's unlimited power and the plight of the serfs had for some time been troubling if not the consciences then certainly the purses of many Russian aristocrats of the day. When Count Vasily Turburov spoke, he voiced the concerns of his peers made all too aware of the rumblings of revolutions in other countries and the words being spoken at home by a small handful of men beginning to share Gregory's ideas.

"My felicitations to you, sir, for your noble ideas," said the count disdainfully, "but isn't it astounding how men who voice your concerns usually have nothing at stake, nothing to lose but their breath in such pernicious political chatter. It is my guess that since you have been in our country but several weeks—according to the princess here—you are completely ignorant and make assumptions about the nature of our country." Count Vasily added, breaking the stem of an orchid dangling from an urn at his elbow, "The English I always believed were noted for their politesse and propriety, but clearly that too is a false assumption."

"Oh, Vasily," murmured his sister, poking him in the stomach, and she glanced shamefacedly at Gregory, whose brown eyes glowed brightly but without rancor. "Please forgive my brother, Mr. Grandison. He is tired from his recent post in Moscow. There he met young Russian officers with naughty thoughts about our beloved country. So you see, you have touched an open wound."

"No, your brother is absolutely correct," said Gregory with smooth sincerity. "I have seen but little of your nation. Readings and conversations do not necessarily acquaint one with the truth. I will hold my tongue until I have seen with my own eyes a little more of Russia. So forgive me my presumptions, and please excuse me. I do not wish to spoil further anyone's enjoyment of the evening." With an elegant bow, he took his leave.

Whatever else, he is certainly a gentleman, thought Sofia Stegorina to herself, watching him depart. She had listened intently to the young men's conversation but had kept her thoughts to herself.

Meanwhile, Tatyana had gone off after Gregory. When

she reached him, she was smiling. "Mr. Grandison, thank you for extricating yourself from that unfortunate conversation with such grace. Won't you please allow me to be your partner in the cotillion?" Not even waiting for his answer, she slipped her gloved hands in his, and they crossed the marble floor to join the dance. As they faced each other, Tatyana said happily, "I am glad you made amends to Count Vasily." Then she paused and smiled with impish delight. "And I hope you will let us all help you with your new education."

Gregory searched the brilliant green of Tatyana's eyes that shined like little magic forests. "I believe I can guess just what form your tutelage would take," he laughed wryly. "You would have all of us men relinquish our ideas and become as docile and obedient as you yourself."

Across the room stood Count Vasily, his sister, and Countess Stegorina, who fanned herself to keep cool from the mounting heat. Irina leaned across to Sofia and whispered, "How handsome that Mr. Grandison is, and so distinguished. And look how well he dances."

"Indeed he does," murmured Sofia. "I hope that he and my husband meet." And then she added in a voice that curiously blended pride and agitation, "They would probably find many subjects of mutual interest to speak about."

"Only, as elegant as he is," returned Count Vasily's sister, "how naughty he is! He always seems to be saying something nobody wants to hear."

"Yes, that is true," assented Sofia, but added half to herself, "That is the thing about him that is so extraordinary."

Then Sofia's pretty, sad gray eyes brightened luminously as a short, slim gentleman wearing gold spectacles approached her. "Ah, Arkady my beloved, here you are," she said, and there was such warmth in her voice it was impossible to mistake that he was her husband. Count Arkady Stegorin was not tall, but after some minutes of talking with him, people tended to forget his inferior height and to think of him as large in stature. This was partly due to his erect bearing and partly due to the influence of his ideas. Though not particularly handsome, his forthright manner and the alert, intelligent expression in his eyes charmed everyone, men and women alike. In the highest circles of society Arkady Stegorin was considered something of an eccentric. As the son of one of the most distinguished families in St. Petersburg, Arkady Stegorin had had the promise of a brilliant military future. But he had checkered his own career and delayed his climb through the ranks by choosing to become a mere justice of the peace. This decision had been unequivocal. Arkady wished to fight the corruption of the Russian courts at first hand and to judge according to his own precepts the criminal cases involving runaway or recalcitrant serfs. This move had gained him the respect of some and the derision of many. It was finally at the age of twenty-eight that he suddenly abandoned this course of action and returned to military life. Arkady received a commission as a captain in the Izmailovsky Regiment, quartered in the city. Only his most intimate friends knew why Arkady Stegorin had made this about-face. The one thing everyone did know was that he was highly respected by his fellow officers and beloved by the soldiers in his company and that he had freed his serfs.

When Arkady joined his wife he was drawn into conversation with Count Vasily Turburov, who stood fretting as he watched the Princess Tatyana dancing on the arms of the trouble-making Englishman.

"These foreigners with their high-brow, idealistic gibberish," he commented to Arkady, "are an irritable cross to bear for us respectable Russian landowners. Why, they begin to think they can get away with bandying their dangerous words around at a court function. What will things come to next?"

He, like many in the top circles of society, knew Arkàdy's reputation for being more liberal than conservative, and he spoke his words partly to test the captain.

"What dangerous words are these?" asked Arkady, and Count Vasily related the conversation that had taken place with Gregory.

"He is one of those idle mouths who, because they have a modicum of talent or brains, sweep masses into uncontrollable fury. Another Marat, another Robespierre," sneered Vasily. "We have enough problems here with our own hotheads without his kind stirring up wicked, bloodthirsty thoughts in the feeble minds of our peasants."

If Arkady disagreed in any way with the count's statement, he didn't show it, for he had learned from sad experience that one word spoken was worse than two words withheld. And discretion was now a policy with him.

But long after Count Vasily escorted Arkady's wife to dance, Arkady stood on the edge of the crowd beside a Grecian column and watched Gregory Grandison. He was still dancing with the princess, moving Tatyana in complex maneuvers through the crowd. Across the room from Arkady liveried lackeys raised long hooks and opened the uppermost windows. Instantly a breeze wafted through the stultifying air of the room. Arkady could even feel the coolness in his nostrils.

"Ah, a breath of fresh air," he mused, his eyes still narrowed thoughtfully on the Englishman who spun his partner across the floor. "A breath of fresh air is just the antidote needed."

* * *

Later that evening, after an eight-course dinner served to four thousand seated guests, Tatyana and Sofia sat together on a gold-threaded divan in a small but beautiful anteroom of the Winter Palace.

Tatyana stretched out her dark green satin slippers and moaned. "How my feet hurt from all the exquisite dancing. I wonder, Sofia, where can the men be?"

"*Nichevo, milenkaya, Tatyana,*" commiserated Sofia, using Russian since Tatyana had lapsed into it and because they were on intimate terms with each other. "You know no moderation when it comes to dancing! But I wonder, also, what can be taking the men?"

"I've hardly seen my brother all night," said Tatyana, trying to maintain a decorous pose, though she longed to undo her stays, throw off her slippers, and stretch her legs.

"I saw him dancing with half a dozen ladies," laughed Sofia, "but I imagine by now he's off somewhere with the gentlemen."

"With General Miloradovich, I hope. Father so wanted him to see him while he is in St. Petersburg," yawned Tatyana.

"But aren't he and his friend Mr. Grandison staying in the capital several days?" asked Sofia.

"Yes, at my father's house."

Sofia had often been a guest at Prince Korbatsky's lavish residence on the Great Morskaya, one of the more prestigious addresses in St. Petersburg.

"Well then, he will have a chance to meet the general again and any other people your father wanted him to see," reassured Sofia. "But tell me, Tatyana, can't I convince you to stay with Arkady and me a few days longer?"

"No," said Tatyana decisively. "Father will want me back. This is the first year he's missed the New Year's

Ball, and he will want a thorough account. Goodness, I ate too much caviar at dinner!''

"How often you put your father before you,'' scolded Sofia gently, worried that her lovely young friend spent so much time in the country with only her father as a companion, rather than in the capital where she could have more fun and be admired.

"Perhaps,'' said Tatyana, loosening the ribbons of her slippers and retying them around her ankles, "but papa is the most perfect of all fathers in the world.'' And she added, seeing her friend's questioning gaze, "He may growl a lot, but that is because his leg hurts him. I am all the world to him, I know it.''

Sofia lowered her eyes and said nothing before changing the conversation. "Your brother's friend, Mr. Grandison, is an accomplished dancer.''

"Yes, he's wonderful,'' said Tatyana, "almost as good as Mitya. How excellent Mitya looked tonight. Oh, if only he was in uniform!''

"Tell me, Tanya, what is his background, I mean, Mr. Grandison's,'' interposed Sofia. "He is not snobbish, as the English sometimes are, and yet he has a certain air. . . .''

Tatyana adjusted the pearls in her hair. "I really know very little about him. Dmitry could tell you. All I know is that he is the only son of an English tradesman and that he seems to be quite uninterested in England. He has a stepfather, I believe, but never sees him. Apparently he has spent many years in France.'' Tatyana laughed. "He has the most insufferable French valet who just drives Dunyasha wild!''

"Wild?'' laughed Sofia in spite of herself. "You mean your dear Dunyasha has finally fallen in love?''

Now Tatyana laughed again. "I did not mean wild in that way at all. Why, she can't stand him!''

Sofia returned to the subject of Mr. Grandison. "A tradesman's son?" she mused. "By his speech and manner, the way he dances, one would think him an aristocrat."

"Well, he is a little conceited," quipped Tatyana, rolling her eyes with impish gaiety. But then she added in a more serious vein, "Actually, Mr. Grandison has some of the strangest notions. Father is not overly fond of him and is not sure he is the best friend for Dmitry."

Sofia leaned forward. "Why do you say that?"

"Mr. Grandison, as you may have noticed, has rather radical English ideas. Father thinks it's all babble and will die away once Mitya is reestablished in society. I certainly hope so. Ah, here they are!"

Into the anteroom and across the parquet floor came Prince Dmitry, Gregory, and Arkady, followed by two other gentlemen who seemed to know Sofia and greeted her easily.

"Mitya, where have you been?" asked Tatyana.

"Mostly dancing," he replied, "but I came upon Arkady and Gregory talking with these two gentlemen. We got to talking because one of them is a very good friend of the great Pushkin."

Tatyana knew the name. "Of course, the young writer. He is the one with the beautiful wife."

Dmitry laughed, "That is one way to define him. Now let me introduce you to these gentlemen."

Tatyana turned and looked at the first young man. He was a tall, narrow-chested man in military uniform. He had orange hair, slightly protruding teeth, and a nose that reminded Tatyana of a platypus. But his large, pale eyes looked gentle and kind, and his manner was simple and straightforward. Tatyana instantly liked him.

"This is Prince Sergei Trubetskoy, I don't believe you know him," said Dmitry.

"I know cousins of yours, but I am not sure if I have had the pleasure," began Tatyana, perusing her memory. She was surprised she did not know him. She had recognized his name, for Trubetskoy like Korbatsky and Stegorin was a distinguished old Russian family. Tatyana did not know that they had lately fallen on bad times and that to mitigate his plight the young Sergei Trubetskoy had married an heiress. Posted to France in 1819, he had only recently returned to Russia, bringing back as his wife a cheerful French countess who had more money than she knew what to do with.

"There is no need to rack your brains, princess," said Prince Trubetskoy jovially. "I have been absent from the capital a long time and am now posted in Kiev. My wife, though, comes frequently to St. Petersburg."

"I hope I shall have a chance to meet her," said Tatyana. As he bowed she saw the white enamel cross pinned to his uniform. She recognized the Cross of St. George, one of the highest medals awarded for military valor. This pleased her, and she thought to herself, "Very good. Mitya is in good company at last."

"Princess Tatyana," said Arkady, stepping forward now, "let me also introduce to you another friend of mine, Kondraty Ryleyev. I particularly wanted him to meet your guest, Mr. Grandison. I found your brother with them already, so our encounter really does seem like fate."

Tatyana turned her attention to this second gentleman. Kondraty Ryleyev was dressed in civilian clothes like her brother and Mr. Grandison. He was slightly built, and his dark skin and dark features almost made him look Persian. His eyes were extraordinarily expressive and flitted everywhere with nervous interest. His teeth were perfectly white.

"I also recognized your name," said Tatyana, as he

kissed her hand in a graceful movement. "You are a poet, I believe, and edit a literary journal called the *Polar Star?*"

"Yes, yes, that is true," said the poet, with somewhat staccato speech. "Do you know it well?"

Tatyana shook her head. "No, no, but I have heard of it." She did not add that she had only recently heard her father damning the magazine for its liberal stance. Though he had a pleasing manner, Tatyana found herself not so drawn to Ryleyev as to Prince Trubetskoy.

Arkady spoke up. "We are sorry, ladies, to be so late, but we were all in Paris after the liberation, so we had many memories to share, and then one idea led to another idea—" He stopped himself. "Well, you know how such things go."

Tatyana wondered why her friend Sofia suddenly shivered but realized it was late, nearly three o'clock in the morning, and everyone was tired. Sofia seemed to confirm this for now she said gently, "The hour is late. Perhaps your conversation can be resumed another day."

Arkady seemed to take his wife's words literally and, turning to Gregory and Dmitry, said, "We must indeed, while you are in St. Petersburg. You must come to my house or to Ryleyev's"—and here Ryleyev inclined his head—"to dine, to talk, to play cards as well." And he added meaningfully, "The stakes may be high, but the play will always be fair."

Gregory and the Korbatskys took their leave.

When they were in the carriage Tatyana addressed her sibling. "Dmitry, you are quiet tonight. What has happened to my happy-go-lucky brother? Were there not enough pretty ladies at the ball?"

"A bevy of pretty ladies, though not quite so pretty tonight as my sister," said Dmitry gallantly.

Tatyana smiled with pleasure, but then a frown crept into her voice. "So you are going to spend your time gambling while you are in the city? Papa would be unhappy if he knew it. Is that poet Ryleyev a gambler?"

"Well," began Dmitry, unsure how to proceed.

"A gambler of ideas, not money," interjected their English guest, who had been very quiet toward the end of the evening.

"Tell me, Mr. Grandison," said Tatyana, feeling prickly with him. "Did you find anyone tonight whose society you found pleasant or worth remembering?"

"You have an excellent friend in Countess Sofia Stegorina, and I liked her husband very much," was Gregory's succinct answer.

"And I suppose you found the poet Ryleyev to be interesting?"

"Yes, that is exactly what I found him."

"He did not seem so very interesting to me," said Tatyana, surprised at herself for being so ornery with their guest.

"That is only because you did not speak to him," said Dmitry, affectionately. "To you Ryleyev must have appeared a tipsy poet, and Prince Trubetskoy only a bon vivant. But believe me, they were very thought-provoking."

Gregory leaned his arm upon his knee and pressed his knuckles against his teeth in concentration. He gazed out the window of the sleigh, at the bright and gaudy lights of the Winter Palace. The sleigh began to pull away. In his thoughts he echoed Dmitry's words, Yes, they were very thought-provoking gentlemen. Strange, he thought to himself, as the Winter Palace drew out of sight, to find in the belly of the beast such kernels of truth.

"How somber you both are," chided Tatyana in the ensuing silence, for she was too excited by the ball to think of sleep. "One would think by your silence you were deciding the fate of nations."

Tatyana never dreamed how close her idle remark came to the truth.

Chapter Five

OTHER THAN ITS IMMENSE SIZE, PRINCE KORBATSKY'S ES-
tate at Starlina was no different from a thousand others in
the Russian countryside. Like most of the country houses, Starlina was large, low, and rambling, with a ground
floor made up of one lofty-ceilinged room after another.
In addition to the huge drawing room was a similarly
huge dining room where forty people could be comfort-
ably seated. Also on this ground floor were more than a
dozen bedrooms which opened onto one another in the
European style while still having access to a corridor that
ran through the center of the house.

At the back of the house were the kitchens and
quarters for the house serfs. And under the house was a
vast network of storerooms stocked with enough food for
the household to last all winter. Vats of cheese, butter,
and linseed oil lay stacked on top of each other in the
cool darkness. One whole storeroom was a complex
pyramid of casks, one on top of the other, and all
contained fermented cabbage leaves. Racks of cool sand
hid turnip and parsnip roots, while hefty sacks of flour

hugged the cold plaster walls. Still farther on were endless barrels of salted meats and dried vegetables and fruits. As a child, Tatyana with her hearty appetite had loved to wander these cool, musty corridors, dipping her hands into the crates brimming with sweetened, dried cherries and greengage plums.

Behind the house, away from the vast lawns now hidden under two feet of snow, was a cobblestone courtyard shoveled clear, with a dairy, a forge, an outhouse, a large wooden shed for curing meats, and an ice house. Beyond the courtyard and some farm buildings was a road whose trace could only be determined from the parallel snowbanks on either side. This track led to the nearest of Prince Korbatsky's peasant villages. Here, the serfs' *izbas*, tiny cottages, clustered together on either side of the road, their thatched roofs sunk under snow and gray smoke curling from their chimneys. On all sides of Starlina stretched the property, endless fields of wheat and corn and oats, now hidden under a vast crust of icy snow. And beyond that, to the north, stretched the Razlin forests, dense with the spiky tips of evergreens.

This was the Starlina that Tatyana came home to after the ball at the Winter Palace, and she sighed with happiness to find it so. Tatyana loved Starlina dearly, loved it in the summer when the swifts and starlings flew overhead and the nearby brook, from a tributary of the Neva River, gurgled and splashed over the millwheel. She loved the ever present smell of pine and honey, the eternal drone of the bees. And always her heart leapt to see the white Doric columns of the house itself. It was framed against the lush leaves of the birch trees that skirted it and looked out from the slope on which it was situated at the lush green and gold countryside.

But Tatyana loved Starlina even more in winter. To her Russia was winter and winter was Starlina. For six months out of the year the glistening snow wrapped itself around the house, burying it almost completely in its chaste and silent bear hug.

The fierceness of the cold excited her. At night, lying in bed, Tatyana listened to the plaster-covered wood walls groaning and creaking as the beams of the house shrank with the cold. And Tatyana loved to open the *fortochka*, a window pane left unsealed during the winter months, and feel the frigid air rush into the often suffocating rooms. The warm inside air would instantly freeze and fall into tiny heaps of snow on the furniture and floor. On the coldest days, Tatyana would finger the curiously twisted icicles she found beside the house. These were made when a house serf flung a bucket of water outside the door and the water froze instantly in the air before hitting the snow.

Though Prince Dmitry and Sofia Stegorina pressed Tatyana to stay in the capital, and though this would have pleased her, Tatyana's return to Starlina did not plague her with any doubts. She really was happiest at Starlina. Besides, her father, she knew, would have a score of questions for her.

One afternoon after her return Prince Korbatsky had his house serfs carry him into the drawing room. He now sat in his high-backed chair listening to his daughter play the clavichord.

"Charmante, charmante," he praised her, for though there were many technical imperfections in her performance, she played with spriteliness and style.

Five weeks had elapsed since her return home from the capital, and still Dmitry and Gregory had not returned. Nor had Dmitry sent word of their activities or imminent arrival. In spite of this, the household seemed contented. Dunyasha was happy to be free from the superior attitudes of Anatole, and the old prince felt that no news was good news and that Dmitry would return with a choice commission in the Guards. Only Tatyana seemed less than cheerful as the days wore on.

Now she spoke. "Oh, father, I feel so bored with myself," and she turned around from the bench of the clavichord. She felt too fretful to do any of the things that had kept her so engaged before Dmitry's return from Paris. She had scarcely touched her embroidery and had only played chess once with her father, though he had offered to several times. Even her precious album, full of anecdotes, sketches, poems, *bon mots,* and the affection- ate outpourings of her friends, lay forgotten. All the rage among her female acquaintances, even the album failed to enlist Tatyana's interest.

Tatyana had been in such a hurry to return to Starlina, and now that she was here she was at a loss how to spend her time. The only activity to which she had applied herself was reading a leather-bound book containing the poems of the English poet Lord Byron. The poet's work had been recommended to her much earliér by Sofia Stegorina, but Tatyana had always preferred to read the French novels of Madame de Scudéry and the Marquise de Sévigné. Tatyana had been tutored in English, but it did not come easily to her, so she had never pursued Sofia's recommendation. But since her return to Starlina, Tatyana had spent several afternoons lounging on the stuffed leather ottoman, trying to read the poems of Lord Byron. She was tackling a very long poem and feeling impatient. In her stilted English she read out loud, half to herself:

> And the whole world would henceforth be
> A wider prison unto me:
> No child, no sire, no kin had I,
> No partner in my Misery;

"Oupph" said Tatyana rolling her eyes. "How difficult English is! There is no consistency in the verbs. How do the Americans and English ever learn it?"

"It certainly lacks the musicality of French," remarked her father distractedly. He was sorting through his correspondence. "But no doubt it serves its purpose. Why are you trying to read in English, when you have Moliere, Racine, and the writings of the Précieuses at your disposal?"

"Sofia Stegorina recommended this book. But how hard it is!" She went back to painfully translating the verses. She had applied herself to this difficult task more assiduously than to anything else.

So that afternoon when she sat at the clavichord and said, "Oh father, I don't know why, but I feel so terribly bored," he scarcely lifted a bushy eyebrow.

"There are many things to do. There is no reason to be bored. Your embroidery, for instance—"

"Oh my embroidery, somehow it seems so useless." She sighed. "Why haven't we heard from Mitya? He is taking ever so long. Besides," she added, changing the subject from singular to plural, "they were supposed to be back ages ago."

"That's nothing to fret about," said the old prince. "It is very good for him to be seen in society. If for some reason General Miloradovich can do nothing for him, there are several others who will be glad to."

"Father, are you so sure he will find a commission? He scarcely seemed interested."

"I know that he will," said the prince with assurance.

"How can you be sure?"

"I told your brother before he left for the ball that when I asked him to return to St. Petersburg it was so that he would reenroll in the Guards. And I told him that if he did not, I would hold to my original position."

"To disinherit Mitya?" said Tatyana, her brow furrowed.

The old man nodded, licked his thumb, and turned another page in his sheaf of letters.

"Father, isn't that harsh?"

"I am only harsh to those who disobey me. Am I not kind to those who do not contradict my words or wishes? Am I not kind to you, little snow princess?"

Tatyana sighed. "Indeed you are, father. But would you be unkind to me if I were ever to disagree with you?"

The white bushy eyebrows slanted with a look of dissatisfaction, then promptly smoothed out again.

"My dear, I know that you love me. And because you love me, you would never disobey me, would never cross the father who loves you so." The tone of his words, however, was more strict than loving.

Tatyana smiled faintly and was silent for a while. She drummed her fingers on the rosewood lacquered lid of the clavichord. "I do hope they return shortly." She turned around completely on the bench. "Father, do you think the Emperor Alexander is a good man, a really good man—honorable and well intentioned?"

"Alexander is an excellent man and an excellent czar. You must never doubt that," said the prince decisively. "But why do you ask, daughter? Has Alexander not been a good godfather to you?"

"Yes, a very good godfather to me," and Tatyana's voice lightened. "How he honored me at the New Year's Ball! I have told you about that, haven't I?"

"Yes, daughter. Well then, he has been a good godfather to you, and that is all you need concern yourself with."

Tatyana nodded, crossed the room to sit down by her father on the couch, and flipped idly through the little book of English poems by Lord Byron. "But father, are

all czars good? Do they always know what's best for
you?"

"Of course they do. What curious questions you ask
today."

"Well then, why did the great Peter sacrifice so many
lives to build our imperial city?" burst out Tatyana.

The old prince turned toward her with a look of
consternation on his face. He put down his ink pen and
began to pull on his moustache. In a rigid voice he
instructed, "It is not for us, Tatyana Ivanovna, to question
the czar, or history. The czar commands at the will of
God, and we in turn submit to the will of the czar. Each of
us has his duties, and yours are very clear. You need only
to keep yourself amused and be a credit to your father,
your family, and country."

He turned back to his papers briefly, then trained his
quizzing glass on Tatyana, which always made her feel
uncomfortable. But when he spoke his words were mild.
"I think, my dear, that I have been remiss. I do not
provide you with enough diversion here in the country.
Maslanitsa begins next week," he said, referring to the
eight-day Russian mardi gras that preceded the seven
weeks of fasting for Lent. "I want you to enjoy yourself
during Maslanitsa. This was brought over to us today."
He held out a creamy envelope on which was printed an
invitation. "It is an invitation from Count Vasily Turburov
and his sister. They are having a fete and apparently plan
to have built an eighty-foot ice hill in honor of Maslanitsa."

All of Tatyana's worries and thoughts vanished at her
father's words, and she clapped her hands. "An ice hill?
How wonderful, how wonderful!" Tatyana loved no
other Russian outdoor activity so much as sledding down
manmade ice hills. Built of wood and glazed over with
ice, they sometimes reached gigantic heights, and
Tatyana adored whisking down their steep icy faces and

for the sled to go so fast she could not breathe. "Oh, father, I am so excited." In the next breath she added, "But what of Mitya and Gregory? What if they have not returned by then?"

"Surely you'll be able to enjoy yourself in spite of that, eh?" asked the prince. "After all, Count Vasily will be there, and I am sure you hold him in high esteem?" He peered at her and then at the little book of English poems in her hand to which she had unexpectedly taken a fancy. He frowned.

Count Vasily Turburov was young, but on the death of his father some years back he had become a rich and powerful landowner. With forty-five thousand serfs and hundreds of thousands of acres of land, he was the most powerful man in the province. His lands adjoined the Korbatsky estate, and one morning Tatyana was driven by Platon along the road that crossed the boundaries to the Turburovs' country estate. The air was crisp and very cold, and she snuggled down into her sable pelisse with its mink-lined hood and dug her hands into a cozy knot in her mink muff. On her feet she wore thick furry boots.

Tatyana felt particularly happy today because she loved Maslanitsa, when everyone from the richest prince to the poorest serf feasted and stuffed for eight days before the long bleak days of Lent. The only thing to mar her joy was that Dmitry and Gregory had still not returned to Starlina. But she even felt hopeful about that. A letter in Dmitry's energetic and disorganized handwriting had arrived to tell Prince Ivan that he and Gregory would arrive in several days.

Tatyana did not know the Turburovs all that well for they like many Russian aristocrats spent more time in the capital than on their country estates, which they generally left to the jurisdiction of their stewards. But Tatyana liked the Turburovs' house. Everything there was splendid, almost like being in St. Petersburg. And their musician serfs were the most accomplished in the area. Her feet began to tap with impatience as the open troika flew along the track toward the Turburovs' big colonnaded house.

Once there, Tatyana was ushered into the huge drawing room appointed in the latest European style. The sumptuousness was far greater than at Starlina, but it lacked the charm of Tatyana's beloved home. And it seemed cold to her. But perhaps, she reasoned, that was because they were there so infrequently, choosing instead to spend their time at their mansion in St. Petersburg, where they were close to the court with all its balls and intrigues.

In their absence the estate and its villages of serfs were overseen by Count Vasily's trusted steward, a weasely man named Fastov. Tatyana had met him once and without knowing why felt uncomfortable in his presence. Fastov had a tight, pointy moustache, which he kept slicked with kvass, and cruel, small eyes. Count Turburov thought him an excellent steward, for the production of grain on his estates was always high and the expenses of running an agricultural community like his were kept almost impossibly low. The steward's management was highly praised, but it took no great talent. With the count's unspoken approval, he simply overworked and underfed the serfs. In his office he kept a knout, the Russian version of a heavy leather whip, which was liberally applied to any serf who proved lazy or recalcitrant. By such methods Fastov had made his master richer than he was before. A steward like him was worth his weight in gold, and he was paid accordingly.

Tatyana was greeted by Count Vasily and his sister. Though even Tatyana had to admit that Irina was not pretty, today she was blessed with a particularly lively air. Without considering whether she was worth having as a friend, Tatyana had always been friendly to her. And because of her own nature it never occurred to Tatyana that her amicable feelings were not returned, or that the politeness of the countess might be only skin deep. When Tatyana was not watching, Irina kept her eyes skewered on Tatyana with envy and dislike.

"Are you ready to climb up the ice hill?" asked Count Vasily, his voice oily, which it always became when he was around the princess. "The ice is hard as a rock."

Tatyana did not notice the hungry look in his eyes, and she laughed. "Is it built then?"

"Yes, yes," said Count Vasily, and guiding Tatyana by the elbow he took her out onto the balcony. Beside the house, on the flat white stretch of lawn before the river, stood an enormous wooden structure. Steps climbed to a platform eighty feet high, and then a long, wide wooden slide descended from the platform to the ground, a length of nearly one hundred and fifty feet. The slide was decorated on either side with boughs of fir.

Dozens of peasants were still hammering away at the wooden beams, while dozens of others carrying heavy buckets of water climbed the steps and spilled the water down the slide. The air crackled each time the water hit the ice and froze. "Watch and see," said Count Vasily proudly. "It will be smooth as glass. They have been out since five this morning polishing and shining the runners on the sleds. We will go very fast, very fast indeed."

During Maslanitsa these ice hills were erected everywhere, particularly in St. Petersburg. But it was not many a private household that had them built just for the occasion. The ice hill seen from the balcony was just one more reminder of Count Vasily's wealth and prestige and his love of display. Only the ice hill at Tsarskoe Selo, another residence of the czar, was any larger.

Soon other guests began to arrive from all over. They arrived in their gaily painted sleighs, bells tinkling in the cold morning air. On the snow-covered lawns, bonfires were lighted, and the burning birchwood sent spiraling the familiar and curious smell of yeast into the air. This spurred the appetites of the guests, some of whom had traveled far, and the party seemed finally launched with the arrival of the food.

As with everything else done by the Turburovs, the food was presented in excess. An army of *mujiks* staggered under the weight of silver trays heaped with all kinds of blinis stuffed with meat and sour cream, mushroom concoctions, herring, and Beluga caviar. The guests immediately pressed forward, for these little pancakes smothered in butter were eaten with delight and reckless abandon by all Russians during Maslanitsa.

"Eat up, eat up," urged Count Vasily to Tatyana, as the guests gobbled down one after another. "You know you'll have no butter all during Lent." And he added slyly, "You wouldn't want to lose your shape."

Tatyana's eyes were on the ice hill, which was just being completed. "Those delicious, fat little blinis will just have to wait," she said with excitement. "I want to slide!" A moment later, "Oh, hooray, they've finished."

Tatyana had been sliding down ice hills since she was too young to walk. Now, as she sat on the sled at the top of the ice hill, looking down its steep shining face, her heart almost skipped a beat. But she cherished this excitement.

"Down I go," she breathed, and giving herself a push, she went over the lip of the ledge. Down went the tiny sled. Tatyana's stomach dropped, and the cold ice blasted into her face. The sled shrieked and whizzed down the immense hill of ice. Faster and faster went the sled. When Tatyana's face was so cold, her breath so frozen, her heart so constricted she thought she would die, the sled suddenly leveled out, skimmed a distance over the flat snow, and came to a grinding halt on the sand that had been thrown down to halt her.

"Again!" she said rapturously, her cheeks red from the wind and ice. "I want to do that again!"

Even after the fourth ride, this was still her refrain. She seemed indefatigable. After she had gone down a half-dozen times she stood up sick and dizzy with delight. "Oh, Irina, do try it?" she implored the countess, who had not budged from where she stood at the bottom of the ice hill. "It is so fun!"

"No, go on without me," said the sallow little countess, brushing Tatyana away without looking at her. "Maybe I will later." She seemed to be watching for something to come from the house. Tatyana's eyes followed her gaze, and a moment later she exclaimed, with joy, "It is they!"

Two figures were sauntering across the snow in her direction. One was Dmitry, with his buoyant energetic pace, and beside him Gregory Grandison, with his strangely mellifluous and indolent stride.

Joy flooded Tatyana's heart until it was broken by Irina, who snapped, "Why, of course it is they. I have been waiting for them all morning." And without waiting a moment longer, Irina sped across the snow to them. Tatyana's abundant happiness felt suddenly tainted by the strange revelation she now had. As she watched Irina scurry on her short legs, she remembered for the first time the expression on Irina's face at the ball when Gregory was introduced to her. Why, Irina was in love with Gregory Grandison!

Chapter Six

IT WAS ONLY BECAUSE IT WAS SO OBVIOUS TO EVERYONE else that Tatyana finally even recognized Irina's fascination with Gregory. Tatyana's one great fault was her ignorance of human nature and her inexperience and inability to look into a person's character. Because she herself was basically good, she assumed all others to be so. And this was one of the reasons she felt no antipathy or distaste for the Turburov brother and sister. So when she understood suddenly why Irina had taken no interest in the ice sliding, her next thought was, How wonderful for Irina. It did not occur to her to wonder whether the feelings were reciprocal. She stood still where she was, momentarily daunted by this discovery, and then held back, resisting her initial impulse to run to them. She felt curiously ill at ease. Perhaps I have been ice sliding for too long, she thought, looking tiredly up the slope that only moments earlier had thrilled her. A moment later, she was grabbed in a bear hug from behind, and she turned and embraced her brother. They kissed each other's hands, and impromptu tears suddenly filled her eyes. "Oh, Mitya, I am so glad to see you," and she again threw her arms around her brother. "Why have you been gone so long? Where have you been? Never mind, you are home, you are forgiven." She laughed and brushed away her tears.

"Your cheeks are rosy. I bet you haven't gotten off the ice hill all morning," chided Dmitry affectionately. In the background, about twelve yards away, Gregory had been waylaid by Irina and stood in conversation with her.

"So tell me, Mitya," said Tatyana, "have you received a brilliant appointment with a brave general who will raise you to fame and fortune and award you the Cross of St. George for some future exploit?"

Dmitry's big smile vanished. "That is the first thing father asked me as well."

"So you have been home this morning?" asked Tatyana. "Then tell me the good news."

Prince Dmitry sighed. "Little sister, there is no good news. At least no good news of the kind you and father are expecting. And you are going to be disappointed if what you wanted for me above all things was to be a commander of some regiment, distinguishing myself at the expense of my fellow man."

Tatyana's lips parted. "No commission?"

Dmitry nodded.

"Then what were you doing all this time in St. Petersburg?"

"We weren't in St. Petersburg the whole time. We traveled around a bit."

"During the whole six weeks?"

"Yes, much of that time."

"Did you travel far?" asked Tatyana.

"Yes, in more ways than you can guess," said Dmitry earnestly, and he swept his blond hair out of his eyes.

"And no appointment?" Tatyana felt heartbroken.

"Well, not yet, and not ever if I have my way!" burst out Dmitry. He paused for a deep breath. "I wish to become an elected assessor on the courts. The poet Kondraty Ryleyev has done as much, and Arkady Stegorin spent six years as a justice of the peace. Now it is my turn."

"An elected assessor?" countered Tatyana. "You are going then to abandon a military career?"

Dmitry took Tatyana's mittened hands in his. "My dear sister, you cannot imagine how so many of our people suffer. While I was in France I was oblivious to Russia's actual woes. But returning from Europe I realized how being abroad unveiled my eyes." Dmitry's voice continued eagerly. "Oh, Tatyana, we sat in on several trials. The corruption of the courts is unbelievable. We heard the case of a young peasant, punished to the full extent of the law. He was sent to Siberia because he knocked down his master, who was attempting to"—he stumbled with embarrassment—"to . . . defile . . . the young man's fiancée. There were even more heinous cases than that. Bribery is rampant. A murderer can buy off the judge, and innocent people are put in prison because someone has the money and the interest in sending them there. And do you know why all this can happen? Because the men who sit in judgment, the civil clerks, are all so grossly underpaid." Dmitry ran his hand through his hair. "Somewhere though, there must be reason and justice. And if I can do my part to help, I will do so gladly."

"But, Mitya, your career!" gasped Tatyana. "To throw it thus away!"

Dmitry shrugged.

"Please, I beg you, you will break father's heart."

"He has threatened to disinherit me," said Dmitry grimly, caught in the moral quandary outlined by Tatyana. "Believe me, it is not an easy decision."

Tatyana smiled hopefully. "Perhaps you will change your mind, Mitya. I hope so, for your sake and father's. Will you stay here until Lent at least?"

"Yes, I hope to, or until I have resolved this question with papa."

The conversation was interrupted at this point by Gregory's approach. He had hung back, seeing the brother and sister embrace and anticipating the conversation that would be brought about. But now that they lifted their heads, he joined them. Count Vasily's sister dogged his heels.

Tatyana gave Gregory her hand, looking up into his sculpted face, the fine nose, and wide forehead, and her emotions teemed within her. She guessed he was partly responsible for Dmitry's drastic new plans, and yet, and yet . . . something in his eyes. Did he return Irina's fascination? she suddenly wondered. "Welcome back," she said out loud, and to Gregory her bright green eyes and red cheeks were a welcome sight after so many weeks on the road. But before he could even compliment her on her coloring, Count Vasily appeared at her side.

"I would not have thought you would deign to visit our humble Russian countryside," he interjected, barely offering Gregory his fingertips.

"I could not refuse your sister's invitation," returned Gregory with infinite politeness. Irina cast her eye furtively on her brother. She had not told him of the invitation she had mailed off to Mr. Grandison of her own accord.

The count turned his icy eyes from his sister and planted them on Gregory. "How very English of you."

Count Vasily's contempt was more than obvious, and even Tatyana felt it. When a peasantwoman came rocking by under the weight of *pryaniki,* gingerbread cut in different shapes, she took a gingerbread man and quite unconsciously bit the head off one. Gregory saw her impulsive movement, and the corners of his lips turned up in a smile. He did not say anything to Count Turburov.

"I learn that you and Dmitry Ivanovich have been not only in St. Petersburg, this whole time, but traveling about. I hope you have enjoyed our country," pressed the count.

" 'Enjoyed' is not the word I would have chosen," said Gregory, casually helping himself to a piece of *pryaniki,* "but it has certainly been an edifying month and a half." He took a bite from the gingerbread cut in the shape of a star. "I feel I have barely scratched the surface."

"How very modest of you. But perhaps you have already come to some judgment. Surely you will share it with us." The count's shrewd eyes would not leave the Englishman.

Gregory's forehead and jaw began to work, which usually happened when he began to organize the wide-ranging panoply of his thoughts for public consumption. His brows knit together in concentration, and he seemed about to say something as he finished the gingerbread. His eyes strayed to Tatyana, and he noticed the look of apprehension in her face. He turned to Count Vasily and relaxed into a smile. His innocent answer to Vasily's loaded question was, "I have never enjoyed myself more in all my life."

Tatyana's face relaxed. "Mr. Grandison, I hope that you and Dmitry have brought your skates."

A little while later, while the others had something to eat, Tatyana left Dmitry and Gregory, who was still preyed upon by Countess Irina, and returned alone to the house to fetch her skates. Walking across the snow, Tatyana saw an old peasantwoman trudging along under the weight of a tray. It was piled high with small cakes in the shape of larks. These fat little cakes, which had currants for eyes, were another favorite of Tatyana's during Maslanitsa. She stopped the woman and, choosing one, bit into its soft, heavy insides. "How delicious these little larks are," she said.

"Little mother, it is you," said the serf woman in surprise, recognizing the princess.

Tatyana peered at the old woman and did not recognize the haggard, wrinkled face that smiled at her. "Lizanka," she said at last, finally recognizing a serf of her father's from a distant village whom she had not seen in almost a year. "Lizanka, I hardly recognized you. What are you doing here at the Turburovs?"

"The count bought me from your father last winter, along with a dozen other serfs from our village," answered Lizanka.

"I didn't know," said Tatyana, ashamed not to have even known of this transaction. And because Lizanka was holding the tray, all Tatyana could do to greet her was to press her arm warmly. "How are you, Lizanka?" she said, thinking she looked much older than she remembered.

"Glory be to God, but I am alive," said Lizanka. "My husband though is dead, not that I saw much of him during his last few months—him still being at your father's." She paused, as if searching for something happier to relate. "Glory be to God, my son is alive and healthy. At least he was last I heard."

"What do you mean by that, Lizanka?" asked Tatyana with a concerned expression. "Were you separated from him as well in the sale?"

The old peasantwoman shook her head slowly. "No, little mother, but my new master, the *barin*, sent my Vanya to be a soldier. How my Vanya wept when they shaved his beard. Oh, little mother, he buys his freedom, but I will not see him again in this life." This was an allusion to the twenty-five year service that was mandatory for conscripted peasants. A tear gathered in the old peasantwoman's blue eyes. "Glory be to God, but it is the will of our little father the czar. God bless him."

Tatyana looked at her grimly. "And are you well, Lizanka? You look very tired." And suddenly she felt uncomfortable that she should be standing there, young and healthy and empty-handed, while the old woman was sinking under the weight of the tray. "Glory be to God, but I am still fit and strong," said the poor fragile old lady.

Tatyana suddenly took half a dozen of the lark cakes off the tray. "These cakes are very good, very good," said Tatyana rapidly. Lizanka nodded in the vague way of someone who does not know whether to agree or not. She had clearly not even tasted them.

Lizanka was about to speak, but out of the corner of her eye she saw her master's steward approaching, and her eyes tightened in fear. "God bless you, my child," she said hurriedly. "You are a good girl, you always were, and your father was a good man, honorable. He was stern, but he let us marry who we would, did not force our men into the army, even gave our men little plots of land to work themselves." She took in her breath, glancing fearfully toward the steward who was approaching nearer and then looked imploringly at Tatyana. "But tell me little mother, why in the name of the Good Lord did he sell us away?"

"I—I—" stuttered Tatyana, who did not have the answer to Lizanka's desperate question, but before she could go on Lizanka hastily stumbled away bent under her platter, and the steward passed by.

Tatyana stared after her. For the first time in her sheltered life, she saw that not all serfs held sway over their masters as Dunyasha did. She felt awed by that simple recognition.

"Just because I am happy doesn't make the rest of the world so."

Deeply troubled, Tatyana gazed at the cakes in the shape of larks which she held in her arms. They had always seemed such cheerful confections to her, larks that could sprout wings if they wanted to and fly away. Tatyana held up a lark cake to eat it, but now the red currant eye seemed wistful.

Though Tatyana was no longer hungry, she ate the cake, and then another, savoring each one carefully. As if performing some ritual, she ate every crumb. "Lizanka, our dear old Lizanka, carried these little lark cakes out for us to eat," she repeated to herself. And then she began to eat another, until she had finished all the cakes at last.

It was three o'clock, but already winter evening approached and dictated that the afternoon's festivities come to a close. Skaters were still skating on the river, cutting up the ice with their blades as they turned in semicircles and pirouettes. Others stood in groups around the dying embers of the bonfires, throwing their nut shells and orange peels to the wind. Hot tea, carried forth in boiling samovars, warmed the few remaining guests, while others had long since comforted themselves with vodka and kvass.

Prince Dmitry, ever gregarious, had fallen in with a group of old family friends, and Tatyana had never returned with her skates. "Probably with Count Turburov," decided Gregory, who had caught himself waiting for Tatyana to reappear.

Gregory had wanted time to think, but his thoughts kept straying like idiotic sheep toward the house, through whose door had disappeared the dark pelisse of Prince Dmitry's sister. But his insubordinate thoughts were not Gregory's only problem. His high brow, furrowed with ennui, the curl of his hair, and the dark intensity of his eyes had drawn all the ladies to him. His melancholic air, so different from his lazy and sardonic words, his handsome, casual stride, were beguiling to the Russian women who were accustomed only to the vigorous, open handsomeness of their countrymen. By the end of the afternoon Gregory found himself in purgatory, beseiged by Countess Irina and a fawning circle of feminine chatterboxes.

"Enough of civilization," he growled to himself. Extricating himself, he went off by himself for a walk.

This was habit with Gregory, whenever he felt morose. No matter what concern, great or small, plagued his mind or his heart, a walk—that English birthright—always restored comfort to his soul. Besides, he found he was getting used to the Russian cold, and even the pervasiveness and insistence of the snow had a certain charm. Gregory walked along the river bank, beyond where the snow had been cleared off the ice for skaters, and downriver, where he could hear the gurgle of running water. He scanned the winter landscape, the blue sky deepening in the distance.

When Tatyana was shocked by Lizanka looking so pale and worn, it was only because there was such a frightful difference between the peasant's present and former conditions. The dire change had forced Tatyana, if only briefly, from her snug little cocoon. But Gregory was different. He looked at himself, others, and the entire world from an innately critical point of view.

He had seen in flashes of bright images the pleasures of the afternoon, the young children sledding down the ice hills, and the skaters doing cartwheels on the ice. But such happiness felt apart from him, as if glimpsed through a dream. More clearly than these things, he had seen the serfs bending under the weight of buckets of water as they carried them up the long ladders of the ice hills. And he glimpsed the other *mujiks* sinking under the massive trays of food. Once he had witnessed a peasant boy booted by the steward when he sank down out of fatigue and rested his head in his arms. And later a peasant had furtively reached for a small cake and put it in his mouth. Gregory then saw Count Turburov fling out his arm and smack the man's jaw, which sent the cake flying into the snow. Gregory had witnessed both these incidents and even others. He had frowned but had not said a word.

Now, though, as he walked along, he thought of the men he had just met in St. Petersburg and Moscow. They were young officers, landowners, and other aristocrats who shared his idealistic views and interest in reform, which they wished to adapt in their own country. Many had been to Europe during the Napoleonic wars, and what they had seen impressed them. These men, most of them quite young, were ashamed of serfdom. Like Gregory, they had immersed themselves in the works of Rousseau, Montesquieu, Edmund Burke, and other writers with liberal viewpoints and progressive notions. Many of the young officers were Anglophiles, impressed by England's parliamentary government and social progress. Gregory's articulateness and his words, which flowed like satin ribbons on the subjects dear to his soul, had shaken many preconceptions and prejudices of the young men. The breadth of his reading and of his thoughts, combined with his elegance and grace, made him particularly attractive to the romantic and youthful gentlemen who still hoped the czar would follow through on his earlier good intentions.

But Gregory was no longer proud of his facile words and his vivid imagery. Even as he watched Vasily Turburov strike his own serf, he thanked him. He thanked him for the lesson he had been taught so succinctly: that an armchair liberal is almost worse than no liberal at all. In the weeks succeeding the ball, the words had tripped easily from his tongue and vanished just as easily into thin air. And though a cluster of young men had been listening to all he said, to Gregory, rehashing all his old ideas felt stale to him. There must be something more, he kept thinking, and had looked around him at the young men he met to find a clue to his frustration and unease. Prince Dmitry and he had been introduced by the orange-haired Prince Trubetskoy they met at the Winter Palace to a young man named Pavel Pestel. The young major was brilliant—a pure idealogue. But Gregory was not as impressed with Pestel as Dmitry was. Gregory imagined Pestel scribbling furiously at his "Russian Pravda," the radical constitution he was writing. While he sat, scribbling furiously away, thought Gregory, outside the window his idealized dream of revolution would become carnage, spilling blood upon the pavement of the street.

Gregory's feelings for Dmitry, on the other hand, had gradually changed as well. He had always patronized his friend's naive zeal, essential goodness, and impulsiveness. But this inclination on Dmitry's part always to act before he thought stirred Gregory's thoughts. Dmitry's actions would always be laudable because his motivations were pure. But Pestel, with the complex moral machinery of his brain, was an unknown quantity. Gregory's spark of admiration for Dmitry grew. He wished now of himself that he had Dmitry's nerve or will to act, but he had put himself in a bind. As a guest in a foreign country, his hands were tied. He could only participate vicariously in the dreams of these young Russian noblemen. And he knew he could only be of use to them as a sifter of ideas, while they would use their own men for grape shot—if it should ever come to that.

Gregory had walked along the bank of the river toward the sound of falling water. Now he spied ahead of him a millhouse and a dam. The ice of the river here began to crimp from the movement of the swollen water. He came abreast of the dam and stopped to gaze at the waterfall. But the serenity of the splashing river was instantly marred when he looked down the embankment and saw two men standing beside the water. They were beating a peasant. Beyond them, a couple of other *mujiks* holding buckets watched with evident fear.

One of the men was Vasily Turburov, the other his steward, Fastov, who struck the peasant with a stick. The serf was holding up his arms to deflect the blows and seemed to be remonstrating weakly in Russian. From his dark, clinging clothes he was evidently soaking wet. His hair and beard were already frozen, and his lips were blue. He was shivering wildly as he raised his yellowish hands to ward off the stick.

"Lazy vermin, son of a dog, defilement of the earth," raged Count Vasily, giving him a kick. "You want to save your tender skin, but for my good steel pail not a thought! Base creature. Crafty fox, trying to give your comrades wicked ideas!"

"Little father, do not beat me. I did not do it on purpose. I only let go of the pail by mistake," cried the peasant, his teeth clacking from the cold.

"I should make you go in there after it," threatened Count Vasily, while his steward applied another whack. "I'd throw you into that turbulent water, too, if I thought your stupid soul would have any luck in finding it."

"What has happened?" asked Gregory in French, standing on the incline.

Vasily turned toward him, caught off guard by Gregory's arrival. Then he glowered with irritation. "We found this lazy dog on the bank without his bucket. And it was only after beating it out of him that he admits it fell into the water."

"Your excellency, it was just a poor man's fear of drowning. The pail was heavy, and when I lost my footing, it would have pulled me under. I do not know how to swim!" wailed the man. Though Gregory did not understand every word the peasant said, he understood the gist.

"Fool, do you think I will be the dupe of your tall tales? You lost the bucket on purpose, to spite me, to put evil ideas in the heads of your fellows. You will suffer for such insubordination. A wretched lying serf like all of them. Well, they will profit from your example," and with his heel he knocked the man backward as the peasant tried to stand up.

By now the peasant was so weakened by the cold, he did not bother to rise. Even from where he stood, Gregory saw the sickly hue that had come over the peasant's face.

"I do not intend to interfere with your meting out of justice, count," said Gregory calmly, descending the incline toward them, "but your peasant will shortly be no use at all if he is kept out here in this cold. I have seen that color on his skin before in other men, and they did not always live to tell of it."

"Kept out here in this cold," mimicked Vasily in anger. "Why, I have half a mind to send him into the river to find that pail!"

"He would drown of course," said Gregory simply, glancing at the surging white water.

"He stumbled in the water to make a fool of me and lost a bucket belonging to me. Drowning would be an appropriate punishment."

Gregory saw that the count was becoming unhinged and tried to steer the conversation onto saner ground.

"Whether it was intentional or not, I imagine the serf is more valuable to you than a bucket."

"A sturdy bucket with no holes in it is worth ten lying, scheming peasants." He stared vengefully at the serf. "He'll go inside when I'm damn well ready to send him."

"If you wait much longer your serf will be beyond where even you can send him," said Gregory, his jaw beginning to twitch.

As Vasily and Gregory spoke a number of *mujiks* carrying empty buckets who had returned from the ice hill collected on the incline above. They were watching with interest the strange interaction between their master and the foreign stranger. Though they spoke no French, they understood from the tone of voices what the altercation was about, and they could see that something unusual was going to happen.

Count Vasily turned to Gregory. "Are you standing on my land, Mr. Grandison, telling me how I should treat my own serf, my personal property?" challenged the count, letting go of the peasant's hair, whose head he had been shaking.

Gregory remained quiet. "Your bucket is lost. All I am suggesting is that you might not wish to forfeit your other property as well." And Gregory stepped forward to help lift up the peasant who had just fainted away. Gregory removed his own coat and covered the man with it.

"Get away from that man," threatened the count.

"I cannot stand by in good conscience and let a fellow human being die if I can possibly help him," Gregory replied, with quiet firmness, now quickly wrapping the man's head with his scarf. But as Gregory started to raise the man up, he felt a blow to his back, and when he turned his head, he was suddenly hit in the jaw. Count Vasily stood quivering with rage. "I have had enough of your meddling and your insolence, Englishman. You will not show me up in front of my own peasants," and he struck Gregory again.

Gregory, aroused to anger, shot back with his fist, and soon the two went rolling along the embankment. When Gregory disengaged himself and stood up to go, he was again jumped on by Vasily, whose arm went around his neck.

"You're a God-damned dirty fighter, aren't you?" swore Gregory in English, and in frustration he picked up Vasily bodily and sent him reeling. Vasily staggered, lost his footing, and went over the embankment and into the water.

The steward, who had backed off when the fighting started, barked at the serfs on the bank to go in after their master. Vasily was chest high in the freezing river, and flailing with his arms. The current threatened to drag him down and under the ice a little distance downstream. But the peasants would not budge, even when the steward started shouting at them. Hatred and contempt were plain upon their faces, and Gregory saw that they were more than willing to stand by and watch their master drown.

"Vasily has trained them nicely by his own example," thought Gregory with vexation. He threw off his boots and lunged into the water. Moments earlier Vasily would have scorned the help of the Englishman. But he too did not know how to swim, and now he grabbed desperately at the arm held out to him. Against the current, Gregory dragged the blubbering, sputtering mass by his collar, until they were both safely out of the turgid water.

Once the count was back on shore, with the peasants staring and tittering behind their hands at his bedraggled sight, Vasily looked with spite at Gregory. "You have made a laughing stock of me," he snarled, "and all because my sister was foolish enough to invite you here today. I will not condescend to ask you for satisfaction. But get out of here, and hope you never cross my path again."

Wringing his coat out with his hands, the count stamped away, while his steward followed at his heels.

Chapter Seven

THOUGH HE WAS SOPPING WET, GREGORY RETURNED TO the poor peasant over whom the ruckus had ensued. Using gestures and a few simple words of Russian, Gregory made the other peasants understand that they must now carry their comrade back to his *izba* and warm him if he was to survive. He indicated he would join them later.

Gregory again felt a touch on his back, but this time it was an affectionate pat. He looked up to see Prince Dmitry.

"I have just gotten wind from some serfs of what happened."

"I am sorry about all this," said Gregory tiredly, putting his boots back on. "I will explain it all to you later."

Dmitry glowed with pride. "There is no need to explain or to apologize, my friend. It is very clear who was at fault. But let us get you dry; you could perish in this cold."

Gregory was watching the peasants depart with their

sick comrade. Unwilling to save their drowning master, the peasants were all too glad to help one of their own, and four men carried him carefully between them. Gregory remembered the savage look of cruelty in Count Vasily's eyes and the look of resentment and hatred in the peasants'. "What a rotten system this is," he muttered to himself, as he let Dmitry lead him back to the carriage to search for dry clothes.

"I wonder if what happened today, here, between master and peasant, is par for the course *chez les Turburovs*," Gregory observed sarcastically.

"Apparently so," answered the young prince. "The serfs are terrified and hate him. When he has anything to drink at all, they say he turns into a veritable Beelzebub." Dmitry glanced about him. "Apparently the serfs have an affectionate nickname for Count Vasily's estate. They call it White Hades."

Gregory snorted in agreement. "Yes, even I scorched myself a little today."

Tatyana clenched and unclenched her hands in frustration and anger. "Gregory did such a thing? How is it possible he could have behaved so badly!" She was in the sleigh driven by Platon, having just taken leave of the Turburovs.

Tatyana had spent the rest of the afternoon inside the house, for she had lost all enthusiasm for skating or for the party. She had wandered into the library and found there were no books in it, only shelves filled with bibelots and bric-a-brac. But she had settled herself into one of the overstuffed sofas and listened to the tune of a music box. Her thoughts wandered about the room, returning always to the image that stayed in her mind of Lizanka bent under the heavy tray and her insistent question, "Why did your father sell us away?"

But now, in the sleigh, mortification had given away to

indignation. Her ears tingled as she remembered the arrival of Count Vasily at the house, who stood sopping wet in the foyer, and the account made to her by Count Vasily's steward.

"Gregory, drunk, and to behave like such a madman." It was incredible to think. But Fastov recounted what had happened by the river near the dam. He told how he had seen the Englishman, Gregory Grandison, downing a good deal of vodka during the afternoon, and then that he had approached his host, the count, and insulted him. When Count Vasily politely suggested Mr. Grandison leave, Mr. Grandison had punched the count not once but half a dozen times and then thrown him purposely into the river. It was only through his own valor that his master was rescued from the water or was even still alive. "If it weren't for me, he would be dead now," bragged the steward. When Tatyana expressed disbelief, he hastened to reassure her. "I saw it all with my own two eyes, princess. His excellency was grossly assaulted by that Englishman."

"How despicable of him," said Countess Irina, "but I am not surprised, I saw how he kept at the bottle." Irina was not a charming person, but she could not have been accused of being stupid. After several hours of tagging after Gregory, she soon realized he had no interest in her—the richest heiress in Russia. And now she hated him with all the spite in her character she could dredge up.

"Gregory drunk," repeated Tatyana to herself. "I cannot get over it."

Now in the sleigh, she could turn over the events of the day to her heart's content, and all she felt was shattered. It was such a rude awakening to Tatyana, just when some of Gregory Grandison's words were beginning to have some meaning for her. In fact, she had planned to go in search of him earlier in the afternoon, but Irina had detained her with accounts of the new furniture and paintings she had added to the household.

Now Gregory had revealed his inferiority, and somehow it made all he stood for, or had seemed to stand for, tarnished by his behavior. "How shameful for Gregory, for Mitya, for all of us," she kept repeating to herself.

On arriving home, Tatyana's flushed face was not lost on Prince Korbatsky. He interrogated her until the whole story finally gushed out of Tatyana. By then, she was almost crying.

"A fine friend for Dmitry," muttered the prince, as he had himself lugged into his study. "Full of madcap ideas was bad enough. But going around getting drunk and attacking Count Vasily? Aieeee! Count Vasily of all men! That cursed son with his choice of pals will be the ruin of me."

Prince Korbatsky suddenly started to tug viciously at a lower righthand drawer under the shadows of his desk. "The count will make things even harder on me," he said enigmatically. The drawer handle would not budge, and the prince collapsed back in his chair, suddenly seeming relieved. "I must remind Timofey not to give me that key." He yanked on his moustache, and only his butler would have had any idea what these strange comments had to do with.

It was completely dark when Dmitry and his friend arrived at Starlina, only an hour later than Tatyana. Though Gregory was chilled, he had insisted on staying behind until he was certain the poor *mujik* was being taken care of and would be all right.

When Gregory and Dmitry entered the house, they were summoned immediately to the study at the orders of the old prince. This was not a good sign. The study was Prince Korbatsky's sanctum sanctorum, where he

worked on private estate matters or held audiences with
those who had incurred his anger and whom he wished
to intimidate. The room was all walnut paneling with
bookcases on either side jammed with papers and books.
The desk was huge, covered with a massive piece of
marble at which he sat while he trained his quizzing glass
on the offending person.

Gregory and Dmitry were issued inside, and the door
closed heavily after them.

At the other end of the house, Tatyana waited. With
her chin in her hand, she flicked nervously through her
little leather book of English poems, then threw it aside in
frustration.

Dunyasha, who was oblivious to what was happening
at the other end of the house, bounced into the room.
She seemed distraught, but her blue eyes danced brightly. "Oh, little mother, that scamp of an Anatole is back
only half a day, and already he has gone and hidden my
outdoor boots. He says the *domovoy* spirited them away
to eat them." Here she briefly crossed herself. "But I am
certain he is fibbing. I think the shoe-eater is not the
domovoy"—and here she again crossed herself—"but
that Anatole. And all because I took his coat and hung it
in the mud room where it belongs." Dunyasha seemed
more excited than upset. "What am I to do, what am I to
do with that scalawag?"

"*Nichevo, nichevo,*" sighed Tatyana mournfully.
"Never mind, never mind. That valet's hours here are
numbered anyway. I am certain father will ask Mr.
Grandison to leave."

Dunyasha's expression changed to surprise and dismay. "Leave, leave? Whatever for, little mother?" Her
mouth dropped open. "And taking Anatole with him? I'll
never get my shoes back! Why leave?"

"Dunyasha, it is too complicated to explain," said

Tatyana, and unable to bear Dunyasha's questioning look, she ran from the room.

Tatyana's steps led her unthinking through one room after another until she found herself in the apartments of Gregory and her brother.

On their arrival that morning the young men had dumped their things. But in Gregory's rooms, through which Tatyana had to walk to reach Dmitry's, everything had been neatly laid out by Anatole. Even the lamps were lit to welcome him. Tatyana sank down on the bed, with its covers turned back, beleaguered at the thought of what must be happening in the study. She felt unhappy at the discord in the house since there had rarely been any. And all for a simple reason. Prince Korbatsky's word had always been law, and he had always been obeyed—until now.

Tatyana's eyes strayed to the bureau beside Gregory's bed. Seeing a stack of books, she picked them up one at a time to read their titles. *Two Treatises on Civil Government,* by John Locke, was one; *Esquisse d'un tableau historique des progrès de l'esprit humain* written by some French philosopher was the next mouthful of a title that greeted her. She picked up a small tome written in Italian: *Tratto dei delitti e delle pene,* by someone named Cesare Beccaria.

"God, no wonder Gregory consoles himself with drink," thought Tatyana looking at these lugubrious books. "How can he read anything so deadly dull?" The rest of the books she turned through were in German, but lastly she found a volume in her own language, *Puteshestvie iz Peterburga v Moskvu.* "Journey from St. Petersburg to Moscow," read Tatyana. She thought she recognized the title.

This travel account had been written by a Russian named Alexander Radishchev thirty years before. The

book had been censored by Catherine the Great for what
she saw as its pernicious attack on Russian society. But
the wily writer had snuck it through the presses anyway.
Though most of the copies had been rounded up and
burned, a few copies found their way to sympathetic
readers in Russia and in Europe. "How can Gregory
have obtained this book?" Tatyana asked herself, and
her interest piqued, she glanced through its pages.
Almost every sentence had a Russian word underlined
and translated into English in the margin. And when
Tatyana opened the other books, she found similar
translations, comments, and passages underscored in
lead pencil. He clearly had a reading knowledge of at
least six languages and was now trying to learn Russian.
Though Tatyana was dismayed by his afternoon's behavior, she couldn't help but be impressed by his persever-
ance with these books in so many different languages.

Tatyana's eyes strayed to the few objects on the table.
There were several silver rubles, a penknife, a brass boot
hook, a snuff box, and his passport, stuffed with Russian
travel permits.

Tatyana was surprised, and she opened up the passport to examine its pages. It had been stamped at least six
dozen times. Though Dmitry had told her they had
traveled outside of St. Petersburg, only the passport
revealed how much. "Novgorod, Moscow, Smolensk,
Mogilev, and Minsk," said Tatyana, repeating the names
of huge western provinces in Russia covering hundreds
of miles. "All these places in six weeks. My God, they've
been all over."

Minsk had been stamped several times, and she
remembered Prince Trubetskoy at the Winter Palace
mentioning his regiment was stationed there. Tatyana
flipped through the passport until her eyes fell on an
open letter penned in small, precise handwriting. It was
written in French. Tatyana would not have read it except

that Prince Trubetskoy's name was mentioned in the top
line.

I am very glad Prince Trubetskoy provided an opportunity for us to meet. It is not every day one meets a
man whose thoughts on subjects little understood in
my country have developed to such a high degree of
refinement. You are not Russian, true, but Justice
and the Search after Truth is a universal hunger.
These are my aims as well, and my goal is that they
should be understood one day as a common language. Your strength and interest mean much to us,
for disagreement and cloudiness of thought threaten
to destroy our universal goals. We look forward to
your next visit.

Pavel Pestel,
Moscow, January 1825

"What a strange letter," thought Tatyana, finding it too
abstract for her tastes. "And what a funny name." But
her questions about Prince Trubetskoy had been answered by the letter. She replaced the passport on the
bureau. What is this goal he speaks of? she wondered,
until her eyes were distracted by a smooth, shiny object
on the bureau. It was Gregory's pocket watch. Tatyana
liked pocket watches, and she opened it up to examine its
face. But the Roman numerals and delicate needles of its
hands proved far less interesting than a miniature portrait
fitted within the lid of the watch.

It was a portrait of a young woman with dark blond
hair and brown eyes. She had a beautiful expression. By
the tiny details at the shoulders Tatyana recognized the
empire style of her gown, so much in vogue twenty years
earlier. The eyes seemed familiar, they were so dark and
romantic, and Tatyana realized it must be Gregory's
mother. "How lovely she is," thought Tatyana, and then

a moment later felt ashamed at herself. There had not been anything very personal about the books, or even the passport, but this tiny portrait of his mother? Tatyana pressed the watch closed, and stood up to go. She had dallied here long enough. And what had become of Gregory and her brother? Was their fateful interview with her father not yet over?

The door to the study had remained closed for more than a half-hour. The house serfs, sensing trouble brewing, would not even knock on the door after all this time, and though they could not hear the conversation within, they could hear the rise and fall of masculine voices.

At last the door was thrust open by Prince Dmitry, though the interview apparently was not over. Prince Korbatsky sat at his desk, trembling violently. "I no longer care which is the truth, yours or Count Vasily's or anybody else's. I tell you, you are both to apologize to him. Apologize, I tell you!"

"As I have said, for your sake and your family's, I will apologize for attending the festivities without a specific invitation from the count, and I will be glad to send him a new coat. But prince," said Gregory quietly, though his face was pale with fatigue and anger, "I will not apologize to him or anybody else about the fight since I was not in the wrong."

"Dmitry Ivanovich," said the prince to Dmitry, who stood with his hand grasping the doorknob, "since your English friend is so stubborn and pigheaded and refuses my request, you must apologize for him. You brought Mr. Grandison as your guest and so were responsible for his conduct. You must apologize for him. You must do this for your family. Count Vasily is our neighbor, and this appalling mistake must be redressed!" It was clear this dialogue had been going back and forth for some time.

The young prince's face was flushed with outrage. "As I have said, father, if any apology is due, it should come from Count Vasily to Gregory. My friend is right, and I stand by him. Count Vasily may be our neighbor, but he will receive no apology from Gregory or from me."

"Well then, be gone!" thundered Prince Korbatsky. "And I do not want to see your faces until you have cooled your heels. Do not step across this threshold until you, Dmitry, are in uniform, and you both have had some sense knocked in your heads. To think that my own son, and a Korbatsky, would show the judgment of a pea hen. Get out, I say!" Dmitry and Gregory did as they were ordered, not even looking back at Prince Korbatsky, whose heavy jowls were shaking with rage.

Tatyana heard steps along the passageway to Dmitry's rooms. But it was not Dmitry's tread. When she looked up, she saw Gregory standing on the landing. He ran his hand through his hair before he noticed Tatyana at the doorway. She could see that his coal-black eyes were angry, though he tried to hide it behind his patronizing smile. That smile, and the way he stood there, as if he didn't care about anything, made her angry too.

"Where is Dmitry?" she asked.

"He has gone to get Platon, your coachman. We are leaving Starlina."

"So," she said abruptly, "you will not go beg forgiveness of Count Turburov?"

"Beg forgiveness, of that ill-bred and cowardly man? Certainly not," he retorted, and he passed Tatyana to go to his rooms. And because Anatole was nowhere to be seen, he began to repack his bags.

This remark seemed only too unfair to Tatyana, considering his behavior according to the Turburovs. She followed him into the room and said indignantly, "You must still be drunk then."

Gregory laughed, but it was not a genial sound.

"Drunkenness? They added that to the charges? How ingenious, but I should think in Russia no one would even bother with such a poor excuse." ˙

Tatyana smarted under this insult, knowing well her countrymen's reputation for drinking. Her eyes began to sparkle with irritation in the lamplight. "You are a guest in my father's house, Gregory Grandison, so it is not for me to challenge your opinions. But from what I have been told, your behavior this afternoon was shocking! If, Mr. Grandison, you have no regard for yourself, I wish you would at least consider what effect your behavior might have on my brother. Count Vasily Turburov is a neighbor, and highly respected at court. His opinion of Mitya could have some bearing on my brother's future. Though it may not seem important to you," she concluded bitterly, "my brother's future should be a consideration."

Gregory's jaw twitched, but he ignored her while he flung some of his clothing in a satchel.

"If the account made against you is untrue, you might explain yourself," added Tatyana, disconcerted by his silence.

"You insult your brother and me both by even asking for an explanation," he flung at her. "First of all, your brother will never be judged by my behavior, and second of all, as to my effect on him, you insult us both on that subject as well."

Tatyana was taken aback, and Gregory continued. "Your brother, princess, is his own mentor, and I at least respect him enough to know he would not let himself be maligned for thoughts which are not his own. You talk about your concern for his future and yet show no genuine interest or concern for him." Gregory shook his wet crumpled shirt at her. "Your future, princess, is more in jeopardy than your brother's. For you, princess, are the virtual slave of obedience and propriety. And those two criteria are the only criteria you use to judge your brother." Seeing her obdurate look of anger, he stormed, "The sun will melt the December snows of St. Petersburg before you are endowed with genuine concern for others." He flung one satchel to the floor and began to pack another. "Since you have so little faith in your brother or his choice of friends, I did throw Vasily Turburov into the water! And though you may doubt my word, it was a dunking he well deserved—even if I cannot claim to have taken the initiative in the matter. I stand by what I did and have no need to apologize or to explain, and neither does your brother. It is you, Princess Tatyana, who have disgraced your brother by having so much regard for what your father wants of him and so little regard for what is wanted by your brother. Your ignorance—"

Tatyana had stood stunned to silence by this huge outburst of words, but finally she exploded. "My ignorance? I love my brother better than myself, and you accuse me of being ignorant of his own good, the best hopes for his future?" Tatyana perched her hands angrily on her hips. "You have come, disrupting our family, Gregory Grandison, distressing my poor father, reading strange books, and setting Dmitry against everything that was always dear to him. You know nothing about Dmitry, nothing about our family, and yet—"

"It is you, princess," thundered Gregory, turning on her, and shaking her by the shoulders, "it is you who know nothing, nothing about what is happening even in your own backyard, let alone this entire country. You are as ignorant as a goose, shallow as the most absurd little coquette. Everything must stay the same, even to the point of suffocation with you, so that your own comfort, your own prejudices, are not in any way disturbed. Your father is to be coaxed and cajoled, your brother unthinkingly pursue his military career, and you, you? I dread to think what marriage you will hasten into!" He suddenly drew back from her and collected his thoughts, which were getting away from him. "Yes, I call you ignorant," he said, not looking at her. "For I as a foreigner have seen more and learned more about your country in six weeks than you have perceived in your whole lifetime!" He now flung the jackets that Anatole had so carefully hung onto the bed. "All you ladies, how you bedevil one. You read your frivolous little novels and shed copious tears but are inured somehow to those about you who cry out in hunger and genuine despair. It does not trouble your cotton candy souls." He came close to her again, and gripped her arm. "Well, princess, you may look out about you with pink rabbit eyes, but even if it shocks you, some day you'll learn this world doesn't revolve about your ignorance, and your petticoats and laces. Little idiot!" he muttered, and pushed her away again in disgust.

Tatyana was stunned. Her arm hurt from where he had crushed her in his grip, and the image of Lizanka kept rising in her mind along with his words. For a moment she could not find her voice. Then her mind cleared as she watched him finish packing. Ignorant, she had been called, with a cotton candy soul!

"Ignorant am I?" she challenged again, her small nostrils flaring and her eyes blazing. "You dare to call me that?"

"Yes," retorted Gregory over his shoulder, and by now he was returning to his old manner of cold cynicism. He picked up one of the books on his bureau and brandished it. "A book written by one of your countrymen, Radishchev, and I hazard a guess you have never read it, nor the poetry of a talented young countryman of yours named Pushkin."

"No, probably not," retorted Tatyana, "for I have been wasting my time with one of your own countrymen named Byron."

Gregory scarcely seemed to hear her, still brandishing the leather volume. "I can't pretend it's a giddy little travelogue about your country, but if you wish to be any less of a ninny, you might try reading this." He flung the volume at her. Tatyana caught it, glanced at the title, stamped her foot, and dropped it on the rug. "No, I shall not read your Mr. Radishes or Carrot top! I have no desire to. Such books spoil people's temper, make them unreasonable and badly behaved. Your own example, Mr. Grandison, is no inducement!" And here she gave the book a spiteful little kick.

Gregory suddenly stopped what he was doing, glanced at the book on the floor, and strode across the room to her.

While Tatyana swayed angrily in her softly fitted gown, her face in the candlelight glowed with indignation. Gregory leaned over to pick up the book, and when he stood up, he towered over her. "Women like you think you can get away with anything," he said in a furious undertone, "because you're so damn pretty." His eyes suddenly raked hers and in an instant Tatyana felt herself crushed in his arms. He kissed her hard.

Terrified by a kiss she had never before experienced, Tatyana struggled. But he held her fast, impervious to her resistance. Then, some deep animal instinct began to pulse within her, and a feeling of bliss came over her. Gregory's lips stayed on hers, plumbing the depths of her feelings. Her arms went slack, all that was real was their embrace, as the world seemed to vanish. Just as she put her arms about him, Gregory flung her away from him.

Tatyana thought she would fall, and she grasped a chair. With dazed but smoldering eyes she looked at him. "Why do we fight when—"

"Forgive my effrontery," cut in Gregory with his iciest voice as he turned away from her. "I don't know what came over me." And before Tatyana could come to her senses, Gregory had picked up his satchels and strode from the room.

An hour later, Dmitry and Gregory were gone.

Tatyana sat by her window, still stupefied by the events of the afternoon, and watched the sleigh drive off. Images, smells, and words jumbled in her brain: the sight of Gregory walking across the snow in her direction, the little red eyes on Lizanka's lark cakes, her father's wrath, and the sweet and salty smell of Gregory's body as he had kissed her. Tatyana shivered as all these things swirled in her mind. She pushed the curtain farther, looking out into the still darkness, and remembered her father's words that afternoon. "If they refuse to apologize, they must leave, and they will not return until they have some sense knocked into those wild heads of theirs." This ultimatum sank heavily in her heart. Onto what paths, she wondered, had her father inadvertently flung them, and would they ever return? Sitting in the darkness of her room, Tatyana touched her fingers to her lips, as if discovering some wondrous new part of her. And still they burned under the touch of Gregory's kiss.

Chapter Eight

AFTER SIX LONG MONTHS OF COLD AND DARKNESS, THE smell of wet grass and the unexpected cry of birds in flight was the welcome sign that winter had come to an end. It was the middle of May, and Tatyana breathed in deeply the smell of jonquils in the garden. When her father was carried out to the terrace, she turned and asked, "Still no letter from Dmitry?"

This question had been uttered by Tatyana almost every day, now that the weeks since their departure had turned into months. "No," was the invariable answer of her father, "and just as well, if your brother's decided to throw his life away."

In that quarter-year, Prince Korbatsky had used his time arranging ways to placate the indignation of his young neighbor, Vasily Turburov. The prince had written him a formal apology, sent him small tokens of his esteem, and entertained him and his sister at Starlina.

When Tatyana put aside her wool and velvet, and tried on her summer tulle, batiste and muslin dresses, she was startled to see how much weight she had lost. The expression in her eyes seemed slack, her skin no longer luminous. "How tired and old I look, Dunyasha!"

"*Nichevo, nichevo,* little mother, that will pass," said Dunyasha. "You are young and so is the spring weather. Wait and see, the sun will shake the winter from your bones."

One morning, Tatyana awoke early and saw the familiar droshky of the Turburovs drive up in front of the house. "Dunyasha, who can that be so early in the day, driving in Count Vasily's carriage?"

"I couldn't say," answered her *nyanya,* who was busy dressing her hair.

But Tatyana saw by her evasive eye that she was not telling the truth.

"Yes, Dunyasha, tell me, or I shall go down right now and demand it of father. Why this mystery?" She frowned. "Is father selling off some serfs again?"

Tatyana had not had the courage to broach her father about Lizanka after her brother's dismissal, seeing how upset he was by the insubordination of his son. But she was waiting for an opportunity to speak to him, and if he were selling serfs again, this would be the moment to mention Lizanka.

"No, little mother, no serfs are to be sold," said Dunyasha, and she crossed herself. "It is for good things." But her puzzling expression did not reassure Tatyana. Dunyasha could never tell a lie, but Tatyana knew she could also be obdurate.

"Tell me what this is all about," she insisted.

"No."

"Yes, tell me."

"No."

Tatyana turned and faced her. The familiar stolid expression on Dunyasha's face and her compressed lips would reveal nothing before it was time.

"Oh, Dunyasha, you are as stubborn as a mule."

But because there was no sense banging on a locked door, Tatyana let Dunyasha finish curling her hair.

When she was finally dressed, Tatyana went downstairs. Some house serfs were removing storm windows, while others washed and swept the walk up to the house. Tatyana went to her father's study door. It was here he spent his mornings going over his ledgers and other estate papers. Today she found the door shut. She could hear a lady's voice from within. Who can that be? she wondered. She was tempted to tap at the door but knew how her father hated to be interrupted when the door was closed. Just when she was about to go away again, the door swung open. A small, elderly woman, excellently attired, popped out of the study.

"There's my daughter," said Prince Korbatsky from inside, seeing Tatyana in the morning sunlight. "Did you sleep well, my Tanya?" His voice ran like honey.

"Yes, papa, thank you," said Tatyana entering the study unbidden and kissed her father's hand in greeting. Then she turned to look at the new arrival. Her father hastened to introduce her to the lady.

"Let me present my daughter to you. Madame Mesatoni, this is Tatyana Ivanovna."

The elderly lady scrutinized Tatyana—from her pretty pistachio gown with its open collar to her eyes and the color of her hair. Then she took Tatyana's slim hand in her own small bony one. "Yes, she is a beauty, of the Russian type," she pronounced, with not a shred of affectation in her voice.

Tatyana blushed at the cool appraisal.

Madame Mesatoni read the look of inquiry in Tatyana's green eyes, pale as her gown in the morning sunlight. "I have come on behalf of the Turburov family."

"Is there some communication, some message for us?"

The little woman continued fixing Tatyana with her gaze, which Tatyana found disconcerting.

"Indeed, princess," said Madame Mesatoni. Then as Tatyana waited for further explanation, the woman wished them both good day and marched outside to her waiting droshky.

Tatyana turned back to her father as the woman departed. "What a curious visitor, father. Who is she?"

Prince Korbatsky smiled and cleared his throat. But he did not answer.

"Is there good news, father, or bad? Has Count Vasily been promoted again? Is Countess Irina ill?" She paused. "Are you . . . selling some land, or some serfs?"

"No, no, no, none of these," said the old prince hastily. "Come sit down." He held out his old soft hands, and Tatyana seated herself beside him on an empire stool. She glanced about her at the walls of his study, ornamented with watercolors from the Napoleonic wars, and the Gold Sword her father had been awarded for bravery. All his other medals, including his Cross of St. George, were in a case beside his desk. They did not often sit together in his study, and she sensed something important was about to happen and that it concerned her.

"This is a day I have long awaited—both with pain and pleasure," began the prince in an official voice. "Fortunately for me it has come rather later than expected. In a moment the expression of wonder on your face will be replaced by understanding, and I hope happiness. And your ignorance of this matter will be put to rest. Why do I delay the moment?" he asked rhetorically, while stroking his moustache, but there was something artificial in his tone. "Madame Mesatoni has been instructed by Count Vasily Turburov with a particular commission and comes in regard to you."

The open planes of Tatyana's face, her wide-set eyes, and parted lips suddenly shifted in astonishment.

"Papochka nye svakha!" said Tatyana, jumping up as she did so.

"Yes, my daughter. Madame Mesatoni is a marriage broker, er, I mean, an arranger of marriages."

Tatyana's hand flew to her mouth. All the afternoons she had spent at the Turburovs or with them at Starlina unraveled in her mind. "Vasily?"

Prince Korbatsky nodded, pulling more heavily on his moustache. Tatyana walked to the study window and gazed out on the lawns. With this proposal spoken, the memories crystallized for her. She remembered his attentions to her at the New Year's Ball, his solicitudes toward her at his skating party, his endless compliments, which she had never taken personally. All his little gestures, which were now so meaningful and of which she had been so ignorant. Yes, ignorant, to borrow Gregory's cruel word. Now, as she stood at the window, she upbraided herself for her inattention and her ignorance of the world.

"Surely you are not surprised, *mon poussin,*" said her father, reinstating their use of French for the formality of the occasion. "But perhaps your silence is a sign of your immense joy."

Tatyana leaned against the window, but turned toward her father. "Father, I must admit I did not expect this. But must I be married, so soon?"

Prince Ivan, understanding Tatyana's natural reserve and modesty, chuckled. "My little snow princess. Three years ago you were introduced into society. I thought I would surely lose you then. Well, God has been good to me in postponing a separation that can only be a loss for me. As you know, I have refused other suitors for your hand, guessing something splendid awaited my little

Tanya. Now a proposal comes from a young gentleman of the very highest social standing who has climbed the ranks quickly and who has a brilliant military career in front of him."

"Father, I can see from your face that his proposal comes as no surprise to you. Is it then something that you have wished for?"

The prince cleared his throat again. "Yes, I believe it is an excellent match. Of course, any man would be fortunate in gaining your hand, but Count Vasily is so . . ." He could not seem to think of the word, and concluded lamely, "so very . . . right."

"Are you very fond of Count Vasily? I knew you respected him as a neighbor but did not guess you had such a high regard for him," said Tatyana naively. She crossed the room and took a seat again by her father.

"The count is a talented young man, destined for an exalted position at court."

"But father, I am speaking of his character, not his position."

The old prince frowned and tweaked his moustache. "Well, I am certain he would make a very fine husband."

"To me in particular, or to anybody?" murmured Tatyana. She felt something was sinking within her as the conversation unfolded.

"The count is a distinguished young man, it is certain. And you, Tanya, would undoubtedly bring out the best in him."

But perhaps he would not bring out the best in me, she thought to herself. Tatyana stood up again and wandered back to the window. She felt unusually perverse and irritable, and that made her angry with herself. This was not the conversation she had pictured she would have someday with her father about her intended groom. "Father, I like Vasily Turburov, he is always courteous to me. But I cannot say the attachment goes much further, and I cannot say I love him." She seemed disappointed to have to admit this.

Prince Korbatsky until now had felt loving and patient toward his daughter, his prize child. But now he began to stroke his moustache with small quick jabs. It was a gesture, coupled with his expression, that Tatyana recognized.

She quickly ran back and sat at his feet. "Father, I hope it is not I who have made you angry."

"No, not at all," assured her father, but his voice was brusque, and he looked at her hard. "Is there someone else, someone who I may have overlooked in my natural enthusiasm for this match?"

"Someone else" murmured Tatyana, the faintest blush rising to her cheeks. "No, papa."

"Someone who has some claim, however slim, to your affections of which you have not spoken or confided in me?"

"No, father, absolutely not. You know I would never keep a secret from you," said Tatyana excitedly. Then her voice was soft and sure. "No, father, there is no one else," and she pushed Gregory from her mind.

"No one who might have been so bold as to speak to you before addressing me?"

"None."

"Then what reasons can you have against the match?" demanded the prince who quickly returned to Count Turburov's proposal of marriage.

"None, except that I feel as a friend and neighbor to the count. Not as a would-be wife. Father, I do not love him."

"Ah, but that is no obstacle, my dear, where there are benevolent feelings, a lifetime shared, compatibilities of every kind. And, my Tanya, you would be a very rich,

very important lady." Prince Korbatsky had hoped by
the simple directness of his statement to underscore this
advantage. But Tatyana did not seem particularly fazed.

"So that I could have my very own ice hill in winter,"
responded Tatyana ruefully.

"No, that is not what I mean. Ice hills are all very well
and good, but I thought of its much larger benefit to you.
We have never been rich on the scale of the Turburov
family, so I do not expect you to conceive of what
luxuries real money can buy."

"But father," remonstrated Tatyana, putting her arms
about her father's neck. "I have always been singularly
blessed by all that I have. A loving father, a dear brother,
a home I love. I do not need to marry, I do not wish to be
rich." Her voice was warm with affection.

Prince Korbatsky did not return his daughter's embrace.

"So I understand that you do not mean to accept
Count Vasily's excellent, excellent offer, and that it is
summarily dismissed?" he said frostily.

Tatyana drew back, hurt. A myriad of emotions played
on her face, as she battled with her feelings. At last she
spoke. "No papa, his proposal is not dismissed with if you
don't wish it to be. I want to do what you think is best."
Her voice was sad but resolute.

"Very good, daughter, I knew you would be reason-
able."

"Only, father?"

"Yes?"

"Please, father, may I have some time to think over the
proposal? It has come so suddenly upon me. . . ." her
voice trailed off.

Prince Korbatsky frowned a moment, then smiled. "Of
course, you may. You are the sensible one of my
children. I know you will make the right decision."

Tatyana felt the weight of his remark, as well as the unspoken allusion to her brother. "Are you very worried about Dmitry?"

"He is my son, so his conduct naturally concerns me. But there is nothing to be done until he decides to be sensible." The old prince paused, but his ideas long brewing would not be held back. He spoke with urgency. "I was patient with your brother after his return from France. Europe went to his head. Well, he isn't the first Russian to fall under Europe's spell. Even Russia herself can be accused of that. After all, here we are speaking *français*.

"So your brother's pot shots at Russia, his wild notions of freeing the serfs, were almost to be expected. As much as his dilettantish ideas were vexatious to me, I was tolerant toward his whims."

He looked to Tatyana unconsciously for confirmation, and she nodded in agreement. He continued.

"I wrote him half a dozen recommendations to present to some of the great men of our age and sent him off to St. Petersburg. It was my belief that while your brother was there he would fall in with other young officers in the Imperial Guard and that soon his thoughts would clear."

Here Tatyana thought of Arkady Stegorin and Prince Trubetskoy, whom she had met at the ball, but she said nothing. The prince went on.

"Instead he comes home six weeks later without a commission. Even then I held my tongue. But I could no longer hold my tongue when he and his friend went insulting the man who will be your future husband." The prince seemed hardly aware of how he had just described Count Turburov, but Tatyana let it pass as he went on. "Your brother has really pushed me to the end of my patience, and the effect of that Mr. Grandison on my family is a real cross to bear." Tatyana half jumped in

her seat as he said this, but the old prince was so lost in
his progression of ideas he didn't notice. "As long as that
Mr. Grandison is with Dmitry, he will muddy the waters
for your brother."

Tatyana remembered with painful, blushing vividness
her own dispute with Gregory on this score and how he
had upbraided her for believing Dmitry incapable of his
own thoughts and decisions.

"You really think Mitya's thoughts are not his own?"

Prince Korbatsky stroked his moustache thoughtfully.
"Dmitry Ivanovich will always be passionate and head-
strong. But at heart he is easily swayed, susceptible to
anything newfangled. Eventually the golden epaulets and
sabers of his comrades will have their effect, and Mr.
Grandison's European luster will be dimmed."

Tatyana was not so sure if this appraisal of her brother
was correct, but she kept silent. The prince, unusually
voluble this morning, had more to say, and Tatyana had
a sense finally of how much he must have been mulling
these issues over. "That Gregory Grandison may hold a
fatal attraction for my son, but Dmitry will come around.
He is a Korbatsky after all, and he will know his duty."
The old prince grimaced and pulled on his moustache,
while concluding cynically, "If nothing else, Dmitry will
come home because he will run out of money."

"Father, I hope he does come home soon—with or
without a commission," said Tatyana. "It would be so
good to have our family back again, with everyone
sweet-tempered, happy. No confusion." But even as she
spoke, Gregory's recriminating words came back to
haunt her—*Everything must stay the same to the point of
suffocation for you—just so your own comfort and
prejudices are not disturbed*—and her voice trailed off.

"Come home with or without his commission," retorted her father, repeating his daughter's outburst. "Not a

chance. Next time your brother comes to our door, he walks in wearing the uniform of an officer. And I hope he comes alone, without that companion of an Englishman."

"But papa, I think perhaps we have misjudged that gentleman," said Tatyana. "There seems more to the story of the fight at the river than meets the eye."

"Oh, I heard Dmitry's side of the story, though that Mr. Grandison was too proud to defend himself. That Count Vasily was beating a serf, and Gregory only went to help the man; that it was Vasily, not Gregory who struck first."

"But perhaps that is what really happened," said Tatyana excitedly, hearing this version for the first time.

"According to Dmitry—though he admits he did not see it with his own eyes. In any case, they were the Turburovs' guests. Vasily's serfs are his to discipline as he sees fit. Even giving your brother and his friend the benefit of the doubt, Mr. Grandison's behavior was unforgivable, and an apology was in order."

Lizanka's words pricked in Tatyana's memory. "Father, I never told you, but I saw Lizanka that day at Count Vasily's."

"Lizanka, Lizanka? I don't recall her. Ah, yes, the laundress."

"She did not look very well."

The prince looked uncomfortable in his seat. Tatyana then asked the question that had long been troubling her. "Why did you sell Lizanka and those other serfs, father? Are you in debt?"

"In debt? Certainly not," exclaimed Prince Korbatsky. "It is not for you to question your father, Tatyana Ivanovna, on subjects of which you have no understanding. Whatever I do is done for the benefit of this family, so believe I am the judge of what is best for us." He saw Tatyana's troubled gaze and added brusquely, "Enough questions for today. Isn't there some embroidery you could work on?"

Tatyana nodded and took her leave. There was nothing more to say.

Chapter Nine

PRINCE KORBATSKY'S PREDICTION ABOUT DMITRY PROVED to be correct. One afternoon a letter arrived at the house from the young prince.

The letter, addressed to Tatyana's father, was brief but polite and informed him that he had received an appointment as lieutenant colonel, in command of an infantry battalion, in the Imperial Army. He did not say which unit he was with or where he had been posted. The letter added that he was waiting for his regimental colors but would stop at Starlina once he had paid for his uniform. There was no word about Gregory Grandison or the confrontation in the study.

"There's my boy, a damn fine lieutenant colonel. Why, he'll be a full colonel in no time," said the old prince, rapping the arm of his chair in enthusiasm. "Order and sense restored at last. He's got the Korbatsky blood in him after all."

Almost three months exactly after their angry departure, a hired droshky drew up under the shadow of the green birches at Starlina. Tatyana was outside, where she

spent almost all her time in good weather. This afternoon
she was seated on a swing suspended from an oak tree;
this had been her favorite spot since she was a small girl.
From the highest point of the swing she could see out
across her father's lands, the peasants working in the
fields, the women near their *izbas*, peeling cabbage
heads, or those washing laundry at the brook. Children
too young to help alongside their parents played in the
road outside the cottages. But Tatyana did not see the
droshky pull up, for she was not swinging, only lolling in
the seat and reading a letter from her friend Sofia. The
countess related news about St. Petersburg and then,
near the end, pressed Tatyana to come visit them.

Tatyana was delighted with this idea. For the first time
in all her life, Tatyana was feeling the need for feminine
companionship. She loved Dunyasha and had cried
herself to sleep in her *nyanya's* arms many times, but
now she needed someone who could offer not just
comfort but wise counsel. Her father's injunction to make
a decision about Count Vasily's proposal of marriage
weighed heavily on her mind. She dreaded a decision
and yet was desperate to please her father. Every part of
her said to accept her father's wishes, and yet each day
came and something kept her from speaking. She knew
that Sofia with her cool, calm head would be able to
advise her.

As Tatyana suddenly looked up across the beautifully
manicured lawns, approaching her she saw the figure of a
young infantry officer of the Imperial Army. He wore a
jacket of green broadcloth with red collar and cuffs and
decorated with gold epaulets and brandenburgs down his
chest. As he strode toward her, she heard the squeak of
brand new black boots worn over slim-fitting white
trousers.

"Mitya," she exclaimed, leaping off the swing. They

embraced affectionately. Dmitry's blond moustache was neatly trimmed, and he had good color in his cheeks. Tatyana had never seen him so handsome, she was convinced of it. "Mitya, I am so happy to see you! You look splendid in that uniform." She gazed at the gleaming gold epaulets denoting his rank as an officer. "How proud I am of you, Mitya, and how happy father is. Every bad word has been forgotten. He brags about you to everyone!"

Prince Dmitry cast his eyes to the ground. But when he finally looked up a smile appeared on his lips. "Tanya, you are a sight for sore eyes," he said swinging her around. His head nodded to the swing. "You know, this is how I always think of you, on that swing. You would not budge from it for hours on end when you were a little girl. How I regret, now that we are both grown up, the times I never pushed you when you asked me to."

This quality of nostalgia was not typical of Dmitry, and Tatyana was surprised. "Ah, but you had more serious occupations to look to, Mitya. Besides, there were always souls to do it for me."

"Yes, I know," answered her brother. He turned briefly to gaze on the house and lawns as if he had never seen them before, or would never see them again.

"Mitya?"

"Yes?"

"No, it is not important."

"Tell me," said her brother, turning back to her.

Tatyana blushed. "I was only wondering, is . . . did you come home alone?"

Dmitry shook his head. "No, Gregory Grandison is in the drawing room with father."

Tatyana's blush rose and her scalp felt prickly. "Now that you're in uniform, Mitya, father will be cordial to everyone—even Mr. Grandison."

Dmitry nodded and seemed preoccupied.

"Mitya, aren't you happy about your commission?" asked Tatyana suddenly.

"I am very pleased by it, but it is not exactly what father expected. I won't be with the Guards in St. Petersburg but with the staff at Staraya-Russa."

"Isn't that a military colony?" she asked, taking his arm in hers and strolling back toward the house.

"Yes, Alexander's brainchild, with Count Arakcheyev as the hatchet man."

"I don't understand. You sound bitter." Tatyana stopped and turned toward him. Her light-hearted, optimistic brother seemed somehow different now from how she had always remembered him. His outbursts of the winter seemed mere deviations from his normal self, but now concern and tension seemed deeply impressed in his person. He was gazing off into some middle distance.

"Sometimes, when I lie in bed at night, when I feel selfish, I wish I had stayed in Paris," he now said.

"Why do you say that, Mitya? Aren't you glad to be back?"

"Yes, but how happy I was then—only three short months ago. I had such dreams and illusions. About us all, the family, the motherland. But it was a false happiness, and where I am going will free me of the last vestige of my illusions."

"Dmitry, I am worried to hear you speak this way. You talk as if the military colonies were like being sent to the Caucasus to fight the Turks, or being exiled to Siberia. Are the military colonies so very bad?"

Dmitry didn't answer immediately, and Tatyana added, "General Miloradovich says all the soldiers live in new-built houses, that they can have their wives and children with them, that they always wear new uniforms, and that they even eat pheasant and suckling pig at meals."

Dmitry snorted in derision. "That is what the soldiers are served when the likes of General Miloradovich pay a visit. Believe me, for the soldiers it is mostly cabbage soup and cabbage soup."

Tatyana put her hand on her brother's arm. "Mitya, what have you been doing these three months?"

"As you may have guessed, touring the military colonies."

"So they are not the model settlements they have been described as?"

"More like a slightly glorified prison, I would say," came a familiar voice. Tatyana spun around to see Gregory Grandison beside them. He wore a bottle green frock coat and a piqué waistcoat. He looked extraordinarily handsome in the soft spring light, his hair and moustache lustrous, his teeth very white. His eyes were just the same as always, slightly veiled and sardonic, while the curve of his lip smiled with faint condescension. There was no trace of the man who had kissed her so passionately at their last meeting.

"Welcome to Starlina," Tatyana said with the utmost formality, but she tingled as she felt his warm breath on her skin when he kissed her hand.

"Yes, Gregory is right," said Dmitry. "They are little more than glorified prisons." Tatyana, looking at him once more, saw in his eyes their light blue consumed by an ardent fire. "They are the emperor's curious fantasy gone haywire."

"What was Alexander's intention when he created them?" asked Tatyana, for the subject of the military colonies was not one that had ever particularly interested her.

"The colonies, Tanya, were supposed to relieve the terrible burden of the twenty-five year mandatory military service for conscripted peasants. It was Alexander's idea to create a self-supporting agricultural community

where the soldiers would have their families with them
while fulfilling their military duties. But then Count
Arakcheyev put his creatures in charge. Many of the able
officers we met at the colonies were so demoralized and
disgusted by what the colonies had degenerated to that
they asked to be transferred elsewhere, even to remote
provincial garrisons."

"But how have they degenerated?" asked Tatyana.
"They sound like a wonderful solution to me."

"They are abominable because the soldiers and their
families have no personal freedom of any kind," exclaimed Dmitry. "The entire day is regimented for every
member of each family. Even the wives are ordered to
give birth to one child a year, and if one miscarries or
bears a girl instead of a boy, she is fined. The conditions
of the serfs are better even with the worst master, for at
least their lives are their own within their own little hovels.
Conditions have so deteriorated that mothers have taken
their children and run away, willing to chance death and
starvation rather than bear the burden of being in a
colony any longer. Meanwhile the men are flogged for
breaking even the most insignificant rule. Of course,
under their clean new uniforms you do not see the welts
upon their backs!" he concluded bitterly.

Tatyana couldn't speak as she glanced from Dmitry's
impassioned eyes to Gregory's cool studied gaze. His
eyes were on the lawns, but it was clear Gregory's
thoughts were on Dmitry's outburst.

"And who is responsible for these conditions?" asked
Tatyana. "Surely not the czar."

"Only indirectly. Arakcheyev is really the culprit."

"Is Arakcheyev really so awful?" asked Tatyana,
doubtful that the czar's most confidential advisor could
be blamed for what Dmitry had described. "I always
thought he was considered to have exceptional talents."

"Yes, he is most certainly exceptional," said Gregory

blandly. "Not every Russian officer when he loses his temper has enough imagination to bite the ear off one of his soldiers."

Tatyana winced. "That cannot be true."

Dmitry nodded, "I have finally learned why Arakcheyev is nicknamed the Vampire."

Gregory lit his pipe.

Tatyana probed her memory, not willing to admit the czar's most powerful minister might have character flaws. "I hear at least that he is passionately fond of music and loves the songs of birds."

"Yes, very true," said Gregory. "He particularly delights in the sound of nightingales." Gregory drew on his pipe, and the little puffs of smoke rose in the air. "That must be the reason he rounded up all the cats in his village—nearly a hundred tabbies—and had them hanged."

"That is monstrous and perverted!" said Tatyana.

"He sees himself as equally responsible for the behavior of his soldiers as his cats," said Gregory coolly. "Unfortunately, he doesn't always distinguish between whiskers."

Tatyana squeezed her brother's arm. "Mitya, it is clear you must not go to one of his colonies," she said, feeling fiercely protective of her brother. "Staraya-Russa is not the place for you. Knowing what it would be like, why did you even accept such a commission? You must wait for a commission that would post you to St. Petersburg, with the Imperial Guard."

Dmitry breathed deeply. "You do not understand, dear sister. I wished to be posted to a military colony. It is what I requested."

"But why?"

"Because that is where I am needed—even more so, I have discovered, than in the law courts. There, according to Arkady Stegorin, one can't even begin to combat the problems. At Staraya-Russa I have a chance to be a good officer to my soldiers, to raise their morale, and to help them in their distress. All the good officers have left, and only the brutal minions of Arakcheyev remain behind, fattening themselves at the expense of the government. Staraya-Russa is where I am needed, where I can do some small but real good for my people."

Tatyana sighed and took some consolation that at least her brother had returned in uniform. And whatever his motives, he had made their father happy. "Perhaps later you can have yourself transferred to the capital," she concluded hopefully.

A week later, Dmitry was gone, off to join his battalion at Staraya-Russa. Gregory had planned to accompany him, but the night before their departure Prince Korbatsky asked Mr. Grandison to accept his hospitality a little longer. Tatyana was surprised at this offer and doubly surprised when Gregory accepted it. She, her father, and Gregory Grandison facing each other over dinner each evening seemed an unlikely combination. Nevertheless, she was pleased at her father's unexpected magnanimity, not considering the invitation might have been extended for less than generous reasons.

That same evening after supper, while Dmitry oversaw his packing, Gregory appeared in the drawing room. Prince Korbatsky was musing over his tea, holding a lump of sugar between his teeth. It was a habit he had picked up from his peasants. Tatyana was at the far end of the room, playing idly on the clavichord. Gregory held out a book to the old prince. "Here is a book I have been meaning to give you, prince. Perhaps this will help you in the management of your estate."

Prince Korbatsky took the book from Gregory. "Where did you get it?" he asked, noticing it was a foreign edition. With censorship of the press so rampant, a book in a foreign language was always potentially a subject for debate.

"At Wolff's on the Nevsky Prospect," said Gregory, referring to a well-known book shop in St. Petersburg.

Prince Korbatsky surveyed the title and name of the author with his quizzing glass. "Who is François Huber?" he grumbled. "Some damn freethinker or philosopher who has managed to slither through the Department of Public Morals?"

"Not at all, prince. François Huber is a Swiss naturalist and beekeeper. Last time I was here I noticed you use the old straw skeps," said Gregory, alluding to the primitive hive design used by Prince Korbatsky's beekeeper. "In this book Huber outlines a beehive that works on movable combs. This new invention allows—"

"New, new, new," snapped the old prince. "Why that word 'new' works like magic on ignorant minds is beyond me. Our straw hives are quite good enough I'm sure. I have never heard the bees complain."

Gregory smiled. "These new combs would double your yield of honey."

The old prince said nothing, but Gregory's words were having their effect on him. At last he said, feigning little interest, "How do they work, anyway?"

"The movable combs would allow your beekeepers to remove the bees' surplus honey without disturbing or killing the bees, or injuring the other combs in any way."

The old prince stroked his moustache. "Well, we shall see, we shall see."

"Father," said Tatyana, now crossing to her father, for she had been listening to this conversation. "Perhaps we should consider these new hives, if what Mr. Grandison says is true."

"All right," said the old prince throwing up his arms,

"you are the mistress of the hives, daughter. I will let you decide as you see fit. Anyway, perhaps a project is what you need." Then he added irritably, "But don't go driving poor Peter the beekeeper out of his mind. One thought at a time is all he can muster."

The next week Tatyana and Gregory worked side by side, Gregory translating into French the text of the book while Tatyana translated it into Russian for the beekeeper and his helpers. At first the peasants were muddled by the complex diagrams, but between Gregory's gestures and Tatyana's coaxings, they grew to understand them. In no time at all, the peasants threw themselves into the work. With their axes they chopped the twelve-inch pine laths needed, splitting the wood with such rapidity and ease that Gregory was amazed. And when Gregory tried his hand with an axe, they were amused and honored at his sorry imitation. Tatyana had never seen Gregory so kind as with the serfs. He had endless patience and, unlike with most people, a complete lack of condescension. In his simple linen shirt, open at the collar, the dew of sweat on his forehead, he seemed in his element: handsome and muscular and vigorous.

Once he had sunk down on the lawn next to Tatyana, and she watched his Adam's apple rise and fall while he swallowed the last of his tea.

"Your father's serfs have thrown themselves into this work with real effort," said Gregory, "and it partly reflects their good feeling for your family."

Tatyana was surprised at a compliment from Gregory. "You see, not all men hate their masters here in Russia, and not all masters abuse their serfs."

Gregory's eyes seemed almost hazel in the afternoon light. "Your brother told me that you and your father have allowed the serfs to keep and sell half the honey that comes from these hives," he said casually. "Is that true? It is a fairly generous amount—by anybody's standards."

"Yes," said Tatyana and smiled impishly. "Is that why you have shown such an interest in building these new hives?"

"I guess I am rather monochromatic in my ideas," answered Gregory wryly. "Yes, that was part of it." And then he looked at Tatyana again. "Is it also true that you were the one who pushed your father to share the yield half and half with his serfs?"

"It only seemed fair," answered Tatyana, shrugging her shoulders.

Gregory gazed into Tatyana's eyes with an intimacy he had never shown before. "Tatyana," he said, using her Christian name for the first time, and gazing at her with an intrigued smile, "you are quite a curious girl."

"What do you mean?"

Gregory smiled and shook his head. "Never mind. In any case, there's work to do, and I had better get back to the men. They're eager to start assembling the new hives today."

From that day forward there was a new gentleness in their manner toward each other, and Tatyana always loved to sit beside him.

Later, when the hives were assembled and the bees transferred to their new homes, Tatyana and Gregory walked among the forty square pine boxes and stopped at the first one from which could be heard the drone of bees.

"How I love that sound," said Tatyana. "They sound so industrious and happy."

"You are only anthropomorphizing them. They are industrious, but happy? Who knows. At least they are fulfilling their own brief destinies." Gregory seemed tired and preoccupied.

"Yes, I suppose," said Tatyana, "but there is something so inspiring about their industriousness, the worker bees' allegiance to the queen bee. Everything they do is for the good of the hive—it is like a society perfectly orchestrated, a utopia."

"A utopia indeed," said Gregory, "but remember, a utopia for bees. Human society requires something different."

"We could learn a lot from the bees," countered Tatyana, resenting the cynical tone that had crept back into his voice.

"What is it you would have us learn from them, princess, blind obedience? You yourself know the spring worker bees have half the life span of those in autumn because they're so damn tuckered out from catering to the queen."

Tatyana frowned. "You just never change, do you? All that talk about abolishing serfdom, putting strictures on autocracy, I hazard you probably still think that way."

Gregory laughed at her naiveté.

"Well, at least Dmitry has changed," said Tatyana, "Dmitry has come around."

"Come around?" laughed Gregory ironically. "You think your brother has thrown up his ideals?"

"My brother is in uniform," challenged Tatyana to prove her point.

"You are a little fool," he said softly. "You probably even think your brother is in uniform only to satisfy your father."

"Yes, and why not? It's as good a reason as any."

"Whatever else you think, understand your brother is not so easily bought off," said Gregory, shaking his head. "You were with him that day. He described the military settlements. He went into the army for only one reason; he felt he had a better chance there than anywhere to help his people."

"I hope he will soon be promoted and transferred out of there," Tatyana thought out loud.

"He is not likely to do so. To accomplish what he wishes to do, he should stay there at least six months."

"Whatever for? Soldiers and officers come and go."

"Yes, but not Arakcheyev, and not the colonies themselves."

"What is Dmitry up to?" asked Tatyana, made apprehensive by his cryptic words. "If it is not just the soldiers' comfort he is after, what does he want?"

"Your brother wants to change the colonies from top to bottom."

"And how, how is he going to do that?" challenged Tatyana, feeling increasingly upset.

"Your brother is writing a draft of a report he will submit to Count Arakcheyev, a petition of sorts. In the petition he is outlining the conditions of the colonies and proposing specific reforms."

Tatyana looked at him blankly. "If Dmitry is not careful, such a work could get into the wrong hands, and he could get into a great deal of trouble. Count Arakcheyev is a very powerful man and is not likely to look well on someone who criticizes his authority or wants to make trouble in the colonies."

"Instead of worrying about the opinions of Arakcheyev, you could try thinking about the opinions of your brother. You should be proud of him!" Gregory's anger was mounting as his last altercation with the princess rose in his mind. "In three months you somehow expected Dmitry to change. But I can see that for all your help on the hives, in three months you're still the same egocentric child." He breathed deeply. "I would be proud to have a brother who wants to beard the lion."

Tatyana glared at Gregory. "And thanks to you, Mitya

may just stub his ears on the lion's teeth!" Tatyana gathered her voluminous skirts and stalked off indignantly.

Two days later Tatyana sat outside rocking in the swing. The sun shone brightly and the air was balmy. Earlier that morning her father had been driven to visit the Turburovs, and Gregory Grandison had been gone all day, having borrowed a horse to explore the countryside.

After that brief promise of warmth between them, Tatyana and Gregory were now just as distant from each other as they had been before. Though Gregory had once tried to approach Tatyana, she had ignored him and walked out of the room. Now he too adopted an aloof manner toward her. When she learned from her father that Gregory would leave the next day, she didn't know whether she was relieved, furious, or heartbroken. Tatyana was not in a good mood. On top of that, she had made a rather strange discovery. Tatyana had longed to reread some of Dmitry's letters. Because her father had already left, she had to ask Timofey the butler for the key to his desk, which was where he kept his letters. The key Timofey gave her seemed the wrong one, until it fitted in the lower righthand drawer. But inside the drawer were not Dmitry's letters but packs and packs of playing cards. The faces of the king and queen and jack stared up mutely at her as she glanced through the decks. Knowing how adamantly against card playing and gambling her father was, the contents of the drawer surprised her. She had never once seen a pack of cards at Starlina, and she remembered an incident in which her father had burnt a deck he found in Dmitry's possession. Tatyana returned the key to Timofey but did not say anything about the matter.

As she sat in the swing outside, she was distracted from her uncomfortable thoughts by the sound of the beekeeper's daughter, who was playing among the old straw skeps, singing to herself. This drew her attention back to the springtime and served to remind her of all that she was grateful for. With spring so short, nature conspired to draw forth the busiest of bees, to make birds build nests without stop and to sing without cease. Everything was accelerated; even the squirrels who scampered about ferreting the ground around the maple and birch trees to lay their store for winter.

In the flush of sunshine only their industriousness spoke of a long deep winter only a few months away. Tatyana was soothed and simultaneously invigorated by what she saw around her, and like the little girl, she began to hum to herself.

There was a movement off to Tatyana's right, near the beehives. Tatyana took no notice of it, lost now in happier thoughts of past recollections. But something in the unnatural movement caused her to raise her eyes. Her song died on her lips.

"*Gospodi pomiluy!*" God in Heaven preserve our souls," she murmured. Hardly twenty yards from her, and only paces from the little girl, stood an enormous bear.

Chapter Ten

THE BEAR WAS RAISED ON HIS HIND FEET, INSPECTING ONE of the old straw skeps that still smelled of honey. He seemed oblivious to the little girl, who was down wind from him. And she too had not noticed him, for she was deeply immersed in her solitary game of laying sticks in rows on the dusty path.

Tatyana stood up very slowly and began walking very slowly in the direction of the beehives and toward the little girl. Her one hope was to convey the child away before the bear should notice her. Leaning down, Tatyana carefully picked up some leftover laths that had not been used for the new hives. She walked closer and closer to the child. When she was just ten yards away, the little girl suddenly sat up and changed the weight on her legs. As she did so, she glanced over her shoulder and saw the bear.

"Iiiiieeee!" The child's terrified scream seared through the balmy air. And the bear, who had been licking the edge of the skep, looked up and saw the child.

The little girl scrambled up and began to run. And the

bear fell onto four paws and began to lope after her. The little girl had not even seen Tatyana. She ran in the only direction that occurred to her—the long distance to her parent's *izba*. The bear's black nostrils flared and he moved faster.

Tatyana streaked after them both. She screamed to draw the animal's attention from the child.

The grizzly had caught up to the child. He was about to give her a swat of his huge paw when he received a blow on his snout. Tatyana raised another lath and flung it at his head. "Don't you dare touch her!" she screamed in fury, using all her strength to hit him with another lath.

The befuddled bear turned slowly in his tracks and saw the larger figure bearing down on him. He was again struck in the head, and opening his huge jaw, bristling with teeth, he growled angrily. Then he came after Tatyana.

Tatyana knew suddenly that it was not worth trying to run. She glanced around her desperately to see if any other people were near. The fields were just on the other side of the hill but out of ear shot. Toward the house, everything looked deserted. Tatyana panicked, flinging the last of the laths as she tried to retreat. Each time he was hit, the bear would pause, then resume the chase. Terrified, Tatyana ducked behind one of the new movable beehives. When the bear was only two feet away from her, emboldened with fear, she lifted up the heavy set of empty frames, and flung it at him. The heavy pine box hit his shoulder and he growled.

She retreated to another wooden hive, and tried to heave it at him also, but this time it was too late. Without another growl, the awkward-looking bear lunged nimbly at her. Lifting its giant paw, and with enough force to fling a full grown man ten feet, he swatted at her. A sudden hot, stinging sensation penetrated to what seemed the very core of her being. The animal's claws had ripped through her blouse and gashed her arm. The searing pain welled up, and Tatyana nearly fainted. Using her last reservoir of strength, she began to stagger away. She stumbled and felt the monstrous creature above her. So this is how I am to die? flashed lucidly through her brain as darkness began to cloud her eyes. Just then an unfamiliar noise echoed and lost itself in the closing chambers of her mind. It was the sound of a single gun shot whisking through the afternoon air.

As she lost consciousness, Tatyana felt an enormous weight upon her, a weight that seemed to push her down into the center of the earth.

It was Gregory who fired the shot that saved Tatyana's life. Gregory had returned to the stables, heard a shriek, and run from the courtyard. His gun was loaded and he fired.

He ran to Tatyana, half smothered by the carcass of the bear on top of her, and he pushed the brute aside.

Tatyana's face was white and limp, and her arm was bleeding badly. Gregory quickly stripped off his linen outer shirt and wrapped it tightly around her arm. "Help, we must get her inside," he commanded her father's *mujiks,* who at the sound of the gun shot had come running from all over. Before too long, Tatyana was indoors, stretched out in the drawing room on her father's leather couch.

Dunyasha came running down the stairs, saw the blood, and threw her apron over her head. "Oh, my baby, my little baby, she is dead, oooooooh!"

"No she is not," snapped Gregory. "But your shrieks are loud enough to send her to Hades. Be silent, woman, if you cannot be of help." Gregory began to unwind the blood-soaked shirt from Tatyana's arm.

Dunyasha was immediately quieted. "We must send for the good doctor, Anton Morabitsky. He is only two versts from Starlina, and I know he will come." Dunyasha scampered off to send for him.

Prince Korbatsky had just driven up in his droshky. He was brought into the drawing room by four *mujiks*, who were so concerned for their master's daughter they nearly sent him spilling out of his chair. "Put me down, right here," barked the old prince, and he grabbed at his quizzing glass as they dumped him unceremoniously beside the couch.

"Please," said Gregory, waving his arm toward the peasants, who stood clustered around, their caps in their hands, "we must give the princess room."

Soon the maids had shooed the poor serfs away.

"I will need blankets to keep her warm. Two bowls of hot water, a clean knife." said Gregory. "And some string. Eucalyptus leaves if you have any, and camphor as well. Have you these things?" The maids were about to scurry off in search of them when Prince Korbatsky stopped them. He looked angrily at the young Englishman. "What do you mean to do? What is this nonsense? She will have to be bled by a doctor."

"To be bled is the last thing your daughter needs," retorted Gregory, becoming angry in turn. "We must staunch the bleeding." He began to fold back her sleeve.

"Such impropriety. Are you a doctor?" demanded Prince Korbatsky, waving his quizzing glass at Gregory.

"I know what I'm about, and at this moment that should be enough for you," retorted Gregory. "And I can assure you of one thing, prince. The princess does not have time for some witch doctor from the steppes to come in and bleed her to death. If you wish to quibble with me about propriety, then expect to lose your daughter."

Gregory's voice was so threatening that Prince Korbatsky sat back in his chair as if he had been slapped. The impatient maids took this cue and scurried off to do the Englishman's bidding.

Dunyasha soon returned, and seeing that Anatole still lingered in the sick room, pointed to the door. Anatole turned his nose up at her and stood his ground. Gregory did not need an altercation at this moment. To Anatole's great humiliation, his master asked him to leave. "Anatole, you know where I keep my medicine kit. Get it for me please." Summoning up his most distinguished gait, he paraded past Dunyasha to go in search of it. Dunyasha shot him a triumphant look, and ran to her mistress.

By now Gregory had ripped back the sleeve of Tatyana's blouse. Her arm was covered with blood, and when he wiped it away he saw four marks made by the bear's claws. "These gashes are deep, but not near any arteries. Thank God for that," he muttered.

Dunyasha meanwhile was holding Tatyana's head in her lap and kept crossing herself and mumbling while she gripped a crucifix in her hand.

"A lot of good that is going to do, Dunyasha," snapped Gregory, as he began to clean the wounds. "If you really wish to be a help to your mistress, start to unwind these bandages." He flung the material at her. Dunyasha immediately began to unwrap the lint. "And use some dampened on her forehead. She must be kept warm, but keep her temples moist and cool. She will have a fever from the infection if it sets in. Bear claws are filthy, so it is bound to."

With the implements and materials brought Gregory by Anatole and the maids, Gregory cleaned the wounds, applied some tincture, and bound the arm.

Dunyasha, who was not noted for her long attention span, listened closely to all he said. And when Tatyana was bandaged, Gregory said, "I was beginning to believe Anatole when he said all you had in your head were hobgoblins, bright-colored scarfs, and crucifixes. Perhaps you will prove him wrong." He watched her apply the compress to her mistress's pale forehead.

Peter the beekeeper, whose little girl had been chased by the bear, came forward after the first emergency steps were taken to tell how Tatyana had saved his daughter's life. Though Tatyana was unconscious, he fervently pressed the hem of her dress to his lips and departed.

Gregory, tired from the trauma of the accident, wiped his arm on his forehead and said to Prince Korbatsky, who waited in a state of stupor, "Your daughter is foolhardy, prince, but very, very brave."

"Parlez-vous français?" Gregory asked, putting his arm on the little Russian man called Doctor Morabitsky.

"Oui, oui, monsieur," he answered, through his spectacles examining the nervous young foreigner, and Gregory sighed with relief.

"Let us talk quickly then." He drew the doctor into the drawing room where they could speak in private.

When Doctor Morabitsky emerged fifteen minutes later, he wiped his glasses with his handkerchief and readjusted his spectacles on his nose.

"So tell me, Doctor Morabitsky, is the young Englishman a charlatan as I suspect?" demanded Prince Korbatsky once the two men sat face to face in the study.

Doctor Morabitsky sighed and cleaned his spectacles very slowly, for he was arthritic. He seemed preoccupied and kept muttering Latin words to himself. "Oh, yes, Prince, I mean no, not a charlatan," he said, suddenly realizing he had been asked a question.

"An imposter then at least, without a degree? Surely you could ascertain that."

Doctor Morabitsky tilted his head, as if the ideas had to run into one side before he could speak. "No, not an imposter," he said. "About a degree, I did not ask to see his papers. He did refer in passing to the medical faculty at Heidelberg."

Then he looked solidly at the prince, pulling all his mental processes together.

"There is one thing I can assure you of, your excellency. That young man treating your daughter knows terms for parts of the body, conditions and infections, and cures I have never heard of." He paused, tilting his head again, so the thoughts could pour down the other side. "From our brief talk, I find that his knowledge of theoretic medicine is astounding. I even had to check my medical texts to check his terms and ascertain if what he said could even be true." He readjusted his spectacles. "In my opinion, Prince Korbatsky, your daughter could not be in better hands. Believe me, I am not needed here." And with a slight, arthritic bow, he turned to leave.

Prince Korbatsky looked flabbergasted. At the door, Doctor Morabitsky stopped.

"Oh, I forgot," and he drew from his pocket a handkerchief from which he unfolded a bullet. "They say he shot the bear from forty yards away? The bullet was found by my assistant, lodged between the cervical vertebrae of the spine. The animal was killed instantly, instantly." He shook his head. "What a shot." Bowing again, the good doctor took his leave of the prince.

Through the painstaking efforts of Gregory, who with Dunyasha kept up a full-time vigil next to the impromptu sick bed, Tatyana slowly recovered.

After the first three days of semi-delirium, Tatyana opened her eyes. She saw through the vague contour of light and shadow her nurse sitting at the end of the bed. "Dunya . . ."

"Tanya, Golubushka!" exclaimed Dunyasha rapturously, and she threw aside her needlework. She ran her coarse hand against Tatyana's lank hair and gazed into Tatyana's eyes. They were flat and expressionless, and

the sign of illness and pain lingered strongly. "You are over the worst of it, my little dove," she said. "Do you feel better?"

"Why am I here?" whispered Tatyana. Then she felt a sharp pain in her shoulder. She groaned.

"Don't you remember the bear?"

Tatyana looked puzzled, then something sparked in her memory. "I am alive?"

Dunyasha planted a kiss on Tatyana's wide forehead. "Very much so, and how thankful your old *nyanya* is for that blessing."

"Have you been with me all this time?" Tatyana asked, sensing that a lot of time had passed.

"Whenever I could be, but there is someone who—"

"And old Doctor Morabitsky, is he here?" Tatyana asked, her voice trailing off from weakness.

"He came once, little mother, but it was not Doctor Morabitsky who came to your aid, it was . . ."

Gregory sauntered into the room to relieve Dunyasha. Seeing Tatyana awake, he removed his hat. *"Zdravstvuitye,"* he greeted her in Russian.

"Zdravstvuitye," replied Tatyana faintly, remembering their most recent quarrel. "I am sick as you see," was all she was able to say.

"But ever so much better than you were three days ago. How does your arm feel?"

"It hurts."

"I should bloody well think so, that bear was no baby or old grandmother."

Tatyana nodded. "Where is Doctor Morabitsky?"

"He is not here, *moi golubushka*. You have had another doctor at your side," said Dunyasha.

Tatyana sent her a sleepy, inquiring gaze and, seeing where Dunyasha's eyes went to, turned her gaze on Gregory.

"You are a doctor?"

"I have a medical degree," said Gregory, sitting down, "but I am not a doctor. Anton Morabitsky is a doctor."

"What is the difference?" she asked sluggishly.

"All the difference in the world. I have a paper that shows I completed a course of study in medicine and physiology. But Doctor Morabitsky has given his whole life to the healing of the sick." He paused. "But now we must examine your shoulder."

Gregory saw the shyness steal across her face.

"Don't worry," he laughed, "Dunyasha has been with me at all times and would have sent me packing if I had transgressed your modesty in any way. But the bandage must be changed. Dunyasha, may I have a second basin of water?"

Tatyana noticed that Dunyasha, who had never seemed particularly sympathetic to Gregory and his valet, was now content to scurry at his orders. While she was gone, Tatyana said, "You have won Dunyasha over."

"She has won me over as well," smiled Gregory. "Her devotion to you is unbounded. She has scarcely left your side the entire time."

"Nor, I gather, have you," said Tatyana, returning his smile.

Gregory, for the first time in his life, seemed embarrassed. He turned his attention to unwinding the bandage around her arm. "Does this hurt?" he asked, and Tatyana saw on his face the remnant of a masculine blush.

"Only a little," she answered, biting her pale lip. Tatyana made no sound as he unwound the last length of bandage from her arm.

"The healing is coming along very well," he said, examining the wound. "The infection is now localized." When he looked up he saw her eyes glaze over near to

tears, but still she uttered no sound. "You were foolhardy
to run after that bear, but very, very brave. And by your
act you saved the little girl's life."

"As you have saved mine," said Tatyana softly.

Gregory could not look in her eyes and concentrated
on applying a salve to her arm. As she watched him, a
thought occurred to Tatyana. "What happened to the
bear?"

"We had to dispatch him. Otherwise I'm afraid he
would have found you a rather tasty morsel."

Tatyana almost giggled, except it hurt her. "But who
shot the bear?"

Gregory didn't answer her directly, as he rewound a
fresh bandage around her arm.

"It was your Mr. Grandison," said Dunyasha, who had
just come to the door. "Doctor Morabitsky said he never
saw a cleaner shot. Mr. Grandison, is there anything else
you need right now?" she asked, putting down the bowl
of water.

"No, thank you, Dunyasha," he said, washing his
hands in the water, and Dunyasha took the basin away
again.

"So you fired the shot as well," said Tatyana when
they were alone again.

He nodded.

"Twice my savior, then," whispered Tatyana, holding
out her hand to him. *"Grigori, spasibo,"* she said softly,
thanking him in Russian.

Gregory paused while he rebandaged her arm. With
his dark eyes he gazed into her own, luminous in the light
that flooded through the window. His eyes strayed to her
lips, and she could see his own tremble. Then he
returned his eyes to hers. Neither of them said anything.
They didn't need to. Soon, with Tatyana gazing on his
handsome face, bent in concentration, Gregory finished

bandaging her wounded arm. He worked unhurriedly, relishing the moment, for time suddenly seemed to stretch out blissfully eternal.

Tatyana's arm healed quickly. After several weeks the pain had ebbed to an occasional tenderness or ache, and soon she was up and dressed.

One morning, early in her convalescence, Gregory found Tatyana sobbing on the couch in the drawing room. She was reading *Journey from St. Petersburg to Moscow*, the book he had flung at her in his room after the Turburovs' skating party. She had been crying because she had read a description of a family of serfs separated from each other when they were sold off the land.

"This is what happened to Lizanka," said Tatyana, wiping away a tear, for the book was full of harrowing accounts of injustices in Russia. "Are so many fathers and mothers separated from their children forever?"

Gregory nodded.

"I never guessed, I never guessed," she said, the image of Lizanka rising up to haunt her. "Father was always fair to our souls—at least the ones he kept."

Thereafter, during Tatyana's convalescence, at moments when her father was absent from the house, Gregory and Tatyana were free to talk about life in Russia compared to the rest of Europe. It was an education for Tatyana. Through Gregory, a foreigner, Tatyana learned more about conditions in her country than she had learned in her entire life. And Gregory too learned something.

He had always accused Tatyana of ignorance and selfishness. Now he saw in her background what had encouraged her to be that way. He came to understand something even more important. While theoretical abstractions about the abuse of liberty and justice could move him to a fever pitch, Tatyana responded instead to concrete instances of these abuses. She was not so superficial and selfish as he supposed, but her mind was more empirical than his. And they both began to gain new insight into the world through each other.

When Dmitry came to visit once, stopping on his way to Moscow on a mission, he sat by Tatyana's bedside, and Tatyana looked at him reproachfully. They were alone together.

"Why didn't you share your new ideas with me?"

Dmitry took her hand in his. "We all learn at our own pace. For me it began with the example of representative government in Europe, for you, meeting Lizanka. I have been guilty of shielding you, partly because the knowledge of troubles in my own beloved country fills me with grief. I also wanted to spare you because I did not want to give you cause to question father's ideas on these matters."

Tatyana wondered what else she had been sheltered from, growing up under the well-intentioned ignorance campaign inflicted on her by both father and brother. But she moved on to another subject that troubled her.

"What are you doing about your military settlement?" She paused. "Gregory told me about your petition. I was upset at first. But now it seems more sensible to me. Even if Arakcheyev is a monster, he will sooner or later have to bow to popular outcry."

"Arakcheyev doesn't have to bow to anything. He has absolute power over the military colonies. I fear my little petition will end up in the dust heap with all the others."

"Then I know what you must do," said Tatyana. "You must write to Alexander. He is my godfather. He wants what is best for his people."

"Alexander has not listened to others' requests."

"There have been other requests and petitions?" asked Tatyana.

"Yes, many of them," said Dmitry, his eyes growing bright, and he said, half in a trance, "I read one report written by a group of colony peasants that was submitted to Alexander's brother, Grand Duke Nicholas. The report read, 'Increase our taxes, little father, conscript for military service a son from every home, take from us everything and send us into the steppes: we should more gladly consent to this than to stay here on this colony. We have arms, we will work and be happy there; do not take our effects, the customs of our fathers, and do not turn all of us into soldiers.' "

"And what did Nicholas do?"

"Nothing. And when the peasants later revolted against the intolerable demands on them, they were brutally suppressed. Hundreds were beaten with the knout, so severely that a number even died."

"Ah, but Alexander is not Nicholas! You must write to him!"

"Believe me, dear sister," said Dmitry tiredly, "There is not much difference. The czar has ignored similar pleas and petitions before."

Tatyana gripped Dmitry's arms. "That cannot be, that cannot be. Even if Alexander has not listened to others, surely he would listen to you. You have seen with your own eyes what these colonies are like. You must tell him. He would not want what is not right."

Prince Dmitry looked at his sister sadly. Her naiveté was overwhelming. But whose fault was it? he realized. She was only a woman whose life had been sequestered and limited to the sphere of women. Her heart was good, but she could not comprehend the enormity of Russia's ills. He felt all the more protective of her.

"Never you fear," he said. "There will be solutions."

What solutions he did not care to say. And in her ignorance, it would not have occurred to Tatyana to ask what they might be.

Prince Dmitry changed the subject and asked, "I hear from father that Count Vasily has asked for your hand."

Tatyana put down her cup of tea and nodded.

"Do you mean to accept?"

Tatyana thought before she answered slowly. "I don't know yet. Mitya, do you like Count Vasily?"

Dmitry felt caught by this question. That he did not like Count Vasily was hard to hide, and he did not think that Vasily, from what he knew of him, would make a happy lifelong companion. But Dmitry hesitated to say this. After all, from a worldly point of view it was a brilliant match, and as a husband, perhaps Vasily would be adequate. Besides, Tatyana brought out the best in everybody. But he was surprised to think his sister would want to marry Vasily Turburov.

"It is, of course, an excellent match," he said guardedly.

Tatyana sighed. "That is what father says."

Dmitry looked at Tatyana hopefully. "Is it possible you are not enthusiastic about his proposal?"

"Well, he is an old friend of the family, but I certainly never envisioned him as my future husband."

"You have plenty of time to decide, so do not rush into anything rashly," urged Dmitry. "Remember, 'marry in haste, repent at leisure.'"

"Except father terribly wants a decision. He seems desperate for the match, just desperate."

"That is troubling news," said her brother frankly, now that he was relieved to see his sister was not in love with Vasily. "Now that your own feelings are clear, I will be honest and say I think him a poor choice. And I am surprised father doesn't think him a poor choice as well."

"I think it is because Vasily is so rich."

"He is rich certainly, but so are many men. And he has at least two vices of which I know father would disapprove."

"What vices are these?" asked Tatyana.

"It's practically common knowledge that Turburov is a lush and an inveterate gambler."

Chapter Eleven

AFTER DMITRY LEFT, TATYANA PONDERED THE DISQUIETING description of Count Turburov's character. It made her more and more resolved to reject his proposal without even having to face the whole other set of new feelings she was beginning to discover in herself. But confusion prompted her to wait; she sensed all these problems would somehow soon resolve themselves.

Besides, there was something much happier to occupy her thoughts the following day. In one of the nearby peasant villages a serf of her father's was marrying his daughter to a young farmer. It was to be a very joyous occasion. The father had come to ask Prince Korbatsky's permission, and after a summary review of the facts, approval had been granted.

Though a peasant *svakha* had made all the arrangements, the young couple knew each other well and were considered a love match. Knowing of this, and knowing the festive quality of Russian weddings, Tatyana wanted to share with Gregory this happy glimpse of the peasants' life. "I have come around to seeing the ills of my country," she said half jesting, when she introduced the subject of the wedding. "Now you must come with me and see some of the good."

So on the day of the wedding, Tatyana and Gregory rode off in the droshky. Old Prince Korbatsky was too busy with estate matters to accompany them. Several versts from Starlina, in a village owned by the prince, they stopped in front of an *izba,* which was where the bride lived. Many of the *mujiks* bent down to kiss the hem of Tatyana's gown, and for the first time in her life Tatyana felt embarrassed by this act of submission on the part of grown men.

All the peasants were gaily clad, with the women in red, blue, and yellow embroidered *sarafans* made from home spun linen. The men wore their best embroidered shirts tied at their waists with sashes, and on their feet bast shoes.

Gregory and Tatyana entered the cottage, Gregory having to duck his head to pass through the low-slung door. Inside, surrounded by family and friends jammed to the walls, were the bride and groom. They had just returned from church. They sat together and, according to custom, did not speak a word to each other. But the occasional look that passed between them was radiant and tender. Everyone congratulated them. Then they all sat down to an enormous meal of *Pieroge,* which were meat pies, *zharkoye,* a baked meat dish, and *krendel,* a sweet pie.

As the guests of honor, Tatyana and Gregory sat at the head of the table during the meal. The mother cried, and her other daughters consoled her, and then the family and guests called gaily through the meal, *"Gorko! Gorko!"* And at each cry the young bride and groom kissed each other on the lips.

"What is *gorko?*" asked Gregory.

"Bitter," laughed Tatyana gaily. "The newlyweds kiss

to sweeten the meal." And her eyes were snagged by Gregory's gaze. She looked away and blushed, feeling suddenly flushed with desire for his dreamy eyes.

After the meal was over, the men and women danced inside the *izba*, and then when it grew too wild, outside under the birches. The women's steps were serene and methodical, but the men danced with great verve and agility. Gregory was surprised to see the peasants, who were so lumbering in their every gesture, suddenly move so nimbly on their feet and leap in spritely, vigorous movements without stepping on each others' toes. It was doubly impressive since most of them were drunk.

Several serf musicians, who even played for Tatyana's father at his own private balls, strummed the balalaika and sang. It seemed to Gregory that all the music and singing, and dancing and drinking, and crying and laughing would ring down the fragile rafters made of mud and straw. Yet even more impressive to him than the vitality and color of the dancers and the music, was the bridal pair.

They drank from the wedding cup, and unable to address each other with words, spoke only in glances. They seemed both charmingly self-conscious about their predicament and completely oblivious to the real world. While their neighbors laughed and drank and sang in jubilation, they gazed at each other with such intimate yet shy, bold yet gentle looks of love in their radiant eyes.

Feeling he had trespassed against something sacred, Gregory looked away. His eyes fell on Tatyana. Her cheeks were rosy from *nalivky,* a cherry wine, and song, and her sparkling eyes careened about in undiluted pleasure of the moment. How I should like to be her, be in her skin, thought Gregory.

"*Carpe diem,* my good lady, *carpe diem,*" he toasted her with his eyes and swallowed the *samoroh,* a potent brew made by the peasants.

When at last they emerged into the sunlight, Gregory realized he was intoxicated from all he had feasted on and witnessed. Tatyana's cheeks were also flushed, and her movements were slow but mellifluous.

To Gregory, who watched what happened next as if it were happening in the past, everything occurred in slow motion. Every gesture became symbolic. Tatyana approached the droshky, followed by the father of the groom. Tatyana was laughing. From her pocket she drew forth a red velvet pouch. Because of the wine, her fingers were a little numb, and she dropped the pouch.

Gleaming silver rubles rolled out onto the ground. Tatyana sank in a half curtsying bend to retrieve them, but the peasant reached down more quickly. He picked up the silver rubles at her feet and handed them to Tatyana.

Gregory, even through the tipsy blur of the afternoon, saw that two coins had rolled under a bush, and he saw the peasant glance at them. In that half-second in his brain, a critical moment occurred. Would the peasant pick them up and return them to his master's daughter? If he does, if he does, . . . he thought, as if the peasant's actions were inextricably linked to his own fate.

"Aha, little mother, here are two more," said the peasant, bending down. He pushed his arm under the bushes, retrieved the two coins, and handed them back to Tatyana. The truth about human nature crystallized for Gregory in that gesture, and he felt flooded with joy for the peasant, for Tatyana, and for himself. Yes, mankind was good, and henceforth he had only to acknowledge his faith in it.

Tatyana laughed a beautiful, rippling sound of joy and contentment. In a tipsy, singsong voice she said in Russian, "No, old Matvei, I saved this especially for your . . . daughter." She pressed the velvet pouch into his hands. "They look so happy. Isn't it a *joy?*"

The old peasant seemed startled by the inadvertent windfall, then kissed Tatyana's hem. She laughed happily again and got into the carriage. Gregory approached, nodded to the old man, and climbed into the droshky beside Tatyana.

"Ooooh," said Tatyana thickly, for she had leaned against her bad arm. Gregory saw a glimpse of her bare shoulder underneath her shawl, which hid that part of her he knew so well—that tiny span of flesh from her shoulder to her arm. He heard her wince, remembering how he had worked to save her, to mend her fragile, mortal flesh. He squeezed her bare wrist, his eyes lingering on her naked throat where he longed to leave a kiss. When he glanced into her eyes, glistening from the wine, they said yes, yes, yes. He kissed her then, first on her throat then on her face, until her lips reached hungrily for his.

"Forward, my pretty little lady," sang out Platon, oblivious to what went on behind him, and the carriage sprang forward.

Where the horses had been stood the old peasant, who bowed and bowed again after the retreating carriage, sweeping his head almost down to his feet. "God is good, praise be to God," he chanted to himself.

Those who have visited Russia have testified that there is nothing grander than the vision of St. Petersburg at summer solstice. These are the illustrious White Nights in mid-June, when the sun scarcely sets before it climbs once more into the morning sky. During this time, all St. Petersburg stays awake at night, even little children and grandparents. The heartbeat quickens, women at balls dance longer, and outside horses frisk along as if on a double ration of oats.

It was at this moment of the year that Tatyana arrived to visit Sofia Stegorina.

Due to Gregory's and Tatyana's reserve with each other in Prince Korbatsky's presence, the old prince did not think to separate them. Besides, he seemed preoccupied with other unnamed worries. His only motive in inviting Gregory to stay at Starlina was to separate him from Dmitry. So when Tatyana decided to visit St. Petersburg and Gregory decided he would go join her brother at Staraya-Russa, the old prince generously offered him instead the use of his house on Great Morskaya.

And so Gregory escorted Tatyana to St. Petersburg. It was agreed that Tatyana would stay with her friend Sofia, who had a small but beautiful house on Gorokhovaya Street. The location was ideal, situated as it was near Senate Square. This would put Tatyana within easy reach of her favorite haunts in the capital: the Summer Garden, Nevsky Prospect, the Moika Canal, and the English Embankment on the river. Tatyana loved especially St. Petersburg's open vistas, which during the White Nights of June seemed almost celestial.

When Gregory handed her down from the barouche in which they had come, Tatyana looked up at him with regret. From the corner of her eye she saw Sofia at the window, and she waved. Then she held out her hand to Gregory. "Sofia is planning a fete on the twenty-first. It is the solstice then. Will you attend?"

Back at Starlina, after their kiss at the wedding, Gregory and Tatyana had assumed a formality with each other. This was the manner that had quieted any suspicions the old prince had. And yet they had not adopted it in order to deceive. Their inner excitement and anticipation prompted it instead, for both sensed something strange and wondrous was beginning to happen.

Now Gregory kissed her hand. "I will be there," was all he said, and he drove away.

Tatyana was ushered upstairs to the countess's apartments, where Sofia awaited her in her lilac sitting room.

Tatyana's thoughts about Gregory were briefly forgotten, so caught up was she with Sofia's own wonderful news. Sofia had kept it hidden from Tatyana in her letters, but now it was impossible to hide her condition any longer. Tatyana's eyes grew round with amazement as she stared at her friend's curving belly.

"With child?"

Sofia smiled happily. "Your expression was worth the waiting, my dear Tanya," and she squeezed her young friend's hands in hers. "We have so wanted a baby!"

Her eyes were glistening and evoked in Tatyana's memory how eager Sofia had been to have a child and the many dissatisfying months that had come and gone without producing any sign of pregnancy. So though it came frustratingly late, this was indeed wonderful news for Sofia and Arkady. "Due when?" asked Tatyana excitedly, plonking down beside Sofia on her Madame Récamier couch.

"December."

"A December baby! What a wonderful month." And Tatyana clapped her hands. "Just think, you're going to have a baby." Then Tatyana began to swirl her friend around. After two turns, with both of them laughing, she stopped suddenly. "Oh, but Sofia, you must sit down. Forgive me. I forgot you must not be getting tossed about in your condition."

"I am not an invalid, my dear," said Sofia, her gray eyes warm with exultation, "though everyone treats me with such care and attention, I profit from the false position you all put me in." Sofia then turned her thoughts to her best friend. "Tatyana, how would you like to take a walk up Gorokhovaya Street to Palace Square? There will be a military review before the palace, and later we can walk down the Nevsky Prospect and back along the Moika. How does that sound to you?"

"Sofia, only you would remember my particular passion when I am in St. Petersburg." Tatyana ran to fetch her bonnet.

Arm in arm, Tatyana and Sofia began their promenade up Gorokhovaya Street. They looked charming together, Tatyana in her favorite pistachio gown and ivory shawl, Sofia in pink with a shawl of cerise. But to the outward observer, the friendship between both women was a surprising one.

Both young women had in common the fact that they "belonged" to what was termed the best society of St. Petersburg. Sofia's aunt was a lady-in-waiting and most intimate confidante of the empress dowager. As such, she was a member of the inner aristocracy. Sofia's aunt had known Tatyana's mother, and both girls had met in their teens at the aunt's house in the chic Admiralty Quarter.

But otherwise, both girls did not seem to have much in common. In looks and personality they were entirely different, but that was perhaps what had attracted them to each other in the first place. While Tatyana was outgoing, impulsive and generally optimistic, Sofia was more reserved and cool-headed. But within her quiet frame she was capable of deep affection, and she won the hearts of all who came to know her.

Tatyana loved in Sofia what she herself lacked—calm and judgement, while Sofia warmed to Tatyana's exuberance. Both young women found in each other the part of themselves that remained unexpressed.

Sofia, being a few years older than Tatyana, had been able to guide her, like a benevolent older sister. It was Sofia who was able to polish what had been lacking in Tatyana's good-hearted but ignorant upbringing, and to add a certain finesse and tone to her natural grace and vitality.

Sofia even helped steer her in such worldly considerations as how to choose fine fabric, or a good milliner, and how to dress. The possibilities offered by color, shape and style were an enigma to Tatyana, but Sofia knew just what would bring out the brilliance of Tatyana's green eyes and the marvelous planes of her face. In everything practical and spiritual, Sofia was able to advise and guide Tatyana.

Tatyana also influenced Sofia in turn, helping her base decisions not only with her head but with her heart, whose impulses she did not always trust. Sofia had adored Arkady from the moment that she had met him, against the wishes of her parents. Tatyana had given her the impetus to marry the eccentric man who she loved, and she had never regretted the decision.

"Arkady must be crazy with happiness," said Tatyana, almost frolicking along the street. As they walked, they passed the classical facades of private houses plastered in stucco and yellow ochre.

"Tatyana, you look radiant," said Sofia. "Your recovery from the bear attack seems absolutely completed. There is something about springtime at Starlina that always brings out your beauty."

"Yes, I love Starlina," laughed Tatyana. "But oh, Sofia, it is a relief to be here with you."

Sofia looked at her narrowly. "That is unlike you, Tatyana Ivanovna." Sofia only used Tatyana's patronym whenever she had anything serious to talk about.

Tatyana glanced at her, "Why the Ivanovna?"

"Forgive me," said Sofia, shaking her head, and laughing self-deprecatingly. "I am such a sheep dog. I always want to rally those I love into the tightest, safest little circle around me so that I can growl for them at the outside world."

"Who needs growling at in my corner?" laughed Tatyana.

"I am not sure," answered Sofia meditatively, "but I have observed that for all your laughter and gaiety, something is a burden to you."

"How can you tell?"

"I don't know, it's instinctive I guess." And then Sofia laughed gently as she looked at Tatyana, "Maybe it's only because you twist your necklace so."

Tatyana dropped her hand from the cross on its gold chain. "How well you know me, Sofia. Anyone can see I have no secrets from you."

"Is that true?" pressed Sofia gently.

"Yes, you know everything there is to know about my life. I have even told you about Vasily Turburov sending a *svakha* to my father searching for my hand in marriage."

"Yes, very antiquated, I thought, from such a comparatively young man," said Sofia. "But that does not make the offer any less significant." She cast a sideways glance into Tatyana's face. "Have you accepted his offer yet?"

"Oh, Sofia, don't test me," said Tatyana, distress now evident in her voice. "You know that I did not. There is no need to be so diplomatic." Her hand went to her necklace. "But oh, I must decide, and soon, very soon."

Sofia held Tatyana's arm more closely in her own. "The decision should be a simple one, you know. Only ask yourself, do you wish to marry him?"

Tatyana let some people pass them in the street before answering Sofia. "No, I don't. I know that now. Unfortunately it is more complicated than that. Father is practically insisting on the match, and yet, I do not love Vasily. In addition, Dmitry confided to me that Vasily Turburov is not the most principled person, and that he gambles."

"Does your father know?"

"I thought not. Otherwise, I couldn't imagine that he'd be so enthusiastic about the proposal. He is so violently against gambling. But when I told him, he said that perhaps Vasily had once played cards for money—that everyone did so in the army. He added that he had no reason to believe that Vasily gambled any more, and concluded by saying, in any case he is so rich that it doesn't matter."

Sofia frowned, but said nothing, while Tatyana rattled on, making her upset with her ideas. "I have virtually promised father I would accept. I told him I would give Vasily my answer on my return from visiting you in St. Petersburg. That is the only reason he approved my visit here. Plus, he respects you so."

"Does your father think I will encourage you to accept Count Vasily's hand?"

Tatyana turned, "I don't know. Will you?"

Tatyana and Sofia had just arrived at the corner of Palace Square. At the far corner, troops of soldiers were beginning to line up in formation. But Sofia turned her attention on her friend, and fixed her soft gray eyes earnestly upon her. "I do not know Count Turburov very well. I have only heard exaggerated reports about his wealth—that he is as rich as Croesus. Based on that reason alone, no one can deny the Count is indeed a brilliant catch—at least from a worldly point of view. And your father's wishes, since they are so strong, cannot be lightly dismissed. Give yourself ample time to think. But remember, that in the end you must absolutely, *absolutely* do only what feels right to you."

Sofia and Tatyana stepped apart to let a nurse and a perambulator pass.

"But I don't know what is right for me," sighed Tatyana, as they resumed their walk. "One minute I decide to, the next minute I can't bear to."

Sofia patted her hand. "Don't worry. It will all come clear to you. For you will ask yourself, is Vasily the man you wish to share your bed with for the next forty years?"

Tatyana shuddered.

Sofia pressed her arm. "Is there anything else you

haven't confided in me that you might wish to—
something that might also be influencing your indeci-
sion?" Sofia remembered the way Tatyana had descended from her carriage, and her unusually long handshake
with Mr. Grandison.

"No, Sofia, not just at present," said Tatyana, her
fingers climbing once more to her gold necklace. Sofia
had never seen Tatyana so distraught before. It had
always seemed to go against her buoyant, optimistic
nature.

Tatyana looked up at her. "I can tell by that quizzical
look in your eyes, Sofia, that you doubt my word. And
yet I believe it is you who are holding back some secret."

"In fact, I am," said Sofia mysteriously. "But first—"
and here she adjusted her shawl "—tell me, how is your
guest?"

"You mean Mr. Grandison?"

"Of course, unless you have had others."

Tatyana blushed. "He is very well." Tatyana glanced
up across the Palace Square. "Look, Sofia, here comes
Alexander."

Both young women gazed across the square where
they could see the Czar arrive, followed by his entourage.
Rows of troops stood in line, while pennants ruffled in the
breeze and sabers gleamed. The infantry soldiers stood in
green uniforms like Dmitry's with the color of the cuffs
and collars indicating the different regiments. There was a
drum roll, and the Czar on his white horse rode past
them, and up and down between the lines of green
jackets, and in front of the cavalry, outfitted in scarlet
tunics. When he was finished, he roared, "Well done, my
children," to each formation. In unison, the soldiers
boomed back, "Thank you your majesty. We will try to
do better."

Tatyana was moved by this spectacle, and thought for
a minute, "Gregory may be right about the things he

says, but he cannot understand really how great a thing it is to be a Russian." And with love and renewed devotion, Tatyana watched the blessed Czar exit from the square.

With the military review over, the admiring crowd dispersed, and Tatyana and Sofia strolled down the Nevsky Prospect. This wide and long commercial street, where Gregory had bought the bee-keeping book, was the most bustling in the capital. Below the apartments and mansions of the rich, were stores and boutiques that sold everything from Russian ikons and Chinese silks to French kid gloves and English soaps. Tatyana and Sofia walked on the sunny side of the street, and passed bookshops, chemists, wine shops and churches of every denomination. All the shops were hung with gaily painted and gilded signs that swayed in the breeze. Nearby, pigeons strutted under the elm trees that lined the boulevard. Sofia and Tatyana stopped briefly at Filippov's bakery to buy *pontchiki,* Sofia's favorite pastry. Then they stopped briefly in a tea shop to buy a brick of caravan tea before they made their way back home along the Moika.

The water of the canal reflected the pastel facades of the rowhouses, and added a shimmering brightness to the walk.

"I have never been to London, Paris or Rome," said Tatyana, invigorated by their walk, "but I cannot imagine any city being so beautiful as St. Petersburg. But tell me, Sofia, you said you had a secret for me."

Sofia smiled enigmatically. "A confidence, really. It is about Mr. Grandison." She waited to see the expression on Tatyana's face, and sure enough, pink crept into her cheeks.

"I would not ordinarily mention what is essentially gossip," said Sofia, "but I tell you because, well, he is a guest of yours."

"Tell me what?"

"Do you know who Gregory Grandison is?" came Sofia's cryptic question.

"Know who he is? Whatever can you mean?" responded Tatyana.

"Do you know about his past, his background? That is what I mean," said Sofia correcting herself, and stopping, she leaned on the wrought-iron fence to watch the ducks in the canal.

Tatyana leaned on the railing beside her. "What is there to know, other than what I told you before? That he was raised in London and that his father was a trader who left him a little money. And of course, that he has a medical degree." Tatyana tried to speak as casually as possible. "That is all I know—why, is there anything more?"

"Indeed there is," said Sofia thoughtfully, "if what I have learned has any bearing on the truth."

Tatyana grew nervous and impatient. "Tell me, what is this terrible news you have heard about Gregory, I mean, Mr. Grandison?"

"Not so terrible, really, more sad," answered Sofia. "It certainly bears out my original hunch about your guest. He was in fact the son of a tradesman, but certainly not a rich one. But his mother, who is now dead . . ." and she paused a moment to consider how her friend would take this.

"Yes go on," implored Tatyana, now quite vexed.

"His mother was the Marchioness of Bellefort."

Tatyana stared at Sofia. "How can that be?" Tatyana knew little about families outside of Russia, but even she recognized the ancient and distinguished English name. "His father was an impoverished tradesman, his mother the Marchioness of Bellefort? I do not understand."

"Apparently it was quite a scandal, though it was hushed up for many years."

"Wait, how do you know of all this?" interrupted Tatyana.

"In the most surprising way. At my Aunt's, I met an English nobleman who had heard the story, and knew a little about the tragedy."

"Tragedy? I thought you called it a scandal," said Tatyana. "Which is it, a tragedy or a scandal?!"

Sofia sighed, "Both, I'm afraid. I see that I had better tell you all of Gregory Grandison's story."

Chapter Twelve

"PERHAPS I SHOULDN'T HAVE TOLD YOU," ADDED SOFIA,
worried at Tatyana's reaction.

"No, you must tell me, since you have begun. Tell me
everything you learned!"

"Well, I don't know much," said Sofia, taking Tatyana's arm in hers as they began to walk along the canal
again. "The Earl said it all happened thirty years ago, and
was promptly hushed up. Apparently Gregory's mother
was an earl's younger daughter, born to great privilege
and distinction. Somehow she met and fell in love with a
handsome young commoner. She became pregnant,
married him secretly, and had the baby. When her family
found out they were appalled, but managed to arrange
through the ecclesiastic courts a legal divorce. The
child—Gregory that is—was left with his father, and all
connections were broken. Nobody knows what the
young mother's thoughts were about the arranged divorce, but she seems to have obediently complied with
her family's dictates. By all reports, she was a beauty,

and before too long she married the Marquis of Bellefort. The scandal finally broke later, but the young man she had married in secret was already dead. He had committed suicide."

Tatyana frowned. "And what happened to Gregory's mother?"

"Surprisingly, nothing at all. The Marquis seems to have loved her very much, and by the time he found out it was all water under the dam. Apparently he was sixty anyway."

"And so what happened to Gregory?"

"The English Earl told me that he had heard all this story through the mother's side of the family, so his facts about Gregory were sketchy. But he gathered that the boy—I mean Gregory—lived with his father's family for several years. Then small sums of money began to arrive for him, enough to provide for his education. He spent most of his early life at school. He was never acknowledged by either his mother or her family, but with the money they sent him, he received a gentleman's education and distinguished himself at Oxford."

"And since then?"

"The Earl had not heard of him since his college days. He was not surprised to learn Mr. Grandison had spent most of his adult life in France. Being an Englishman himself, the Earl suggested how difficult it must have been for Mr. Grandison to live with the stigma of divorce, and to be the child of two separate classes, not quite belonging to one, and ostracized from the other."

"What a terrible story," said Tatyana, staring off into space, as she remembered the pocket watch with the portrait of the beautiful lady.

"Yes," said Sofia. "And terrible to think of how a woman could abandon her own child."

Tatyana nodded, lost in thought.

"The story shocks you even more than I expected,"
said Sofia with concern. "I feel remiss in having told you.
It is Mr. Grandison's secret after all."

"No, I am very glad you did," said Tatyana. "For your
intentions were not to harm him."

"Certainly not. I have the highest regard for Mr.
Grandison." She gazed back at her friend.

Tatyana was still pensive.

"This account certainly explains his veneer of coolness
and his cynicism," said Sofia as they reached the end of
the canal. "Look, we are nearly home. We have reached
Gorokhovaya Street." They turned right at the end of the
canal.

Yes, it certainly does explain those characteristics of
his, thought Tatyana as the two ladies turned right at the
end of the canal—and a number of other things as well.

The next couple of days at Sofia's were busy, and the
two young women spent a good deal of time together.
Tatyana soon noticed that even with the advent of the
baby, a faintly worried expression crossed Sofia's brow
whenever Arkady was present or his name was mentioned. It was obvious she loved him dearly, even
passionately, but something on her husband's account
was troubling her.

Each night, whether they spent a quiet evening receiv-
ing at home, or off to the ballet, he would leave the house
afterward to visit with his men friends. Of course, at this
time of the year there was no night to speak of, and all
kinds of people kept later hours. But even Tatyana
noticed that he excused himself from the house more
than would have been expected of a loving husband.

Tatyana would see Sofia standing at the bay window
until the early morning hours, waiting for Arkady to come
home.

"Where is your Arkady off to this evening?" asked

Tatyana when she and Sofia were left alone the third night of her visit. His frequent departures were now too obvious for her not to ask her friend.

"To Kondraty Ryleyev's."

Tatyana thought back to the winter ball, and the poet with a nervous, inspired look in his Persian face. "What is so fascinating there? Do they gamble, or dance with gypsies?"

"No, they drink a little, play cards a little, and mostly they just talk."

"What do they find to talk about, night after night?"

"Politics, and philosophy," answered Sofia, looking apprehensive.

Tatyana heard the clock strike one, and guessed that Gregory Grandison was also visiting at Kondraty Ryleyev's. He had not come to visit her at the Stegorins' and she felt nonplussed by this.

"Talk, talk, talk," said Tatyana. "All they do is talk of Russia's ills. And yet for all that, they don't ever seem to do anything about it. They are against serfdom, yet do any of these young men—excluding your husband of course—ever give or sell their serfs their freedom? Their concerns are justified, but where on earth does all this talk ever lead to?"

"Their trouble and distress are genuine," said Sofia, coming away from the window. "Their wishes to redress the wrongs of our country are heartfelt and sincere."

"I do not doubt their motives or intentions," said Tatyana wearily. "And certainly Arkady, who gave six years of his life to working in the courts, is above reproach. But what of these other men? They should return to their family estates, and at least become good landlords to their serfs if they are not willing to free them. That is how they can effect good in our country."

"Yes, that is one alternative," conceded Sofia dubiously, wandering finally to the stairs. "But while they dream,

we should think of sleep." The two young women kissed
each other good night and retired to their rooms. Later,
when Tatyana went in search of a glass of water, she
passed Sofia's door, and thought she heard Sofia crying
in her sleep.

On June twenty-first the sky was blue, the clouds
promised to be soft and amiable. The air was warm and
sweetly smelled of roses. It was a perfect day for the
solstice festivities planned by the Stegorins which were to
take place on Krestovsky Island. On this island the
Stegorins had a *dacha*—a large drafty summer house
with lawns overlooking the Gulf of Finland.

Late in the day Tatyana, Sofia, and Arkady arrived at
the Embankment, where they were to hire a gondola to
take them to the island. The Neva glistened in the late
afternoon sun, and bobbed with boats of every color.
Boatsmen dressed in vivid colors plied the waters with
their oars while their partners played on tambourines and
sang. Once out on the water, Tatyana shaded herself
under the striped canopy. She glanced behind her
several times to see if any other boat carried Gregory
Grandison in the same direction. But so far, there was no
sign of him.

They landed in an inlet on Krestovsky Island, which led
to the Stegorins' *dacha*. They went up the stone steps
which led them to the gardens. They passed Greek
marble statues of nymphs and satyrs that lined the pebble
walks, and through the flower gardens until they reached
the lawn. This large stretch of grass overlooking the bay
was ringed by weeping willows that dangled their long
strands of leaves into the water. Everything seemed to
glow rich and peaceful in the golden light.

Tatyana, who kept glancing toward the inlet, finally
caught sight of Gregory's dark curls and sideburns. He
crossed the lawn, kissed Sofia's hand and then Tatyana's.

She wished to ask him why he had not called in the interim at Sofia's house, and he seemed to want to answer her. But neither of them spoke, for as they gazed a little longer into each other's eyes, they both knew the answer. Tatyana blushed, and floated away to help Sofia. Because the Stegorins had dismissed their servants for the evening, it was Sofia who, with the help of the ladies, unwrapped the food and laid the dishes out on the muslin blankets.

Soon everyone, each family arriving in a separate gondola, was there. Tatyana found the company included Prince Trubetskoy and his French wife, Catherine, and Kondraty Ryleyev with his dark-eyed, dark-haired wife, Natasha.

Because they were in the company of the ladies, the men restricted their talk to light conversation. Even so, it was evident by their light repartee and the quality of their jests that these were no ordinary young men. There was one thing that set them apart from the other dozens of young men that Tatyana had met in the last few years. At first she could not tell what it was. But when somebody else used the word in another context, she suddenly understood. They lacked all trace of pettiness. Gregory spent all his talk on Ryleyev as the picnic began, and so Tatyana turned for interest to the women. Natasha Ryleyeva was quiet and solemn, so Tatyana let herself become monopolized by Princess Trubetskaya. Having had a rich, pampered childhood herself, it was easy for Tatyana to sense it in those who had a similar background. And it was clear that Princess Trubetskaya, the former Comtesse de Laval, had been raised in the lap of luxury. It was nothing that the well-bred Frenchwoman alluded to directly, and yet Tatyana inferred it. Strangely enough, riches did not seem to have ruined her disposition, and Tatyana found her engaging. Of course, Tatyana did not know the aphorism uttered by Sofia's worldly aunt: If you want truly good friends, look for them where you are bound to find them—among women who are both rich and ugly. Perhaps in this instance the aunt was right, for the princess was less ravishing than roly poly, and yet she could not have been more at ease or more affectionate. She also had a certain brashness to her that attracted Tatyana and that seemed typically French.

Princess Trubetskaya seemed equally enchanted with Tatyana.

"How is it, I wonder, that we have never met?" she gushed. "I would certainly remember you if we had ever been at the same party. Of course, we came to St. Petersburg via Paris and Kiev, but from what Sofia Stegorina says, you hide yourself out in the countryside. *Mon Dieu,* doesn't a pretty young thing like you die of boredom in the steppes?"

Tatyana could not help but smile. "St. Petersburg's delights are many, but the countryside at Starlina has much to offer."

"Ah, *chérie,* of course," said Princess Catherine in her exquisite Parisian French, "but you are young and should be in society. After all, part of enjoying one's youth is to be seen doing so! It is a crime for your family to deprive St. Petersburg of your company." In another woman such comments would have been cloying or suspect, but with the little French princess it was clear she meant it.

"Do you like our capital?" asked Tatyana.

"Well, nothing will ever replace my beloved Paris, but St. Petersburg has wheedled her way into my heart. She is truly an enchanting city! I simply cannot imagine how one lives deprived of a cosmopolitan existence, the ballet, the theater. . . . I should simply expire without it."

Tatyana laughed at this vigorous little woman, and

then she helped Sofia remove the rest of the food from the wooden picnic baskets.

The feast spread before them was breathtaking, for Sofia had gone to a lot of trouble in its preparation. First they ate *zakuski,* Russian hors d'oeuvres, which was a meal in itself. These were followed by smoked salmon and sturgeon, *pirozhki,* little pies stuffed with meats. The meal went on and on, and finally for dessert the guests were offered *pastila,* a jam, and pastries. All through the picnic Arkady poured the drinks, which included Veuve Clicquot champagne, which had a special flavor so loved by Russians.

Tatyana enjoyed herself immensely, even though she was seated by Natasha, Kondraty Ryleyev's wife. Tatyana was generous by nature, but even she failed to summon a spark of animation or pleasure in the woman's dour expression. It seemed to Tatyana that Natasha kept her eyes on her husband in a most unhealthy manner of possessiveness. What can she be afraid of? Tatyana wondered to herself. What does she think can happen to him here? That some huge eagle will swoop down out of the sky and eat him?

But she was soon distracted again by Princess Trubetskaya, who chatted on merrily about her favorite French champagnes.

At last Arkady pushed his gold spectacles back on his nose. "Before we finish the last of the Veuve Clicquot, let us drink a toast."

"Yes, yes," said Tatyana, who had already had three glasses of the champagne. She raised her flute. "I propose one to the health of his majesty, our beloved Alexander."

Through the bubbles beginning to fizz slightly in her head, Tatyana noticed an awkward silence, for Arkady had not raised his glass. He readjusted his spectacles and

seemed about to propose something along different lines.
Gregory, though, saw Sofia's worried glance at her
husband, and he interjected, "As the one foreigner here,
let me do the honors, and propose a toast to the health of
all of us, and to all the Russian people."

"Here, here," was the general murmur of approval,
followed by the clink of glasses, and Sofia relaxed back
onto the grass.

Throughout the meal Gregory watched Tatyana often
and was amused to see her pick up one of the balalaikas
and begin to strum it. She did not play well, but she
played with such enjoyment that the others began to sing,
and Tatyana forced each of them all to sing a verse. Even
the nervous, sallow Natasha Ryleyeva joined in and
clapped her hands when they were finished. It was a
happy ending to a lovely night.

The picnic over, they regained their boats. Now the
current would be with them, and all the oarsmen had to
do was steer back to the city from Krestovsky Island. The
Ryleyevs climbed into one boat, the Trubetskoys into
another. Tatyana was ready to join the Stegorins with
whom she had come but suddenly found Gregory at her
side, and he wordlessly helped her into his boat. Tatyana
did not resist, and she only laughed to hide her relief and
pleasure.

It was nearly eleven o'clock at night, and the sun was
just beginning to set. The water was golden, the sky a
mauvish pink, and Tatyana sank into the gondola's
graceful bow on velvet cushions. The oarsman steered
from the back. Their boat floated serenely out with the
others into the middle of the Neva and drifted with the
incoming tide toward the city spires.

Unlike Tatyana, who became more extroverted and
lively on champagne, Gregory had become more medi-
tative and silent as he watched her. He sat in the middle
of the boat and felt painfully aware of the promise, side

by side, of both happiness and sorrow. Here, on the water, he could feel the enchantment of the moment: the sound of the music wafting over the breeze, the gondolas rocking in the golden light, and Tatyana, barely inches from him. She lolled among the cushions, humming to herself. One bare arm dangled over the side of the boat as she let her fingers dimple the water. The delicate sound tortured his nerves, and Gregory longed to drink the gurgling water under her fingertips. In the evening light, her face looked luminous.

He remembered her the first time he had ever seen her, standing so immobile in her *kokoshnik* on the terrace steps at Starlina waiting to greet her brother. What vitality and faith she had, and he had been so awed and frightened by it then he could only list her defects. Six months ago, he mused, in a late December. Now it seemed like forever to him. He felt, at this moment, that he had known her his entire life.

He had come to Russia on the spur of the moment, on an idle whim—or so it had seemed to him as he and Dmitry glided over the snow that cold December day. And yet he knew now that from the moment he had seen Tatyana their meeting and the whole outcome of his life was not a random happening, but fated and inexorable. She had cast her line across an entire continental waste-land of snow, and he had come to her, almost as in a dream. Even now, with her so close beside him, he felt that same strange sensation: that all of it—even this moment in the gondola—was preordained. For the first time in a strange, cruel, but beautiful country, to the sound of an instrument he had never heard of, he felt his heart beat with euphoric dread. Gregory glared at Tatyana in her lazy, contented pose and knew with excruciating agony that this moment could never last and that she could never love him as he loved her. For if she did, she could never look so peaceful and happy. Perhaps she didn't love him at all, crossed his mind. Perhaps her amorous response that day he kissed her in the carriage was only because of her ardent nature. After all, she clasped everything to her wholeheartedly. Perhaps she was like the rest of womankind, whom he had found so easy to resist with all their inconstancy and fickleness. Perhaps he had chosen the queen of them all and his fall would be all the greater.

His black eyes moved out over the water like thunder-clouds. There in the boats floating off to the left and to the right were other couples in gondolas. Sofia Stegorina in her husband's arms, Kondraty and Natasha in another, Sergei and Catherine in yet another, a man and a woman in every boat, rocking on the open waters. How did they find happiness, he wondered desperately, since love was never equal, and only pain could come from being separate from the object of one's love. As the boat rocked, he could see first the gondolas containing the Ryleyevs, the Trubetskoys, and the Stegorins, and when the boat rose out of the dip, Tatyana's profile against the sky, eclipsing them. Here were the two opposing forces of his life. The one, reason with all its safety and familiarity; the other, passion, which had no bedrock. As one came in the view, and then the other, rising and sinking each in turn, he tormented himself with this opposition.

But already the Ryleyevs and Trubetskoys and Stegorins seemed so far away, tiny buoys floating on the distant ocean, inanimate. Whereas Tatyana sighed with pleasure, her voice drowning out the sound of the distant oars. His heart was full of fear and rage. Why did her hair blaze in the light and her eyes devour him like emeralds eating fire?

"Gregory, what is the matter?" asked Tatyana, her lovely face looming close to his, for she had sensed some terrible grief welling up within him. "Your fists are clenched."

Gregory took her face in his hands and pressed her Slavic cheekbones between his knuckles; he would not let her go until she returned his kiss.

"What is the matter, Gregory?" she asked, letting her palms slide down his chest. "You look angry, or almost frightened of me."

"No, foolish little Russian mermaid," said Gregory thickly. "It is only that you look so self-satisfied I could throw you back into the water."

Tatyana's eyes wavered between joy and fear as she felt his own so fiercely on her. "How strange you are tonight, my Englishman," she said lightly. But under his adamantine gaze she almost wished they would both be swallowed up by the sea.

At midnight the gondolas brushed up against the English Embankment, and the weary passengers disembarked. Tatyana was separated from Gregory at the Stegorins' door. Though he barely uttered words of good night, the eyes that raked hers frightened yet mesmerized her. Yes, it was happening, she was being sucked into his vortex. Instinctively she kept her arm through Sofia's to delay the moment. Arkady, who had been preoccupied during much of the party, also left them at the door and drove off in a hired droshky. So the two young women were left to mount the stairs alone in the house on Gorokhovaya Street.

As they crossed the dark, soft Persian carpet, Tatyana still felt as if she was rocking in the boat with Gregory, and every detail of the evening was vivid to her. Her own feelings heightened her perceptions, and when she looked at Sofia she saw for the first time the magnitude of her friend's unspoken fears.

"What are you worried about, Sofia? What is Arkady

doing to upset you? Are you worried he is with another woman?"

Sofia pressed her hand to her pale forehead, and a tear rolled down her cheek. "If only it was that."

"What is it then? You cannot doubt his attachment, do you? He obviously loves you."

"Yes, I know he loves me, but more than me he loves the fatherland." Now she sobbed. "Arkady is so good he would do anything, even sacrifice his life to make life better not only for the two of us, but for everyone—all the Russian people. I believe in his ideals and goals, but oh, Tanya, I am so afraid for him."

"Afraid for him?"

"Yes, afraid of what may happen," she said gripping the bannister. "Afraid of where their brave ideas and bold designs will lead them. Sometimes I think that if they could they might even start a revolution!" She said the word as if uttering a blasphemy. "I see images of my dear Arkady in mortal danger." Sofia wept, clinging to her friend's arm. Tatyana stroked her hair, then drew her up straight.

"A revolution? Don't worry, they would never do anything so foolish. You, Sofia, know more about life than I do, I often think, but I am sure that Arkady will not come to any harm. He loves you too much, he is too sensible. Anybody can see that. He would never do anything to hurt you. So you must have faith in him. I too worry about their talk at times, but believe me, nothing dangerous would come of it. The reforms they wish so dearly will be arrived at in a peaceful way."

Sofia's eyes brightened, and she hugged her friend. "I love you so, Tatyana. I love your strength. I wish I was as strong. In Kondraty Ryleyev's wife Natasha I also see my doubts."

"It is clear from her expression she is just a worrywart. But you are strong, Sofia! You only think that you are weak! Sometimes I think you are the strongest person I know, even all the men included."

Sofia laughed at Tatyana's droll way of expressing her convictions. "You really are my good, true friend."

Tatyana squeezed her hand and let Sofia move down the hall to her empty bedroom. Sofia stopped at her door and turned around. "I didn't even think to ask, did you enjoy this evening?"

Tatyana ran to her. "Not only are you strong, Sofia, but more perceptive than anyone I know, and more truthful. I have in my slow turtle's way discovered something I think you knew but which I kept hidden from myself." Tatyana's voice threw off sparks of excitement and awe.

"Yes?" Sofia urged, knowing what Tatyana would say.

"Blind as I have been all along—as wretchedly stupid as I have been—tonight I learned, with such clarity it is impossible to convey"—she bit her lip with ecstasy— "that I love Gregory Grandison with all my soul."

In the early hours of the morning, in the few hours of dark, a lone carriage drew up quietly in front of a private residence on Great Morskaya Street. A passenger in a hooded cloak alighted, paid the driver three kopecks, and entered the house. Up the grand staircase the figure went with sure steps, as if certain of the course. Across the length of several corridors the interloper walked, then paused at a door. Waiting a moment in the darkness, the figure then gently pushed it open and entered.

It was a bedroom, and moonlight through the window shone on the mahogany bed. Under a single muslin sheet lay Gregory Grandison naked and fast asleep. The trespasser approached the bed and stood resolutely staring down on him. The cloak that concealed the person's face dropped upon the floor.

Gregory moved in his sleep. Then sensing a presence

through his dreams, he awoke. In the dimness he could not remember where he was. Then his eyes focused, and in the soft silvery light he looked up and saw the figure.

"Tatyana," he whispered with wonder. Gregory's eyes grew dark and he sat up brusquely on one elbow. To Tatyana, his stance seemed a challenge, to demand if she knew she entered the lair of the tiger. But she was not daunted. She stood immobile, her hands at her side, gazing at him.

"Do not tempt me, princess," he said softly, as his eyes suffered over the ridiculously skimpy dressing gown that clung to the curves of her body. He brushed one hand over his eyes.

Tatyana kneeled down beside him and her scent eddied up to his nostrils. "I am so frightened, but please, please let me be with you," she whispered. She ran her hand tentatively along the sheet to his naked thigh. When he looked at her again his eyes were dangerous, and made her feel weak in the knees. She almost drew back in fear. But it was too late. He held her body between two strong hands. In an instant she found herself stripped of her diaphanous gown and naked in his bed. His fierce kisses burned her cool flesh as his mouth seared across her neck and shoulders and down her breasts.

"You will regret this," he breathed. He felt mad with love and desire, now that there was nothing between them but his urgent need for her and her exquisite skin. His hands slid down around her hips with a steel grip.

Suddenly he arched up in anger. "No, I must not, I must not."

"Yes, you must," said Tatyana with a sweetness and surety. She lifted her arms and stroked the veins that rose in knots along his neck. "Yes, you must," she commanded with a sigh.

He entwined his long fingers in her silky hair and gazed at her desperately in the darkness and moonlight. Her eyes were glistening and seemed to invite him. Yes, yes, yes. Just as they had done in the carriage after the peasants' wedding.

"Really?" he whispered gently.

"Yes," she murmured. "Please believe me."

He no longer held back from her and began to make love to her. But he was no longer fierce and touched her with unexpected gentleness. Taking her in his arms, softly so as not to hurt her arm and shoulder, he kissed her tenderly.

"How I do love you," he uttered.

Then his caresses, insistent, strong, and gentle, replaced Tatyana's fear and excitement with excitement and desire. She clung to him. Something that pulled and fluttered within her wanted every inch of him and his entire mysterious body. She arched her back with desire, opening to him. At last she felt the aching emptiness within her penetrated, smoothed, and caressed by the most intimate part of Gregory's body. She swooned with this new sensation, but his kisses drew her back. He held her close, held her when her body suddenly twisted and trembled under him. At last, knowing she was fulfilled, Gregory surrendered himself entirely to Tatyana. He pressed himself once more into the intoxicating beauty of her body, groaning deeply, and sank within her arms.

Chapter Thirteen

A FOUNTAIN DIMPLED THE SURFACE OF A POND, LARKS sang overhead, and a gauze curtain flapped idly in the morning breeze. These were the sounds Gregory and Tatyana awoke to as they lay half-asleep entwined in each other's arms.

Tatyana ran her hand wonderingly along Gregory's flat belly, then along his chest rising and falling with each breath. She marveled at all the thick hair a man could have on so many different parts of his body. She kissed the cranny of his shoulder, trying to bury her nose in his smooth soft hair which smelled so curiously sweet but masculine. Then she kissed his Adam's apple, which she had fallen in love with, watching him build the hives, and tugged at his ear. He opened his eyes and let them bask in hers like a cat purring in the sunlight. She tugged at him again. "More," she said, like a little child wanting chocolate. Gregory turned over, his blood rising as he saw the delights of her flesh in the morning sunlight, and they made love again.

So it was that Tatyana seduced Gregory. And once she

had a taste of the delights of love, spiritual and physical, Tatyana suddenly felt the thirst and hunger she had long kept hidden from herself in her role of dutiful daughter.

That night, before she came to him, Tatyana had known she was on the brink of something with Gregory richer, more intense, more frightening, and endlessly more satisfying than anything she had yet experienced. And without stopping to analyze or reconsider, she clasped the feeling to her and gave herself completely to Gregory.

As Gregory had presumed, Tatyana was totally inexperienced, but eager and inquisitive. But even as the weeks went by, she instinctively kept their lovemaking a secret. She did not need to tell Sofia, though Sofia had guessed, having heard the hired carriage come and fetch Tatyana to the house on the Great Morskaya.

Sofia did not have to wonder whether Tatyana was happy and satisfied, for she saw the new bloom in her friend's face and movements. Sofia was not at all surprised by any of this. She had seen the look in Gregory's face as he gazed on Tatyana as early as at the New Year's Ball. Sofia had guessed his feelings would only develop further as he grew to know Tatyana. As to Tatyana, she had been more of a riddle. It was only when Tatyana endlessly referred to Gregory in her letters that Sofia decided the fascination might be reciprocal. She had only waited to see when Tatyana would realize it as well.

But so caught up in her allegiance to her father, Tatyana had denied her feelings for Gregory all those months. It was only when she sat in the boat returning from the picnic that she could no longer hide the truth from herself. And once admitting it, she embraced it wholeheartedly.

Several weeks later, after an evening of opera, Tatyana told Gregory what she had learned from Sofia about his past. They were lying in bed at the house on the Great

Morskaya. While she spoke, Gregory listened to her, his eyes hard and betraying no emotion. When she finished with her account, he turned away from her and sat up in bed.

At last he spoke. "Doesn't my past ever tire of pursuing me?"

"It is all true then?"

Gregory nodded. "Strange that gossip which has traveled so many miles, across so many years, should stay so relentlessly intact. Your account is accurate to every syllable." In his voice Tatyana detected his old measured tones of cynicism. "It is a handsome legacy, is it not? A father who shot himself for love and a mother who abandoned her husband and child for the lecherous advances of a rich aristocrat." He snorted.

"Certainly neither parent was an example for me of any path I wished to follow. So it's not surprising I suppose that I have such mixed views toward my fellow creatures." Gregory threw back the bed covers. "So you see at last, Tatyana, who I really am, a man who drifts about the Eastern Hemisphere trying to keep one step ahead of the gossip, while idling my time away. 'Brilliant at everything,' they always used to say," he concluded with bitter ruefulness, "but useless to myself and to this planet we live on."

Here summed up was all the anger Tatyana had ever glimpsed in his cool manner and sardonic tongue. But now the source of all that bile was being voiced in the intimacy of their bedroom. She breathed with relief. Unexpressed it could poison their love, she guessed. And she loved him all the more for what she had learned of him. "Hardly useless to me," she said half-seductively, half-gently, reaching out her hand to him.

But he stood up and began to dress. "Is that why you have been good to me, out of some sense of guilt or pity?

Believe me, such charity is futile, for I regard my fellow man absolutely pitilessly."

"Gregory, why are you so bitter?"

"That is the way I am," was all he answered.

"No," said Tatyana firmly. "That bitterness is only part of you. I have seen another part of you which you've kept hidden for so long. But you trusted me with it, thank heavens."

"No," said Gregory, "I didn't trust you with anything. With you, I have simply lost my head."

"No, Gregory," said Tatyana, reaching for his hand. "You like to see yourself as hard and mean. But you aren't that way really. You can't fool me any longer. I know about that soft underbelly." And her eyes sparkled with love and indignation.

Gregory, in his shirttails, let Tatyana pull him, and he sat back down on the bed. "My crazy Russian princess, I was right to be terrified of you," he said, half laughing in spite of himself. "You can't imagine how I talked and talked myself into disliking or being angry with you. Now look where you have me—in a fine predicament." And with a finely tuned English sense of humor, he flourished a hand to their love nest. Tatyana laughed and embraced him. Then she looked at him seriously again, and her hand reached out for the pocket watch on the table beside the bed. But before she could open the lid, Gregory's hand closed around hers. "Yes," said Tatyana, "I saw her portrait."

Gregory took it from her and put it back on the table. "I only keep it because my father cherished it." He did not look at Tatyana, and she saw his jaws work in anger again.

Tatyana gazed at his handsome profile. "She was very beautiful, your mother. You inherited your looks from her."

"Perhaps, but I hope not her character."

"Did you ever see your mother?" Tatyana pursued.

Gregory got up from the bed and went and stood by the window. "Only once," he said at last, as if it was hard for him to speak. "When I was eight years old and away at school. The other boys had gone home for the holidays and I was there alone. It was the day before Christmas." He stopped and after the long silence Tatyana nearly spoke, but he continued. "She came. She was beautifully dressed, in a green velvet gown. Strange how I remember that so well. It was the color of the Christmas tree in the housemaster's den, which I was allowed to peek in at."

"And then what happened?"

Gregory turned back from the window. "Nothing. She gave me a box of toy soldiers."

"And then?"

"And then she went away."

"And you never saw your mother again?"

Gregory shook his head.

"Your loss must have been very great for her."

"Hardly," said Gregory with derision, and he returned to his dressing.

"No mother would give up a child easily," countered Tatyana.

"That is a very pleasant notion, but it is only part of the mother myth. She gave both my father and me up to marry a doddering old marquis."

"It was not an *affaire de coeur* then?" asked Tatyana, who stayed in the bed.

"How could it have been? She was twenty when I was born and married the marquis two years later. He was over fifty. But God did punish her in his way."

"How is that?" asked Tatyana.

"Because my mother never had any other children

and died when she was thirty-two—the same age I am now."

"Were you sad when you heard she had died?"

"Of course not," said Gregory, who was buttoning his shirt. "I never loved her."

"All children love their parents."

"Yes, every child loves his father and mother," said Gregory with unexpected fierceness, "loves them blindly, unreservedly, adoringly. But it is up to the parent to deserve that love. And when they prove they do not deserve that simple adoration, then it is time for the child to stop loving them. So you see," he concluded with finality, "I have never loved her."

"Neither have you forgiven her," whispered Tatyana.

"She never asked forgiveness," replied Gregory. "But what does it matter? I never loved her, I never think of her, I have no feelings for her memory," but in his voice was the same bitterness she heard before.

She looked at him quizzically. "I think you did love her, and that you love her still."

"Impossible."

"No, not at all impossible. I think it's the truth. There you go, wishing to seem devoid of all feeling—mean and heartless. But it's clear. You love her, otherwise why do you seem so angry, so grieved?" Tatyana went and put her arms around him. "Oh, Gregory, admit just once to yourself that you have loved her all along, she who did not deserve your love. And then you will be able to forgive and to forget, to put your grief aside for good."

Gregory neither spoke nor moved.

"Your love for me is not happy but tormented, and all because of her. She left you and your father for her family and station, and for another man. That is the only injury she did you. All that has come since has festered in your heart because you let it. Admit not only the anger, which you've held up like a beacon all your life, but that love you felt and feel. I want it, Gregory, for myself."

Still Gregory did not move.

"Gregory?" Tatyana looked up into his face. She saw tears running down his face.

"Oh, Gregory," she sighed, putting her arms tightly around him. "Forgive me for intruding where I have no right to."

Gregory squeezed her tight. When he spoke his voice was hoarse. "I only knew that there was pain in love. That is why I pushed you from me. That is why I fell in love with you only against my will. Lately I have begun to think that there may be joy and happiness—happiness, what a foreign feeling that is. Oh, but Tatyana you must never leave me." And Gregory crushed her in his arms as if he would never let go.

Strong feelings, feelings that dog the heels of one's life, die long and hard. But on that day, Gregory saw in the future a promise of serenity for a weary exile of the heart, and a promise of gladness.

Tatyana's stay in St. Petersburg had intended to be brief, but the seven days turned into several weeks.

Now urgent letters from Prince Korbatsky kept arriving at the Stegorins' house every other day, urging Tatyana's return home. Tatyana, true to form, answered each epistle. Her answers never varied, "Yes, papa, in just a few more days you shall see me at Starlina." But still she lingered in the imperial city, for she could not bear to tear herself away just yet from Gregory.

One morning in August, a letter arrived informing Tatyana that Prince Korbatsky was coming to the capital himself. Tired of waiting for her return, her father had decided to precipitate a response to the Great Unanswered Question concerning Count Turburov.

Tatyana was flabbergasted. The last thing that should

happen was to see her father's droshky drive up to the house on Great Morskaya where Gregory had been staying. Tatyana promptly had a servant pack a valise for her and kissed Sofia three times on the cheek. Their parting was not dismal; it was agreed Tatyana would return the following week, her excuse being a fete given by Sofia's aunt in the Summer Garden.

"What are you going to tell your father?" asked Sofia.

"Now it seems so simple!" said Tatyana. "Of course I'm going to refuse Vasily's offer. I love Gregory, after all. Oh, Sofia, how I love him."

"And you're going to tell your father that?"

"Of course!"

Tatyana was off. She drove in the hired barouche to meet Gregory, as had been agreed, at Senate Square, on her way out of the city.

Senate Square was a handsome place right in the heart of St. Petersburg. The classical yellow facade of the Senate fronted the western side of the square, and on the other side stood the imposing Admiralty building. At the other end of the square stretched the English Embankment where they had hired the gondolas and the wide St. Isaac's bridge, which spanned the Neva River.

Tatyana's barouche passed the half-built church of St. Isaac and passed into the cobblestone square. At this hour of the morning it was almost empty. A few people were promenading along the quay, a dog barked intermittently at the corner of Galernaya Boulevard, and a vendor was hawking *kalachi*, sweet twisted rolls, to the passersby, who ignored him.

Tatyana's eyes scanned the square in search of Gregory and came to rest on the Bronze Horseman, Falconet's famous statue. The equestrian statue of Peter the Great dominated the square as it rose imposing from the center. It had been erected by Catherine I at great trouble and expense. Atop a huge granite rock reared a larger than life-size horse on which was seated the founder of St. Petersburg. Peter's enormous size and will were captured in the bronze casting, which flung its arm imperiously over the city. The monument was surrounded by a black wrought iron fence, and it was here, leaning against the rails, that Tatyana found Gregory. He wore a frock coat and top hat and stood rocking on the backs of his heels, watching for Tatyana. His face broke into a self-conscious grin when he saw her, and he lifted his hat in the graceful, polished way perfected only by Englishmen.

Gregory kissed her hand. Tatyana held her hand out decorously while he did so but, unable to resist, threw her arms about him. "I am not even gone, and already I miss you!"

Gregory laughed at her effusiveness but was clearly in love with it. "So you have decided to go to Starlina?" he said, betraying by his tone what he thought of this decision.

"Yes, I must see my father. But I won't be long, *rodnoy moy, Grigori,*" she said, uttering the most intimate endearment as she stroked his moustache with her fingertips.

Gregory looked at her quizzically. She let her eyelids drop. She had not told him about Count Turburov's proposal of marriage. The proposal had become so insignificant the last several weeks she had scarcely thought of it, and now she did not want its mundane reality to intrude on their happiness together.

"You will hurry back?" said Gregory, scanning her face.

"Very very soon. And you will be here?"

"Of course. Having taken so long in my life to find you, do you think I'd go jaunting off to Moscow?"

Tatyana laughed.

"Have you written about us to your brother?" he now asked.

Tatyana shook her head. "Let us tell him together."

Gregory seemed pleased at this idea. He kissed her hand, and impulsively she raised his to her lips. "Gregory, how I shall miss you, even during so few days."

"Good, that is just what I want. You will come back all the sooner."

Tatyana could not bear to relinquish his hand and squeezed it tightly. She longed to have him return with her to Starlina. But reason and delicacy prompted she should break the happy news to her father by herself. Now that she was actually going she was nervous, but also relieved. For she was impatient to tell her father about her love for Gregory. Tatyana had never hidden anything from her father in all her life, and now she longed to share her secret happiness. It was true he hankered after this marriage with Vasily, and Tatyana had never gone against her father's wishes, but she felt sure he would understand her feelings once she explained them to him. And that he would even come to share her inclinations.

For the moment the only pain was leaving Gregory, but it was now time for her to go. She glanced around at the empty square. The sky had grown overcast, threatening a summer thundershower. "You must put on your hat and get home again," she said tenderly. "I do not like this weather."

He watched her for a moment, as if trying to imprint her image before he let her go. "Off with you then," he said at last, "before it turns into a gale."

The barouche rolled away, and Gregory watched until it disappeared down Admiralty Boulevard. The rain began to drizzle. His eyes strayed back to the bronze statue of Peter the Great rearing up lonely and titanic above a sea of mute cobblestones. Some rain fell on his hand, and he glanced down at the cool, translucent drops. He rubbed the wetness on his fingers and frowned. "Why is there something so portentous in this rain?" he wondered. "Bah, it is only my morbid imagination." And putting on his top hat, he left the square.

Several hours later, Tatyana arrived at Starlina, where the rain had preceded her. The birch trees were wet and glistening in the late gray afternoon, and the forests of pine smelled sweet from the rain.

As soon as she arrived, she was besieged by her *nyanya*. Dunyasha scolded her for remaining so long in the capital and in the next breath questioned her on the comings and goings of Gregory's valet. "Accompanies Mr. Grandison everywhere, I see. That'll only add to the rocks in Anatole's head. Tell me, little mother, what did the Stegorins' maids think of him?"

"I don't know if they even saw him," sighed Tatyana.

"A good thing too," huffed Dunyasha. "One sight of that stuck up little Anatole, and they would have given him the drubbing he deserves. Do you know what he did as a good-bye present just before you all left?"

Tatyana shook her head. "I can't imagine."

"In my sewing basket he put a toad! And I wouldn't have known it except while I was at my prayers I kept hearing a croak near my head. When I looked up, there on the bed, sitting on top of my open sewing basket was the slimy parcel, grinning at me. That Anatole is the devil incarnate, I am sure of it."

"A man who was courting couldn't have done any better," laughed Tatyana. "I venture to say you haven't lost a minute not thinking of him."

"He is such a scalawag, little mother," exclaimed Dunyasha. "It is a wonder Mr. Grandison can put up with him."

Questions that touched on Gregory were too delicate to contend with just at that moment, at least until she could talk to her father. So she interrupted their conversation to ask for him.

But in spite of the barrage of letters, her father seemed in no hurry to talk once they were reunited. They spent the evening with the samovar boiling between them, talking in generalities. The prince seemed unusually loquacious that night. He discussed life in St. Petersburg during his youth, old acquaintances, and the latest reports that the empress was not in good health. Tatyana listened but was mostly preoccupied and silent.

"Elizabeth was always a beauty," said the prince, referring to the czarina. "But always frail, never in good health. And of course, their marriage was never a very happy one. It is a great loss that none of their children survived."

"Yes, it must be terrible to lose one's children," said Tatyana, thinking of Sofia's and Arkady's extraordinary excitement about her coming baby.

"The personal loss is, of course, great, but that is not what I mean," remarked her father. "I am talking about the loss for our people. After all, the fate and future of this nation rest on the czar and czarina's progeny."

"Why is it any greater a problem than for a simple family? If they have no children, the crown passes on to the next brother," said Tatyana simply.

"You speak only out of naiveté," remarked her father. "If you knew anything about the history of your country, as well as of other countries, you would know that the right of succession has been one of the untidiest issues in the history of civilization. Surely you have heard of the War of the Roses. Why English history is fraught with skirmishes all relating to the rights of succession! Think, the Plantagenets in France. And here in Russia, the imposters to the throne, pretenders like the False Peter. There has been so little constancy in heirs throughout our history, we have something no other nation has—palace revolutions, where the Guard puts into power the man or woman they wish. It is a sorry state of things, I tell you, when a man like Alexander has no children—we could be catapulted backward a hundred years."

"But father, Alexander is young yet, and if the czarina, God bless her soul, is as ill as the reports say, he may marry again. He may have other children."

"Of course, of course, I am only commenting in general, how the czar undoes all his handiwork by not begetting children, by not ensuring who will inherit the throne when he dies."

"Father, aren't the rights of succession fairly simple where Alexander is concerned? He has three fit and able younger brothers. Won't the eldest, Grand Duke Constantine, eventually come to the throne?"

"Not necessarily," said her father. "I have heard rumors for the last several years that Constantine is happily ensconced as Governor of Poland and has signed an official manifesto of abdication."

"Well, if such rumor turned out to be true, wouldn't Grand Duke Nicholas succeed him?"

"Presumably. But Nicholas has never been popular with the palace guards—they find him strict and unsympathetic. Who is to know if they would tolerate this second brother? Perhaps they might instead favor the youngest, Grand Duke Michael."

Tatyana shook her head in confusion.

"Ah ha!" said the prince, shaking his finger at her. "You see how complicated become the rights of succession!"

"But Alexander is only forty-eight. It seems rather early to be worried about his successor."

"Of course," conceded her father, as he stroked his moustache. "But with the empress ill, I can't but think it would be a godsend—the Lord forgive me—for her not necessarily to recover."

Tatyana looked surprised. "Father, I thought you liked Elizabeth."

"I do, very much, she is a charming woman—I am not speaking against her personally, only for the good of Russia."

Ordinarily Tatyana would have been flattered to be privy to her father's political conversations, in which he did not usually include her. But tonight, hereditary succession was not the subject she wished to speak of. Something far more urgent and important was on her mind. Her heart was almost bursting from the secret she kept concealed from her father. "Papa," she said at last when there was a pause in the conversation, "in all your letters you requested a decision regarding Count Vasily, but I have things that I must talk with you about."

"Hush, my daughter," said Prince Korbatsky, interrupting Tatyana's urgent appeal. "Let us not talk of these matters tonight, on your first evening home. You have had a long journey and need your rest. We will have our tête-à-tête by and by."

With that the old prince clapped his hands to summon his house serfs, and soon after he was lugged in his chair from the drawing room. Tatyana sighed. Her love for Gregory would have to remain a secret one night longer.

The following day and then the next passed without further allusion to a tête-à-tête between father and daughter. Prince Korbatsky was cordial to his daughter but seemed anxious, as if waiting some particular mail. Tatyana found him lost in thought several times while he sat pulling on his moustache, and he would start up in his chair when he was brought any mail. There was something he was waiting for.

On the third day home Tatyana sat through a long dinner with Count Turburov and his pointy-faced sister.

This was uncomfortable for her, knowing what her answer would be, and she was unhappy that both she and the count were put in this compromising position. She tried to be cordial without seeming particularly moved to see them. When Irina made an unfavorable remark about the manners of Englishmen, Tatyana turned crimson but said nothing. Her blush was not lost on the three pairs of shrewd eyes that watched her through the evening. And she did not see the look that passed between them. Twice during the dinner Prince Korbatsky had to summon his daughter's attention back to their guests and the dinner conversation.

After the dinner was over, and when at length the Turburov brother and sister left, Prince Korbatsky settled himself in his study. He did not have a pleasant look in his dark beady eyes, and his lips were chalky as he drummed the edge of a letter on the marble surface of his desk. Finally Tatyana was summoned to his study, and the door closed behind her.

Ten minutes later the serfs who hovered nearby the study heard something hit the door—a sign of summons from the prince. Confined to his chair, Prince Korbatsky often heaved a book or onyx paperweight at the door to gain the servants' attention. A house serf immediately popped in.

The old prince sat glowering at his desk. "Get someone to carry my daughter to her rooms," he ordered. "She has fainted." And he waved his arm toward Tatyana, whose head drooped in her chair.

"Should we send for Doctor Morabitsky, your excellency?" asked the house serf.

"No, there will be no need. She has had some news not entirely agreeable to her, so she must be allowed to rest. Be quick about it."

Tatyana was lifted up and carried to her room, where she was handed into the loving arms of Dunyasha.

"Sometimes the old prince goes too far," thought Dunyasha to herself, seeing Tatyana's limp body placed upon the bed. "From his daughter he expects the obedience of a serf and the behavior of a saint. Holy Mother of Vladimir preserve us."

When Dunyasha conferred a little later with the butler, Timofey, she found out from him the news told by the prince that had made the princess faint. The old prince had received a letter from his old friend, General Miloradovich, and had read it aloud to Tatyana.

"This letter is in part to advise you that your former guest, Mr. Gregory Grandison, is being watched. There is every reason to believe he is a spy for the English government. We have received a confidential report that he has infiltrated a Russian secret society based in St. Petersburg whose purpose is the downfall of the czar."

Chapter Fourteen

"IT IS SIMPLY UNBELIEVABLE, UNBELIEVABLE," SCREECHED Prince Korbatsky, waving the letter from General Miloradovich at his visitor. "In General Miloradovich's own words! It is unbelievable, I tell you. All that mindless twaddle and posing was more pernicious than I even imagined!"

"Perhaps you could tell me what you are talking about," drawled his visitor. It was Count Turburov.

"To think that the snake is within the very bosom," heaved the prince. "Our own milk-fed asps."

"Who are you talking about?" said Vasily impatiently, who was lolling with his knee up in an armchair.

"Why, young men of the Imperial Guard, your own subordinate and fellow officers, the pampered youth of St. Petersburg, members of some of the finest families. Aieee! And even my own son," the prince groaned.

"Let me at least see the letter so I can make head or tail of what you are droning on about," said the count.

The prince reached over and handed it to him. When the count finished reading it he tossed it back.

"What of it?"

"What of it, what of it? The emperor's life could be in danger, and what of it?!"

The count had drawn out a gold nail file studded with emeralds with which he proceeded to clean his finger-nails. He was immensely proud of his plump white hands.

"Let me just put it this way. All of this is old news to me," answered Count Turburov, and he added pointed-ly, "I am surprised to find you so out of touch, prince, with what is happening in the government. Everyone who is really important has known about these secret societies since 1820. Why do you suppose Alexander punished the Semyonovsky Regiment for disobeying their commanding officers?"

"That is not a very good example," said the prince, piqued by the count's insidious allusion to his waning influence at court. "You and I know those boys, the *crème de la crème* of the Imperial Army, had nothing up their sleeves. That Colonel Schwartz that Arakcheyev appointed was worse than a dummkopf, and the soldiers were within their rights to lodge a complaint against him. Alexander should not have had them all imprisoned. It is the only time he has ever erred in judgment, to my mind."

"On the contrary," said the count. "They probably did have nothing up their sleeves, but shutting them up in the Peter and Paul Fortress was not a bad lesson."

"Not much of a lesson, I'd say, when my own son and other boys in the army have organized a society whose raison d'être is the downfall of Alexander. These young men should be rounded up and imprisoned more justifia-bly than the Semyonovsky Regiment!"

"You do not understand, of course, that it is much more clever to wait and watch them. Let these incipient Robespierres and Riegos drown in their own drivel.

Believe me, it will come to nothing. I have met some of these dreamers. Withal their being officers in the Guard, these men couldn't find their way out of a wet paper bag. As to that insufferable Gregory Grandison, what the general said was to be predicted. It will be interesting to see the trap they set for him. In any case, prince, I weary of this trifling conversation. Tell me now about your daughter."

"It is just as we suspected. I invite that Grandison under my roof, in order to get him away from Dmitry, and he goes after my daughter instead. A pleasant fellow. I didn't even let her sully my ears with her tender avowals. Don't worry, this letter set her straight."

"Good, so she has abandoned all notions about that Englishman?"

"Absolutely. She was in shock at first, which was to be predicted, but time heals all wounds, eh? Today she even ate an entire meal."

"Yes, yes, but what about in regard to me," snapped Vasily.

"You will be most glad to hear that today I wrested from her an assent to your proposal," said the prince with evident satisfaction.

Now the count looked up with real interest, and put his nail file away. "Finally," he said with a mixture of irritation and pleasure. "I waited long enough, prince."

"Yes, yes, I know," said the prince hastily. "But now you see it all works out all right for both of us?"

"Indeed it does," answered Vasily slyly, tweaking his pointy nose.

There was a moment of uncomfortable silence, and Vasily added, "May I see my future wife?"

Prince Korbatsky scrutinized the young man who would be his son-in-law. His bulky shape, flabby flesh, and oily skin were hardly prepossessing. But it was that pointy nose and the small harsh eyes on his lumpish features that were most damning.

"Perhaps you had better wait a few more days, count," said the prince, wary of what an interview with Vasily at this moment could do to Tatyana's distraught nerves.

The count looked at him suspiciously.

"Take my word—though you may have doubted it before. My Tatyana will be your wife before the season's over."

The count rubbed his plump white palms together briskly. "Very good, prince, very good. In the meantime, I have arranged for, let us call it an engagement present, to be delivered to her. Ladies are so susceptible to these little amenities. It should help her recover all the quicker. In any case, since I must be with my regiment in St. Petersburg, it will serve as a nice reminder of me."

Prince Korbatsky bowed to his young neighbor with the utmost courtesy and deference, but under his white eyebrows the look he cast on the count's receding figure was far from complimentary.

Dunyasha ran about her mistress's room, clapping her hands with delight. "Oh, princess, what an inspiration. Who would have thought? Such a gift! It is extravagant."

Tatyana was leaning on her hand, gazing mournfully out the window. "Do you like it?" she asked tonelessly.

In the space of two weeks, Tatyana seemed transformed. She hardly resembled the vivacious, happy girl who had left St. Petersburg only a fortnight before. Her face was pasty white, and her hair, normally thick and lustrous, was wound in an untidy coil around her head. Her lips looked bloodless and swollen, and she had lost weight. With glassy eyes she stared at the gift sent by Count Vasily, which had created such a sensation in the house. It was something only a certain kind of Russian could have conceived.

The engagement gift from Count Vasily was a stuffed bear cub standing on all fours. Its fur was black and felt soft when Dunyasha ran her red hands through it. Tatyana had heard of gouty noblemen putting their sore feet up on the backs of these little black bears. But what had created such a stir at Starlina was the Turburov version of this Russian footstool.

In the place of the glass eyes ordinarily used had been fitted two large purple amethysts from the Ural Mountains. This was extravagant enough, but it had been eclipsed by a more peculiar innovation. The bear's teeth, normally left in place, had been removed from the animal's open jaw. Instead, set in gums made from beaten gold, were two rows of sharp, pointed white diamonds. In the morning sunlight, the bear cub's fantastic mouth gleamed, making it look as if he were smiling.

"Oh, Dunyasha, take the footstool away. It is a monstrosity!" said Tatyana, dismissing the gift with an impatient wave of her arm.

Dunyasha picked up the bear cub in both arms. "But little mother, it is a gift from your fiancé, Count Vasily!"

"I don't care," retorted Tatyana, close to tears. "Take it away."

"But, little mother—"

"Dunyasha, get rid of it, or better yet, you have it!"

"I can have it?" asked Dunyasha, her blue eyes turning round as saucers. "For me to keep, all my own, little mother?"

"Yes, that poor wretched little thing is yours."

Dunyasha looked as if she might possibly burst from happiness, and still holding the bear in one arm, started to heap kisses on Tatyana's hands. "Oh little mother!"

Tatyana sniffled. "I'm glad at least you like it, I couldn't bear to sleep in the same room with it."

Dunyasha held out the bear at arm's length, and a look of utter delight and satisfaction filled her face. "Wait, just wait until that impudence of an Anatole sees me with this bear. That'll curl his tongue!" Blowing hearty kisses to her mistress, Dunyasha rushed out of the room with the bear.

Tatyana sniffed back a tear and lay down on her bed. "Is that what marriage will be like with Count Vasily— baby animals stuffed with jewels? My life is so ghastly it might as well be over."

In the last two weeks Tatyana had felt in such despair she could not conceive happiness would ever come her way again. She hit the flat of her hand against the pillow.

"Oh, Gregory, Gregory, how could you deceive me? How could you, how could you?" And she sobbed all over again.

Whether Prince Korbatsky realized it or not, from his quiver of secret information he had wounded Tatyana with two separate arrows, both of them poison-tipped. Normally Tatyana was not one to torture herself with roads not taken, but she kept wondering over and over again which was more terrible: that the man she loved wanted the downfall of the father of her country, or that he should keep such a secret from her.

Like all Russians, Tatyana had been raised to believe that no matter what else one doubted, the czar was to be loved as if he was one's father. In her nightly prayers she begged the Almighty in Heaven to bless her father, her brother, and the czar. And unlike many Russians, the czar played a personal part in her life as well. He was her godfather, he had always sent her gifts on her nameday. And when she had turned eighteen, she had been invited by Empress Elizabeth to become a lady-in-waiting at the court. This was a rare privilege, for only the daughters of the most distinguished families in Russia were asked. It was only her devotion to her father that made Tatyana

beg exemption from this honor. One could criticize
serfdom, the courts, the censor, the military colonies, but
the czar himself? Never, he was unimpeachable. It had
been hard enough to accept from Dmitry and Gregory
that things might be rotten in Russia, but that either one
of them should even think or wish to strike a blow at the
throne itself was absolutely intolerable.

Now she had to face a cruel truth: that the man she
loved was a spy whose political aim was the downfall of
Alexander. Tatyana covered her ears with her pillow and
rolled in her bed, wishing to shut out the outside world.

Tatyana also had felt the rug pulled out from under her
for another reason. She had bestowed her love indiscrim-
inately. For the first time in her life she had dared to think
and feel differently from her beloved father, and her
reward was to find that what she thought and what she
felt was all a gross mistake, a wicked error in judgment.
For it was clear that Gregory was not who she had
thought him. Since he had withheld the true nature of his
interests from her, what else was he, who was he really?
Who was the man whose bed she had so rapturously
shared? If he was not who he appeared to be, then
neither could their love be. Another sob broke from her
at this thought. As her emotions whirled about her
tempestuously, her heart felt so broken, her pride so
damaged, it never occurred to her to challenge or
question Gregory himself.

So without pausing to sort out her thoughts, Tatyana
handed her destiny back into the hands of her father. It
was he who had been right about Gregory all along, she
reasoned, so he must be equally right about Count
Turburov. To atone for all her sins, Tatyana accepted
Vasily's proposal meekly and without argument. Where
she would live, what views she would hold, would no
longer be in her domain. She relinquished her hold of
these things willingly, in the hope that her father would

forgive her terrible ignorance and stupidity. As the days wore on, a certain blank expression appeared in her eyes, and she became listless and withdrawn. But somewhere deep inside her a tiny flame flickered, not allowing itself to be quenched. It was the tiny little flame, the part of her own true self, that made her suffer.

Prince Korbatsky added to Tatyana's self-immolation by his own distrust and dislike of Gregory. "Another letter from the man who wishes the downfall of your godfather," he would announce harshly, handing her the third envelope that week, and she would wince and fight back tears. He would glare at her as if he couldn't believe she would even touch the infected envelope. Tatyana would gaze at it, and hand it back to her father. "I do not wish to read it. Please return it to Mr. Grandison or destroy it."

"Sensible girl," he would say in his most honeyed voice and then pat her pale hand. After three weeks of envelopes, they stopped coming.

And so the days dragged by through September. The autumn leaves fell at Starlina, and the weather grew colder. Cold mists lay over the lawns in the early morning, and the prince's serfs began to harvest the summer wheat.

Slowly the pain subsided in Tatyana's heart, numbed by her return to her familiar duties at Starlina and by the round of social obligations precipitated by her impending marriage to Count Vasily. Madame Mesatoni, the *svakha*, who both awed and chilled Tatyana, was an occasional visitor at the house, her shadow popping into Prince Korbatsky's study at the oddest hours. There was something formidable about this tiny woman fastidiously dressed. She seemed to judge everything, material and abstract, only by its marketable value.

Tatyana sensed Madame Mesatoni measured in the scales of her mind the exact number of rubles everything was worth—from Tatyana's pearl *kokoshnik* to the innermost secrets of Tatyana's heart. Tatyana did not like her. But she was a distant relative of the Turburovs who had married an Italian and been widowed, and now she seemed to be handling the details of Tatyana's dowry. So Tatyana was respectful to Madame Mesatoni. She shook Tatyana's hand in her own small firm hand, and when she left, Tatyana was always filled with a sense of wonder. Widows seemed a mysterious entity to her; either they were mere shells, remnants of forgotten femininity, or they were like Madame Mesatoni, who only started to bloom once they had buried their husbands. Perhaps, if one was married to someone like Vasily, it would be easier to fall into the latter category. Tatyana instantly quelled this wicked thought.

One day she idly asked her father about Madame Mesatoni and the terms of the dowry. The prince poohpoohed her questions and told her not to worry over these mundane worries, that he, her father, was making all the necessary arrangements through the *svakha*. There were not many things her father shared with her regarding money or estate matters, so this was not a surprise. She went about doing what was expected of her: sewing, an important pre-wedding activity for Russian brides, and visiting the Turburovs. And now she began to look on them in a new light: as family.

They and their immediate relatives were cordial to her as they had always been. But it was only after being with them on several intimate occasions that something in the family's manner, something in the very house itself seemed actively out of step with Tatyana. At first Tatyana didn't notice it, but the sensation increased until it became a thought in her mind. She realized how little spirit, trust, or warmth entered in their relationships. The conversations at the banquet tables in the ornately festooned dining room were witty and fashionable, but behind the high sheen of its gloss there was a hard, cold vacuum that was constantly mirrored in Count Vasily's face. Count Vasily would look up to find Tatyana's large dark pupils staring across the table at him. It was not a gaze to make one comfortable. He could not guess her thoughts.

Why was Vasily's face so devoid of warmth? Tatyana wondered. Why were his eyes so flat and hard? Why, oh why, did he not have Gregory's eyes, so dark and lustrous and thoughtful? Then she would push the thought from her mind, feeling ashamed of herself. She would rejoin the conversation, listening to it as if the words spoken were stones falling into a deep well. Still Tatyana remained steadfast to her father's wishes. Even when the Turburovs and their relatives sat gossiping about the czar and his activities, discussing how Alexander had gone to Taganrog on the Azov Sea to be by his ailing wife, Tatyana's thoughts were elsewhere. Where was Gregory? she wondered. What was he doing? And then she would remember he was not her Gregory but a spy and would-be assassin.

In early November Tatyana's name day arrived and with it an unexpected flow of guests from St. Petersburg and the neighboring countryside. Now that Tatyana was to marry Count Turburov, making her one of the richest young matrons in European Russia, Prince Korbatsky was assailed with invitations and requests from old friends who had forgotten him.

When Tatyana appeared to greet the guests she was dressed in her red brocade *sarafan* and pearl *kokoshnik*. The last time she had worn them was to welcome Dmitry home from Paris. The memory of this was so strong she almost put the costume aside. She only wore it when

Dunyasha pressed her to, reminding her how much her father loved her in it on ceremonial occasions.

Tatyana sat at the head of the banqueting table with Vasily at her right. At the end of the table was her father ensconced in his chair, with Countess Irina beside him.

A huge mushroom and meat *pirog* was brought in, a requisite at name day celebrations. The pie was followed by platters of different meats and fish and fowl. Because the prince drank little, only tea was poured for the guests from the silver samovar. All drank and ate until they were quite stuffed and sated. All the guests, who had been enjoying themselves immensely, broke into ooh-la-las when a beautiful bombe of ice cream garlanded with candied cherries was brought out for dessert. Cherries were Tatyana's favorite fruit, so she particularly should have been pleased. But throughout the meal she had seemed listless and preoccupied, and even the ice bombe failed to stimulate her appetite.

"Eat up, daughter, eat up," scolded her father. "The count does not wish to marry a cadaver," and because he was nervous, he laughed. Tatyana did not smile at the joke, but then again she had not laughed at any others all evening. For someone who was to be the future Countess Turburova, Tatyana did not strike any of the guests as appropriately ecstatic.

While they were eating dessert, there was a commotion at the foyer. The doors to the dining room were thrown open by the butler, and in walked a tall, cloaked figure.

Tatyana bit down on her spoon, while all the guests turned to look at the intruder. He doffed his top hat and made his most distinguished bow, which was not difficult for him to do. "Mr. Gregory Grandison," announced Timofey the butler.

"Pardon my intrusion at this hour," said Gregory, addressing Prince Korbatsky in French. "I have come on behalf of Dmitry who wished to send greetings to his sister on her name day."

As he spoke, Gregory did not even look for Tatyana in the group of faces.

"You come too late to partake of the meal," said Prince Korbatsky, frowning at Gregory. But seeing the inquisitive looks on the faces of his guests, he added with cold politeness, "Of course, please join us for ice cream and gingered fruit."

There was the mumble of excuses, "Here's a seat," and the scrape of chairs rearranged on the parquet floor. The candle flames darted in the changing currents of air.

Gregory took a seat in the middle of the table, halfway between Tatyana and her father. "I could not of course refuse such a gracious invitation," said Gregory, "especially on such a happy occasion. I don't believe I've had a chance to toast the happy couple." Everyone clapped and laughed and sighed at yet another reference to Tatyana's betrothal, but when Gregory raised a glass to Tatyana, there was no such merriment in his eyes. Tatyana must have found something fascinating on her dessert plate, for she could not bring herself to raise her eyes. Gregory's toast was echoed by the other guests.

"You do not look well, pigeon," said an ignorant, well-intentioned lady, noticing the perspiration and pallor on Tatyana's face.

"She will be well enough, by and by," interjected Vasily. "When the door opened I think she felt a chill." And now he looked long and hard at Gregory. But Gregory did not waste a glance on Count Vasily. His eyes were fixed on Tatyana.

Tension began to fill the room as an uncomfortable silence reigned. Prince Korbatsky glared at Gregory, and Count Vasily tapped on the damask tablecloth with his dirty spoon. Now even though the guests were finished, Tatyana began to eat her ice cream with concentration.

Gregory also ate hungrily, his eye on Tatyana and seemingly impervious to the glances cast on him by the guests.

"The dessert is delightful," he said, after several spoonfuls. "The soft sweetness of the cherries would be cloying, but the ice cream sets them in relief. The cold sweetness is an unanticipated combination but goes down easily on the palate. I commend your cook, Prince Korbatsky."

Tatyana had grown paler and paler, and just when she was convinced that she would faint right into her plate of ice cream, her father clapped his hands. The serfs had been summoned, and the dinner was over. Prince Korbatsky had himself carried out in his chair to the drawing room, where there was to be dancing. And then the guests began to file out of the dining room.

Tatyana folded and refolded her napkin, hoping Gregory would get up and leave with the other guests. She was relieved when he did stand up, but then he lingered at the door. She saw if she stayed too much longer she would be left alone with him. This thought terrified her. And she could not lean on Count Vasily. An elderly baroness had grabbed his arm to escort her into the drawing room.

Tatyana jumped up from her seat and followed in the wake of a neighbor's billowing skirts, half hoping Gregory would not notice her among the flounces. But as she passed him her heart thudded. She felt his hand suddenly upon her wrist.

"You didn't think I'd let you escape so easily, did you?" he whispered harshly.

"Please let go," she said, imitating her father's frigid politeness toward him.

"Not on your life," said Gregory in a harsh undertone. "At least not just yet." And he squeezed her wrist tighter.

Some of the ladies still lingered in the entrance hall, so Tatyana could not make a scene.

"Please let go," she repeated in her proudest voice, turning obliquely aside so as not to face him.

"Don't worry, I am not staying long," he said, splinters of ice in his voice. "I came from Staraya-Russa, and this time am indeed on my way to Moscow. But I wouldn't have dreamed of missing this occasion to congratulate you."

Tatyana glanced up at Gregory sideways and saw for the first time how his handsome face looked gaunt and drained. His dark eyes were trained on the foyer door which led to the drawing room. Count Vasily lingered there, detained by the baroness while he kept an eye on Tatyana in the dining room. Gregory and Tatyana stood in some strange relation to each other, but it was clear by the position of their bodies that they were engaged in no affectionate tête-à-tête. If anything, Tatyana looked angry. Count Vasily was satisfied.

"Your Count Turburov has us both squirming under his gaze, like beetles stuck and spinning on pins," said Gregory. "There, very good, he's smugly pleased with your look of haughty displeasure. Any moment we will be relieved of him." Sure enough, Count Vasily wandered into the drawing room.

"You are hurting me!" whispered Tatyana angrily, her wrist aching from Gregory's hold.

"Not enough to please me," said Gregory through clenched teeth, "but I am sorry to crease your dress. It looks so fetching on the future Countess Turburova."

"Why did you come here?" demanded Tatyana in a fierce whisper, not looking at him.

"I'm not entirely sure," was Gregory's sardonic answer. "Perhaps I'm just after a hair of the dog that bit me."

Tatyana said nothing, though her eyes were beginning to glisten with tears.

"So tell me," continued Gregory in an undertone. "From your own sweet lips. Tell me you are going to marry Count Vasily."

"Yes, with pleasure," Tatyana whispered fiercely, wanting to hurt him as much as he was hurting her now, and for all she'd suffered in the last weeks.

"Perfidious lady," he assailed her, jerking her harshly. "Be glad you're here in the safety of your father's house and not alone with me."

Tatyana's eyes flashed to his own, which were black with rage. She met his with a blaze of hurt and indignation. "How dare you, how dare you call me perfidious?!" Her voice rasped as she tried to contain her shriek to a whisper.

"Is it not perfidy to lie in one man's arms while you proclaim your love for him and then marry another? I know no other word for it." His voice was low and deadly. "But perhaps in mad, fashionable Russia breaking hearts is *de rigueur.*"

Tatyana could barely stand it and wanted to scream or slap him, but they were only yards from the drawing room door, which stood ajar.

"Break people's hearts," she almost blubbered, "break people's hearts our national pastime? Well it is not our national pastime to break the heart of the father of our people!"

Gregory stared at her, and his anger was mingled with a look of perplexity. He was trying to think and his silence only enflamed Tatyana. After all the weeks of pain she had been through she begrudged him the luxury of a single moment. "At least you have enough shame not to contest what you are accused of," she demanded, facing him full on.

Gregory looked at Tatyana narrowly. "It is not from

shame that I do not speak. Just that I am not certain of the charge, princess."

Tatyana was made furious by this remark. "Fortunately, not only England has her spies, but Russia too. And my father as you know has friends in very high places. Otherwise we would have all remained deceived by you. Well, no one could accuse you of modest aims. Not just a little information gathering was it, but actually setting your sights on the czar himself."

Gregory loosened his hold of Tatyana's wrist and rubbed his forehead with his hand. Finally he sighed and said enigmatically, "Now it all comes clear—and all of these weeks wasted." This thought seemed to tire and anger him, and he passed his hands over his eyes again.

"Well, is it not true, is it not true?" Tatyana demanded in a whisper as she rubbed her wrist. She felt dismayed by the look of exhaustion that had come over Gregory. She almost preferred his indignant anger.

His silence, for he was deep in thought, oppressed her. At last he spoke.

"To believe, Tatyana, that I am a spy for my country or any other is to show not only how little you trusted me but how little you understood of my nature. How could you think me the instrument of government bureaucracy, someone to follow orders, since it is totally alien to my nature? How could you?" he demanded.

Tatyana felt the warmth of his breath on her face, and the familiar perfume of his body made her head giddy. She longed to drown out the concerns of the world, her memory of the past few weeks, and to sink her head in Gregory's arms. So it was all false, all false, she began to wonder.

Gregory sensed the softening in her body, longed for it after so many weeks of silence and pain and with a quick deft stroke wheeled her to an alcove with a window,

where they could not be seen from the drawing room
door.

"Oh, Gregory," sighed Tatyana, overcome with remorse at what she had believed of him.

"Tatyana, doubt me if you must, but do not withhold
your love from me just now, just now," said Gregory. He
suddenly crushed her in his arms and forced her to kiss
him ardently.

With the sound of voices, laughter, and violin music
hardly more than a room away, this was an audacious
maneuver. But all Tatyana could do was succumb to his
devastatingly familiar body and the richness of his embrace.

Gregory pulled back. "Forgive me," he said quickly,
drinking her beauty in but aware of the danger of
compromise in which he placed her.

"Tell me, then, swear to me that none of the charges is
true," Tatyana whispered urgently. "Tell me it is not true
that you and Dmitry and those other young men are
organized with the intent to topple the czar. Swear to it,
Gregory, I beg you!"

Gregory placed his hands gently on Tatyana's shoulders and looked her in the eye. "No, Tatyana," he said at
last with quiet resolution. "That second charge is not one
I can wholeheartedly deny. It is true that some of your
countrymen have reached a state of desperation, and it is
also true that I have been meeting with them."

Tatyana stared at him silently.

"But you must also believe, Tatyana, that many members of this secret society—which is not so secret—have
no wish to harm the czar or his position. These countrymen of yours, many of them talented, courageous young
officers, have always wanted reform over revolution. And
several are still intent on drafting and resubmitting consti-
tutions based on representative government. It is they
who have been leaning on me as an Englishman from a

parliamentary system to advise them. None wants bloodshed, but confidentially, a few are increasingly convinced that reform alone is no longer possible, that violence will carry over endless reams of unread paper."

"Is my brother one of these young . . . radicals?" Tatyana asked, her mouth trembling.

Gregory looked at her a long moment, then nodded. "Yes, but again, only after endless patience and despair. He has not told you this, but the petition on which he spent so many months and which he presented to Arakcheyev was thrown out, and a copy submitted to the czar and his ministers went ignored. He and other young men have reached a point of desperation. There are others, like me, less heroic but perhaps more levelheaded too, who wish to dissuade the more radical among them from such a course—if only because it could not mean victory to them. From an objective point of view they are not prepared, just tactically, to wage an insurrection, and they lack a base of popular support."

"Insurrection," muttered Tatyana aghast, "insurrection? I don't understand."

"Yes, on the contrary, you do," said Gregory urgently. "For you understand the conditions of your country and your people. Liberty does not exist in Russia. And while freedom brings with it problems of another kind, it does not poison the human soul. No insurrection is ever likely to take place, as the czar guesses, for they are not prepared, and that is why they will not be arrested.

"But respect these young men at least for their heroic idealism and their honorable intentions. For the first time in the history of your country, you have members of an intelligentsia whose one altruistic aim is the betterment of their people. Their talks and dreams are not the machinations of Russia's age-old palace revolutions representing only cliquish personal ambitions. These young men are after something much loftier—a life that is better not just for a select handful but all the Russian people." Gregory was practically shaking her.

Tatyana knew that she could never betray her allegiance to the czar, even if the cause was worthy, but she also knew how much she loved her brother and how much Gregory really meant to her.

"Oh, Gregory," she said despairingly, "perhaps their dreams are laudable, I can't refute that. But you must stop your own involvement and Dmitry's in these secret meetings. The czar knows your names. If anything happens of any kind, you, my brother, all of you will be held accountable, and who knows what the punishment would be. For my sake you must promise you will stop all this. Promise this to me!" Tatyana gripped the lapels of his frock coat as if she would not let him go until he agreed.

"I am not in a position to promise," said Gregory stern-faced. "Something is happening in Kondraty Ryleyev's drawing room that I heartily believe in. I who until I met you hardly believed in anything. This is not my country, but their aims are universal. Your countrymen like all people have a right to freedom and to justice, and I will help in any way I can, no matter how insignificant. I will not turn my back on what they and I believe in."

"You must not pursue this drastic course," Tatyana implored.

"I must pursue what I believe in—in spite of even you," he said and dropped his hands from her shoulders. But he searched her eyes for some sign of abiding love or understanding.

Their earlier kiss, that moment of rapture, was over. Tatyana and Gregory clung each to their own fierce beliefs, which neither of them would shake. Yet Gregory could not be angry at Tatyana's selfishness, seeing how it was born out of her love for him. And Tatyana could not dismiss Gregory forever from her heart for his untimely principles. They stood face to face, gazing at each other, longing to obliterate their differences, to drown in one another's touch and smell and taste. But the seconds ticked by, and both held steadfastly to their convictions and their pride.

Just then, Count Vasily and his sister came sailing into the dining room. "So sorry to interrupt this tête-à-tête," was Count Vasily's caustic greeting when he saw Tatyana and Gregory in the alcove. But they gave him no further reason for anger. They stood in no incriminating embrace. In fact, quite the contrary. They looked as much at odds as they had a quarter-hour before.

"You interrupted nothing. I believe we have just finished our conversation?" There was the faintest look of reproach as Gregory glanced at Tatyana.

"Yes," she said, looking him in the eye. "We were just about to join the guests." Their pride kept them from each other.

"A very good idea," said Vasily. "I will escort you, princess." Count Vasily took Tatyana's arm in his plump white hands and led her away.

Irina was left in the room alone with Gregory. Although she had found nothing flattering to say on Mr. Grandison's account the preceding months, she now unexpectedly began to sway. In another minute she would droop upon his arm.

Gregory looked at her small hard eyes and pointed chin and the false and twisted simper on her face. "Forgive me, countess," he said sardonically, "but I must be gone. I may be wrong, but there are others I believe who have more urgent need of my right arm." To Countess Irina's mortification, he flung his cloak upon his shoulder and disappeared out the door into the cold November night.

Chapter Fifteen

Whatever great upheavals were going on in the hearts of Gregory and Tatyana, their problems would have seemed inconsequential to anyone surveying general developments in Russia during the next several months.

One morning, on November twenty-eighth, shortly after Tatyana's interview with Gregory, a messenger came galloping up on horseback to Starlina. The courier was admitted to Prince Korbatsky's private study, where he delivered his astounding news. Prince Korbatsky's jowls quivered, and he sat speechless. Then he remembered to clap his hands—not briskly as was his habit, but as if it were a great strain to do so. Tatyana was summoned along with the entire household, from the steward down to the most menial scullery maid.

Tersely the prince announced, "The Almighty in Heaven, bless and forgive us at this moment of great misfortune. His imperial majesty, the Emperor Alexander . . . is dead."

There was no sound in the room, as everyone stared at

the prince, disbelieving. A murmur arose as they regarded the prince's stern and resolute face. Then a moan
could be heard, and then another, and one serf after
another began to sob.

"Father, it is not possible," said Tatyana, trying to
catch her breath. "He is only forty-eight. What has
happened, what has happened?"

Early in the fall the czar had gone to Taganrog on the
Azov Sea to be by the side of his ailing wife. But at this
seaside resort Alexander had put himself unknowingly in
jeopardy. He, who had worried so about assassins, came
down suddenly with malaria. And to the astonishment of
his retinue, it was the czar, not the czarina, who expired
and suddenly died on November the nineteenth. This
was what Prince Korbatsky explained to his daughter.
The news of this calamitous event took a full week to
reach St. Petersburg, but when the report arrived, it
spread as quickly as the ubiquitous fires that constantly
menaced Russia's wooden towns and cities. Prince Korbatsky was informed of the czar's death not many hours
after Alexander's most important ministers.

Tatyana sank down in her chair. "Oh, thank God,
thank God," she muttered.

"Why do you thank God, my daughter," berated the
prince. "The father of our country is dead, and at a most
untimely moment."

"I only meant, father, what a Godsend he was felled by
swamp fever and not an assassin's bullet." Tatyana
crossed herself. When Tatyana's terror was past, her grief
consumed her, and she cried off and on during the
afternoon. But she was not alone. Everyone in the
household wept, candles were lighted beside the holy
icons, and the sound of chanting and prayers emanated
throughout the house and from the tiny *izbas* of the
nearby serf villages.

Alexander I had not accomplished what he had set out

to do with his handsome looks and youthful idealism. At the beginning of his reign Alexander had made the people dizzy with joy. He reopened the borders to travelers, he allowed the import of foreign newspapers and books, and he abolished censorship of native presses. Ukases and manifestos were issued by him that repealed trade restrictions and limited police dictatorship. Most importantly, he had begun in earnest to take the first steps toward emancipating the serfs.

But Alexander soon succumbed to his own worst instincts, to mysticism, and to the reactionary conservatism of his ministers. The restriction on literature and public education became worse than before, and censorship became so excessive even conservative statesmen regarded it as a folly. And it was Alexander's disastrous idea to create military colonies that would be self-sufficient and not dependent on the government for money.

In twenty-five years the czar had dragged his country not forward but backward in time. Even so, in the minds and in the hearts of many of his people, Alexander was still the hero of the war against the monster Napoleon still fresh in their memories. He was "Alexander the Blessed," and the "Little Father" of his people, and if he had not done what he set out to do, it reflected less on him and more on his conniving ministers.

But while the country mourned, those in high places were being more sensible than sentimental. They scratched their heads and pondered the next significant question. Who would be the new czar?

Alexander had no children, and by the rights of succession the crown should go to the first of his three brothers. This was the Grand Duke Constantine, who had fought in the Napoleonic wars and was considered cantankerous but good-natured. But Constantine was presently in Poland and momentarily out of reach. Grand

Duke Nicholas, Alexander's second brother, received news of the death of Alexander while prayers were being said for the czar in the Winter Palace. Nicholas immediately made a declaration of allegiance to his absent brother Constantine and commanded the generals to make their officers and troops do the same. This was not an insignificant request. The backing of the Guard had long been of importance in Russia to ensure a smooth accession. Constantine was expected to arrive in St. Petersburg to accept the crown at any moment.

Meanwhile, though, another development had taken place. For several years rumors had been circulating that suddenly flared up again at the moment of Alexander's death. It was again being whispered among the courtiers that Alexander had previously issued a manifesto proclaiming Nicholas heir to the throne and not Constantine. Constantine, they whispered, had years earlier abdicated. This secret manifesto, long a rumor, proved to be correct. Now, just after the news of Alexander's death and to the astonishment of the court, the manifesto was brought forward. But Grand Duke Nicholas, backed by General Miloradovich, nobly continued to swear allegiance to his brother Constantine. But still there was no sign or word from Constantine in Poland.

"But I don't understand," said Tatyana. "Who is the rightful czar?"

"Constantine, of course," said her father. "Unless he makes a formal abdication. General Miloradovich is quite right to urge Nicholas to stand by his brother."

Finally, on December the third, a formal renunciation of the throne arrived in St. Petersburg from Constantine in Warsaw. Constantine, having no children either, and perfectly content to be Governor of Poland, abdicated his right to the throne of Russia.

Prince Korbatsky learned all this from a letter written to him by General Miloradovich.

Nicholas is in a quandary. His younger brother the Grand Duke Michael and many other important personages berate Nicholas now for having ordered an oath of allegiance to Constantine, because if Nicholas assumes the throne he will have to cancel the first oath and demand another.

"How can the Guard undo one oath and take another?" asked Tatyana perplexed. "Would either oath be valid?"

"I have not finished the letter," snapped Prince Korbatsky, irritated by the reasonableness of Tatyana's question. "Let me continue."

The general's letter went on.

They are concerned about what will happen now if the troops are ordered to repudiate their first oath to Constantine and take a second one instead to Nicholas. And then there are worrywarts who want the issue resolved quickly because they say members of a secret society would welcome a schism to spread harmful gossip about rights of accession. I say, let those brats read their wretched rhymes aloud to one another. A small parcel of schoolboys can hardly do much harm with their wagging tongues. Believe me, prince, with sixty thousand bayonets at my disposal, I can vouch for the safety and tranquillity of St. Petersburg. I fear no harm from any quarter. Let Nicholas take his time. It is clear that he must write to Constantine again and demand his older brother accept the crown.

"Very sensible advice. I agree with Miloradovich entirely," said the prince, and he put aside the letter.

But one day rolled by after another, and still nothing

was heard from Constantine in Warsaw, and still Nicholas would not take the crown.

Prince Korbatsky began to stroke his beard, asking of everyone who drew up at his door if they carried any news or any letters. The interregnum dragged into its second week.

"This is preposterous!" exclaimed the old prince after scanning a letter that brought no new information. "Absolutely preposterous. A mighty ship adrift in the ocean, with no captain to take the helm. It is a fine thing, a very fine thing indeed, when a crown is treated like a hot potato!"

"What is to be done?" asked Tatyana, her own nerves on edge at the way state affairs were dragging on, and secretly worried for Gregory and her brother.

"What is to be done?" retorted her father. "Why, it is obvious. Since Constantine drags his heels, let Nicholas accept the blasted crown and be done with it. What nonsense all this posing and dillydallying is!"

"But father, there are many people who are worried about such a move. Nicholas swears allegiance to Constantine. But the Grand Duke Michael doesn't and keeps disappearing and reappearing in the capital. And not a word from Constantine himself," exclaimed Tatyana. "No wonder people think something is amiss between all three brothers. Perhaps they're right. Perhaps some strange plot is brewing in the royal chambers." Tatyana's eyes were wide with alarm.

"Nonsense, daughter," prompted her father. "It is simply political folderol. Nicholas would love the crown! But he is not as popular as Constantine among the Imperial Guardsmen. He has always been considered hard and unyielding. But to take the crown Nicholas should have the backing of the Guards. He is undoubtedly biding his time so as not to appear overly eager to assume the throne. The last thing he wants I'm sure is yet another palace revolution. I have already told you once before where that kind of thing leads to." The prince stroked his moustache. "But Constantine should certainly send word and settle the matter. And once he does, if Nicholas is half a man, he should have no problems with the Guard. They are not beset with the foolish liberal notions of your brother and Mr. Grandison. The Guard can be depended on to take an oath to Nicholas. The second oath will immediately cancel out the other."

Tatyana wondered if everyone would see the matter in the sanguine manner of her father, but she said nothing.

On Saturday, December twelfth, Prince Korbatsky received a second letter, this time in Count Turburov's small, almost illegible hand. The prince bent over it with his quizzing glass. "A letter from your fiancé," he grumbled. "I will be fortunate if I can piece a word of it together."

Tatyana sat anxiously beside her father in the drawing room. Something was brewing, she sensed, from the urgency with which the letter had been sent from the capital.

Prince Korbatsky read the letter slowly, often stopping to make out the words. "'A second reply has finally come from—' constantly? No, it must be Constantine. 'He has again abdicated in favorite—' No, in favor, 'of his younger brother Nicholas. Nicholas would wait longer, for further concern,' damn it, 'confirmation, but he has recouped,' er, 'received news disturbing to him. It was discovered . . . yesterday . . . that there exists in the Second Army a vast . . . conspiracy to overthrow . . . the czar.'" Here the Prince paused. "Damn it, I can't make out the next word."

Tatyana's trembling hand reached for the letter. "It says, 'and exterminate the royal family.' Father, do you wish me to finish the letter?" Tatyana asked, looking white as a sheet.

Prince Korbatsky handed it to her, and Tatyana read while she twisted the cross around her neck. She repeated the whole passage. " 'It has been discovered yesterday there exists in the Second Army a vast conspiracy to overthrow the czar and exterminate the royal family . . . by means of an organized and armed *coup d'état.*' Oh, it cannot be," breathed Tatyana.

"Go on, go on," said her father, waving his arm. "What else does the count say?"

Tatyana picked up the letter and continued. " 'There is reason to believe that the oath of allegiance will be questioned in order to create upset in the capital. They may launch their own insidious campaign against Nicholas, but the report received indicates that their ultimate goal is not only to thwart Nicholas's accession, but to rip asunder the groundwork of the monarchy. Apparently these men are after nothing less than a constitutional republic. It may have worked in France, but Russia will not allow it. We are prepared to confront the possibility of an insurrection and to annihilate it at its inception.' "

Insurrection, annihilation. These seemed dreadful words in Tatyana's ears.

"Finish up, daughter," barked the old prince, rapping the arm of his chair.

Tatyana's hands were trembling, but she continued to read out loud.

" 'Nicholas will wait no longer, as all are urging him to take the crown. The fate of our country and the crown may be in jeopardy. Therefore, tomorrow Nicholas will draft a manifesto of accession, and on Monday, December fourteenth, the Senate and the Guards will take their oath to him. Nicholas will then take his rightful place as the new father of Russia.' " Tatyana paused to regain her breath. " 'All will go smoothly. Additional troops are being brought into the capital, to safeguard Nicholas and ensure his accession. Your son's regiment, incidentally, is being summoned, since Nicholas, as their former commander, trusts in general to their allegiance to him. While this conspiracy seems more far reaching than we all originally guessed, there is no need for worry. God is with the czar.'"

"Why that worried look on your face?" demanded Prince Korbatsky, as Tatyana sat motionless with the letter in her hand. "What are you worried for. Your fiancé and his artillery men will come to no harm."

Tatyana was jolted by the discrepancy between her father's words and what she had actually been thinking. She flushed. "Oh, father, do you think there will be an insurrection?"

"Certainly not. You read of General Miloradovich's sixty thousand bayonets and of the resolve of your fiancé. Nobody, not even a liberal, would be so foolish as to start a revolt at this late hour. By God, Nicholas practically has his seat on the cushion of the throne. There is nothing to fear. Soon this interminable interregnum will be over, and Nicholas will be czar."

Tatyana did not look reassured by her father's words. "This vast conspiracy Vasily refers to, do you think it includes Dmitry's secret society?"

"Who knows? They're all windbags, but they might be idiotic enough to be involved with some radical group. Even if your brother thinks like an idiot, I'd hardly consider he would try to back his mindless drivel with grapeshot. And if for some unfathomable reason he does, he will have to pay the consequences."

These harsh words from her father cut Tatyana to the quick. It seemed awful that her father could speak in such a way of his only son. But when she finally handed Vasily's letter back to her father, her hand was steady.

The word "insurrection" kept beating in her brain like a tiny hammer all through dinner. She hardly touched her food. She remembered Gregory's words: "Your countrymen have a right to freedom and to justice, and I will help in any way I can—no matter how insignificant." She tried to imagine how Gregory and Dmitry would behave if an occasion presented itself to suit action to words. For so long, all their ideals had seemed fodder only for drawing room or barracks conversation. They had seemed more enamored of their thoughts than of the possible consequences. But now, from her recent conversation with Gregory about Dmitry, and from what she had seen of Gregory himself, she sensed both their priorities had shifted. They seemed tired of speech, more impressed by deed. She felt sure that if his comrades lifted up their muskets, so would Dmitry, who could be so hot-blooded. And she also wondered, would the Englishman fight alongside his Russian friends? The answer that kept pounding in her heart made her feel faint and lightheaded.

It began to snow again that evening, and Prince Korbatsky eyed his daughter as she went once or twice to look out the window. But otherwise she seemed composed and after dinner took up her usual evening activities. She played on the clavichord, read from a lighthearted romance by Madame de Scudéry, and worked on her embroidery. To her father's superficial questions and conversation, her answers were easy and serene. Soon he stopped worrying about her.

At midnight it was time to go to sleep, and Tatyana kissed her father's hands as she said good night. In a sudden impulsive gesture she leaned forward and kissed his jowly cheek.

Reassured by this sign of docility and affection, the old prince said gruffly, "Don't worry about that brother of yours. He'll come to no trouble. You'll get a good night's sleep, won't you, my snow princess."

Tatyana kissed him again, and the old prince, finding

order in his house, went off to bed and to thoughtless slumber.

That night, the coachman Platon was asleep in his usual place, a cast-off couch in a corner of the winter kitchen. But early in the morning, while it was still dark, his snores were interrupted. He awoke to feel someone tugging on his shoulder.

"Platon, wake up, wake up," he heard, whispering fiercely at him. For an instant he was terrified, for it could be the voice of a *rusalka* or other enchanted sprite deciding to play tricks on him. But when he opened his old puffy eyes he found his master's daughter, the Princess Tatyana. She held a lantern, which showed she was wrapped in her sable pelisse and fur galoshes.

"What is it, little mother, is the house on fire?" he asked, suddenly sitting up in the semi-darkness.

"No, no, Platon," answered Tatyana, and she was about to continue, but her reassurances had been enough for the old coachman. He immediately flopped down again and was asleep. Tatyana had to shake him again. "Platon, get up. I need your help!"

Platon was utterly faithful to his master, Prince Korbatsky, but he loved his master's daughter even more. Besides, it was not for him to question her orders, this famously dutiful daughter of the prince. Now he nodded to the short requests she made of him. His hair stuck out on all sides, but the expression in Tatyana's face showed there was no time even to neaten his appearance.

Shortly before five in the morning, he hitched up his beloved gray Orlovs, yawned, scratched his head, and helped his mistress into the *troika*.

"To St. Petersburg," said Tatyana, and soon the troika sailed over the moonlit snow, the horses cantering as fast as they could go.

Tatyana crouched in the cold darkness of the carriage,

her body snug in its sable pelisse, her mind in a flurry of anxiety. She was terrified and had been so all last evening, though she had tried to hide it. Instinct had compelled her deception of her father, something which she had never done in all her life. It would be midday before he wondered where she was, and by then, by then, the mission she had set out upon would be accomplished.

"Volki, Volki," she heard Platon shout, and she held her breath. But the sleigh kept sliding quickly through the darkness. Then she remembered her father had offered bounties this year for wolfskins. So the wily animals now knew better than to attack a fast-moving sleigh. They slunk away into the forest. Tatyana sighed to think how her father had unknowingly helped her on her flight from Starlina.

When dawn broke at seven, the sky was gray and bleak, a typical winter morning. After several more hours and a change of horses, the sleigh drew up at Prince Korbatsky's house in St. Petersburg. She ran breathlessly up the staircase, calling, "Gregory, Dmitry, Gregory, Dmitry." Only silence answered her.

Back in the coach again she ordered Platon to take her to Sofia Stegorina's house. A maid answered the door at Gorokhovaya Street. "No, princess, Arkady and Sofia are not here. They were supposed to be back yesterday, but the snow has probably blocked their course." Sofia will be ever indebted to our Russian winters, thought Tatyana, and regained the sleigh. She thought and thought. "Platon, though I have never been there, take me to Voznesensky Prospect. We shall pay a visit to the Ryleyevs."

The door to their apartment was answered by Kondraty Ryleyev's wife, Natasha. Tatyana recognized her from the Stegorins' picnic on Krestovsky Island. Madame Ryleyeva held a little girl by the hand. Natasha's large

brown eyes were red and swollen, and Tatyana saw that
she must have been crying.

"We have only met once," said Tatyana rapidly, "at
the solstice picnic last summer. I feel sure you may know
the answer to my question, or I would not have bothered
you. My father and I heard rumors yesterday that there
may be a campaign—maybe even an uprising against
Nicholas." Since Madame Ryleyeva did not seem to look
baffled by her words, Tatyana quickly continued. "I am
looking for my brother, Dmitry Ivanovich, and for Gregory Grandison. I believe you know them both and . . . I
am very worried for them."

The distraught woman nodded. "Yes, I know them
very well. They were even here last night until all hours
with my husband." Now she began to sob. "Theirs is a
hopeless cause. Kondraty Fyodorovich has foreseen his
own death. I cannot bear to think of it."

"Where are they now?" Tatyana demanded, her voice
rising in response to Natasha's disquieting words. "Are
they all planning to help if there should be an insurrection?"

"God forgive your ignorance," exclaimed Natasha
hysterically, and added in a grief-stricken whisper, "They
are the insurrection."

Chapter Sixteen

TATYANA LEANED AGAINST THE DOOR HANDLE TO KEEP her balance while Natasha rambled distractedly on.

"Kondraty at this very moment is out scouring the streets for more recruits. Imagine!" She squeezed her daughter's hand so tightly the child yelped. "Many of the soldiers are still in their barracks and have refused to take the oath to Nicholas."

"They want Constantine that much?"

"No, no, that is just their pretext to set their men against the czar. They want the downfall of the government!" Natasha Ryleyeva put her face in her hand and wiped away her tears.

"They are all in the barracks?" asked Tatyana, for her aim above all was to find Dmitry and Gregory.

Natasha shook her head. "No, the Moscow Guardsmen are in Senate Square. That is where they plan to confront the czar."

Tatyana shivered. "Well then, my brother will be with them." She remembered Senate Square as it had looked that summer, empty and serene, abutted by eighteenth

century facades. A mutiny to take place on its cobblestones? Tatyana began to take her leave.

"Please, please," begged Natasha Ryleyeva. "If you
see my husband, beg him to come home to me."

"I will."

Without waiting another moment, Tatyana resumed
her place in the sleigh. As she gazed back at the
grief-stricken face of Madame Ryleyeva, she commanded Platon, "To Senate Square. Immediately."

The troika whisked up Voznesensky Prospect and past
the Church of St. Isaac, which had still not been completed since the summer. The coach passed scaffolding
erected beside it and drove into the square itself. What
greeted Tatyana's eyes stunned her.

In the middle of the square stood nearly a thousand
soldiers, a mass of plumed shakos, green jackets with red
cuffs and collars, and dark green breeches. These were
the soldiers and officers of the Moscow Foot Guards, and
they had formed themselves into a carré, directly in front
of the equestrian statue of Peter the Great. On their
outskirts stood groups of civilians. When Tatyana left the
coach, she ran across the icy cobblestones to this mass of
people.

The soldiers stood at ease, stamping their feet to shake
the cold. Some were being plied with vodka, sausage,
and bread by the civilians, to help them keep their spirits
up. Many had left their barracks in such a hurry they had
no greatcoats, and Tatyana saw the civilians give them
the coats off their backs. A small meek man in uniform
seemed to be in charge. Tatyana did not recognize any of
them and saw no sign so far of Dmitry, or Gregory, and
none either of Ryleyev or Prince Trubetskoy. As she
searched the crowd, she was distracted by the movements of a young man with handsome features and a
receding chin who stood nearby. He wore a purple frock
coat and kept pacing wildly back and forth beside the

troops, his hand playing on the pistol he had jammed in his belt.

Tatyana heard the thud of horse hooves and turned around to see a horse and rider come cantering out of Admiralty Boulevard and into Senate Square. Tatyana recognized the Governor-General of St. Petersburg, her father's old friend Count Miloradovich. He rode his horse up to the Moscow Foot Guards and pulled his horse to a full stop with absolute authority. He was so close to Tatyana she could see the features of his familiar face, his fine aquiline nose and ruddy complexion.

"Are there any among you who were with me at Borodino, or at Tarutino, when we chased the tails off Bonaparte's Grande Armée? Are there any among you who would trust my word?" he called loudly.

"Here, here," said a few voices from the crowd, and many nodded. Russians were still easily moved by memories of the war against Napoleon, and it was common knowledge that Miloradovich had distinguished himself for the glory of Russia during the campaigns he cited. "We were there," repeated other soldiers enthusiastically.

The general lifted his sword and unsheathed it. Holding it by its golden hilt he read aloud from an inscription on the blade. "'To my brave friend Miloradovich, from the Grand Duke Constantine.' Any of you who wish to may see it."

No one seemed to doubt his word, and he carefully resheathed the sword. At last he spoke. "I too would prefer Constantine as emperor. He is my dear, dear old friend, and as many of you know, an excellent commander. But he has renounced the throne. I saw his manifesto of abdication and all his letters with my own eyes. Nicholas is the czar, and you must all swear your allegiance to him."

Tatyana, like others in the crowd, was increasingly

moved by the simplicity and bravery of the general's words. But the small meek man who seemed vaguely in charge of the Foot Guards seemed displeased. Now he spoke up in a lisping voice.

"Your exthelenthy. You mutht move away. There can be no accounting for acthons taken againtht you by thethe men. Pleathe move off now, Genewal. Your prethenthe can only lead to twouble."

But General Miloradovich had sensed the sympathy within the crowd. He pretended not to hear the young man in charge, who Tatyana later learned was Prince Yevgeny Obolensky. Miloradovich continued to address the troops.

"You must now return to your barracks, my boys, and entreat your comrades to stay there as well. There is still time to save your backs. Return to your barracks at once and carry on with the necessary oath of allegiance to Nicholas."

"I tell you, genewal, be gone fwom here. You are in gweat pewil," called out the diminutive Prince Obolensky.

Still the general ignored Obolensky, and Tatyana saw anger suffuse the prince's narrow face. He grabbed a musket from one of the guardsmen beside him and in his haste and irritation pricked the general's horse behind the saddle. The animal jerked away, forcing Miloradovich to gather up his reins.

A sudden explosion made Tatyana jump, and she saw Miloradovich slump in his saddle. He wobbled in his seat until a couple of Guardsmen lifted him off the horse. Tatyana stared beyond him to the young man wearing the purple frock coat. He held his gun, which was still smoking, triumphantly up in the air. The gaze he fixed on the fallen general was the most resolute and desperate Tatyana had ever seen. It was this look, even more than the gun-shot itself, that disconcerted her. It was this look that convinced her that what was happening out there on the square might become a lot more ferocious than anyone anticipated. From the eyes of the young man it was clear he would, without the least remorse and without cruelty, shoot any and every man who did not share his cause. So here was one of the young *enragés* that Gregory had alluded to at their last meeting. Here was a man who had shot one of Russia's greatest heros. Now Tatyana managed to push herself through the crowd to where the general was being lifted into a hack sleigh.

"Count Miloradovich," said Tatyana, bending over the general. Miloradovich was in great pain from the gunshot wound, but he recognized Prince Korbatsky's lovely daughter. "Tatyana Ivanovna, *Comme c'est étrange de vous retrouver ici en ce moment,*" he said with difficulty, but still using French.

"Our meeting seems less strange than many things that are happening today," said Tatyana. She saw with alarm that the blood was seeping quickly through his richly brocaded military coat. "We must send for a doctor!"

"It is too late for that," muttered the general, who then asked, "Who fired the shot?"

"A man in a purple frock coat."

The general fluttered his eyelids in pain and anger. "A mischiefmaker in civvies? Not a soldier then."

Tatyana kissed his hand and held it. "You, General Miloradovich, who fought so bravely against the monster Bonaparte? No officer or soldier would have raised his gun to you." And tears were collecting in the lids of her eyes. "General, you must not let an assassin take your life!" But even as she spoke she saw the life ebb from the beloved general.

His eyes were slowly opening and closing as his words gradually faded. "There are worse deaths, I imagine, for at least I die under a Russian sky. Ah, well, these rebels, these civvies, these soldiers, perhaps their cause is greater than we suppose. . . ." His words died away. Tatyana gazed into his face, defying that he should die. He must have felt the intensity of her look, for he looked dimly up at her. Her soft, feminine, pretty face became blurry, and he imagined she was his own daughter, and then even his beloved wife. The image of his family appeared evanescent like warm breath in the cold morning air, their faces poised before him, with looks of love and admiration. And then he closed his eyes.

One of Tatyana's tears fell on his hand, which she was still holding. "Quick, you must find a doctor," Tatyana ordered the young Guardsman with the sleigh. Yet she knew that it was too late for that. She gazed after the sleigh as it moved slowly through the crowd that gave way for it. The people looked in at the fallen general with curiosity, unable to decide between a feeling of triumph or dismay.

Tatyana did not wish to stay in the square any longer. She had seen no sign of Gregory or Dmitry. They must still be in the officers' barracks.

Platon's sleigh could not cross through Admiralty Boulevard for already a large crowd was beginning to collect on the eastern side of the square, many of whom had come from the Winter Palace. Instead Tatyana made Platon take her the long way around to where Dmitry's regiment was being quartered. But when they finally arrived there, Tatyana found his battalion was gone and the barracks empty. Feeling disconsolate as she came out the door, she suddenly bumped into a gentleman. "Please forgive me," he said.

"Kondraty Ryleyev," said Tatyana.

It was indeed the poet. He was dressed in civilian clothes but wore no greatcoat, and around his shoulder he wore a soldier's cartridge pouch. His arms were crossed because of the cold, and he was rubbing his hands briskly on his upper sleeves. Tatyana had not particularly liked him on the two occasions she met him, but now she was almost glad to see him, to see a familiar face. Instinctively she touched his arm with her mitten. "I am Tatyana Korbatskaya, we met—"

"Yes, I have often heard of you," he said, suddenly recognizing her, "through Mr. Grandison." He spoke in clipped sentences.

"Your wife is looking for you."

"Yes," said Ryleyev, briskly patting his hands on his sleeves, "but there is one more regiment, the Izmailovsky, that must be rousted from their lethargy and blindness." His words were impassioned, but his tone of voice was serene and inspired. There was in his dark hazel eyes with their thick dark lashes a look that was gentle, but just as determined as in those of the man who had shot Miloradovich. Ryleyev's whole face seemed to be lit up from the inner world of his ideals and reminded Tatyana of the glow of a Chinese lantern.

"I am so worried for all of you," said Tatyana in a hushed whisper.

"There is nothing—nothing to worry about, princess," he said rapidly. "The czar's forces will not attack us. The soldiers are all comrades after all. And by nightfall, many secret sympathizers will come over to our side, even soldiers in the Preobrazhensky Foot Guards. And the public as well—just as we had hoped. They have gotten wind. They will be there. Witnesses."

"Do you think that you can possibly win?" asked Tatyana, not even sure herself what answer she wanted to that question.

Ryleyev looked in her eyes. "No, princess, we cannot win. Mr. Grandison was right to try to dissuade us. We are not organized as we should be. The peasants, who many of us would risk our lives for, have no knowledge that someone is fighting for their rights. No, princess, we will not win." There was not the slightest trace of bitterness of dejection in his voice.

"But then, why fight? Why not give up this madness and go home to your wives and children? We are so worried for you. The czar would still forgive. Nothing has happened yet," said Tatyana urgently.

Ryleyev shook his head. Already he was distracted by the thoughts that impelled him toward the next barracks. "The czar would not forgive us now. And what is the value, the glory of being arrested in our comfortable beds? This will be a grand show, a gift to posterity. The peasants do not know our names today, but they will someday know what we were fighting for."

Tatyana saw by the gleam of his dark hazel eyes that if the young man in the purple frock coat was ready to kill for their cause, Kondraty Ryleyev was ready to die for it.

Tatyana stretched out her arms toward him, and he took her mittens in his bare hands. "I believe I see a glimpse of what Mr. Grandison could not resist in you."

Tatyana was touched at the absurd gallantry of his words, for this was not a moment he would even remember. His thoughts were with his comrades and with their dreams.

"Do you know where Gregory is?" she asked, realizing her time with him was running out.

"I have implored him to go to the English Embassy, where he would be safe. It is madness for him to risk his neck for a country that is not even his. Minds as great as his should be put to use selfishly, in his own country. Even England could use a man of his imagination, of his integrity." He paused, thoughtfully. "That madman is probably in the square."

Tatyana nodded. "That is what I thought you would say."

"I must go," said Ryleyev urgently, and a moment

later Tatyana watched him running down the street, rubbing his arms, as he turned in the direction of the Izmailovsky barracks.

Tatyana returned to Senate Square. It was now surging with people.

Much had happened in the brief interval since her departure. The Marine and Grenadier Guards had joined the insurgent Moscow Foot Guards. But they were being surrounded by troops who had taken the oath of allegiance to Nicholas. In front of the embankment of the Neva River and the Admiralty Building stood two squadrons of Horse Guards, the Chevalier Guards, and the awesome sight of the Preobrazhensky Foot Guards. To Tatyana's left, on the western side of the square, were the Semyonovsky Guardsmen, the very regiment that Nicholas's brother had thrown into prison five years before for lodging an official complaint against their cruel commander. But they too were on the side of the czar. As the figures mounted on both sides, the square seemed crushed by two opposing tides of human life. Though Tatyana could not guess the number, there were fifteen thousand men who stood for Nicholas and government and only three thousand insurgents. The only question now to be answered was how many of the czar's troops would finally betray Nicholas and join the mutinous Guardsmen.

Tatyana's sleigh was barred at the top of Gorokhovaya Street by a young officer who with his company had just returned from swearing-in ceremonies at the Winter Palace. "Madame," he said politely, "you are advised to turn your troika around and return home promptly. Senate Square will soon be no place for a lady."

Tatyana gazed at this young man with sand-colored hair and a blond moustache dressed in the uniform of a lieutenant. It could have been Dmitry standing there.

Instead, her brother was somewhere in the square near Falconet's famous statue. Something in the young man's expression was disarming, and Tatyana asked, "Our new czar will not let it come to blows, will he?"

"It is no one's wish to fight, madame, certainly not the czar's on the first day of his accession." The young lieutenant cast down his eyes. "And not our wish, either. They are our brothers after all."

"My own is somewhere there on the side of the mutineers," said Tatyana, the young officer's gentleness and the peril of the moment inviting intimacies.

"I have three cousins on their side as well," said the young officer, nervously ruffling his sandy hair.

"What are their names?"

"Alexander, Nikolay, and Mikhail Bestuzhev. One is a poet, one is in the Marine Guards, and one, like me, is a member of the Moscow Foot Guards." He spoke calmly, but the timbre of his voice betrayed his torn allegiances. So these are the young men Ryleyev hopes to win over to their side when the sun goes down, thought Tatyana. "What does the czar hope will happen?" she now asked, as she leaned on the open window of the sleigh.

"That a show of arms on his side, and the rebels' own fatigue and hunger, will make them rethink their actions and so surrender. But I think he is also afraid. He is loathe to put the loyalty of the Guard to the test unless he has to."

"Will he have to?"

The young man shook his head gloomily. "He will if the rest of the insurgents are like my cousins."

Or like Dmitry, thought Tatyana.

She took her leave of the anxious young lieutenant but ordered Platon to take her to the Galernaya Quay. This would give her access to the square and put her closest to the mutineers. Platon implored her not to, making signs of the cross as he did so, but Tatyana would not be swayed. She was going into the square, and nobody, not even the czar himself, would keep her out of it.

"Let me at least accompany you, I beg you, little mother," said Platon when they arrived there, thinking of what the prince would say when he learned his coachman had assisted the princess in her folly. "I beg you little mother, stay, and if you won't, let me go with you." Even now he could hear sporadic musket shots going off in the square, and his horses shied.

"Absolutely not. Drive to the Stegorins' house, give the horses a rest, have something to eat, and wait for me there." And then she added with naive valor, "I am going to get Dmitry and Gregory out of there." The next moment she had disappeared into the mass of people.

Now that she was immersed in it, Tatyana could tell how much the feeling of the crowd had changed since morning. The citizens who had at first been merely inquisitive, now noisily voiced their approval of the outnumbered mutineers. Many hung from lampposts, drinking and cheering them.

Through the crowd could be heard the shout, "Constantine and constitution. Down with Nicholas, the false czar." The stonemasons who were perched up in the scaffolding of St. Isaac's Church were also abusing the czar's men. "Brass blockheads," they jeered loudly when new breast-plated troops marched into the square and joined the czar. They pelted the soldiers as they passed with stones and hunks of wood torn from the scaffolding.

Pushing her way slowly through the motley crowd, Tatyana kept her eye on the statue of Peter the Great. For if Dmitry or Gregory were in the square at all, near the statue is where they would be.

Nicholas must have become worried about the increasing rancor of the crowd, for orders were made to clear the square with a charge of cavalry. Tatyana's heart leapt up into her throat at the ominous line of men in their red-trimmed white jerkins and copper-colored breast plates. They looked regal and forbidding mounted on their jet black horses in front of the Admiralty Canal. They drew their sabers and prepared to charge.

"Oh, please God, make Nicholas wait," prayed Tatyana, for she was now halfway through the crowd and it was too late to retreat. "And please God, protect Mitya, and Gregory, please be in the British Embassy!"

But the insurgents, seeing the gleaming sabers, now began to fire their guns overhead. A command was given, the horses' hindquarters dropped in that instant before breaking into a canter, and suddenly the line of black horses started forward. The crowd began to sway but then stayed put, and the sound of laughter rose into the air. Tatyana looked back at them and saw that all the horses were slipping and stumbling on the patches of ice and snow on the cobblestones. After a few ineffectual charges and musters, the cavalry retreated to the taunts of the crowd.

Tatyana's prayers seemed to have been answered, and now she pushed through the mass of people more ardently than before. But the going was difficult. The thaw of midday and the slush underfoot had begun to freeze as the afternoon wore on, and Tatyana's progress was slowed. Many soldiers and civilians made lewd remarks as she passed. For her sable pelisse trimmed with ermine, her bearing, and her beauty proclaimed her high station, and she might have been herself a member of the royal family. Vodka had loosened their tongues and latent class hostility. But Tatyana ignored their catcalls; something else worried her far more. Though it was only mid-afternoon, the sun was quickly setting, and soon it would be dusk. Not only would she not be able to find Dmitry or Gregory if they were there, but this strange standoff would have to be resolved. By the looks of the crowd, there might be no peaceful resolution. She must at all costs find Dmitry and Gregory and somehow get them out of the square. This was the thought she kept repeating to herself as she stumbled through the people pressing her on all sides, and over the lumpy cobblestones. When Tatyana had come within yards of the insurgent guardsmen, she suddenly caught sight of her brother. Her heart soared with relief. He was standing in uniform beside Prince Obolensky, and though he was still a distance from her, his voice carried. Tatyana heard him shout, "Yevgeny, we must seize their cannons. Now they mean business. We will be blown to bits!" Now Tatyana saw the czar's four large cannons had been wheeled up Admiralty Boulevard and were being positioned.

"They will not fire on us, we mutht wait for darkness, printhe," argued Prince Obolensky.

"Mitya, Mitya," called Tatyana, but since she was downwind he didn't hear her. Now with desperation she made her way toward him.

Across the square stood the czar, who was mounted on horseback. He looked irritably toward the Senate building and behind toward the yellow-gray light of the setting sun. Already the square was beginning to darken. "We have given them enough warning, and we have waited long enough. Prepare to fire!" He waited for his orders to be followed and adjusted the blue ribbon of St. Andrew that spanned diagonally across his chest. The czar was doubly angered because the Izmailovsky Foot Guards, of which he was commander, had not even appeared on the square. It was not a brilliant way to ascend the throne. "A fine way to begin my reign," he muttered under his breath. "Gun number one, gun number one!" he commanded.

There was a long silence.

"Why the devil are my orders not being followed?" demanded Nicholas of his aide-de-camp.

The answer came back. "They do not wish to fire upon their comrades."

"I will repeat my orders a second time, and that is all I will repeat them," said the czar through compressed lips. "My orders are to be followed, unquestioningly, and those who do not obey will be court-martialed."

His order was repeated a second time to the master gunner in charge of gun number one. The young man held the wick, unable to ignite the firing pan. He let it burn in his cold, trembling hand.

"Fire, I said," shouted his captain.

"I cannot, your honor, I cannot," said the young gunner, and tears began to stream down his cheeks.

"You don't deserve the epaulets upon your shoulders," barked the commanding officer. It was Vasily Turburov. Grabbing the wick from the gunner, Vasily struck the firing pan himself. It ignited easily, and the square suddenly rocked with a huge boom.

Unfortunately for Vasily Turburov, the guns had been deliberately aimed away from the crowd by the sympathetic gunners, so the shot went wide. The first cannonball hit the second floor of the Senate building. Windows crashed. Tatyana, who had nearly reached her brother, looked up aghast toward the Senate building. But her eyes were distracted by something that made her heart leap to her mouth more than the sound of the boom. Directly in her view, only twenty feet away from her, she saw him. "Gregory!" she said, almost swallowing his name in her excitement.

There he was, so close to her, that profile that she adored standing in the anonymous crowd. He had not seen her.

"Gregory, Gregory," she called, but her voice was drowned out by the burst of a second cannon. The cannonball landed on the edge of the square, sending up a cloud of smoke, dust, and snow into the chilly air.

"Damn it to heaven," swore Count Vasily at his artillerymen. "Aim those cannons into the crowd, or you'll know what's good for you!" His orders were now obeyed.

Tatyana pushed through the crowd toward Gregory and called him again. But a third cannon sounded and this time landed in the center of the square. Until that moment, no one had moved or reacted to the cannon explosions. But with a fourth cannonball fired immediately on the heels of the other, people began to scream. Now the insurgent Guardsmen fired their muskets back.

One person after another began to fall with each blast, and Tatyana saw a man hurtled backward onto the icy cobblestones. His warm, red blood creaked and hissed as it hit the cold snow. Tatyana's eyes strained for Gregory. But now the whole crowd had begun to shift, and she could no longer see him. Panic-stricken men and women, some of whom had their children with them, began to run in every direction.

The czar's troops, irritable from standing in the icy weather and from dodging missiles thrown at them by the crowd during so many hours, now threw themselves into their tasks. The rebels were no longer their brothers and their comrades-at-arms with whom they shared their barracks and the agony and glory of having fought side by side at Austerlitz and Borodino. They were now simply the enemy of the czar, the enemy of Russia. The Guardsmen fired directly into the crowd.

"Mitya," shrieked Tatyana, for just then another cannon sounded and she saw her brother disappear in a blast of dark smoke. Her legs wobbled, but she tried to press forward to where he had fallen.

Now though, all independent movement was impossible. The crowd saw with desperation that they were hemmed in on all sides of the square by government troops. Now the only chance of escape was to break through the cordon of troops near the embankment and head for the frozen Neva. The tide of human life shifted with sudden energy in this direction, and Tatyana found herself shoved backward with it toward the river. Throwing all ideals aside, every human life now sought to save itself.

"No, no," she yelled. "Mitya, Mitya, where are you?" She tried ferociously to fight the relentless pushing of terrified people.

Women shrieked and men grappled over each other to escape the red bursts from the troops that fired into them. As Tatyana fought to return to where her brother had fallen, she was suddenly shoved hard. In an instant she lost her balance and was swept under the stamping feet of the crowd.

Chapter Seventeen

TATYANA MIGHT HAVE BEEN TRAMPLED BUT FOR AN ARM that reached down and, encircling her waist, lifted her up in the crowd.

"I'd hoped I was the only one going to sweep you off your feet," was the sardonic voice in her ear. Tatyana looked up at the man who had rescued her. "Gregory!" She sighed, seeing his handsome face full of the contrary signs of cynicism and relief. She longed to kiss him but felt too weak, "Gregory please forgive—"

"There's no time now for touching reconciliations," he yelled in her ear. "And it's too late for heroism. We must go with the tide. Hang on to me."

Tatyana felt herself wafted along, with Gregory holding her up through the mass of thronging people. She clung with all her might to his greatcoat, like a baby oppossum to its mother. Gregory's presence and strength seemed to lessen the terror that surged around them. But her exhaustion, hunger, and the ordeal of the day began to spin in her head, and Gregory felt her mitten loosen on him. Tatyana had fainted. He picked her up in his arms and at last got her away from the crowd and beside the embankment.

The whiteness of the Neva stretched before them in the dusk, and people began to stream across it. Gregory stopped briefly to see a platoon of insurgent Guardsmen rally on the ice and form a column. But this was useless. Already the czar's artillerymen had rolled the cannons up the embankment and were firing onto the frozen surface of the river. The cannonballs thudded on the ice, and the shrieks spiraled into the twilight air as people struggled helplessly in the freezing water. Tears welled up in Gregory's eyes at the sight of this. Does Nicholas have no sense of moderation? he wondered, as he saw Platon the coachman waiting on the side.

When Tatyana opened her eyes, she found herself in a moving sleigh rolling along in the darkness. She realized it was her father's, the same one she had come in. The afternoon's events rolled groggily into her mind, and she suddenly sat up rigidly in her seat. She rapped on the little window, and when the sleigh came to a stop, she jumped out. Platon was driving the sleigh, and it looked as if they were on the outskirts of the city.

"Platon, where is Mr. Grandison? Where are you taking me?"

"To safety, little mother. Praise our Father in Heaven you are alive and safe. To safety now, at Mr. Grandison's orders."

"But where is he?"

"He's in the square, little mother. To see if he can help the last of the rebels."

"And you let him?" demanded Tatyana, stamping her furry boot.

Platon nervously adjusted the beaver hat on his head. "I told him he courted the Devil, but he refused to listen to me—an old coachman of no account."

"Well, then, I'll court the Devil, too. Take me back to the square."

Platon quickly crossed himself. "You don't mean that little mother," he said, fearing a thunderbolt would come out of the sky and strike his sleigh. "I cannot take you back to the square. It is not safe there. Oh, little mother, hundreds are dead." And Platon started sobbing.

"Very well, then I will go back alone," said Tatyana, and she started to march off down the ill-lit street in the direction of the center of the city.

"No, little mother, let me take you," begged Platon, desperate at the sight of the young princess stalking back alone to that scene of carnage. Soon Platon was urging the troika back along the streets to Senate Square, and inside sat the exhausted princess with the will of iron.

Near the end of the English Embankment the sleigh could go no farther. Tatyana jumped from the sledge and told Platon to wait for her. It had grown dark now. In the moonlight she walked along the bank and saw Guardsmen dragging what looked like bodies across the frozen surface of the river and then push them down the holes in the ice. This seemed impossible, but now she came upon the square itself. The silhouette of Peter the Great rose up immovable in the darkness, unruffled by what had just taken place under his gaze. At the feet of the statue and all around the square lay bodies of the dead and wounded. There were soldiers, men, women, and children, and even a few dead horses. Some groaned pitifully on the blood-stained ice.

As Tatyana stared with disbelief upon the scene, she saw soldiers walk about, picking up the bodies, even some of those which were still moving, and lug them toward the river. The full horror of what was happening in the silver light of the moon was only deadened by the cold which had entrenched itself in Tatyana's body.

Her feet felt on fire. She walked forward dully. "Mitya," she whispered hopefully into the darkness as she passed the bodies stretched out on the ice. None of them answered. Her fingers trembling, she turned a couple of them over, expecting to see the face of her dead brother. But she did not find Dmitry.

Then she looked up across the square beyond the statue and saw a man kneeling over a fallen figure. The man raised himself onto his knees, and something in the movement sent a geyser of warmth through Tatyana. With a last burst of energy she ran toward him. It was Gregory. He looked up and recognized her in the moonlight.

"My brave and foolish princess," he said tiredly, "I thought I'd sent you to safety." He opened his arms to her.

"Gregory," said Tatyana desperately, "What happened today . . . will you ever forgive me? I never want to leave you. . . ."

Then she saw he was holding bandages and she looked down at the body.

"Mitya?" she whispered hoarsely.

Gregory shook his head, but his eyes strayed to the embankment and the luminous Neva.

"Is he dead?" Tatyana asked.

"I don't know," answered Gregory. "I looked but I couldn't find him." He went back to bandaging the man's head. "Many are dead," he said.

"Yes, Gregory, even women and children. They are pushing them under the ice in the river."

Gregory nodded.

Tatyana shook him in terror and frustration. "Gregory, Gregory. There is nothing you can do about it. None of it is your fault. You never meant for it to come to this. Come, come at once, while there's still time. The sledge and Platon are waiting."

Gregory covered her mouth with his hand. "Shhhhh," he said gently. He bent back over the wounded man.

Tatyana saw at the end of the square a contingent of soldiers making their way through the bodies.

"You see," said Gregory, without lifting his head. "It is too late for that. But you can help me."

"How?" begged Tatyana. He handed her a roll of lint. She gazed at the oncoming soldiers, then at Gregory's tired but resolute expression as the moonlight showed all the curves and hollows of his face. With a trembling hand she took the roll of lint and slowly began to unravel it. Gregory continued carefully to bandage the young insurgent's head. Tatyana began to sob, and the approaching soldiers flickered and danced through her tears.

"My poor naive child," said Gregory. "You are so tired and have been so brave already. Let me take this from you."

"No," said Tatyana obdurately, pushing her tears away with the back of her mittens. "I want to stay and help you."

"Good girl," said Gregory, and they both unrolled the bandages and helped the wounded until the soldiers came to get Gregory.

They walked up to him across the ice and addressed him in French. *"Votre nom, monsieur?"*

"Gregory Grandison," he answered calmly, and he went on with his work.

"You are under arrest and must come with us."

Gregory asked, "What is the charge?" But something in his tone seemed rhetorical.

"You are charged with aiding and abetting the members of the Decembrist conspiracy in their uprising," was the mechanical answer.

"Decembrist conspiracy?" he said with a half-mocking smile. "Not inaccurate I suppose, since we are within the last month of the year." He paused and asked serenely, "Have you a warrant?"

The soldiers paused, discomfited by this question. Then one of them said angrily, "We are charged by the czar, Nicholas himself, and you will be interrogated in the Winter Palace."

"Ah, then of course there is nothing else you need," he said, gazing up at their stiff, earnest faces. Having finished the bandaging, he now stood up. He turned to Tatyana. "Now I must go with these gentlemen."

Tatyana clung to his arm. "Oh, Gregory, please . . ."

Gregory glanced at the soldiers. "May I have a word with this lady?"

They nodded and Gregory drew her aside. "Now that I am being taken off to prison, what are these last confessions you have for me?" His voice was tired, yet ironic.

"Gregory, please understand—" Tatyana whispered ardently.

"Understand why you drove off from Senate Square on an August day and never returned?"

"Oh, but Gregory, I loved you all along, though sometimes I didn't know it. You hurt me—I had to learn from my father all your high ideals were contributing to a secret society against the czar. And he told me you were a spy. And then, when I saw you on my name day, you still wouldn't abandon this society, though I begged you—"

"I see I must never underestimate your pride or your patriotism," he said in a soft sardonic tone. "Did you come today to St. Petersburg then at your father's wishes?"

"Oh, Gregory don't be cruel, when I am about to lose you again. I didn't even tell my father I was coming. I knew he would try to stop me."

"Then why did you come?" Gregory challenged quietly.

"Gregory, I was so worried for you both."

"At the eleventh hour?" he chided her.

Now the soldiers stepped forward. "You must now come with us. There are other suspects to be rounded up."

As they handcuffed him, Tatyana pleaded, "Gregory, did I come too late for you?" The tears began to roll down and freeze upon her cheeks.

Just then the bells of St. Isaac's began to chime in the darkness. And Gregory, though he was handcuffed, leaned forward and kissed her on the lips, a long lingering kiss to make up for all the kissing they had wasted in three months.

When their lips parted he whispered, "No, Tatyana, you did not come too late, for since the eleventh hour, what an hour we have shared." His voice, still rueful, but now touched with a certain sad triumph, lingered in the frozen air, while under the moonlight Gregory was escorted by the soldiers to the Winter Palace.

Tatyana's dreams were frightening in the oblique way of nightmares that skim the surface of half-waking. Tatyana woke to the sound of someone crying, a distant echo of grief that threaded its way into her sleep.

She opened her eyes and looked at the high white ceiling. I am at Sofia's, she thought mechanically, but she was aware of something unpleasant that plagued her without remembering what it was. She felt drugged but groped in her mind for what made her feel so ill at ease. Something is wrong, she remembered. It was the crying that reminded her.

She climbed out of bed, so quickly she lost her footing, careened, and fell back on the eiderdown. The crying continued. Tatyana did not even reach for her dressing gown but rose again, and on shaky legs ran to the sound which came from down the hall. At the end of the corridor the morning light flooded the elegant lilac sitting room where Sofia Stegorina spent her mornings at embroidery or reading.

But this morning Sofia sat bent over the Madame Récamier sofa, her face in her hands. She was sobbing. When she looked up at Tatyana her face was puffy and streaked with tears. Her eyelashes glistened.

Tatyana ran to her. "Arkady?"

Sofia nodded. "They took him away this morning."

"But he didn't even participate in the insurrection."

"I know. He was desperate that we were snowbound yesterday, and when we arrived last night, he ran to the square. He went to help the insurgents on the ice, but it was too late."

As Tatyana gazed on Sofia she now remembered that it was Sofia who had come out the night before in search of Arkady with Platon at her side, who had come to entreat her help. They had found Tatyana wandering in a daze about the square. She had been going from one body to the next, murmuring her brother's name, and sometimes Gregory's.

It was Sofia who had brought Tatyana home to her house and put her to bed. Not once had Sofia mentioned her own terrible fears for Arkady, who had not reappeared till the early morning hours. He had arrived too late to help his friends in their uprising and so had spent the night trying to help some escape.

"The police were here when he returned and took him to the Winter Palace for interrogation. Hundreds have been placed under arrest." Sofia's voice quavered. "The punishment for all of them will be severe." She sat still, holding her breath. A moment later, she flung out a silk-draped arm. "No, I cannot bear to think of it!" She was sobbing again. She flailed her arms around as if to

fight off a terrible army of thoughts that threatened to
crush her. Tatyana grabbed Sofia.

"Stop it, Sofia. Stop it!" Tatyana commanded and
pushed her firmly back onto the couch. "Arkady would
be grieved to see you so," Tatyana added urgently,
remarking Sofia's protruding stomach now eight and a
half months pregnant. She was worried what a hysterical
outburst could do to Sofia's health and the unborn baby.
"You must think of the baby, Arkady's baby!"

Tatyana's urgent words calmed Sofia. She subsided
back into her seat and began to pluck aimlessly at the
dressing gown that draped over her belly. Then she
rubbed her stomach. "Poor baby, poor little baby," she
murmured as she began to rock on the couch. She
seemed to find solace in the reminder of what she carried
within her, a testament to the love between her and her
husband.

Soon the lilac room was quiet. Tatyana sank down
beside Sofia. The two women wove their arms about
each other's waists, and both rocked gently, basking like
wounded animals in the winter sunlight. Tatyana finally
spoke again and said in a hollow voice, "I think that
Mitya is dead."

Sofia squeezed her. "No, Tanya, maybe not, maybe
not." But she did not add that even Arkady had found no
sign of Tatyana's brother the night before.

Finally Tatyana sighed out loud and stood up. "I must
go see Gregory."

Sofia turned her gentle gray eyes, which were now
bloodshot, on her friend. "By now they will all be in the
fortress." She whispered this last word as if she hardly
dared speak the name.

The Fortress of Saints Peter and Paul was the prison
situated on the Island of Hares, across the Neva from the
Winter Palace. The fortress had been built by Peter the

Great and was notorious for its deep dungeons built
below sea level and surrounded by walls ten feet thick.
No one had ever escaped from it, and many had died
within its walls.

But Tatyana did not flinch at the word. "Yes, I know,"
she said dully. "You stay here, Sofia, and take care of
yourself and the baby for the time being. I will go to the
fortress to see Gregory and inquire about Arkady."

"Thank you," whispered Sofia.

Tatyana kissed her on the forehead and left Sofia
rocking in the sunlight and rubbing her belly while she
crooned a lullaby to Arkady's unborn child.

Tatyana, who had been half-mad the night before,
suddenly became very businesslike. She wrote a short
letter of explanation to her father and sent Platon back to
Starlina with it. Then she hired a sledge to take her to the
fortress. The sledge had to pass through Senate Square
to reach the Island of Hares. Tatyana's bleary face looked
out on the pristine whiteness of the square. It did not look
as if an uprising had taken place there only the night
before. There were no bodies, not even bloodstains in
the snow. Even the broken windows of the Senate
building had been replaced. Tatyana almost fancied, and
longed to fancy, that what had happened on December
fourteenth was only a lurid figment of her imagination.
Why was there no trace of the insurrection?

The sledge turned east along the English Embankment. Here too, the night before, Tatyana had seen the
soldiers pushing the bodies through holes in the ice of the
river. But of this, too, there was no trace, and all she saw
was the smooth and placid surface of the frozen Neva.
They crossed the Troitsky Bridge to the Island of Hares.
Before her the outer walls of the fortress with their soft
pink hue looked strangely beautiful. And the cathedral
dome within the fortress gleamed in the winter sun. Its
slender gold spire pointed loftily into the blue sky.

Tatyana was driven through the great stone arch with its stone medallion of the Romanov double eagle.

Once inside the fortress, Tatyana identified herself to the guard on duty. He told her Mr. Grandison was being held in the Alexis Ravelin. From the little Tatyana had heard, this could not be a good sign. The most suspect of all political prisoners were usually imprisoned and forgotten within the walls of this compound. But Tatyana took solace from the one thought that had been brewing in her mind all morning: that Gregory was an Englishman, and though not a diplomat, might be subject to the allowances of diplomatic immunity.

After an hour's wait, a guard led Tatyana down a dark hall and down a flight of steps into a cold and dank stone corridor that curved as they walked along it. Water dripped from the walls.

"Why does the water drip?" asked Tatyana of the guard.

"We are now under the Neva, princess," he answered.

At the end of the curving corridor, past a number of cells, they came to a door which was covered by a curtain of dark green felt, and it was covered with moss. The guard unlocked the door, which grated as he opened it, and they entered the darkened cell. The guard lifted up his lantern.

"Prisoner, you have a visitor."

Tatyana peered into the humid darkness and heard nothing but silence. Then there was the creak of someone rising from a bed and the clank of chains. The haggard face of Gregory emerged through the gloom.

Chapter Eighteen

BY THE SOLITARY FLAME OF THE GUARD'S LANTERN, Gregory leaned stiffly over and kissed Tatyana's hand. She was too shocked to move. Then she put her arms around him.

In his memory, grown dim from recent turmoil and present pain, Gregory recalled the way Tatyana had reached for her brother on his arrival, exactly a year ago. And he remembered for the first time, even though he denied the thought then, that he had wished that Tatyana would someday clasp him that ardently. Now, in this wretched, cold cell, she was doing so.

Tatyana looked at the guard to see if he would leave them in peace. "What is he waiting for?" she asked in her rusty, stilted English, which Gregory had never heard before. She had spoken in Gregory's language so the guard would not understand her.

"He is waiting for a little gift," said Gregory tiredly.

"A . . . bribe?"

Gregory nodded.

Tatyana quickly opened her reticule and with a look of

surprise handed a gold imperial to the guard. He looked
at the valuable coin with admiration and promptly left. As
soon as they were alone, Tatyana took Gregory's face in
her hands.

"What have they done to you?" she demanded,
seeing the bruises on his forehead and on his chin.

Gregory reached up and clasped Tatyana's hands in
his own. His fingers were cold as a dead man's.

"What have they done to you?" Tatyana repeated in
alarm.

"Nothing that any one of the other prisoners hasn't
been subjected to. Ten hours of interrogation, no sleep,
no blanket, and no windows or lights. I cannot even
read," and he added with irreverent irony, "And yes, I'm
fettered."

Tatyana stared hard at him. "You will be unfettered,"
she announced in the autocratic way she sometimes used
when she felt cornered.

Gregory laughed softly. "You passionate, determined
little thing. You think my freedom can be gained so easily,
even if you are one of the great Korbatskys?"

Tatyana nodded fiercely and helped him sit down.
"Yes, I am going to the British Embassy. We will have you
out of this hideous place in no time."

"The British Embassy can make overtures, but my
release depends entirely on the will of the new czar."

Tatyana's voice lifted. "Well, that is a very good thing.
He will pardon you all, and you, as an English citizen, he
will turn over to the embassy. Nicholas will be compas-
sionate, he will understand you were motivated from
high ideals."

Gregory was touched at the naiveté that still beamed
from the beautiful wide planes of her face. She loved the
czar, even after what had happened yesterday, and was
still devoid of cynicism. "I'm afraid I don't think the czar
will pardon any of us, at least not to begin with," he said,

shaking his weary head. "It was he who interrogated us last night at the Winter Palace."

"And he was not at all sympathetic?"

Gregory snorted at this remark, recalling the humiliating scene that had taken place in the palace. All the Decembrists, as they had been dubbed overnight, had been taken before the czar and questioned. Even men who had not had anything to do with the secret societies for several years. There were rumors that even Alexander Pushkin, who had only sent sympathetic letters to some of the Decembrists, might be arrested.

The czar's anger and bad humor were to have been expected. But Gregory flinched as he recalled the paranoia and pettiness Nicholas had also exhibited. The new czar was not a man who would mete out justice impartially. He would bestow favors and dispense punishment with startling cruelty and capriciousness.

"Was it not at the czar's orders that the dead and even the wounded were pushed through the ice of the Neva last night?" he observed coldly. "And this morning it was announced that only two people had been killed by government forces, and only thirty-three wounded."

"Two people," said Tatyana. "But that is impossible. I saw the bodies lying there with my own eyes. It looked like scores, at least."

"No, not scores, ignorant child, but hundreds, and most of them dead. Tell me, what does the square look like this morning?"

Tatyana recalled the pristine orderliness of the square when she had passed it that morning. "Gregory, it looked as if . . . there had never been an insurrection."

"Precisely, and that is what the czar wants everyone to think. What happened yesterday, in which hundreds were killed, is only a dream. I saw it in Nicholas's eyes that night of the ball in the Winter Palace."

Tatyana was astounded by what Gregory had explained. Gregory was feeling cynical for other reasons as well, and now he voiced them. In a seeming non sequitur he demanded, "You met Prince Sergei Trubetskoy, didn't you?"

"Yes, at the Winter Ball, and at the Stegorins' picnic," said Tatyana vaguely, still mulling over Gregory's previous comment about the new czar.

"Prince Trubetskoy never even showed up on the square yesterday."

"Was he supposed to?" asked Tatyana.

"He was to be the provisional president of their new republic, chosen for his calm and bravery for that position. Instead he went and locked himself in at the Austrian Embassy." He paused. "Apparently the Austrian ambassador is a relative of his wife's."

"Prince Trubetskoy who wears the Cross of St. George?"

"The very same. And then, when Trubetskoy was arrested, he groveled at the feet of Nicholas and gave the czar his comrades' names."

Tatyana found this a revelation. "Prince Trubetskoy?" she repeated doubtfully.

"Even a prince can have the scruples of a pauper," said Gregory bitterly, distressed that Trubetskoy had abandoned his ideals as fast as he had abandoned his friends. "And another mutineer, named Yakubovich, swore allegiance to the czar and to the mutineers and then incited both sides to fight each other. Yet, when interrogated, he would not inform on anybody. Curious."

Gregory ran his hand through his hair, a gesture familiar to Tatyana when he was upset or deep in thought.

"But you know, Ryleyev was indefatigable, and even Arkady, when he finally arrived. The Bestuzhev brothers —how remarkable they were at the end. No one knew what to do—whether to fight the czar in Senate Square or try to storm the Winter Palace or even to run and hide. But the Bestuzhevs took the last remains of the Moscow Foot Guards out onto the ice and fought back, even with the cannons facing them." Tatyana listened to this with interest, as she remembered meeting the young cousin of the Bestuzhevs the night before. She wondered briefly whether he would now be ashamed or proud. "Last night, too, they behaved with honor throughout the interrogation." Gregory's earnestness dissolved into a laugh. "And even my giddy Anatole. There he was, just as the cannons were put into position. That little Frenchman pushed through the crowd, shouting, 'Monsieur, you must not be out without your muffler!' and he was waving my yellow scarf at me."

"Is he all right?"

"I haven't seen him, but he must be. The scarf was delivered to me this morning."

Tatyana laughed softly at the valet's allegiance.

Still Gregory was pondering the behavior of his Russian comrades. "I will never understand you people," he remarked with almost affectionate wryness. "Last night that crazy man Kakhovsky, even after he was arrested for shooting poor General Miloradovich, stood up before the czar and demanded he release all the serfs."

Tatyana smiled, but Gregory noticed by the candle flame that she was silent. "You haven't asked about Dmitry," he said gently.

Tatyana impulsively clapped her hand on Gregory's mouth. "I cannot, I cannot ask." Tatyana's voice trembled.

Gregory understood. "I know it is not from want of feeling, my curious girl."

After a moment's silence she asked, "He has not been found?"

Gregory shook his head. "Not as of this morning. But perhaps he will."

"Yes," said Tatyana, stifling a sob, "when the ice melts on the Neva." She had lifted Gregory's hands to her mouth, and when she said this, the tears she had long suppressed came gushing out onto his hands. They were hot and salty as she kissed his fingertips with grief. "My father was so cruel," she swallowed. "He said if Dmitry fought, he would have to pay the consequences. Oh, Gregory!" Having been strong all morning, she finally could no longer contain herself and cried on the shoulders of the one person who could be stronger.

"There, there, Tatyana," said Gregory, stroking her hair. And a little later he confided, "Do you know, I became your brother's friend for all the wrong reasons. Because I was flattered by his admiration for me. It was only within the last few months I came to see his great strengths." He paused. "Of all the young men yesterday who fought in Senate Square against injustice, Dmitry was the bravest."

Tatyana went to the British Embassy and was granted an interview with the ambassador's secretary. The young diplomat politely assured Tatyana that as an English citizen Gregory Grandison would be put under their jurisdiction. He would be safe from any drastic consequences of the Decembrists' uprising. The secretary felt sure Mr. Grandison would be released shortly and that his detention in the fortress was just a matter of protocol. No, there should be no problem, he reassured her, and they would make inquiries. This was the general tone of the brief interview. Tatyana was told she could come back at the end of the week and they should have an answer for her then. Tatyana felt a great weight taken off her shoulders.

The next few days she spent traveling to and from the

Peter and Paul Fortress, bringing Gregory a pen and some paper and a silver candlestick from Sofia's house. He was not allowed books, at the czar's particular order. Nicholas had agreed to the first two amenities after the first angry day when he had denied the Decembrists any considerations. Now he seemed to take a zealous interest in meticulously overseeing the restrictions and gratuities allowed or withheld from each prisoner. But the errands Tatyana made for Gregory kept her occupied and her mind off Dmitry as well as the fate of the other Decembrists imprisoned in the fortress. Reassured by the British Embassy, Tatyana was no longer worried for Gregory, and she turned her extra attention to Sofia, who was in an anxious state about Arkady.

That Friday Tatyana returned to the embassy and sat serenely in the oak-paneled waiting room outside the ambassador's offices. At last a clerk approached her. "Princess Korbatskaya, this way please," and he led her again into the secretary's handsome office.

At last the secretary emerged through a side door. He seemed somehow embarrassed to see the princess there, and he rubbed his temples with a handkerchief.

"Yes, yes, yes," he said, as she reminded him of why she had come, smiling confidently at him. "The Gregory Grandison affair. Yes, yes, yes." He rubbed his temple. "Very troubling."

"Troubling?" questioned Tatyana.

The secretary rubbed his forehead again. "Princess, we have had some difficulties making inquiries of him," he said.

"I don't understand."

"It is rather unusual, I'll admit, but the czar's representatives will give no confirmation of Mr. Grandison's incarceration. Therefore, we are not yet in a position to proceed in requesting his release."

"But he is imprisoned in the Alexis Ravelin," said

Tatyana taken aback. "I have visited him several times myself."

"I do not doubt your word, princess. We are speaking of official confirmation of his status."

"I thought he would be released within a day or so," said Tatyana, at a loss.

The secretary raised his eyebrows while he touched them with his handkerchief. "From the little we have heard here at the embassy, several days appears to be unrealistic, dear lady. There is reason to believe that many who have been arrested will be confined until a committee submits a report to the czar."

"How long would that take? Several weeks?"

The secretary mopped his brow. "Probably much longer. Estimates are that the procedures could be very time-consuming. It may take as much as three to four months." He leaned forward in his seat and lowered his voice. "I beg your pardon, but we are in Russia, after all."

Tatyana stared at the secretary. "Mr. Grandison is an Englishman. Surely he will not be tried in a Russian court along with the other Decembrists?" She had begun to twist the gold chain around her neck.

The secretary beamed. "Oh no, princess. Mr. Grandison will certainly be turned over to our authority to be returned to England. Timing is the only issue. The palace is in an uproar, as can be easily imagined. So his release may simply take longer than expected. We have to go through the proper channels, as you understand, I'm sure. If you will wait a few more days, we will see what we can do for you."

That afternoon, after Tatyana returned from the embassy, a letter was waiting for her at the Stegorins'. It was from her father. Platon had delivered it and now stood nervously by, adjusting his beaver hat on his head.

Tatyana opened the letter and saw her father's familiar scrawl.

Daughter:

I am instructing Platon to bring you home as soon as this letter is in your hands. The news of the uprising in Senate Square leaves us all aghast and humiliated that the sons of our finest families could stage such an absurd and criminal event, notwithstanding that it backfired. Thank God that Russia has a few sensible men at least. You should be proud of your fiancé, who distinguished himself in quelling the mutineers.

As you may know, Dmitry took part in the event, but on the side of the conspirators. He is reported dead, and from what I hear of the punishment to be meted out to these criminals, his own fate must be regarded as an act of clemency. That your brother, a Korbatsky, could so betray me, his family, his name, his country, is unfathomable to me. As far as I am concerned, your brother does not exist, even in memory. I bid you never to speak his name again.

Tatyana's heart ached at her father's callousness and cruelty, but she continued the letter:

I am astounded to say that rumors have reached me to the effect that Mr. Grandison, the man who dragged your you-know-what into all this rebel's mess, has received visits from you at the fortress. These visits will of course cease, and once you are back at Starlina you must never have any correspondence with him again. He is going to be in a lot more trouble than you think.

We must now put the past behind us. I will speak to you further on this matter when you arrive home.

It is time you were married, and we must go forward with our plans.

Ivan Dmitrievich Korbatsky

Sofia's plea that Tatyana remain until her baby was delivered rose in Tatyana's mind when she finished her father's letter. Sofia's condition was too risky just now, compounded with her worry about Arkady. So Tatyana resolutely dipped her pen in ink and wrote the following note:

Dearest father,

I have received your letter this morning. Unfortunately, I cannot return today with Platon, or for several days yet. Sofia Stegorina's interesting condition promises to resolve itself most happily within the next few days. The turbulent events have badly unnerved her, and her delivery may not be an easy one. She has begged me to stay by her side. Her husband, Arkady, has also been arrested, and she needs me here. I will be home, father, as soon as I can.

Please understand and believe me.

Your loving daughter,
Tatyana Ivanovna

Tatyana made no mention of Gregory Grandison, her brother, or the wedding plans. There would be time enough to discuss these things when she returned to Starlina. She sighed, enclosed the letter in an envelope, and delivered it to Platon. I hope he will understand and forgive me, she thought, and she went to see Sofia in her sitting room.

The days dragged by, and Sofia's pregnancy went on

until Tatyana grew concerned. In addition, St. Petersburg learned that a second insurrection had taken place near Moscow. Though its ringleader, who was Pavel Pestel, had been arrested earlier, officers and soldiers from the Chernigov Regiment had revolted and were marching on Kiev. All of St. Petersburg held its breath to hear what would happen. Finally the news reached them. Two battalions and miscellaneous soldiers had been squashed before they even reached Kiev. Those arrested were brought to St. Petersburg, and the interrogations began all over again.

Tatyana was now also worried about Gregory. He seemed, on hearing the news about the ill-fated southern uprising, to become more disheartened by what had happened around him. Tatyana felt exasperated and worried about the ominous silence of her father and of the British Embassy. One afternoon, after visiting Gregory, Tatyana called on the Embassy of her own accord and asked to speak to the secretary.

When he came out, he sat Tatyana down. "There is no point in not telling you what has happened," he began ominously.

"I am listening," said Tatyana.

"Mr. Grandison's status has been confirmed. He is regarded by the czar as a very dangerous political prisoner. We received information that it is in the interest of people very highly placed in the czar's entourage that Mr. Grandison not be set free without a full assessment of his contribution to the Decembrists' uprising. They are accusing him of being a spy. We have denied this charge, but it seems they wish to review all the evidence before letting him leave Russian soil.

"I will be very frank with you, Princess Korbatskaya. We are negotiating some very difficult and touchy trade and shipping agreements with your country that could have far-reaching effects on both our economies. We cannot place national interests in jeopardy by taking a hard line with the czar's people at this crucial moment. What we must do is tide this one out."

"Does this mean he will be brought to trial here and judged on the same terms as a Russian?"

"No, not necessarily at all. It only means that we must wait for the czar, and those influencing his decision, to review his activities for inclusion in their reports and to let them turn Mr. Grandison over to us when they are ready."

Tatyana stared at him.

The secretary paused uncomfortably and dabbed at his nose with his handkerchief. "May I ask, is Mr. Grandison a friend or relative of your family?"

"A friend or relative of our family? No," answered Tatyana, rising from her chair. "But he is the man above all men who I wish to marry." Thanking the secretary for his help, Tatyana took leave of the British Embassy.

Chapter Nineteen

WALKING DOWN THE MARBLE STAIRCASE IN A DAZE, TAT-
yana felt someone pull on the sleeve of her pelisse. She
turned around and recognized the Stegorins' coachman.

"Come quick, princess, please. I was sent to find you
and bring you back. My mistress is about to have her
baby."

When Tatyana arrived at the Stegorins' she heard, as
soon as the door was opened, the sound of a woman
groaning in pain.

Tatyana rapidly crossed herself. "Our Lady of Vladimir," she prayed, pressing her eyes tightly together,
"please bring Sofia Stegorina and the baby through this.
Please make sure she is well, for her sake, Arkady's and
mine!"

Another groan, and Tatyana hastened up the stairs to
the lilac sitting room, which Sofia had made her refuge. A
doctor was already there, leaning over her, and several
maids surrounded the couch. Sofia lay there groaning,
her face shining from sweat, her gray eyes moist. "I am

so glad you are here," she said between breaths, while Tatyana looked at her with frightened eyes.

"No need to be terrified, princess, your friend is going to be fine," said a familiar voice.

"Doctor Morabitsky!" said Tatyana, looking with relief into the elderly man's face. "What are you doing here from the country?"

Doctor Morabitsky tilted his head slowly. "At her husband's request, princess."

"You know Count Stegorin?"

"No," said the doctor, now tilting his head slowly in the other direction, as if this question demanded serious thought, "no, I do not know him. But his comrade-at-arms is a fellow I've met before." He slowly brought his head up straight and adjusted his spectacles. "Here is a letter for you. I almost forgot." And he drew out of his pocket a letter which he handed to Tatyana. She recognized Gregory's bold, elegant handwriting.

My beloved Tatyana,

Doctor Morabitsky and I met earlier this year, when you were recuperating from the wound on your shoulder. Your brave friends Sofia and Arkady deserve the best, and I hold Doctor Morabitsky in the highest esteem.

No romantic he, it was signed simply, Gregory. Tatyana kissed the handwriting on the letter and pressed it to her cheek. No thought for himself or his own troubles, she thought, just as on the night of the uprising when he went around helping the poor men who had fallen. How different Gregory was now from the haughty and guarded young man who had arrived on the doorstep of Starlina a year ago December. Tatyana pressed Doctor Morabitsky's hand. "Thank you so much for coming."

Sofia's labor was long and exhausting, but the doctor and Tatyana stayed by her all night. All night long the whole household waited expectantly, and hardly anybody wished to sleep. Finally, in the early hours of the morning, while it was dark and cold out, the servants who clustered in front of the door heard the faint cry of a newborn baby.

Inside the room, Tatyana leaned over the bed and smoothed back for the hundredth time Sofia's damp locks. "You have a boy," she whispered. Through her cracked lips, Sofia smiled weakly, unable to speak. But the happiness radiated from her eyes.

Doctor Morabitsky was washing his hands in a white porcelain basin and turned to Tatyana. "Has a name been chosen?"

Sofia motioned with one hand, and Tatyana put her ear down close to her mouth to hear the whispered answer. Tatyana kissed her feeble hand.

"The name of your new patient," said Tatyana proudly, "is Arkady Arkadievich Stegorin."

Hours later, the baby lay swaddled and asleep in his new cradle. Tatyana had just come in from the baby. "How does he look? Well?" asked Sofia, who was already beginning to sound more vigorous.

"He is a fine, lusty baby with excellent coloring and good lungs, as you must have heard before." Sofia nodded with pleasure. "You should just see him without his clothes on," said Tatyana, who had watched the new nurse robe him. "He is so dainty and soft!" She leaned down next to Sofia. "His feet are a miracle, they are so little and pink and delicate. Why, his toes look like baby shrimps. I almost could have eaten one!"

Sofia laughed at Tatyana's sense of marvel; somehow now it all seemed so natural to her. She saw a preoccupied expression steal across Tatyana's features. Sofia knew she had gone to the Embassy the day before. "You have been so thoughtful, not speaking of your own concerns. Tell me, Tanya, what did the secretary say?"

Tatyana told her.

When she was finished, Sofia said, "Who do you suppose is leaning on Nicholas not to hand Gregory over to the Embassy? It doesn't make sense."

Tatyana shook her head. "I would have thought Arakcheyev, since he is so suspicious of outside influences on Russia, from what Gregory once told me. But now Arakcheyev has fallen from power, perhaps Nicholas has a different advisor."

Sofia nodded, "Yes, maybe another Iago. There are certainly other Arakcheyevs in this world." In her voice was a new cynicism that saddened Tatyana. "What do you plan to do now, my beloved Tatyana?"

"I know what I must do now. I must go see my father. I am disquieted by his silence, and I promised to return to Starlina after your baby was safely delivered. Besides," she added pensively, "my father still has some influence at court. Maybe he will help me, if I just explain to him how desperately he is needed."

Sofia frowned, for she did not share Tatyana's optimism about Prince Korbatsky, but she would not hold her back. She had already detained Tatyana long enough from returning to Starlina. She squeezed Tatyana's hand. "My poor dear, what a worry this must be to you—I know how much you really love Gregory."

"Oh, Sofia, yes, it is a worry. But no more so than for you. Both our men are in the Alexis Ravelin."

Tatyana couldn't help but feel a wave of admiration for Sofia. It was certain her husband as a leader of the Decembrists would be dealt with more harshly than the rest. How, hardly any one could guess. But the women whose husbands and lovers and sons were locked inside the fortress knew that their fate depended finally on the czar. And nobody knew Nicholas that well. Could he be unexpectedly forgiving, or would he prosecute them relentlessly right through to the end?

"Sofia, surely your aunt, as the intimate friend of the Dowager Empress Marie, would plead on Arkady's behalf to Nicholas?"

Sofia smiled sadly. "No, there is no reason to believe she can help. You know, my aunt has so much family pride. She would never condescend to abuse her station by asking the empress for a personal favor, even if it would break her heart."

Tatyana was appalled that someone should be so principled as not to use her influence to save someone else in trouble. "Well, I have no such scruples," retorted Tatyana. "I would do anything to help any one of those poor men in jail." Tatyana seemed scarcely aware of how her allegiances had shifted.

"I know you would," said Sofia tenderly. "That is why she is my aunt but you are my friend."

Tatyana stood up. "Now I will go tell Arkady how you and his little son are doing. I imagine he is pacing his cell right now wondering if he is a husband or a husband and a father."

Sofia smiled. "Tell him what a thick head of dark hair little Arkadyushka has," she said, already using a pet name for her son.

"Of course, it is just like his father's," said Tatyana, understanding. "There will be one very proud husband and father in the Alexis Ravelin tonight."

The following day, after visiting Gregory in the morning, Tatyana went home to Starlina. She had sent no letter to announce her arrival, and when the hired sleigh drew up, no one came out to greet her. The Turburovs' troika was out front, which surprised her, and she could hear the sound of her father's serfs chopping wood out back. Otherwise, there was no other activity. Tatyana let herself in the front door on the terrace. At the sound of the latch, half a dozen house serfs came running to welcome her home and to remove her wraps. It was good to see their familiar faces, and they reminded her of how much she had missed Starlina in the weeks she had been gone.

"Is my father here?" she asked in Russian, and after an odd delay of several minutes, she was led to the sanctuary of his study. This surprised her because if he was entertaining he should have been in the drawing room. Standing at the study door she suddenly felt unnerved that he should receive her here. She thought of the many days she had been absent from Starlina. Perhaps her father was angrier than she thought.

When she entered the study, her father sat alone waiting for her. The reunion between child and parent was diffident on one side, reproachful on the other. Prince Korbatsky glowered at her from his desk and barely returned the kisses she laid on his old hands.

"Deceitful child," he muttered, treating her just as he had treated Dmitry when he returned after his two-year leave in Paris.

"Father, why are you so angry with me?" Tatyana begged, "I had to go look for Dmitry, and I knew you would never let me. If I had asked, and you had said no, I would never have disobeyed. So that is why I could not tell you. And later, Sofia needed me, so desperately." She paused for breath.

"You guessed I would have forbidden you and yet you went. That is an interesting twist of moral logic. And then, on top of that, you stayed three weeks. In the meantime I have been growing old by the minute."

"Forgive me, father. I love you dearly. I came as soon as I could. Sofia just gave birth yesterday to a healthy baby boy!"

"I pity the child who should be born into the world with such a father as he has," growled the old prince, "and I always thought the Stegorins were sensible people, even with all their eccentricities."

Tatyana let this go by and sank down on the familiar stool at her father's feet.

"Father, Dmitry—" began Tatyana, but her father interrupted her.

"I do not wish to speak of that person," he snapped. "But tell me, is it true that you visited that wretched Gregory Grandison in the Alexis Ravelin?"

"Yes, father."

"We shall have no more of that, you can be sure," pounced her father, yanking on his moustache.

"Father, it is also of him I wished to speak."

He looked at her fiercely while she talked.

"Father, I know you are not overly fond of Gregory Grandison. But he may be in terrible trouble, for something that is not his fault. He is being kept in the fortress when he should be turned over to the English Embassy. Without any help he may be there many more weeks. Father, he needs our help."

"Aha, the prodigal daughter returns home now that she needs her father's help."

Tatyana winced at her father's suspiciousness. "No, father, you are mistaken. But I do indeed need your help if you will give it."

"And what kind of help are you looking for?"

Tatyana only heard the question, since she was desperate, and not its tone, which was one of rising indignation.

"Father, couldn't you write to Nicholas? He would listen to your request to hand Mr. Grandison into the keeping of the British Embassy. You could influence him on behalf of Mr. Grandison. After all, father," she said, lowering her voice, "he was a friend of Mitya's."

"So what of that!" thundered the prince. "They should both have gone to the Devil."

Tatyana almost recoiled. "Father you do not mean that. You cannot mean what you say."

"Indeed I do! The water rats of the Neva are too good for that blasted Englishman. They should have shoved him under the ice with the rest of them. He could use a swimming lesson."

This allusion to Dmitry's probable death and tirade against Gregory was too much. "Father, you must not speak that way of him," she said, her body shaking.

"Really? And why not, why not?" challenged the old prince, now venting all the anger he had been saving up for weeks. "Why not, I ask you?!"

Tatyana's eyes filled with hurt, but at last she said quietly, "Father, I love Gregory Grandison."

"Love him? Love him?" he hissed. "Love that criminal? Do not even use that word if you have any shred of obedience or respect for me, your father."

"Father, I cannot help but love him. I do not love him to spite you. I love him because I cannot help it. So father, for me, if not for him, please write a letter to Nicholas asking for his release. Father, I have never asked for anything before. Please do not refuse me now." She was almost hanging from the brocade sleeve of his caftan as she begged him.

"Enough of this nonsense. You are going to marry Count Vasily Turburov."

"Count Vasily, always Count Vasily. I do not love him, father. Why have you insisted on this marriage with a man I do not love?" she said plaintively.

"He is the best man for you. I know it even if you don't. He is a brilliant match."

"But I should be miserable." Tatyana stood up. "Father, I heard about him at the uprising in St. Petersburg. He was the one who fired the first cannon, the one who started the bloodshed. Men, women, and children, killed.

How can you admire a man like that? I cannot admire him, and I cannot marry him!" Tatyana's green eyes danced with fear, but also with determination.

Prince Korbatsky was momentarily startled by this vehement outburst, but he brought his fist down on his armchair. "Tatyana Ivanovna," he said menacingly, "I will not sit here any longer and argue with you. You will do as I say. You will indeed marry the count."

"Father," Tatyana repeated so softly he could hardly hear her, "I cannot bear to marry him."

"Enough of these games," said a strange voice, and Tatyana spun around to see Count Vasily himself step from the door behind her father's desk.

Tatyana looked at him in astonishment. "Count," she sputtered. "What are you doing here? Why were you behind the door?"

"Ask your father," said the count, helping himself to a chair and putting a plump knee up on one of the arm rests.

Tatyana looked at her father. "Father, what is the meaning of his presence? I thought we were alone."

The old prince looked irritated at this question. He also seemed suddenly nervous as if he would have liked to whisk the corpulent body of his guest back behind the door. He tugged on his moustache and said gruffly, "Nothing, nothing at all. He was visiting before you came and . . ." The old prince seemed suddenly at a loss for words.

"Enough of this rigamarole, your excellency," interrupted the count, raising his arm to sweep the prince's words aside. "Your invocations that I am an excellent match begin to sound like the one line refrain of a macaw. I am getting bored with all this folderol." He stared hard at the prince and then at Tatyana with vindictive satisfaction. "Tell your dear little daughter the real reason you wish to ensure our marriage. Tell her, prince. Unless you would like to give me the satisfaction of telling her myself."

Tatyana turned bewildered eyes from the count to her father.

"Let me handle this, count," said Prince Korbatsky nervously. "Do not offend her sensibilities."

"To what is the count referring, father?" asked Tatyana. "By what would my sensibilities be offended? Perhaps I have a right to hear, if it concerns me."

"Believe me, my dear, I am convinced that Count Vasily is the best man to be your husband." His tone of voice with his daughter had altered. He now spoke with solicitude instead of criticism.

"Father . . ." Tatyana began again.

Count Vasily looked disdainfully at both of them. Then he walked to the window, and his bulk cut much of the light out of the room. He began to speak with evident relish at the scene his words would bring about. "I have been silent this whole time and have not once erred, prince, from my role of attentive fiancé. Now, though, I am tired of your irresponsibility and will speak since my discretion has not procured me what I wished." He now directed his words at Tatyana. "It is indeed true, princess, that I am a brilliant match, though your father has repeated this catch phrase ad nauseum. There are at least two dozen St. Petersburg ladies from the highest echelons who would love to sink their pretty little teeth into me and my fortune. Unfortunately it is my own failing, princess, that you are the one I've hankered to possess.

"In a pique of endless generosity, for I have been all generosity with your father, I allowed him to use unusual collateral in a game of faro, at which he had been losing to me by four hundred thousand rubles. I see by the color, or rather lack of color on your face, princess, that your father's little peculiarities escaped your notice. I don't imagine you guessed your father's penchant for cards, or the desperate stakes he embroiled himself with.

"Well, I've taken half his serfs from him in sloppy games. This time, he could not resist the gamble—seeing as he was losing so badly and his house in St. Petersburg was mortgaged already. Oh, so sorry to let you into that little family secret. Well, to proceed. On this particular night of which I have already made mention, your father was losing, very very badly I might add, and I in my infinite mercy let him stake his best possession. I, gentleman that I am, accepted the terms. He staked his daughter. Princess, his price for you was high—almost the value of five hundred serfs—but I believed well worth it. Princess, you should be flattered at our grand stakes."

The trivial vulgarity of Count Vasily's last remark was lost on Tatyana. She stood completely still, transfixed like a marionette suspended in air. The whole time the count was speaking she had not removed her eyes from her father. There was an oppressive silence when Vasily finished.

"Sold, father?" said Tatyana softly at last, ignoring Count Vasily.

Her father hung his head and said nothing.

Tatyana for the first time saw on the desk beside her father a pack of cards. Tatyana picked them up. She turned the cards in her hands a moment, as if she were holding some curious, imported object which she had never held before. And she stared at the meaningless red and black symbols as if they were Egyptian hieroglyphics.

"Sold me as you would a serf," she said in that same low breathless voice.

Still her father did not answer.

"Exactly," quipped Count Vasily. "I can answer for him since he seems surprisingly tongue-tied. Yes, that's what he did, because he would have lost his fortune, his family's fortune actually, for that included what should have been your dowry. You are indeed fortunate that one such as I not only does not expect a dowry but will cancel your father's horrendous debts once you are my wife." Still Tatyana seemed impervious to the count and his vulgarity, and was gazing at her father.

Then Prince Korbatsky, who had always ruled his household and his family so imperiously from his chair, sank forward on his knees. He lifted the hem of Tatyana's mantle and pressed it to his old wrinkled lips. "Forgive me, daughter," he said meekly. "Cards have been my only weakness."

Tatyana watched her father's abject kisses applied to her pelisse with the same gaze she had cast on the unfortunate cards.

"Your duty is clear, princess," said Count Vasily, the satisfaction oily in his mouth, for he knew that now that Tatyana understood the truth, she would become his wife. Princess Tatyana, the ever dutiful daughter, would rescue her father from his dreadful predicament. Already his plump white hands tingled in anticipation of the tender sensuality of Tatyana's flesh.

Tatyana did not even hear Vasily. She had gone beyond grief or outrage to a state of shock. Suddenly her whole life flipped through her mind, shuffling like the pack of cards in one image after another that blurred into one haze of color. All her values—home, family, her country—everything she had cherished, everything that had made up her being, suddenly seemed startlingly clear and artificial.

When she finally spoke again her voice was quiet but resolute. "Father, I still will not marry Count Vasily, for I do not love him. And I will not throw away my life, even for the father I have loved always." Here her voice caught as she remembered in that instant her entire lifetime of love for her father and the way she had wept when her gift to him, the snow princess, had melted in the spring air. She was quiet again until she retrieved her calm. "No, father, I cannot even marry him to make you happy, or to settle your debts. I will do all I can to help you with this debt. I will even become a governess. But no, I will never be sold to anybody, not even by my own father." She stopped. "I was not yours to barter."

Tatyana took the pack of cards and quietly dropped them into the fire. She watched them spark and curl in the flames, till there was nothing left of them.

Tatyana had never seen her father cry, but now, still on his knees, he sobbed. "By my weakness, daughter, I have done you a great injustice. Forgive me if you can."

Tatyana said nothing and left the room, ignoring Count Vasily, who had been made speechless by her words. Now he rushed out after her on to the terrace and grabbed her arm. Tears were rolling down her cheeks.

"Undutiful daughter. Your father is in dire straits, and you leave him like this!"

"Dire straits that you, not I, have put him in, and dire straits that you, not I, have the power to rescind!" she said, grief and anger struggling in her voice. "Good day, Count Vasily."

She quickly walked down the steps to the waiting sledge.

Count Vasily's eyes screwed up as he saw Tatyana escaping from him. "Don't think that in spite of this you will have your Englishman," he threatened, and he barred her way to the coach.

"You have dishonored me, and you have dishonored my father. Leave us to our separate griefs," commanded Tatyana, now casting a look so fierce that even Count Vasily wavered, and Tatyana climbed quickly into the carriage.

But Vasily would not let her close the door, and he shook his fat white finger at her. "You had better listen to me, little Princess Korbatskaya. Your father's ruin means nothing to you perhaps, but it is also in my power to injure the bastard you are in love with."

These words caught Tatyana off guard, and she looked back at him with doubt.

"Yes," continued the count, "I have the means to see that your Mr. Grandison does not escape Russian justice. If you do not marry me, I will make sure that he never sees his country again. And by the time the czar is through with him, he will wish he never left England."

Tatyana fixed him in the eye. "You may own Starlina yet, and you may even own my father, but you do not own Gregory Grandison, and you will never, ever, ever own me!" Then, before he could think to stop her, she leaned forward and wrenching the door, slammed it shut on him.

"Play the proud puss, for all I care," challenged the count, wagging his finger angrily in the air, "but one of these days you will come groveling to me."

Tatyana's face was now white with fury, but she ignored Vasily. "Off, driver," she commanded. Instantly the horses lurched into motion and the sledge careened down the drive and away from Starlina.

Chapter Twenty

ONLY THREE MONTHS HAD GONE BY SINCE TATYANA'S VISIT to her father. But even in that short time Tatyana had undergone a change. The transformation began in the sleigh when she was leaving Starlina. As she sat in the *troika* tears rolled down her cheeks from the strain of the interview with her father and Count Vasily. But even as the teardrops dried on her face, Tatyana felt something stretch and break within her; she did not realize until much later that it was her lifelong submission and blind allegiance to her father. She felt like a snake that has shed its skin, or like a bird poking against its shell to propel itself into the open air and the outside world. The feeling was not a happy one, and it frightened her at first. For she realized intuitively that the past was over, just as her father said in his earlier letter, though not in the way he had anticipated.

When she arrived at the Stegorins' that night, there was a new firmness about her—that certain firmness she had always admired and found mysterious in Sofia. Tatyana did not yet realize the trait was acquired through suffering, and she did not know as Sofia did that she was also finally growing up.

Tatyana stayed with Sofia in St. Petersburg the entire spring, and her experiences in that short interval swept the last veils of illusion about her native country from Tatyana's eyes.

She spent her time visiting Gregory in his cell in the Alexis Ravelin or simply watching him from afar as he walked along the fortress ramparts once a day. Her love and admiration for him grew as she understood what he and the other Decembrists were going through. She learned that bribery, so rampant in Russia, could make Gregory's state more comfortable. This was the way she provided him and the other young men, whenever she could, with paper and ink, books, and even a few surreptitious oranges. The underpaid guards who received their salaries in devalued paper money welcomed the sight of the lovely young princess, who rewarded their deviations from the written rules with silver rubles and Russian imperials. And when her gold and silver ran out, Tatyana tore the oriental pearls from her beloved kokoshnik and offered them instead.

Tatyana soon found another way of helping the young men as well. Aside from when they crossed paths at the endless interrogations now going on within the fortress walls, Gregory and the other prisoners were not allowed to see or speak to one another. So it was Tatyana, with her youth and beauty, her family name, and the gold coins discreetly slipped here and there, who was soon able to visit many of the prisoners and to carry messages back and forth between them.

She met Major Pavel Pestel, the ringleader from the southern insurrection. It was his letter she had read months before in Gregory's passport. Major Pestel's ideas burned brightly from his magnificent mind, but they were like cold white flames, amoral in their perfection.

Tatyana was less drawn to him than to some of the others, like the brave and energetic Bestuzhev brothers, who reminded her with a bittersweet pang of Dmitry.

A certain fondness and gallantry developed between her and Ryleyev, and she often took messages to his wife for him. Ryleyev along with most of the other men had a high regard for Gregory, who due to his ambiguous position they now began to refer to as the December Guest. Gregory's admiration turned particularly toward Ryleyev and to a strange Muscovite named Lunin. Gregory had never met this lieutenant-colonel from an elite regiment of Hussars before their imprisonment, but it was Lunin only throughout the months of interrogation, blackmail, and torture who never abandoned his beliefs or his allegiance to his fellow conspirators.

To Gregory's sorrow, the same high principles and endurance could not be said of all the men. Under the relentless inquisition that went on at all hours of the day and night, many of the young men, including Pestel, broke down. They were being harrowed past endurance by the iron will of Nicholas. Abandoning the clear-headed thinking that had first motivated them, many regressed to their adolescent adoration of the czar. They genuinely began to believe that what had taken place in Ryleyev's apartments and out on Senate Square was the harebrained scheme of temporary insanity. They had all been Don Quixotes, tilting at windmills, and now they groveled in shame at the feet of the all-merciful emperor.

Tatyana was more and more disconcerted by these things and by the appalling slowness of the investigation as the members of the czar's secret committee wrote, collated, and filed endless reports, charges, and testimonies. When she was not at the fortress, Tatyana wrote letters to everyone who might have impact on the outcome of these interrogations, and finally even to the czar himself. She used her former position as goddaughter to Alexander and her family's illustrious name to beg Gregory be handed over to the English Embassy. She also begged clemency for the other men.

Tatyana's illusions were further eroded by the silence of the czar. Neither he nor an intermediary answered any of her letters. All that was done for Gregory in those months was to move him into a larger cell above ground with a window that looked out on a drab inner courtyard. Soon Count Vasily's terrible threat preyed more and more on Tatyana's mind. Now all she and Sofia could do was pin their hope on the tribunal that would dispose of the cases once they went into session June third.

The tribunal of men had been handpicked by the czar, and Tatyana and Sofia learned they would not hear the testimony of prisoners themselves. To try each of the one hundred and twenty cases being brought to trial, the tribunal would rely only on the written reports, whose accuracy was highly doubted. In addition to that, Tatyana and Sofia got wind that there was so much written material that none of the jury members would have time to read the testimony. This final absurdity made the trial of the Decembrists a mockery.

On June eighth the tribunal advised the czar on the verdict for each case, and that afternoon Sofia learned from her aunt Arkady belonged to a "category two" along with thirty-one other men. For them, the death penalty had been recommended. Though all anticipated the czar would lessen the sentences considerably, even this news was too much for Sofia. She was put to bed with a fever. About Gregory's case there was still no news and no one knew if his case would even be brought before the tribunal. The Embassy's recent overtures had gone unanswered. On June tenth the czar was to publish a decree lessening the sentences determined by the tribunal. That morning Tatyana set out alone in a droshky and headed to the Winter Palace to find out the final fate of Arkady.

Sofia was confined to the couch in the sitting room, her baby in his cradle beside her. While she tossed and turned, she prayed to all the saints in heaven that her husband's life be saved.

The afternoon sun went down, and in the late evening hours twilight set in, but still Tatyana had not returned. Sofia twisted on the couch, wondering what delayed her. At last she heard Tatyana's voice downstairs as she was let in the front door by a servant. Sofia raised up on her elbows. She could hear Tatyana's tread on the stairway carpeting. Her footsteps were slow, scarcely moving, it seemed to Sofia, and her heart began to pound in her head.

At last Tatyana appeared in the door of the sitting room. Under her shawl her mint green gown looked gold in the vanishing light. Her cheeks were blotchy, but perhaps that was from the wind, thought Sofia. Could it be Tatyana had good news of Arkady after all? But Sofia could not bring herself to speak. She waited passively for Tatyana to drop the dreaded or desired words.

Tatyana sank listlessly on the couch.

"Arkady?" Sofia just managed to ask.

"How is little Arkadyushka?" Tatyana asked dreamily, using the baby's pet name.

The question made Sofia's flesh crawl. "He is sleeping in the next room. But tell me . . . the verdict?"

Tatyana gazed at Sofia, and her lips moved, but she could not speak.

"For the love of St. Vladimir, tell me of Arkady, tell me the truth."

Tatyana's eyes focused on Sofia, and she seemed to remember where she was. "Arkady, your husband, has been sentenced to twenty years hard labor in Siberia."

Sofia sank back at this news, but when the tears

glistened in her eyes, they were not from sorrow but from relief. "Thank the Almighty in Heaven, my Arkady is saved."

At last Sofia wiped away her tears. Tatyana sat on the divan gazing out the window. "Tatyana," said Sofia, sitting up abruptly. "What is the matter? Have you had news of Gregory?"

Tatyana turned and looked at her dully. Then she nodded.

"What is it, tell me what has happened," asked Sofia. "Have they turned him over to the Embassy at last?"

Tatyana shook her head. "Gregory has been tried by the tribunal as well and convicted as if he were Russian," she said softly.

"Has he been sentenced?" asked Sofia with astonishment.

Tatyana nodded again. "And the czar in his infinite mercy has thought fit to condemn him to Siberia."

"To Siberia?" echoed Sofia in shock, for Gregory had had much less of a role in the secret society than Arkady.

Tatyana nodded again, "To Siberia for life."

There was a long empty silence, for Sofia could not believe what she had heard. But Tatyana's mute face testified what she said was the awful truth. At last she took Tatyana's hand. And all she could think to ask was, "What in the world are you going to do?"

Tatyana smiled, a strange unearthly smile that went beyond emotion. "I will marry Count Vasily."

Sofia was aghast. "Spend the next forty years in the bed of a man you detest with all your heart? You cannot!"

Tatyana looked at Sofia. "Wouldn't you? For Arkady, wouldn't you?"

Sofia was silenced, unable to know what to say to her friend.

Tatyana stood up. "Now I must go write my father a letter to tell him to set the date for our nuptials."

This was the letter Tatyana sent her father:

Dear Father,

This letter is to inform you that I have reconsidered Count Turburov's proposal of marriage. He has made it evident that it is in my interests, not to mention your own, for the wedding to take place. I will arrive by coach at the end of the week and will at that time put myself entirely at your disposal. Let the wedding date be fixed as Count Turburov wishes.

                              Your dutiful daughter,
                              Tatyana

After Tatyana mailed the letter, she realized there was one thing more she must do, and that was to tell Gregory. "I will just say I am doing it to save my father from his debts. No, that's not right. I'll just tell him I've had a change of heart." Tatyana paced her room mulling her stratagem. "Sometimes Gregory can be so cynical and doubting. He has already once doubted my love. Since he thinks he is being sent to Siberia for life, it will be easy enough to convince him of my faithlessness. Then, when at Count Vasily's promise he is turned over to the Embassy, he will be glad to leave Russia and will never think of me again." Tatyana pondered. "Yes, that is how I must do it if I am to save him from Siberia. If he doubts my love, I will be able to convince him of my desire to marry Vasily. I must free him of our love so that he never regrets me."

Brushing the tears that kept springing into her eyes against her will, Tatyana went to see Gregory one last time. "I must convince him," she kept repeating to herself. "I must, I must."

When Tatyana's letter arrived at Starlina two days later, Prince Korbatsky was overjoyed. He immediately informed Count Vasily of Tatyana's change of heart regarding his proposal of marriage. The count anticipated with pleasure the coming scene of Tatyana's humiliation. Even if she held on to her pride now, he consoled himself, there would be time enough after the wedding crowns were placed on their heads to break her spirit. He rubbed his palms briskly with satisfaction and commissioned his sister to order new sheets for the bridal bed. She who had dared refuse his generous offer of marriage would soon suffer for her arrogance.

At the end of the week, Tatyana returned to Starlina just as had been arranged. Her father greeted her on the terrace and was abject and cloying. He followed her around in his chair, plucking at her sleeves and kissing her fingertips. "My dutiful, loving daughter, I have Count Vasily's word that he will make you happy. And you have done the right thing by Mr. Grandison. He will be set free and sent by escort back to England. I have the count's solemn promise."

Dunyasha suddenly popped onto the terrace and kissed Tatyana's hands. "I am so glad to see you, little mother, but I must tell you something." Her voice was low and urgent.

"Shush, Dunyasha," said Prince Korbatsky. "Count Vasily is waiting."

Dunyasha looked worried but let them go in to their guest.

Tatyana was brought into the drawing room where Count Vasily lounged in the leather bolster. He had his feet up on the stuffed black bear cub with the diamond teeth he had given her as an engagement gift. Tatyana realized her father must have wrested it away from Dunyasha. She was offended to see the count make himself so much at home in her father's drawing room, but she said nothing.

Without getting up, Vasily held out his hand, waiting for her to kiss the ring on his pinky. So this was the humiliating return that had been planned for her, she realized, glancing at Vasily's small hard eyes. But she merely shook his hand.

This annoyed him. "If you are going to be my wife, princess, you will have to kiss my hand, just as you will have to do every morning once we are married."

Tatyana glanced at her father in his chair to see if he would defend her, but he was scrutinizing the leaf scroll on his quizzing glass. "I have never kissed your hand before, count," said Tatyana quietly, "and I don't wish to begin now."

"Tatyana Ivanovna," reprimanded the prince, "you must do as Count Vasily bids you."

Tatyana looked at her father again, her face now bloodless at the thought that he too would join in her public penance. "And if the count wishes me to wash his feet?" she asked. "Would you not be ashamed for me?"

Prince Korbatsky pulled on his moustache. "Do not be recalcitrant, daughter. He is to be your husband, and you must show him absolute obedience."

"Just as I have always shown to you, father?"

"Precisely," said the prince, unaware of her irony.

"You are my father, but the count is not my husband, so I do not know why I must kiss his hand today," said Tatyana with maddening logic.

"Yes, you must," said the prince, losing his patience. "Do this for me, your father, and for him, since tomorrow he will indeed be your husband."

Tatyana stood in her turquoise bombazine gown and looked from her father to the count and to Dunyasha,

who stood anxiously in the background, her hands
folded over each other almost as if in an attitude of
prayer. It was a curious moment, utterly defeating to
Tatyana, and yet she did not seem defeated by it. She
seemed, on the contrary, to derive strength from the
humiliating scene. She turned to her father. "I am afraid I
cannot be married tomorrow."

"Why not?" asked her father, his irritation turning to
anger at the petty way his daughter was delaying matters.
"What is the matter with marrying the count tomorrow?"

"Because father," she said, gazing at him in a way that
unsettled him, "I was married today."

Prince Korbatsky stared at his daughter. "Repeat what
you just said," he stuttered.

"With pleasure, father," said Tatyana. "I said I cannot
marry Count Turburov tomorrow because I was already
married today." In the background Dunyasha almost
started to clap her hands with glee, then stopped,
noticing the look on both men's faces. But her eyes
beamed with triumph. Count Vasily had suddenly raised
himself up from his reclining position on the couch.

"You are not serious," spluttered her father. "What is
the meaning of this?"

"It is indeed true, father. I cannot in good conscience
kiss the count. I am sure my husband would not allow it."

"Husband," said the prince, his voice shaking, as he
became more and more overwhelmed.

"Yes, my husband," said Tatyana, her voice becoming
stronger. "Gregory Grandison."

"It is a contemptible lie," thundered her father.

"Not at all," countered Tatyana, "Father Peter My-
slovsky, the dean of the Cathedral of Kazan, performed
the ceremony at the fortress chapel. Gregory Grandison
is my husband. Or if you prefer, I am his wife."

"No, not wife," spit Vasily, rising from the couch, "but

widow! He will be sent to Siberia, and that is farther away than Hell. He will die there."

"Then we will die there together, for he is not going alone. I am going with him," retorted Tatyana, her nostrils flaring. "As for you, Vasily Turburov," she said turning to him, "leave this house. It does not belong to you yet."

"I will leave when I choose to leave," said the count, and his corpulent face turned crimson with indignation.

"You will choose to now," said Tatyana with desperate calm. "There is a houseful of serfs who would be glad to accommodate my wishes, and they would not be nearly so polite as I."

Vasily hesitated, then glared at her and at her father. "I will never trust your word again, prince. Believe me, this time you are ruined, utterly ruined."

"Get out and take your idea of a footstool!" ordered Tatyana, so fiercely the count suddenly quivered. Then seeing a circle of serfs gathering ominously in the foyer, he picked up the diamond-studded bear cub and hastily departed.

Tatyana, her father, and Dunyasha were left alone in the drawing room. "Foolish girl, you are the ruin of me," erupted her father. "You have married a man who will work the mines of Irkutsk for life, and you will be his companion in misfortune. You will not be able to stand it, I tell you, and you will beg to return home. Then you will have to live off what's left of my estate and be dependent on my mercy!"

Now Dunyasha saw something begin to rumble deep within the young woman before her who had once, so long ago it now seemed, been the dutiful little girl put in her safekeeping.

"Father, stop right now!" said Tatyana suddenly with such authority she surprised her father into silence. "You have already injured me sufficiently. Know this one thing of me, that I go with my husband, and I will never leave him."

"Why do I have such foolish children!" raged the prince, then turned wrathfully toward Tatyana. "Go then, die there. You do not know the meaning of cold, of poverty, of misery, of back-breaking work. And have your bastard children, for by Nicholas' decree that is all they will be. Go then, and never let me see your face again. Your life will be hideous!" he exploded.

"Perhaps," hurled Tatyana back at him, "but I will have the man I love and trust by my side. The man who loved me enough to trust my love, who saw through the artifice I created so as to free him. The man who wanted a lifetime in Siberia rather than lose me."

Tatyana came up very close to her father.

"You, you who have always dared to speak to me about devotion? What devotion have you ever showed your children? You erased the memory of a son who loved and honored you in spite of his beliefs, and you abused my love and infinite trust in you. You were ready to sacrifice my entire life away for some contemptible weakness of yours, just as you did with your serfs. Poor Lizanka, if she knew her life had been bartered by a king of spades!" Tatyana turned abruptly away from him.

"If none of this had happened, father, if it weren't for all those young men and their high ideals, if it weren't for Mitya and his passion and conscience, if it weren't for the world containing one Gregory Grandison, all might have been right for you. I would have spent my life by your side, maneuvered by your clapping hands. I would have married Count Vasily, exchanging one life of blind servility for another."

Now her voice sank to a whisper. "I will bend down and kiss the soil of Siberia, for there lies truth and the promise of love and devotion. Here, in my childhood home that I have loved until now more fiercely than anything else in the world, is jealousy, selfishness, and deception." Tatyana's voice slowly softened as she strayed to the window.

"And yet, I will always dream of Starlina, the stars above, and the birds that sing in the birches, not infected by human weakness. Starlina will ever be beautiful in my mind, for Russia's goodness and beauty will always exist, no matter how men think or act. Here at least I lived in innocence, even if it was a happiness born out of ignorance." Tatyana turned from the window, and the softness was gone, replaced by sad revelation.

"What a disservice you wrought, hiding the nature of the world around me and the weakness of the human heart. Did you wish to strengthen me by this ignorance, or make Starlina my prison since no light or truth could penetrate my mind? What is happiness wrought of ignorance? Only a handful of dreams! I would rather be, and feel right now, the saddest person in the world. But now I will cry tears of happiness every step along the way to Siberia. For I will be by the side of my husband. His example of love, selflessness, and devotion will shine like a beacon through the years of my life, no matter how short or how long it may be."

With this outburst, Tatyana ran from the room.

"Come back, come back," called her father from his chair. But his futile words fell on empty air. He had lost his daughter forever. The snow princess had melted into the spring air.

Chapter Twenty-one

FIVE OF THE DECEMBRISTS HAD BEEN CONDEMNED TO death. They were to have been drawn and quartered, by the rules of capital punishment. But Nicholas I knew what public opinion would be in regard to this medieval form of capital punishment, and the sentence was altered. They would be hanged instead.

Kondraty Ryleyev, whom Gregory so deeply admired, was among the number, along with Peter Kakhovsky, the man who had shot General Miloradovich. Major Pavel Pestel, whose cold brilliant ideas had both frightened and awed Tatyana, had also received the death sentence, along with two other handsome young officers from the southern insurrection.

Before the execution, the czar ordered a ceremony of military degradation for the officers whose lives had been spared and who were being sent to the Siberian work mines.

On July twenty-first the prisoners were taken to a small field within the Peter and Paul Fortress and ordered to kneel before detachments of their own regiments. Their crimes were read aloud, swords were broken over their heads, and then their insignia and epaulets were ripped from their uniforms. While drums rolled, they were stripped of their uniforms and put in the gray convict clothes they would travel in to Siberia. Gregory, though not a Russian officer, was ordered to watch the proceeding. He was disgusted to see that some of the swords had not been properly blunted and that several of the men received cuts on their heads. But even more disquieting than this symbolic death was the sound he could hear on the other side of the fence of a scaffold being erected.

Gregory knew the execution of his friend and the four other men would take place early the following morning, and he was unable to sleep. At dawn he rose from his bunk and looked out the window of his cell. There in the early light he saw the two posts with their horizontal beam, the simple but effective design of the gallows. He watched his friends come out at last and have sacks put over their heads and nooses around their necks. The hanging was interminable, and Gregory winced with horror when the operation backfired. Two of the ropes failed, and Ryleyev and Kakhovsky fell into the pit.

Gregory smashed the bar of his window with his fist with grief and frustration. "By God, this country can't do anything right."

Finally Ryleyev and Kakhovsky were strung up again, and their lives shuddered out of them. Gregory lay down and closed his eyes. All that could be said for them now was that they were out of their misery.

Three hours later, a letter was brought to him. It had been smuggled through by one of the guards who had befriended him and Tatyana. The letter had been sent to Gregory in care of the English Embassy. There was a note accompanying it addressed to him from the ambassador's secretary. In it he sent his assurances that they would try to negotiate with the czar for his release, or at least curtail his sentence. The secretary expressed every hope that he would be able to return to England within a few years.

Gregory smiled wryly. "In the meantime we will keep an active file open on you and will work to clear the charges against you. In the meantime accept our sincere apologies. We are also enclosing a letter forwarded here, which has arrived several months late."

Gregory turned to this second envelope with more interest than the first. It was thick and the sender's name was engraved on the envelope. "Jonathan H. Crumm-wait, Esquire, Solicitors at Law, Oxford Street, London." Gregory read the letter by the light of his window. When he was finished he gazed at it thoughtfully, shook his head with disbelief, and then began to laugh—a laugh of amusement tinged with bitterness. "What ironies life is full of," he muttered at last, and he put it aside to show Tatyana.

"I wish to see my husband," said the woman at the fortress gate. It was Tatyana. Soon she was escorted through the now familiar insides of the Alexis Ravelin until they reached cell five, where Gregory was held.

When she was admitted through the door, she clasped Gregory in her arms. "Husband now not only in my heart, but in the eyes of the world." She put her cheek against his breast, feeling his heart beat through the prison garb.

"You do not look like a lady who is about to embark tomorrow on a forty-five-hundred-mile trek to Siberia," said Gregory tenderly.

Tatyana smiled. "Yes I do, for I am happy to think that you and I will never be separated again."

Her words reminded both of them of what had happened in the early morning hours.

"It is done?" she asked softly.

Gregory nodded.

"So Gregory, it is all over? All their dreams are vanquished?" asked Tatyana in a whisper.

"For men like Ryleyev and Pestel, yes, and for a certain breed of eloquent and honorable young men who died with this coup," said Gregory. "But no, the movement is not over, no matter how the czar obliterates the records, how many bloodstains he removes from Senate Square. The first seeds have been sown and will carry in the wind all over Russia. There will be other revolts and other revolutions—maybe not soon, maybe in twenty years or fifty or a hundred—but they will come irrevocably."

Gregory's eyes looked somber.

"Only, when the wave breaks next, it will be neither so gentlemanly nor altruistic as this poor aborted rebellion. On the tailcoats of idealistic reformers will come professional assassins and those who use the ideals of revolution toward their own private and destructive ends." He paused, "There are not many Ryleyevs whose ideals remain pure to the end."

Tatyana nodded. "I learned that the day of the insurrection. He knew he was going to die for his beliefs, and he didn't waver." She thought about Natasha, Ryleyev's wife, remembering her look of fear as she gazed on her husband at the Stegorins' picnic.

"How ignorant I was of Natasha's sorrow even then," she said softly. "I was so spiteful. I thought to myself, 'What is she afraid of, that an eagle will swoop down and carry him off?' And look now, Gregory," said Tatyana bowing her head, "that is what happened, only it was a double-headed eagle that took her husband from her arms forever." Tears began to fall down Tatyana's cheeks.

"Oh, Gregory, you can scarcely imagine the suffering of all the wives. Some of them have sought divorce, it is true, since Nicholas will allow it. But do you know? I am not the only one accompanying my husband. Do you remember Princess Trubetskaya, the merry little one at the Stegorins' picnic who seemed to live for the glitter of city life? She made a marriage of convenience, and yet she will be riding in one of those carts tomorrow next to her cowardly husband." Tatyana brushed aside her tears. "And Sofia—"

"What of Sofia?" asked Gregory, who was cut off from Arkady and learned all his news through Tatyana.

"Poor Sofia. At first she wept for joy to learn that Arkady's life was saved, but oh, I could not live through her present agony. She will be by his side tomorrow as well."

"That is no less than what you are doing, my brave beloved," said Gregory, tenderly lifting her chin and gazing into her vital green eyes, now brilliant with the wash of tears.

"Oh, but Gregory, in all his cruelty, the czar will not allow the wives who accompany their husbands to bring their children with them."

"Sofia will leave her son behind?"

Tatyana nodded. "It is monstrous of Nicholas."

"I imagine she will recover," observed Gregory, more from his own instinctive cynicism about parental love than in criticism of Sofia.

"Oh no, Gregory, Sofia is heartbroken," said Tatyana. "After Arkady, that little boy is all the world to her."

Gregory sighed deeply to think of the lives thrown asunder through the will of Nicholas. And this reminded him of something. "I think it an appropriate irony to tell you on the eve of your departure from the high society of St. Petersburg you leave not only as a Russian princess but as an English marchioness."

"I beg your pardon," said Tatyana in her stiff and archaic English, which she was trying to practice with Gregory. "What is a marching 'S'?"

Gregory smiled. "I feel the same way about it. It means, my dear naif, that the past comes knocking deviously on one's door at the strangest hours."

And here he produced the letter from the London solicitor's office that he had received that morning. Tatyana read it and understood it, her reading of Byron having helped produce this dividend. She looked at Gregory in amazement.

"You see," he said with an ironic smile, "you're now married to a marquis, and a rich one, too. We'll go off to Siberia in style. If we go mad there, we can sit and count the untouched money in our London bank."

"Gregory, a hundred thousand sterling pounds a year. Is that a lot of money?" Tatyana asked, lapsing back into French.

Gregory laughed without merriment. "To use a Russian equivalent, I could buy outright five thousand serfs."

Tatyana's eyes popped open. She was clearly impressed. "That makes you even richer than my father, or rather, than my father was."

"Past tense for both of us," said Gregory gently. "Where we're going it's not going to make much difference."

Tatyana kissed him. "No matter where we went, as long as I was with you, it would make no difference."

Sofia sat in the twilight beside her baby's cradle. She had fallen asleep with her arm still in the cradle and her hand on her son's back.

She awoke when Tatyana came in the room. "Are you packed?" she whispered.

"Yes," said Tatyana, "but there is not so much I'm going to take. The book of poems you gave me, my album, my *sarafan*. The only thing I really need will be in the cart beside me," she said, alluding to Gregory.

Sofia nodded, then her face tightened and reddened as tears came in her eyes.

"Oh, Sofia, forgive my thoughtless words. How terrible this night of all nights must be for you."

Sofia nodded, unable to speak, and went back to stroking her sleeping baby. He was six months old now, her little Arkadyushka. He had his father's hair and eyes, his mother's bones. He would be a handsome child, and someday a handsome young man. Now he lay asleep in his cradle impervious to the conversation that went on above him. He rubbed his mouth sleepily, and Sofia smiled through her tears. "At least I have had him these six months."

"Your aunt will take good care of him until your return," said Tatyana gently to give her strength.

"Yes," whispered Sofia. Her voice was hushed and she spoke reverently. "He will be brought up in the lap of luxury. She has promised to raise him as her own son. I know that she will; she is an honorable woman. He will have his own rocking horse and cavalry soldiers. The best Swiss tutor that money can buy." Sofia sighed. "And then, when he is older, she will enroll him in the Corps des Pages, or the Military Academy, where he can distinguish himself like his father. It will be a good life for him."

Sofia spoke in Russian, but there was no language, French, English, or Russian, that could have conveyed the pain with which she described the future life of a child she might never see again. She turned to Tatyana and whispered urgently. "Do you remember those sacred words from your ceremony, 'To love, comfort, and honor him, to keep him in sickness and in health, to love and to cherish, until we are parted in death?'"

Tatyana nodded, too moved to speak.

"My son, will he understand?" begged Sofia.

"Yes, someday he will understand and be proud to have had such parents."

The following night the stars winked in the dusky sky. It was a perfect evening for a party. Prince Kochubey, the minister of the interior, was holding a ball at his mansion to celebrate the coronation of the czar.

The chandeliers glittered, the champagne was poured, and everyone vied for the honor of being granted an audience with the czar, who was in attendance with his entourage. The strains of ballroom music wafted out the open windows and into the quiet street below.

A small escort of mounted cavalry soldiers suddenly turned the corner, their horses' hooves clip-clopping along the cobblestone street. Behind them, and surrounded by other guards, rattled an open cart carrying a convoy of prisoners. The cart contained Gregory, whose ankles were in chains, and Tatyana, who sat beside him in the straw. They had their arms around each other, and Tatyana's head lay on Gregory's shoulder. They leaned against a trunk that contained their most precious possessions, all they would have for a lifetime in Siberia. Beside them in the cart sat Sofia, cradling her husband's head in her lap.

They looked around them at the familiar and well-loved streets and wondered when if ever they would lay eyes on St. Petersburg again. A czar had built the city, and another czar now dominated it, but St. Petersburg was still their home and a trove of happy memories. When they passed Prince Kochubey's palace, the strain of violins floated out to them through the open windows, and the warm yellow candles of the chandeliers cast a haze of light down on them.

"Your aunt is at Kochubey's fete tonight?" asked Gregory, who from where he sat could see the shadows on the walls of people dancing.

Arkady Stegorin nodded. "The empress dowager would have disapproved if her mistress of the robes missed this celebration in honor of her son. They say Sofia's aunt broke down and wept when her presence was requested."

Soon the music and chandelier light died away and gave place to the clop of the horses' hooves, the jingle of the bells on the harness, and the scrape of the wooden wheels along the street. They rode to the Schusselberg gates of the city, where they would begin their forty-five-hundred-mile journey to Irkutsk in Siberia. The thought of that long journey, which would take several months to complete, awed them into silence.

They left the city behind them, and while Gregory looked at the stars, Tatyana gazed at the road ahead of them. After they had traveled a distance she nudged Gregory with a kiss. "Look, soldiers up ahead," she said, indicating a troop of cavalry traveling in the opposite direction, "they must be coming to relieve our guards for the second leg of the journey."

Gregory looked out through the fading light at the riders who were approaching them, and Tatyana felt him stiffen against her.

"Gregory, are you all right?"

He did not answer. Tatyana saw he was gazing intently at the horsemen who had drawn up along the road just in front of them. Now she understood his odd reaction, for the small cluster of cavalry was no ordinary group of horsemen. In fact, they were a strange assortment of men. Several were in Cossack uniforms, but most wore loose gray caftans with black leather belts and shoulder straps. They carried cartridge pouches and a mixed assortment of weapons. On their dirty caps they wore the insignia of the Romanov double eagle. All of them had beards.

"Those, Gregory, are *opolchenie*," said Tatyana, for

she had recognized them. "They are peasants who were levied during the Napoleonic wars to fight alongside the regular army."

Tatyana knew that the *opolchenie* had often been braver than the front line infantry. But she also knew how they had been awarded for their patriotism and valor at the end of the war by being returned to their masters to resume their lowly career as serfs. Tatyana had not seen *opolchenie* in uniform in a decade.

"I wonder what they are doing here," she said, and she peered into the dusky light with curiosity and interest. "Are they going to be our new escorts to Siberia?"

The lieutenant in charge of the prison convoy reigned in to request the destination and passports of the peasant militia. He addressed a rugged, blond-bearded peasant who rode in the lead. While they were both speaking, Gregory had the strange feeling that they were being surrounded.

Suddenly the peasant uttered a loud shout and flung himself off his horse at the guard. Within seconds three more peasants had jumped on some of the other soldiers and knocked them from their saddles and onto the ground. Gregory stared with utter surprise and then with sudden understanding. To Tatyana's dismay, since he was manacled, she saw Gregory fling himself on the guard riding beside them. His weight pulled the guard from his horse, and they wrestled on the ground. Soon every soldier had been knocked from his horse and was fighting in hand to hand combat with the peasants. Gregory fought beside peasants, knocking another soldier from his horse, and when a second knocked him to the ground, Gregory kicked out with his manacled feet and sent the soldier groaning into the bushes.

The convoy soldiers with their tight-fitting uniforms and fastidious manner were no match for the brawn of the peasants. After a couple of minutes of fighting, all the guards were pinned on the ground and their weapons removed.

"What is it you want?" demanded the young lieutenant-in-command of his peasant captor.

"The release of the prisoners," said the blond-bearded peasant who had initiated the attack. He spoke in the thick guttural voice of the Russian peasant, and yet his voice seemed vaguely familiar.

"You are mistaken," said the lieutenant. "These are not your fellow serfs being conscripted or sent to Siberia. They are political prisoners who have trespassed against the czar. You have no want for them."

"They are exactly who we want," said the peasant fiercely. "Release them, unlock their fetters, or you will never see another day." The guards unwillingly obeyed, and soon Gregory and Arkady were released from the chains around their ankles.

Tatyana suddenly clung to Gregory as if she would faint. Her eyes were riveted on the leader of the *opolchenie*. "Gregory, that blond-bearded peasant," she said, her voice staggering. "Tell me, tell me. . . ."

Gregory had never seen Tatyana's body tremble so much. Suddenly she was out of the cart. She ran sobbing to the blond peasant, who surprisingly held out his arms as she reached him. She flung herself into these arms.

"Mitya, Mitya, Mitya!"

Dmitry smiled, for it was indeed he. "So," he said resuming his normal accent. "You recognized me in spite of my beard, my dress, and my voice."

But Tatyana couldn't answer, between her laughter and tears, which all seemed to be coming out in the same breath. "Mitya, Mitya! Is it true?" She ran her fingers through his blond hair as if only touching him could convince her it was really her beloved brother, alive after all, not frozen under the Neva. She would not let go of him until he gently unfastened her. "Mitya, explain, I don't understand. How is it you are alive?" began Tatyana when she could at last find words.

Dmitry touched his finger to her lips. "You will understand all, but for the moment we have to get you safely out of here." Now he included Gregory in his instructions. "You are going to mount on horseback, we have horses here for you. Most of my men will remain behind to stall the convoy, but I and two others will escort you to a hiding place on the Gulf of Finland. It is several hours from here. An English merchant ship is there, waiting for you."

Tatyana threw her arms around her brother's neck again. Their rescue seemed a miracle, and Dmitry's presence a gift from God.

But Gregory had been distracted by the arrival of a peasant who came out of the bushes leading four horses. The fastidious gait of the small peasant wrapped in sheepskin looked oddly familiar. Only one man in Christendom would lead a horse so daintily. "By God," laughed Gregory, "this Russian climate certainly now agrees with him."

The little figure now stepped forward and flung off his sheepskin coat. *"Quel affreuse odeur,"* he exclaimed, pinching his nose. "These Russian sheepskin coats smell worse than some of our best cheeses."

"Anatole!" exclaimed Tatyana. "Gregory and I thought you had returned to France. What are you doing with my brother?"

Dmitry stepped forward to explain. "I am alive because of him. He found me wounded in the square after the rebellion and whisked me off to safety. Because of him, I was able to keep hidden from the police these past six months."

"Where did you think to hide him?" asked Tatyana in

astonishment. Anatole hardly seemed like the epitome of resourcefulness.

Anatole shrugged his shoulders in a typical French gesture. "*Eh bien,* I asked myself the question, Who would help Dmitry? Who loved him like a son—without it being his papa?"

"Dunyasha!" exclaimed Tatyana.

Anatole shrugged his shoulders again but looked coy. "I was forced to enlist her help."

"You sly one," laughed Gregory. "No wonder I have not heard a word from you since."

Anatole blushed and grinned. "What a woman," he said in English, and Gregory and Tatyana laughed. But this seemed to offend him and he drew himself up huffily. "I am no spring chicken it is true, nor is Dunyasha, but somehow we suit each other. And I might also say, *monsieur,* that we have both been working very hard. It is no laughing matter to go from being a gentleman's valet to a revolutionary's accomplice. I have had to go running around in the bushes wearing these putrid jackets made of sheep."

"You can return to being a gentleman's valet," said Gregory with a smile.

"Forgive me, *monsieur,* but when you are safely off I intend to settle down. See life as a husband, is what I mean."

Tatyana clapped. "Oh that darling. High time she was married too. I give you both my blessing!"

Now Dmitry had turned to Arkady and Sofia. "We have two horses for you as well, but you must come now."

After the initial shock, Arkady and Sofia had quickly surmised the situation, and when Arkady answered his manner was decided. "No, Dmitry, we decline your generous offer"—and here he looked at his wife—"but

Sofia and I are going to stay. We are Russians and belong here. If we leave now, we will never be allowed to return to Russian soil. And our little son waits for us in St. Petersburg."

"Sofia," entreated Tatyana with dismay.

Sofia grasped Tatyana's hand. "What Arkady says is true. Our place is here. If we left now, we would forever lose our rights to our child. Someday we will return and claim him. But you—Tatyana—you and Gregory must go. He is an Englishman, and you are an Englishman's wife. Before you lie your entire lives and another country that needs you."

Sofia spoke so calmly, so resolutely that Tatyana knew it was no use trying to dissuade them. "When will I see you again?"

"Someday," said Sofia gently.

Tatyana sobbed.

Sofia chided her. "Do not cry, Tatyana, if you love me. Nothing should be measured by how or when it ends, since all things mortal have their endings. So do not think sadly of our parting—a few trivial moments in time—but of our years as friends. That is how I want to be remembered by you. Believe me, when I think of you, it will be with fondness, respect, such joy—enough to last me forever." The two friends kissed each other's cheeks and hands reverently. "Now go," said Sofia. "That boat is waiting for you."

Their farewell was over. Now Tatyana found herself raised by Gregory's strong arms onto a saddle. "Dmitry has explained the route to me. Hold on to the saddle and follow me. We are going to ride like the wind." He attached a lead on her horse to his own saddle, and soon they were off, following Dmitry. In their tracks came several of Dmitry's peasant comrades.

The horses cantered a long time, then stopped and were replaced by other horses provided by peasants who appeared from out of the forest. Dmitry seemed to expect them and to know them all by name. Even the route he took through the forests and marshes seemed well known by him. As the hours went by and every aspect of their flight seemed so well prepared, Tatyana realized their escape must have been much rehearsed.

As the dawn rose, they rode out of the forests and to a promontory. Before her Tatyana saw the quiet blue mists of the Baltic Sea shimmering in the early morning light. Below them through the copse of birch trees lay the glistening bay, where a handsome frigate lay at anchor. From the top of its mast waved the blue and red of the British flag.

It seemed hardly any time before they were rowed across the inlet and placed on board the ship. Dmitry hovered near the gangplank.

Now Tatyana turned to her brother, whose hands she kissed again. "Isn't it time the three of us were leaving?" she said tenderly. And yet there was something in her voice that betrayed she was not entirely sure of his answer. As they had ridden endlessly in the darkness she had realized how much he had changed from the little boy she remembered, even from the young man he had been a year before. Something burned within him still, a mission, an object of intense importance.

"No, sister, I am staying here."

Tatyana looked at him a long time. "Mitya, I knew in my heart, without knowing why, that that would be your answer."

"Finally you have come to understand me," he answered gently.

"But dear brother, what can you hope to change by staying here? You would be arrested if they ever caught you. The dream is over. It died that night in Senate Square."

Dmitry shook his head. "I know that Nicholas has

suppressed it, which is why I must stay. Our beliefs did not die in Senate Square, or in the Winter Palace, or yet again in the fortress where those brave comrades died for their beliefs. And it doesn't die in the likes of Arkady Stegorin and his wife.

"We cannot fight like gentlemen anymore for our beliefs, we cannot fight out in the open. I am an outcast, I must live now in the shadows, underground. But someday we will flourish. Not the czar, not all the rulers in the world will keep us down, because the truth will win out in the hearts of men like these"—and he pointed to his band of ragged peasants—"and in all those who have the strength and courage to believe in their ideals."

Tatyana kissed Dmitry on the forehead and on his hands. "I understand."

Dmitry smiled, for Tatyana did understand what she had never understood about him, that his beliefs were larger than the limits of his lifetime.

Gregory and Tatyana watched Dmitry row across the water to the inlet. He and his men climbed onto their horses, separated, and then vanished into the woods.

To Tatyana and Gregory, this disappearance did not seem an ending but a beginning, for they both knew that the invisible ideals of these renegade men carried the future of Russia.

Tatyana slipped more fully into Gregory's arms and sighed, "And a new beginning for us also." The green eyes that looked up into his mingled love and hope.

Gregory hugged Tatyana gently. "I came to Russia to glimpse into her future, never guessing I would find there my own future as well." He paused to kiss her tenderly as the frigate set sail into the Baltic Sea. "And this time, I'm never going to let her go."

About the Author

Victoria Ravenhill Foote grew up in Paris and New York. She was educated at Wellesley College where she won the Johanna Mankiewicz Davis Fiction Prize for an experimental novel about the French Revolution.

She has worked in journalism, publishing and in public relations for travel, foreign film, and wine accounts.

Ms. Foote lives in Nyack, New York.